Praise for *The Lor*

"Absolutely beautiful! An exquisite t
fully told! This is the kind of book th
stays in your heart after you finish. I loved it!"

—Sarah Beth Durst, *New York Times* bestselling author of *The Spellshop*

"With the backdrop of an enchanted but deadly forest, *The Lord of the Wood* by E.M. Anderson is a lyrical quest supported by a diverse and memorable cast, each experiencing full-on terror while finding strength through unexpected friendship."

—B.R. Myers, Mary Higgins Clark Award–winning author of *A Dreadful Splendor*

"E.M. Anderson's *The Lord of the Wood* is darkly delightful. Compelling cozy queer horror with fairytale echoes of 'Beauty and the Beast.' Fabulous, frightening and hopeful."

—Angela "A.G." Slatter, multi-award-winning author of *A Forest, Darkly*

"*The Lord of the Wood* is the epitome of cozy horror, unsettling and tender in equal measure. This genre buster is perfect for fans of *Over the Garden Wall* and *Princess Mononoke.* A prickly hug of a book."

—Rosiee Thor, co-author of *Dead & Breakfast*

"*The Lord of the Wood* is a perfect cozy horror—it's a warm, strong hug as the world falls apart outside. Even though the tale revolves around a haunted forest, Anderson imbues the novel with grace: grace to discover who you are, and grace to arrive when you're ready."

—Mia Tsai, author of *The Memory Hunters*

"E.M. Anderson has delivered another gorgeous and heartwarming tale rooted in love—for one's family, for one's partner, and for one's self . . . a wholly original tale that tackles pollution, conformity, chronic pain, and generalized anxiety in a thoughtful, fresh, and delightfully queer manner. One of the best books of 2026, hands down."

—Kamilah Cole, *USA TODAY* and national indie bestselling author of *An Arcane Inheritance*

Also by E.M. Anderson

The Keeper of Lonely Spirits

Author's Note

As you've (hopefully) noticed, *The Lord of the Wood* is my first horror novel. Admittedly, it's cozy horror/fantasy, but it still comes with potentially heftier content warnings than books past.

The world of this book is not queernorm, so the characters grapple with homophobia, internalized homophobia, a homophobic slur, and an instance of misgendering. Additionally, despite the prevalence of disability in the setting, there's ableism and internalized ableism. In particular, there's a lot of internalized ableism on the part of a character struggling with the impact of a new physical disability on her life. There's also more coded internalized ableism on the part of the main character, who has undiagnosed autism.

Beyond that, there are the content warnings you'd probably expect of a horror novel set mostly in a sentient forest that keeps murdering people: anxiety, body horror, attacks by various creatures, illness, injury, blood, death, past parental neglect, past parental death, past spousal death, mentions of bullying, mentions of drowning, and animal death.

(Spoiler alert: The pets are fine.)

Overall, I like to think this is a fun and cozy book—but please do step away while reading if you need to, and take care of yourself. The book will still be here for you if you decide to pick it up again.

to the late bloomers,
the Weird Girls™,
and everyone who's a little afraid
to become the person they want to be

and to Baby E:
this was the story you were trying to tell.
you just didn't know it yet

Thirty years ago

It had been an awful day. Most days were awful for twelve-year-old Arthur Throckmorton. In the seaside fishing village of Seacliff, where most boys his age were already strapping and calloused from working the sea with their fathers, Arthur was a slender pink thing with soft hands, a mop of golden hair, and watery blue eyes behind wire-rimmed spectacles that never sat quite right.

This late summer evening, his spectacles were more crooked than ever, having been forcibly removed, peered through, jeered at, and stomped on. The frames had bent; miraculously, the lenses had not broken. Arthur had been walking home from the convent after lessons, forgetful of his usual care because Mother Superior, aware of his deep interest in timepieces, had given him an old clock that no longer worked. He'd been trying to figure out what was wrong with it when a group of boys hardly older than he had accosted him. It was difficult to say what, precisely, their gripe with Arthur was, but almost everyone in the village found him odd. He didn't understand why, except for his bastard status and a vague feeling of *difference.*

He'd snuck past his mother on the way into the house, bruised, bloody, with bent glasses. If she saw him like that (again), she'd fuss and worry. Rather than joining her in the sitting room, Arthur called a greeting from the kitchen and crept into the bedroom he shared with his five-year-old half sister. He'd been there ever since.

As bedtime approached, Arthur was lying on his stomach in bed, finishing his homework. Maths. Always maths. Sister Mary Paul insisted on it. The numbers, which had a nasty habit of rearranging on the page before his eyes, blurred as his spectacles slipped yet again.

Someone knocked on the door.

Arthur bolted upright, trying to straighten his glasses. "Don't come in!"

Too late. His stepfather—the only father he'd ever known—had cracked the door, entering the room with Charlotte in his arms. At the sight of Arthur shamefaced on his bed, with a split lip and bruised eye, George Throckmorton sucked in his cheeks.

"It's nothing," Arthur mumbled.

George tucked Charlotte into bed without comment, kissed her forehead, and withdrew. Charlotte clambered out of her bed and into Arthur's. She cocked her head at him, eyeballing his bruises.

"Does it hurt? It looks like it hurts."

"Yeah."

To his relief, she ceased her examination and snuggled into his side. "Are you okay?"

"Yeah," Arthur repeated, even though he wasn't. But he had his sister. That was something.

Their father returned, his medical kit in hand. He was a doctor, not a fisherman. A proper doctor who'd gone to university in Port Lorne and everything, not that that held much weight in Seacliff: Since his return, the villagers had thought George too high-and-mighty, too book-learned and citified.

It didn't stop them from coming to him for every injury

and illness, however. This was his first time home since morning; a bout of flu had swept through the village. Tomorrow he was off to Port Lorne to restock his medical supplies—a trip he took every year—so today he'd seen his patients.

Shedding his coat, George nudged Charlotte aside and sat on the edge of Arthur's bed. A silver acorn on a chain gleamed on his neck.

"Why aren't you in bed, my little love?" he asked Charlotte.

"I'm not sleepy."

George shook his head with a chuckle, but his expression sobered as he turned to Arthur. "Let me see, son."

Arthur set his glasses aside. There was George calling him *son* as he always did, because to George they were kin, the same as if he had sired Arthur himself. That simple appellation always made Arthur feel better, no matter how bad a day had been.

George was grave but calm as he examined Arthur's bruises. He was a comforting presence, a big man whose belly shook when he laughed. His skin was the same warm brown as the tip-tilted eyes he shared with his daughter. They had the same rounded chin and high forehead, too, although Charlotte had ochre skin and her mother's freckles and button nose.

Not for the first time, Arthur wished he took after George. He resented looking (he supposed) like the man who'd run out on his mother before Arthur was born. Alas, he didn't take after George in any respect. His one ill-fated foray into medicine two years ago had ended in ten minutes. He'd trailed George through Seacliff, intending to visit patients with him. The first cut of the lance had sent Arthur fleeing outside, where he'd sat with his head between his knees until rain had chased him into the general store for shelter. He couldn't stomach the sight of blood. At the ripe old age of ten, he'd found following in his father's footsteps as a doctor out of the question.

If George was as disappointed in Arthur as Arthur was, he

never showed it. Now, he dotted cream onto Arthur's lip and eye. Arthur winced.

"Who was it?" George asked, but Arthur shrugged. It hardly mattered who. Snitching would make things worse. Nothing could be done anyway.

His father sighed but didn't ask again. He packed the cream away, straightened the frames of Arthur's glasses (more or less), and kissed Arthur's forehead. Maybe they were alike in one way, Arthur thought hopefully. The villagers never said George was odd, because he was a proper doctor and a respectable man—even if he'd married, as they termed it, a fallen woman—but the villagers were never so soft with their sons. All George was to Arthur was softness, and that was all Arthur was, too.

"You won't tell Mam, will you?" Arthur said.

George tucked Charlotte back into her own bed. Despite her insistence she wasn't sleepy, she'd fallen asleep curled in her brother's quilt.

"She'll want to know," George said. "She worries about you."

"That's why I don't want to tell her."

George shook his head. "I think she'll notice, unless you figure on staying in this room until that bruise heals."

Arthur snuggled into his bedclothes, feeling better except that tomorrow was Wednesday. Lessons. Another opportunity for the boys to jeer at him.

And likely more maths.

He thought of Port Lorne, the great city at the northern tip of the forest abutting the Throckmortons' garden. His father had told him about a clock shop in the city that sold not only clocks but parts and tools for their building and repair. George had brought Arthur a travel repair kit after last year's trip; Arthur had been itching to see the shop ever since. He imagined it walled in ticking timepieces, with tools and gears shining on the counters.

"Dad," he said, "can I come with you to Port Lorne?"

George gave a small smile, and Arthur's heart sank.

Sure enough, his father said, "I'm afraid not, duck. Not this time. I'll take you when you're older."

He'd been saying that for years.

"That's what you always say."

George's smile disappeared.

"Please?" Arthur said. "I'm practically grown now."

George's mouth twitched. "You're twelve, son, and there are your lessons to think of."

"Most of the other boys aren't even in school anymore! They work with their dads. Why can't I go with you?"

"Because I said so."

"But—"

"No."

Outside, a wind blew in off the sea to the west. The windowpanes rattled in their frames.

George pinched the bridge of his nose, took a breath, and gave a small smile. "I'll have to fix those when I get back. I'll teach you how."

"Dad—"

His father's voice was firm, final. "Good night, Arthur."

George clasped his medical kit and left the room.

Something small and aching cracked open in Arthur's chest. He always hated it when his father went to Port Lorne; he hated it all the more because George kept promising to take him but never did.

Arthur listened to the rattling of the windows. His father would teach him to fix them, and he would try to learn, but such masculine pursuits always seemed beyond him.

Behind the cottage garden, the forest's silhouette was faintly visible, a black shape against a blue-black sky. In the morning, George would vanish into its depths as he did every year at this time.

He'd told Arthur so many stories about the forest. Its dangers and enchantments. Its lord, whom George had met once, long ago. He'd given George the silver acorn.

Do you think he'd like me? Arthur had asked once. *The Lord of the Wood?*

Of course, his father had said.

Unlikely Arthur would ever meet him, however, since his father wouldn't take him to Port Lorne.

In the other room, his parents murmured together, their words a low rumble. Arthur slipped out of bed, pausing when a floorboard creaked to make sure Charlotte hadn't awoken. She sighed and turned over.

Arthur cracked the door.

"—pack a bag for Arthur?" his mother was asking.

His heart leaped; perhaps his father had changed his mind.

"Not this year," George said. "Maybe when he's older."

That *maybe* hadn't been there before, Arthur noted. His eyes stung.

"I worry about him, Eileen. He's so . . . You know what he's like."

Arthur's heart stuttered.

"Yes." His mother's voice was soft, concerned. "I had hoped the other boys might take to him by now, but . . ."

Silence. Arthur pressed his ear to the door, desperate to hear more. To know what words clung to the end of his father's *so*, his mother's *but*. To know what, exactly, his parents thought he was like. Whether they had an answer for his uneasy relationship with Seacliff.

"I think he'd like Port Lorne," George said, "but I worry

he'd be worse off being here after. I'd rather take him when he's grown—seventeen or eighteen, maybe—when he's old enough to make his own way if he wants."

Seventeen or eighteen! Arthur's hands balled in his nightshirt. He'd thought, when his father said "older," that he'd meant soon. Thirteen or fourteen, since twelve evidently wasn't older *enough*. Seventeen or eighteen might as well have been a hundred, it seemed so far off.

His father was speaking. Arthur pressed his ear back to the door.

"—bring back that new medicine Maclure wrote me about. I hope they'll be open to it, seeing as how sick everyone's been for the past week. I've never seen the flu hit so hard. But if it's not herbalism plain and simple, they don't trust it."

"They will." A creak of bedsprings. "I'm sure if you keep trying—"

"I will, dove. All I've ever wanted was to make life better here. It's improved a little—hasn't it? You remember what things were like when we were young . . . But it's an uphill battle. Seacliff doesn't change."

Arthur crept back into bed; evidently, he'd hear nothing more about himself. On the table between his bed and Charlotte's, the frames of his glasses were dented. He'd have to find a different route home tomorrow, if he could.

He lay awake for a long time, wondering how to change his father's mind.

He still hadn't figured it out when morning dawned.

Charlotte had already stumbled out of the room, half asleep but lured by the smell of eggs frying. Floorboards creaked as George emerged from their parents' room.

His footsteps paused at the children's door. Arthur squeezed his eyes shut.

A soft knock.

"Arthur?" A brief pause. "I'm going now."

Arthur's eyes prickled, but he clenched his jaw. He cried far too much for a boy his age, about any number of silly things. Like when he accidentally stepped on an ant going about its little ant life and squished it. An innocent victim of his day-dreaming and plodding human feet. His father going to Port Lorne without him was undoubtedly sillier than that, since it didn't involve murder.

"I know you're disappointed," George said. "You'll understand one day, when you have your own bairns." A long pause, more unbearable than the last. "Well . . . I'm off. Be back in a fortnight or so."

Arthur was determined not to go out and see him off as he usually did, but he couldn't help saying, "Bye, Dad." But the floorboards' creaking swallowed it, he said it so quietly, and his father didn't hear him. The back door slammed.

Arthur turned over in bed, burying his face in his pillow. He should've gone out and said goodbye properly, but boys his age were supposed to be stubborn, weren't they, and everyone thought he ought to be more like other boys his age.

The window muffled his parents' goodbye out in the garden. Charlotte asked their father to bring a doll back for her; George promised he would. Arthur's ears snagged on his own name, but whatever had been said was finished before he could sit up and strain for a better listen.

Another knock. His mother, this time, but she didn't wait for a response before entering. She was short and slender, with ruddy, freckled skin and blue eyes warmer and less watery than her son's. She disliked her freckles and had tried any number of things to do away with both her own and Charlotte's (none successful), but Arthur wished he had freckles like they did. Having been warned too much sun would cause them, he'd spent most of last summer outdoors with his face turned skyward. All he'd achieved was the most magnificent sunburn of his young life.

"Well, now!" Eileen said. "Sulking in your room while your father goes off without so much as a fare-thee-well. I'd never have expected it of you."

Arthur reddened, regretting it, but she cried out; she'd caught sight of his bruises. Perching beside him, she grabbed his chin.

"Mam—" Arthur wriggled free. "Mam, it's all right. I'm fine."

"The state of you! And still you'd not let your father in? I'm sure he could've done something for you."

Shame burned through him. "He did. Last night."

Arthur hunched, mussing his hair with his hands.

"I just wanted to go with him," he mumbled.

His mother softened. "I know. One day. Here."

She pressed something into his hand. His father's silver acorn on its chain, which George had worn around his neck every day for as long as Arthur could remember.

"He wants you to hold on to it until he gets back. Mind you don't lose it." Eileen bit her lip. "Might be best to leave it home for lessons."

She touched his cheek, too close to his bruised eye. Arthur flinched.

"It looks awful," his mother said.

He shrugged, certain it had looked worse before his father had dotted cream onto it. He clutched the acorn so tightly it dug into his palm. A lump swelled in his throat.

"If you're sure you're all right—" Eileen glanced at his split lip, a wobble in her own as she stood "—you'd best get dressed. Lessons start soon."

Arthur swallowed. He didn't give a fig about lessons, or what might happen today when he left them. All he could think of was George, tending his bruised eye and split lip. Not mentioning it to Eileen because Arthur had asked him not to.

Arthur flung himself out of bed, still in his nightshirt, and dashed through his father's workroom at the back of the cottage and outside.

"Dad!" he shrieked. "*Dad!*"

The garden glistened with dew. Grass dampened his feet and the hem of his nightshirt. The garden gate was swinging, but the small stretch of heather between the fence and the forest's edge was empty. The only sign his father had been there was the narrow trail of flattened heather from the gate to the trailhead.

Arthur's chest heaved. He barreled through the gate, but his mother gripped his shoulder.

"He's gone, Arthur. Come, now, or you'll be late for school."

"I have to tell him." Arthur clutched the acorn to his chest, eyes welling. "I didn't mean it."

"He knows, sweetheart. Come get breakfast, won't you? Charlotte's eaten so much sausage already there won't be any left if you don't hurry. You can tell him you're sorry when he gets back."

Arthur wiped his eyes. "Okay."

A fortnight. Just a fortnight. Then George would return, and Arthur could fling himself into his father's arms and tell him he was sorry. He'd ask George to tell him more about Port Lorne and his journey through the forest, whether he'd seen the Lord of the Wood, and the whole thing would be forgotten.

For two weeks, that was what Arthur told himself would happen.

Instead, his father never came back.

1. In which Arthur tells a bedtime story

August was a disappointment.

Arthur looked forward to it every year. In August, the world held its breath. Anticipating something—promising something. To the west, the sea glittered in the late summer sun, still and silent like an empty church, seething with expectation. The first storms rolled in, black clouds on the horizon, lightning forking out to sea. As crimson and gold limned the first autumn leaves, Arthur stood in the garden with bated breath, waiting for a storm to burst on the vacuity of his life and fill it with adventure and romance.

But every year, when August ended, his life was exactly as it had been before.

He'd voiced this to Charlotte once, but she'd said, *Of course it is. You never do anything to change it.* Arthur hadn't brought it up again.

He kept thinking it, however. August had heralded so many changes in his youth: school starting, however much he didn't want it to; his father preparing for his annual trip to Port Lorne, taking stock of his medical supplies to see what needed replenishing; a time of plenty for the fishermen down in the village, their boats overflowing with pollack and salmon.

Now, from his place by the laundry line on the second-to-last evening of August, Arthur gazed down at Seacliff. He'd gone out to bring in the day's washing, leaving Charlotte in her armchair; she'd had another dizzy spell.

What was the point, he wondered, unpinning a pair of trousers, of trying to change one's life in a place like Seacliff? The slate-gray rooftops and narrow cobbled streets half a mile downhill from the Throckmorton-Prentices' cottage were exactly the same as they had been in Arthur's childhood, as were the villagers. All merely shabbier. The cannery that had opened two decades ago spewed smog over everything and always smelled of fish guts. The commercial fishing venture that had opened five years before that had long since cleared Seacliff's fishing grounds and moved on to richer waters.

Lights twinkled down in the village as darkness fell, so much fewer than they used to be. Half the shops in Seacliff had closed in the last decade. Most of the young people left, going to Port Lorne or Glenwhistle to seek their fortunes.

Arthur finished taking down the laundry and put a hand to his lower back, massaging the twinge that had flared up. Beyond the garden and laundry line, the trees rustled. Arthur bit his lip, feeling as if they were gazing back at him.

He remembered his father's many stories about the forest. The enchantment. The trees going about their business, uprooting themselves to walk about like men. The Lord of the Wood. Despite the dangers the forest held, Arthur couldn't let the stories go.

Not for the first time, he imagined a magnificent stag appearing at the wood's edge, its pelt burnished gold. It would gaze at him with large, liquid eyes. Then, suddenly, it would transform into a man. The man would smile, and beckon Arthur close, and say . . . and say . . .

I've been waiting for you, maybe. Like they were old friends, though of course the Lord of the Wood would not know who Arthur was just because Arthur knew who he was. Or, *You're not like anyone I've ever met*, but it would be a compliment. Whatever was said—whatever Arthur decided he would most like to hear—the Lord of the Wood would smile and welcome him, and they'd have a splendid time of things.

With a soft sigh, Arthur hauled the laundry basket into the cottage, ignoring the goat bleating at him as he went.

Inside, Charlotte's children sat at the kitchen table. Jonas was having Sasha read a book aloud to them for practice before school began in another couple of weeks. Sasha was a mirror image of her father, with cool, dark brown skin and dark brown eyes ever twinkling with curiosity and excitement. Jonas favored Charlotte, but their curls were brown instead of black and their eyes green instead of brown.

The laundry basket tipped over as Arthur set it down. He narrowly stopped clean clothes from falling all over the floor and sent the children to get ready for bed. It wasn't quite their bedtime (Sasha informed him promptly), but bedtime was an eternal struggle. Best to get an early start.

As usual, Jonas went without fuss. Sasha, however, was in and out of bed several times in the next twenty minutes. At ten past nine, she was finally in her nightgown only because Arthur had put on his nightshirt.

Back in the kitchen, he found Charlotte at the sink, in her shirtwaist, skirt, and boots, with her black hair in its chignon, washing the supper things.

"I could've done that after the children were asleep," Arthur said. "You didn't need to get up."

She grimaced.

"Yes, I did." Glancing at him, she sighed. "Heaven's sakes. Why are you in your nightshirt? It's not *your* bedtime."

Arthur grabbed a glass from the cupboard beside the sink.

Sasha had requested milk and a story and sworn to him she would, at last, go to bed if he'd provide them.

"Sasha made an excellent point about the unfairness of her and Jonas having to be in their nighties while you and I are in our day clothes."

Charlotte pinched the bridge of her nose. "She's eight."

"She's very persuasive."

Charlotte sighed again but didn't argue.

Someone knocked at the front door. Charlotte dried her hands, but Arthur said, "I'll get it."

"In your nightshirt?"

"They ought to expect it, if they're going to call so late."

Arthur did, however, tug on his dressing gown before answering, since he didn't want to scandalize anyone.

At the door, a fisherman twisted his cap in his hands. Weatherbeaten and gruff, he looked near ten years older than Arthur, but they were both in their forties. They'd been schoolmates until the fisherman, name of Cormac Young, had left school at age ten to join the men at work. Arthur had joined them briefly at twelve, having left school when his father vanished, but the fishermen had scared him off after he'd lost a net, sprung a leak in a boat, and cried over the one fish he'd caught. He'd let it go, pretending it had escaped, because the men would forgive a boy's clumsy hands, if begrudgingly, before his tears.

Cormac's eyes swooped down to Arthur's bare feet and back up. Arthur curled his toes against the floorboards. He wished he'd thought to grab his slippers.

"Good evening," he squeaked.

He hadn't meant to squeak, but Cormac had very blue eyes, which had, for unclear reasons, made Arthur desperate to be friends with him back in school. Cormac hadn't been one of his bullies, but he'd ignored Arthur except occasionally for paltry things like holding doors open rather than letting them slam in Arthur's face.

"Evening." Cormac shifted from foot to foot, avoiding Arthur's gaze. "Mrs. Prentice about? Rosie's coughing something fierce."

Arthur nodded, turning to get his sister, but she was already making her way to the door, leaning on her cane. "Good evening, Mr. Young. Rosie?"

The fisherman nodded. "Fever's down, but the coughing . . . She can't get to sleep. If you've anything might help—"

"Certainly. Arthur," Charlotte said, and he snapped to attention, eager to show Cormac Young how helpful he was. "The syrup in the blue bottles."

Arthur rabbited away. Sasha had trailed into the kitchen with a frown.

"Why aren't you in bed, duck?" Arthur asked absently, digging through the cabinet in which Charlotte kept her most-used herbs and medicines.

"You said you'd bring me milk."

"Half a moment. Mr. Young is here for— Aha," Arthur said under his breath, finding several small blue bottles. "I'll be there once we've finished with him, I promise."

He nudged her back toward the bedroom and dashed away with a bottle in hand.

". . . not the sickness, thank the Lord," Cormac was saying. "But I'll feel easier when Rosie stops coughing. She's had such fits as makes it hard for her to breathe."

Charlotte's jaw clenched at the sidewise mention of wood sickness, but since Rosie Young didn't have it, all she said was, "What about when she's not coughing? Has she any shortness of breath?"

Cormac shook his head. "Goes on so cheery between coughing fits you'd not think her sick at all if she weren't so pale, now the fever's broke."

"I hope she'll recover quickly," Arthur said desperately, handing the blue bottle to him. "Here."

A brief glance as Cormac took the bottle, a quiet "thanks" that made Arthur's heart thump painfully. Then, to his disappointment, Cormac jammed his cap on and turned back to Charlotte. "We're sure grateful, Mrs. Prentice. I'll bring a fish by this week, or probably a few if they're so small as the ones been coming in lately."

"There's no need for that."

Cormac hesitated. "You done so much for Rosie already—"

"Which you've already paid me for. She'll recover sooner if she eats well."

Like their father, Charlotte often failed to charge the villagers for her services as a healer. Despite the cannery's promises of work and riches, Seacliff was poorer now than it had been in their youth. The village had been dying a slow death for years.

Perhaps things did change in Seacliff, Arthur thought, but only ever for the worse.

After a long moment, Cormac tipped his cap, slipped the medicine into his pocket, and trudged back downhill, where darkness swallowed him up. Arthur let out a soft sigh.

Charlotte squeezed his arm. She returned to the kitchen, the sink, and the remaining dishes.

"I really can do that," Arthur said.

"I know," she replied, but she didn't stop. Arthur hesitated but poured Sasha's milk and returned to the tiny back-corner bedroom without another word.

A screen was crammed between the children's beds. Since turning twelve that spring, Jonas had become shy about their body and didn't want anyone to see them dressing or undressing. Besides the privacy it afforded, the screen blocked (more or less) the constant opening and shutting of the door as Sasha attempted to avoid bedtime.

Unfortunately, it did little to muffle the sounds of her fidgeting. Snuggled into their bedclothes with the cat, Jonas pulled a pillow over their head with a huff.

Sasha bounced on the edge of her bed. Forgetting Cormac Young, Arthur bit back a smile. Sasha was his darling; his sister often chided him for laughing at Sasha's behavior when he should have been telling her off. He tried to look stern as he handed his niece the glass of milk, but *stern* was not part of Arthur's natural makeup.

"Don't bounce on the bed," he said half-heartedly, because he knew Charlotte would want him to.

"It's fun."

"I know, but Jonas is trying to sleep."

"Yeah," Jonas muttered from the other side of the screen. "*Trying*."

"That's because Jonas is boring." So saying, Sasha stopped bouncing, downed the milk, and held out her empty glass. "Done."

She started getting up, but Arthur pushed her gently back into bed. "Where do you think you're going?"

"I have to wash my face again." Sasha turned her face upward to show him the full glory of her milk mustache. "See?"

Arthur had prepared for this, however, and plucked a handkerchief from the pocket of his nightshirt. "Then isn't it lucky I have one of these?"

Jonas snorted.

"I thought you were sleeping," Arthur said.

"*Trying* to," Jonas said, and fell silent.

Sasha wiped her mouth, looking disappointed that Arthur had thought this far ahead, but she handed the handkerchief back without objection. Arthur waited for her to wiggle into place under her quilt with her old rag doll, which took longer than strictly necessary, and tucked her in.

Sitting beside her, he picked up the novel he'd left on the nightstand before putting on his nightshirt. The battered cover featured an image of a young woman fainting into the arms of a shirtless man with flowing hair.

Sasha eyed it dubiously. "Is this a kissing book?"

"Of course." That was by far his favorite kind.

She groaned. "I want a *good* story, Uncle Arthur."

He chuckled. "It is good. I promise."

It was the first romance novel he'd ever read. His father had brought it back for his mother after a trip to Port Lorne. Eileen had read it once, enjoyed it, and set it aside forever. Arthur, ten, had stolen it from its spot on the side table and been utterly enamored from the first page. But he'd had a suspicion he was not supposed to be reading this book at this age, or possibly at all, a suspicion born of the cover's shirtless, flowing-haired man. The sight of him made Arthur's stomach clench pleasantly but guiltily.

The faint suspicion had grown into full-blown certainty when he'd reached a scene halfway through in which the hero and heroine started undressing each other, at which point young Arthur had flushed, slammed the book shut, and thrown it under his bed. It had lain there for several weeks until curiosity got the better of him and sent him crawling under the bed to find it.

He'd be skipping that bit when he read it to his niblings, of course.

"I don't *want* a kissing book," Sasha said.

Arthur set the novel aside. "What do you want, then?"

"I want Granddad's story about the Lord of the Wood."

Jonas jerked upright. With a hiss, the cat stalked to the foot of the bed to curl up afresh. Her disapproving golden gaze settled on Arthur. She closed her eyes and twisted tighter with a sigh, fluffy black tail curling over her nose.

Jonas spoke in a whisper. "He's not supposed to tell that one. Mama said."

"It's been forever," Sasha insisted. She held up her rag doll. "Besides, Molly wants to hear it, too."

"Mama *said*."

"Mama can't tell Uncle Arthur what to do. He's older."

Jonas was outraged. "You tell me what to do all the time!"

Sasha ignored them. "Please?"

All Arthur's best stories were about the wood. Charlotte had once loved them as much as he did. Though she'd never said so, Arthur thought the stories reminded her of their father as they did him. Her husband, John Prentice, had found them fascinating, too—especially since the villagers had warned him away from the wood without telling him why.

Then the sickness had come. One case, first. Another. More. Now Seacliff saw at least half a dozen such cases every year, despite the measures the villagers took to protect themselves from the forest. Salt in the pocket. A rowan cross in the lining of the clothes. Yellow flowers around the neck. Iron on wrists or ankles, prayers on lips, an elder leaf in the right shoe to ensure safe return. No matter their precautions, those who returned so often returned with the sickness.

Around nine months ago, four cases had hit all at once. Every person who'd fallen ill had died. Not long afterward, Charlotte and Arthur's mother had died, too. They'd found her half frozen by the garden gate, like she'd been dragging herself toward the forest. They'd brought her in to warm her up, but it had been too late. She'd died delirious, calling for George.

The first time Charlotte heard Arthur telling stories of the wood after that, she suggested he might not. The second time, she asked him not to. And the third time—when Sasha had begged for the stories as she did now, and he'd given in despite his best intentions—she forbade him.

Arthur missed sharing the stories. They were a comfort. A reminder that the way things were wasn't the way things had always been. Of the man he'd idolized as a father, who'd loved Arthur despite his many, many failings.

"It has been a while," he said. "Perhaps just this once."

Sasha whooped. He hushed her. If Charlotte heard them, he wouldn't get to tell the story.

"But once I'm done," he added, "it's really bedtime, and no arguments."

"Okay."

Arthur held out his pinkie. "Promise?"

Sasha linked pinkies with him and shook. "Promise."

Turning away, Jonas pulled their pillow back over their head so as not to be a party to the misbehaving on the other side of the screen.

Arthur settled in beside Sasha. She hugged her rag doll, wiggling her toes in anticipation.

"Once upon a time," Arthur said, because his father had always started the story that way, "the forest was far greater than it is now. It stretched for miles and miles to the north and east. The—"

"The Lord of the Wood guided lost travelers!" Sasha said, bouncing.

"Are you telling the story or am I?"

"You are."

"Don't interrupt, then, please, and stop bouncing."

She obliged.

"Thank you," Arthur said. "The forest was so big you simply had to go through it, no matter where you were headed. If you went around, it took weeks and weeks—if you got around at all. But—"

"But travelers got lost all the time," Sasha said with relish. Having recently grown interested in all things macabre, her favorite part of any story was when people were in terrible danger. Given the family's losses, one might have expected her preferences to run differently in regard to this particular story, but Arthur supposed it was cathartic for her in some way. The stories had been the same for him after George's disappearance.

"Are you sure you don't want to tell the story?"

"Get to the good part!"

Arthur laughed. "I'd get there faster if you'd let me tell it how I please. Yes, travelers got lost all the time because the wood was so big . . . and the paths shifted. The trees were alive, people said. No one ever saw them move, but they must have, because the paths were never the same from one day to the next."

The forest had, in fact, been called Shiftleaf for this reason. Now it went by no name at all. The villagers said the man who spoke the forest's name would be its next victim.

"Luckily, the travelers had a protector." Arthur paused dramatically, half expecting Sasha to interrupt again, but she didn't. "The Lord of the Wood."

"I *knew* it," she whispered, like she hadn't heard the story before.

"He was a stag," Arthur continued. "A magnificent red deer who emerged from nowhere to guide lost travelers to the edge of the wood and vanished as suddenly as he'd appeared. As long as he was guiding you, nothing could harm you—not wind nor weather nor wild beast."

The only thing the story needed was a good romance. Alas, unlike Arthur's small collection of novels, this story had no romance whatsoever.

"Your granddad saw him, once." Sasha fidgeted, no doubt because she wanted Arthur to skip ahead to the part where her grandfather had almost died, but Arthur could never resist an opportunity to tell the children about George. "He grew up right here in Seacliff. A long time ago, when he was a young man, he left for Port Lorne to study medicine. But not long after entering the wood, he got lost.

"Granddad was a smart young man, and he knew how to survive in the wild. He'd studied all sorts of plants in preparation for medical school, so he knew which ones to eat when his supplies ran out, which ones to heal his wounds when he got injured, and which ones to avoid. But as the days stretched into weeks, he worried he'd never make it to the city. The path kept shifting, like he'd always heard. Sometimes he thought he was going in circles. Other times he thought he was hopelessly lost in some deep, dark part of the forest. Then he came down with a fever, after a cold, wet, rainy night when he'd gone without shelter, and he began to think he would die."

"Then what happened?" Sasha asked, as if she didn't know. Jonas sighed.

"The Lord of the Wood found him. He led your granddad into the deepest part of the forest . . . and turned into a man."

"What!"

"Sasha," Jonas said in a long-suffering (if muffled) voice from under their pillow.

Arthur chose to ignore both of them. "At first, Granddad thought he was hallucinating because of the fever. But there he was, sure enough—a man who looked like he'd grown from the forest itself. He had eyes like sunlight in the trees, and hair like shadows, and he was dressed all in leaves and flowers."

Try to picture the Lord of the Wood as described by his father though he might, Arthur always envisioned him as one of the heroes on the covers of his novels, complete with flowing hair and bare chest. He wasn't sure why.

"He nursed your granddad back to health," he continued,

"and when Granddad was well, the Lord of the Wood turned back into a stag and led him safely out of the wood, giving him a silver acorn to remember him by—the one that's hanging in my workshop to this day. Granddad never saw the Lord of the Wood again, but he never forgot him. And when he returned to Seacliff years later, he didn't get lost once."

"*Wow.*" Sasha turned onto her side, dark eyes sparkling. "Do you think I'll ever meet the Lord of the Wood? Do you think he'd like me?"

With a pang, Arthur remembered asking his father that so many years ago. He swallowed the memory and smiled.

"Certainly he'd like you, duck." He leaned over her, trying to look menacing. "But to meet him, you know . . . you'd have to enter the forest."

Sasha popped upright, narrowly avoiding beaning him in the nose with her forehead. "I'm not afraid!"

"You should be," Arthur said solemnly, "because in the forest there are . . . *tickle monsters*," and he grabbed her and tickled her until they were both breathless with laughter.

"Arthur."

They sat up guiltily, the laughter dying on their faces. Charlotte stood in the doorway, eyes bruised with exhaustion.

"Bed. Now."

"But Mama—"

"Now."

Even Sasha knew better than to argue with that tone, so she wriggled farther into her quilt silently (if grumpily), frowning when her uncle and mother kissed her forehead. When both children had been attended to and the light turned out, Charlotte and Arthur retreated to the hall, closing the door behind them.

II. In which Arthur makes a promise

The moment the door had shut, Charlotte rounded on her brother.

"I've told you not to tell my children that story anymore."

Arthur flinched. He knew he'd messed up worse than usual whenever she called them *my* children rather than *the* children. *The* left Arthur with some semblance of parenthood. *My* put him back in his rightful place as uncle.

"Lottie—"

"I know what Dad's stories mean to you." Charlotte's voice quivered; she hardly ever mentioned their father. "But you take them too seriously. You think the forest is this beautiful place full of adventure and enchantment, but it's *dangerous*, Arthur."

"Dad used to say the forest—"

"Dad vanished in that forest. Or have you wrapped yourself up in so many stories that you've forgotten?"

Charlotte didn't sound angry, merely tired. She slumped against the wall but snapped upright as the bedroom door opened, revealing a sliver of Sasha's face. Freya, the cat, slipped out past her.

"I like hearing about Granddad," Sasha said. "And I like hearing about Shiftleaf."

"Don't speak its name," Charlotte snapped. "Go to bed."

Sasha looked ready to argue, but Jonas dragged her away and closed the door. Ferocious whispers drifted through the wall, unintelligible, and died away. The squeak of bedsprings suggested Jonas had convinced Sasha to get back into bed.

Charlotte sagged. Arthur tucked his book under one arm and offered her the other. Taking it, she leaned against him as he helped her to her room. She sank onto the bed.

"I know it makes you feel close to Dad, telling his stories. But you never mention the sickness."

Arthur's stomach turned. He'd seen someone with wood sickness once. If he never saw it again, it would be too soon.

"Or the disappearances," Charlotte continued. "You don't even tell the children about *Dad's* disappearance. And I worry . . . Sasha's too curious for her own good." The cat hopped into her lap. She petted her absently. "If you had your own children, you'd understand."

People had been saying that to him his whole life. Most of the time, his niblings were quite as good as his own children, except when Charlotte reminded him they weren't.

It wasn't as if he didn't want a family, but at forty-three he was unmarried. He'd grown from a soft, slender, pinkish boy into a soft, paunchy, blond adult, aggressively average in height, build, and features; the village girls never spared him a second glance. Nor did he have fortune to recommend him, nor his father's education, nor the other village men's brawn. And every year, marriageable girls were fewer and fewer and younger and younger.

Most recently, he'd been half-heartedly courting Mary Tierney, a pretty, good sort of girl whose family had pushed her on him in desperation because she'd reached the age of twenty-five without a proposal. But she hadn't sparked in Arthur any of the feelings his beloved romance novels said he should have when he fell in love. The only women who ever had were unattainable: married women, for example, or strangers who were but passing ships to Seacliff. He wasn't sure why he fell briefly in love with such women, but he suspected, uncomfortably, that it was precisely *because* they were unattainable.

His courtship with Mary had broken off when she'd absconded to Glenwhistle with the cash Arthur had given her and a young lover of whom her mother disapproved. No one else knew what had happened, and he hoped no one ever would—Charlotte least of all. He'd found it dreadfully romantic, the situation between Mary and her beau. Charlotte would've found it foolish.

He sat beside her. "I'm sorry I told the children that story. I won't do it again."

Charlotte laughed wetly. "You will, Arthur. You know you will. The second Sasha asks."

He wanted to protest but didn't, because it was true. He found it hard to deny Sasha anything, no matter how he knew he ought to.

"Well, then—" he bumped Charlotte with his shoulder "—next time I'll make sure you don't hear it."

Chuckling ruefully, she fished a handkerchief from her skirt. She dabbed her eyes, gazing at her still-laced boots with a sigh.

"You had the right idea, getting into your nightclothes early."

"Would you like help with your boots?"

"Not in the slightest. But I suppose I need it. If I bend over at this point, I don't think I'm getting back up." Charlotte grimaced. "My hair, too. My fingers are . . ."

She flexed her hands and rubbed them together, breathing on them for warmth. She'd taken ill back in February; since then, her joints often ached or swelled, or both. She'd had spells of faintness and dizziness, too, occasional palpitations or difficulty breathing, and, on some days, a fog in her brain so dense she could hardly think.

She'd tried to hide it, at first, and still often did. Arthur helped as much as he could—quietly, since Charlotte's answer upon being asked whether she needed help was usually no. Agreeing to it tonight was a sort of accomplishment, Arthur thought, though he knew she felt differently. Agreeing to use the cane, especially down to the village and back, had been another.

He knelt at her feet, unlaced her boots, removed them, and placed them beside her bedside table with its whistle rack and stack of old medical texts. The texts had been their father's; the whistles, three in various sizes, were Charlotte's, not that she played much anymore. Her husband had made the small cherrywood whistle sitting in the place of pride at the top of the rack.

"Are we all right?" Arthur asked.

The corner of her mouth turned up.

"Of course we are." Charlotte spoke so quietly he almost didn't hear her. "I like when you tell the stories, you know. They remind me of Dad, too. It's just . . ."

He patted her knee. "I know."

Exhaustion radiated from her. She caught him looking at her in concern and said, "I'm fine. Help me up."

That *fine* was automatic. She constantly said that—but she hadn't always. When she'd been young, she'd divulged when things bothered her, when she'd hurt herself, when a healing had been unsuccessful. Since John's death, she'd become closed off. Like she wanted to distance herself from their mother, who, after George's disappearance, had wept and wailed over every pain life threw at them. Now, whether it was her body hurting her or life, Charlotte said flatly, *I'm fine*, and moved on.

Arthur waited as she changed behind a screen, in case she needed additional help. She'd been mortified the first time she needed help changing after her illness. The screen had been a compromise so he could be nearby, just in case, when she'd had a bad day. Sasha sometimes helped instead (if it wasn't past the children's bedtime), but she struggled with some of the pieces of Charlotte's wardrobe that, as an eight-year-old, she was years from wearing.

Charlotte emerged in her nightgown and sat in bed. Arthur sat beside her, took her hair out of its chignon, and started braiding it. He hadn't quite gotten the hang of braids, but he practiced on Sasha whenever she'd let him.

"What's your new book about?" Charlotte asked, and Arthur grinned. On nights like this, when she needed help with her clothes and hair, he told her the stories in his romance novels. Agnes Livingston, a wealthy woman with a collection of timepieces to which Arthur could only aspire, had given him a new book this afternoon, declaring it didn't suit her taste, when he'd returned her newly repaired tabletop clock. It was mostly thanks to her library that his small cache of novels had grown over the last three decades.

"I'll get you reading romance yet."

"Thank you, no. I much prefer my radio shows."

"You'll like this one. It's more like your radio shows, listen—"

Arthur launched into an explanation of his new book, in which the intrepid heroine picked her way through a forest filled with creatures that wanted nothing more than to eat her, until a monster saved her. Subsequently, of course, she realized he wasn't a monster (except anatomically) and fell in love with him.

Charlotte raised an eyebrow. "Anatomically?"

Arthur flushed. "Well—it's—he *looks* like a monster, that's all," he said, although, since he hadn't yet reached an intimate scene, he couldn't be sure the love interest's monstrous anatomy *didn't* extend to his nether regions.

Charlotte grinned. "Good heavens, Arthur, what did you think I meant?"

Arthur flicked her shoulder, but he liked seeing her grin. He returned to her hair and his story.

The braids were done before he was. Charlotte slipped into her bedclothes. Though they were far too old for such things, Arthur tucked her in. Her lips twitched, which was why he'd done it. By the time he finished telling her about his new book, she'd sunk into oblivion.

Even asleep, she looked exhausted. The dark crescents under her eyes seemed permanent.

Arthur's brow creased. He kissed her forehead. She was already tired all the time; he didn't need to pile on by making her worry about the children.

"I won't tell Dad's stories anymore," he whispered. "I'll forget all about the forest."

In that moment, he meant it.

III. In which Arthur is a hopeless romantic, emphasis on "hopeless"

The last day of August dawned like any other Sunday. Charlotte shook Arthur awake far too early so the family could wash, dress, and traipse the half mile downhill into Seacliff for Mass. A narrow path was worn into the heather from four decades of the Throckmorton-Prentices going back and forth between the cottage and the village. George Throckmorton had built rough wooden stairs into the steepest bits decades ago, with lumber taken from Shiftleaf back when the forest was friendlier. Now, salt and sea breezes had worn the steps smooth.

Arthur shuddered his way through a yawn. The morning was cool, but he sweated through his shirt. By the time they made it home after Mass, between the late-August warmth and the walk uphill, he'd be soaked. Behind him, Sasha straggled along, hand in hand with Jonas and even more exhausted than Arthur. She stumbled; her uncle hoisted her onto his back, and they went onward.

The grass grew longer and more golden, undulating around them. Farther downhill, the first hovels appeared: half-ruined old fishing shacks abandoned for their proximity to the cliff and the forest thereon. With the wood as dangerous as it was now, the villagers refused to live in its shadow. One of many superstitions, but one of the few not aimed at the sea.

Never whistle into the wind or you'll whistle up a storm. Don't wish an angler good luck or you'll doom him to bad.

(The wishing of good luck on the part of one fisherman to another he was known to harbor some grudge against had been the start of more than one fight in Seacliff.)

No black bags on the boats. No women on the boats. Always throw back the day's first catch. Baptize new gear with whiskey before using it.

So on and so forth, superstitions passed down through generations. Those who'd been out with Charlotte's husband the morning he'd drowned, not long after Sasha's birth, were convinced it was because he'd failed to throw back his first catch.

So important, these rituals. Each one was believed with perfect sincerity and observed with perfect precision (or, not having been observed, counteracted with a different ritual that existed for just such a purpose). Yet none was believed so sincerely or observed so perfectly as *Don't name the wood.*

The shacks gave way to hard-packed dirt paths, then narrow cobbled streets and stone cottages. Charlotte lagged, but when Arthur suggested they rest, she declared they would be late.

Except for roaming chickens, the village square was deserted. Mist twisted over the cobbles. Back up the hill, the Throckmorton-Prentices' whitewashed cottage looked like it was perched in the clouds. Behind it, the tips of treetops jutted darkly into the sky.

The family joined the thin stream of villagers heading toward the spindly stone church spearing upward like a dagger at the village's southern end. The convent abutted it like a fortress. Headstones studding the churchyard looked ethereal in the mist, until Arthur smacked into one and received painful confirmation of its corporeality. He shifted Sasha on his back. His shin throbbed.

The churchgoers were hard and gray like the buildings, with pinched, dour faces and leathery, salt-beaten skin, but they were turned out in their Sunday best. Gaggles of them stopped around the church steps, or just inside, or clustered at the ends of pews for a few minutes of gossip before the service began.

". . . wants to go to school in Port Lorne if you can believe it. I told her proper young girls study at the convent, not university, and anyway how would we come up with the money, and there's the wood to think of besides. But she's—"

". . . see that city friend of Bess's finally left. Her parents are relieved Bess didn't go back with her, but I think—"

". . . worried about this pregnancy. If it's anything like the last I'm afraid what will—"

". . . eldest Tierney girl was finally heard from. Did you know, she's eloped with that no-account Cameron boy—"

At the latter comment, Arthur nearly dropped Sasha. She grumbled, rubbing her eyes as he set her down.

"Sorry, dearest," Arthur said. "We're here."

He hurried after his sister and older nibling, clutching Sasha's hand and willing no one to notice him. It was easy, at first; as a matter of course, people tended to ignore him. But as the Throckmorton-Prentices reached their pew . . .

"Mr. Throckmorton," said a voice he had hoped not to hear.

Arthur squeezed Sasha's hand.

"Mrs. Tierney," he said with reluctance. "How do you do this morning?"

"You look at me when I'm talking to you, young man."

With even greater reluctance, Arthur dragged his gaze from the floor to Mrs. Tierney's forehead. Looking at a person's forehead made them believe he was making the required eye contact without him actually having to do so.

Mrs. Tierney glowered up at him. Shriveled and bent, she leaned heavily on a cane while three of her five daughters towered around her. They were pink cheeked and neat but uncomfortable as their mother prodded him with her cane.

"I'll tell you how I'm doing," she growled. "My Mary finally wrote. She's settled in Glenwhistle, did you know? She eloped with the Cameron boy."

"Congratulations to her," Charlotte said dismissively. Arthur flinched. "Please excuse us, Mrs. Tierney. You're blocking our seats."

"Congratulations indeed!" Mrs. Tierney's nostrils flared. She stood firmly in their way. "Married to the bastard son of a drunk. He's not even employed! You were no catch," she said to Arthur, which might've stung if he hadn't been well aware, "but at least you work for your living, even if it is to tinker with rich people's baubles instead of doing something useful. And lucky for you that doctor stepfather of yours legitimized you when he married your mother, God knows why he did it."

"Ma," one of her daughters said in embarrassment, but Charlotte intervened.

"Forgive me, Mrs. Tierney, but I don't see how it's any of our business whom Miss Tierney has married, unless you mean to apologize for her breaking off her courtship with my brother without a word."

"I assure you that's not necessary," Arthur said hastily.

Mrs. Tierney let out a bark of laughter. The nearest villagers turned, more interested in this conversation than their own.

"Apologize to *him*? Do you know, Mrs. Prentice, who funded her elopement? Your brother himself! Oh yes," she said, and leered at Arthur, who wished he had stayed in bed, "she wrote and told me everything. Asked me to *thank you*, if you can believe it. Thank you! For allowing her to—"

"With what money?"

Turning to Arthur, Charlotte didn't look angry, just exasperated—an expression not unfamiliar to him, but he quailed.

"I had a little saved up."

His sister sighed. "Arthur . . ."

"She gave him some sob story," Mrs. Tierney continued, "about already being courted, by someone her cruel old mother wouldn't let her marry. Did she even tell you who it was? Or did you give her the money without considering what such a match might do to her?"

Arthur wanted to sink into the floor. "She told me, yes."

"You see!" Mrs. Tierney sounded triumphant, though she had clearly expected him not to know. "Good God, what a fool you are. Giving a silly young girl the money to run away and elope with a boy with no family, no money, no standing! She'll be ruined thanks to you."

She might have sounded upset about the ruination of her eldest daughter, which would surely reflect poorly on her four younger daughters—or would have, before Seacliff had suffered the loss of so many eligible young people to far-off cities—but her voice was filled with savage delight.

"And *now*," she said, "my youngest has run off, too, and I want to know what you know about it."

"Nothing."

"A likely story!"

It was true, however. During their courtship—such as it was—Arthur had struck up a sort of friendship with Mary. It had culminated in her tearful confession that her mother was less afraid of her becoming a spinster and more afraid of her marrying Alasdair Cameron. But he knew the missing girl, her sister Brigid, only by sight.

Mrs. Tierney's ire might've made him regret giving her oldest daughter his savings, but Mary's tale had been dreadfully romantic. The chance meeting between the girl from a good family and the boy from a bad one. The discovery of unlikely similarities in their hopes and dreams. The love letters. The anguished confession. It had been so like something from one of Arthur's books that he'd immediately retrieved the cash from the sock at the bottom of his dresser and pressed it into Mary's hands, urging her to elope with Alasdair like she'd hoped to.

Only afterward did Arthur realize he'd have to start saving all over. But he'd been strangely relieved. He had the uncomfortable feeling that, as much as he hoped to relocate to Port Lorne one day, he was afraid of doing so, too.

In the choir loft, the organ started up. The villagers closest, who had ceased all gossip to better listen to Mrs. Tierney's accusations, settled into their pews. Cormac Young, his wife, and three of their children slipped into the pew behind the Throckmorton-Prentices. Rosie, his youngest, coughed intermittently, but she hummed along with the organ. Arthur flushed, not wanting Cormac to witness the ridiculousness taking place in front of him.

"If you please, Mrs. Tierney," Charlotte said coolly, "Mass is about to start. You had better find your seat."

The old woman wasn't done with Arthur, but one of her daughters said, "Heaven's sakes, Ma," and headed for the Tierneys' pew without waiting for her.

Mrs. Tierney cast a final, withering glance at Arthur and said to Charlotte, "If your brother has spurred another of my children into an ill-fated love match, Mrs. Prentice, you best believe I'll do something about it."

Charlotte sighed, but Mrs. Tierney had moved off.

Usually, Arthur sat on the far end of the pew, with Sasha and Jonas between him and their mother so he could keep Sasha (more or less) quiet during the service. This morning, however, Charlotte nudged the children into their seats first, sat beside them, leaned her cane against the back of the next pew, and gestured Arthur in after her. Sasha slumped against her older sibling, on the verge of falling asleep.

Arthur's skin prickled. He was very aware of the Youngs behind him, and Mrs. Tierney glaring at him from her pew farther up. Her daughters kept trying to make her turn around but gave up as the processional started.

When the priest had passed, Charlotte leaned close and murmured, "You really don't know anything about Brigid Tierney?"

Arthur shook his head.

She straightened, tucking a stray hairpin back into her chignon. "Well, that's something."

He flinched. She hadn't known about the money; he'd hoped, when he gave it to Mary, that she'd never find out. Trust Mrs. Tierney to ruin that.

Sure enough, Charlotte leaned back over as the priest gave a short welcome. "We could've used the money."

"It wasn't much."

"All the more reason to have kept it," Charlotte said, but she focused back on the service rather than her brother's romantic whims.

As Mass went on, she stumbled over responses and hymns she'd known her entire life. The fog that had enveloped her brain on and off since her illness had that effect; she'd forget a word, why she'd entered a room, or what she'd meant to add to her medical kit before visiting a patient. Gripping her hand, Arthur responded and sang louder so she could follow along, but her eyes brimmed with angry tears. She kept one hand on the wedding ring at her neck, rubbing it for comfort.

At long last, Mass was over. The sun guttered weakly in the uneasy sky. Long tendrils of mist lifted and burned away; the late-August air had grown clammy rather than warm. Villagers spilled from the church. Their gossip washed around the

Throckmorton-Prentices, but Arthur tuned it out. He didn't want to hear delight over the scandal of Mary Tierney's elopement or speculations about the disappearance of her sister.

He couldn't help speculating himself, however. "Where has Miss Brigid gone, do you suppose?"

Charlotte glanced at him wearily but offered no answer. She'd managed the end of the liturgy without stumbling over the words, but concentrating so hard to remember something she'd known for thirty-six years had exhausted her.

"She was seen heading uphill the other night," one of the other Tierney girls said, drifting toward them. "Then she was gone. Ma's convinced she's eloped like Mary did, but—" the girl's voice lowered "—we're afraid she's gone into the wood."

"Kitty!" Mrs. Tierney snapped from somewhere in the throng of people. The girl jumped. "Where have you got to? Are all my daughters to run off on me now?"

"Tell us if you see her, won't you?" Kitty whispered, then called, "Coming, Ma!" and rabbited away.

IV. In which Charlotte faces wood sickness

The Throckmorton-Prentices hadn't made it past the churchyard when a well-dressed old woman with milky skin and impeccable posture stopped them. She took one of Charlotte's hands in both of her own, warm and welcoming as she'd been for as long as Charlotte could remember.

"My dear Charlotte. I hoped I might speak to you."

"What can I do for you, Mrs. Livingston?" Charlotte asked.

The old woman nearly snorted, but she was too well-bred. "'Mrs. Livingston.' Please, Charlotte, I pray you will call me Agnes. How long have we known each other, yet you insist on such formalities?"

Charlotte's lips twitched. "It seems one of us ought to."

"Silly girl," Agnes said fondly.

Charlotte may have been thirty-six, but she'd been a favorite of Agnes's since childhood. After their father's disappearance, their mother, drowning in grief, had taken to her bed, neglecting her work, her home, and her children. The villagers had offered her no help or sympathy. Twelve-year-old Arthur had dressed himself and Charlotte in their best clothes, taken his sister's hand, and walked up to the Livingstons' manor door to ask in a trembling voice whether they had any clocks in need of repair.

Agnes's husband had wanted to turn them away, but Agnes had hushed him. Pulling an old mantel clock out of storage, she'd told Arthur she'd pay him to fix it. She'd played a game with Charlotte while he'd worked, made him stop so they could have supper, and, when he'd managed the repair, paid him far too much and told them to come back the next day.

Agnes was the main reason the two of them hadn't starved, since Arthur's only notable skill was clock repair and Charlotte had been just five years old. Back then, Charlotte had wished the old woman was secretly their grandmother and would adopt them once the truth came out. But she wasn't, and she didn't.

The old woman smiled at Arthur, offering her hand.

"Arthur, dear boy." He kissed her hand, bowing, and she turned back to Charlotte. "Do you have a moment to come by the house?"

"Is everything all right?"

Charlotte hadn't visited in some time. As she and Arthur had grown, and Charlotte had become a healer, they hadn't relied so heavily on Agnes. Then, too, Charlotte had become more aware of the differences between them; Agnes could sail about doing whatever she pleased because she had money. Though Arthur cared for her ever-increasing collection of timepieces, she'd never had need of Charlotte's services before: She'd long kept a live-in physician who'd tended her husband's poor health. Agnes had outlived her physician (and her husband), but surely she'd send to Port Lorne for a doctor if she needed medical attention now.

"It's poor Gracie—my cousin, you know. Gracie Buchanan. I don't think you've met her yet, Charlotte. Arthur has, of course, he comes by so often. I do wish you'd visit more."

"Gracie Buchanan?" Charlotte prompted.

"Yes, of course." Agnes's smile faded. She wrung her hands.

"A tad under the weather, I'm afraid. If you wouldn't mind taking a look . . ."

The area over Charlotte's left eye throbbed with a threatening migraine, but she was a healer before she was anything else. "Of course."

Her brother bit his lip, but she attempted a smile. Her facial muscles felt stiff. She hadn't smiled much in the last six months.

"I won't be long, I'm sure. You go on home with the children."

"Well," he said helplessly, but Agnes said, "As it happens, I'd like to talk to your brother, too, on another matter. The children are welcome. You know how I adore children."

Charlotte would've really smiled at that, if not for that throbbing over her left eye. Agnes had spent hours playing games with her when she was a child, or lying on the floor of her drawing room, pretending to see shapes in the clouds painted on the ceiling. Arthur said she still asked after Charlotte whenever he visited.

Agnes hurried toward the Livingstons' manor. Charlotte lagged, fatigued from her muzzy-headedness during Mass and the headache now.

"Are you all right?" Arthur asked.

She gritted her teeth. "Yes. Of course."

Luckily, the manor wasn't far. At the sight of its magnificent wooden door, carved with the family coat of arms, Charlotte froze. It made her feel five years old, walking up to that door hand in hand with her frightened but determined older brother.

The door had seemed magical then, a harbor in the sudden storm their lives had become. Arthur had spun such stories about the wondrous things they'd find inside. Reality had fallen short, as it often did; the manor was, even then, staid and prissy. Agnes's husband hadn't wanted them to touch anything, though

Arthur had washed their faces and clumsily darned their clothes before they'd come.

"Come in, come in," Agnes said, with uncharacteristic impatience.

Charlotte tore her eyes from the door. The old woman's brow was furrowed.

"Mrs. Livingston," Charlotte said, "what's going on?"

Agnes's mouth twisted. "It's the sickness."

Charlotte's heart sank. If it was wood sickness, she could do nothing. She didn't know why Gracie Buchanan should even have it. In recent years, an increasing number of villagers had entered Shiftleaf, despite their suspicion of it, for firewood or meat. But Agnes had more than enough money to buy such things, or to send someone else for them. A wealthy woman had no need to risk the forest's dangers.

Agnes pushed the door open. Inside, the manor was shabbier than Charlotte's childhood memories of it, and less lived in. Sheets covered half the furniture. An entire wing was unlit and closed off.

"The housemaid left us some time ago," Agnes said.

She offered no explanation as to where any of her other servants might have gone. Charlotte suspected they had fled the sickness. She'd never seen it spread from person to person, but that didn't stop the villagers from staying far from any house with a black rag on the door.

Automatically, Charlotte turned toward the spare bedchamber in which Agnes had sometimes laid out old clothes, tutting over how out of fashion they were but promising to have them resized for Charlotte or Arthur. Charlotte had barely opened the door, however, and glimpsed a bedchamber long out of use, when Agnes said, "This way. She's in my room."

Charlotte's skin prickled.

"Well, gosh," Arthur said. "That's awfully kind of her, letting her cousin stay in her own room when she's ill."

Charlotte flushed, grateful for her own sake that Arthur didn't have the suspicions she suddenly did about the nature of the women's relationship. If he didn't suspect anything amiss about them, likely he didn't suspect anything about his sister's proclivities, either.

At the door to Agnes's bedchamber, Charlotte fumbled in her pocket for the masks she always carried in case of unexpected house calls like this. While the sickness didn't seem to spread between people, she still knew so little about it that she preferred not to take the risk. She put a mask over her nose and mouth and offered one to Arthur, but he said, "I'll take the children and wait in the drawing room, shall I?"

"Can I come with you, Mama?" Jonas asked.

"Of course, dearest." Charlotte turned to her brother. "You'll be all right with Sasha?"

Arthur smiled, grasping his niece's hand. "Of course. We have great fun together, don't we, duck?"

"Can we play pirate?" Sasha asked.

"Not in Mrs. Livingston's drawing room."

"When we get home, then."

"If we get our chores done."

"Okay. But only if you let me use my sword. Jonas never lets me use my sword."

The sword in question was a stick bigger than Sasha, with which she was excellent at whacking people very hard. Before Charlotte could suggest, however, that it might be best if she did *not* whack her uncle as hard as she could with said stick once they got home, they disappeared around a corner. Sighing, she handed masks to Jonas and Agnes.

Agnes knocked on the chamber door but entered without

awaiting response. She hurried to the luxurious four-poster bed, where a lump was piled with blankets.

"Gracie, dearest?" Agnes leaned close to the lump, lowering her voice. "The healer's come, love."

Charlotte's skin prickled again at the endearment not meant for her ears, the tenderness in the old woman's voice. The throbbing in her head worsened.

Gracie Buchanan turned over in bed, revealing a tanned, withered face threaded with black.

Jonas stepped back with a soft gasp. Charlotte drifted forward instinctively, her uncomfortable thoughts forgotten in light of a patient who needed her care.

She peeled the blankets back. "It's all right."

The black veins extended down the sick woman's throat to her chest. Her neck was bandaged, but the veins concerned Charlotte far more. Even the whites of the woman's eyes were threaded with black.

Charlotte's skin crawled. Blood, pus, the throes of a difficult childbirth, a limb mangled during a shift in the cannery—none of them affected her, beyond the thought of how best to take care of them. The black veins characteristic of wood sickness, however, made her shudder. This was her eighth case this year, but she'd never get used it.

At least with those other things, Charlotte knew she could do something.

She felt Gracie's forehead. No fever; there never was. But the woman's breath rattled like a pot boiling over on a stove.

"How long has she been like this?"

Agnes wrung her hands again, her dark eyes fixed on Gracie's face. "Since last night. She returned from a hunt two days ago—she loves hunting, you know, and she was itching for fresh venison—I told her we could send a boy, but she *would* go—"

"Last night," Charlotte prompted.

Agnes swallowed. "Yes, my dear, forgive me for prattling so, I can't help myself—she returned two days ago with the most horrid claw marks on her neck. I was all a dither about it, but Gracie laughed and said it was fine, she'd had worse. But the next morning she shivered no matter how many blankets the servants brought or how much they built up the fire—she could hardly get up without leaning on me, insisted she was fine, but by afternoon I'd made her get back in bed, and around sunset—"

She broke off. Charlotte was about to nudge her when Gracie's voice came, like a rusty pulley.

"Aggie?"

"I'm right here, love."

The other old woman's lips cracked into a smile. A thin, wrinkled hand crawled through the blankets, searching for Agnes's. Agnes surged forward, shunting Charlotte aside.

Charlotte turned away. The sick woman needed whatever help she could give. That had to be her focus right now.

She reached into her pocket for her travel kit, a small leather case in which she kept general-use herbs and teas, an ointment for pain, a paste to prevent infection in wounds, a tincture for sleep, tweezers, sewing scissors, thread, bandages, and gloves. She slipped it into her pocket each time she left the house.

"You understand I can only do so much."

Agnes perched on the bed, smoothing her companion's hair. She blinked but didn't cry.

"Anything to ease her, however little. She can barely breathe."

She squeezed the other woman's hand then sailed away in a rustling of petticoats.

Charlotte let out a breath. Life had long blown her about like a ship in a storm. The sea had stolen her husband, the forest her father and, in a sidewise fashion, her mother; her own illness had left her weakened. Her work as a healer was the one thing that gave her a sense of control. No matter how bad an injury or illness, nine times out of ten she could heal or cure it. If she couldn't, she learned something from the failure and was more prepared next time.

The sickness reminded her it was an illusion. She had no control. No matter how practical she was, how proper, how determined, how learned, she was at the mercy of forces beyond her ken. No different than the fishermen whose lives and livelihoods were at the whim of the sea. The villagers who had been impoverished by the very ventures that had promised to enrich them. She'd lost every person who'd fallen ill to the sickness, barely able to do more than ease their passing—sometimes not even that. And despite the increasing number of cases, she knew so little about it.

It affected only those who entered the wood. The villagers' many precautions had no effect—of course; Charlotte had admonished herself more than once for thinking it could be otherwise. The sickness took hold quickly and killed quickly, in weeks, in many cases, but just as often within the week. Aside from the telltale black veins, it caused headaches, pain, fatigue, and difficulty breathing, but not fever. It was so like yet so unlike the myriad other illnesses she'd treated over the years.

"What do we do, Mama?" Jonas whispered.

With a groan, the sick woman turned back over, hiding her black-veined face in a pillow. Charlotte rubbed her forehead. The throbbing had spread over her right eye now.

"Heal-all and meadowsweet. To help with the pain and ease her breathing."

Jonas bit their lip. "But how do we make her better?"

Charlotte faltered, but if Jonas continued shadowing her work, they would learn sooner or later that sometimes nothing could be done. "I'm afraid we don't, my love."

After they applied an ointment of heal-all, Charlotte sent Jonas to boil water for meadowsweet tea. She wasn't sure how far Gracie's pain extended—asked twice, but Gracie had expended all her energy clutching at Agnes's hand. Usually, with how quickly the sickness took hold, Charlotte couldn't ask her patients what had happened that might have sickened them. It was the same case here, although Charlotte had the first inkling of an answer.

While Jonas was gone, she peeled the bandages from Gracie's neck. Despite what Agnes had said, the claw marks were shallow; Agnes was no outdoorsman and had probably thought them far worse than Gracie had. Under any other circumstances, they wouldn't have worried Charlotte. If she'd seen them before Gracie had fallen ill, Charlotte would've cleaned the scratches, dabbed an antiseptic paste of sweet amber onto them, bandaged them, and called it good.

Now, however, black veins unfurled from them. The veins were thickest around the claw marks, spooling thinner as they traced across Gracie's throat and up her face.

Charlotte might have thought the wound infected, but there was no fetid stench, no redness, no sign of gangrene. Instead, the wound appeared to be the source of the sickness.

She'd seen it before. Infection from an animal, she'd thought the first time, or some eldritch creature with dark magic in its veins. The latter would certainly explain why nothing in Charlotte's arsenal could cure the sickness. But the wounds differed from patient to patient, offering little insight into what creature might have left them, and some patients had no wound.

Perhaps the sickness had multiple causes. The only certainty was that it came from the forest. Even there, Charlotte faced frustration and confusion. Were those who returned without the sickness immune, or had they not had whatever experience had infected the others?

She treated the claw marks with antiseptic—not certain it would help—and re-dressed them.

When Jonas returned, Charlotte poured a generous mug of tea for the sick woman, drank the rest, and rubbed a fingertip of ointment on her own forehead before helping the woman sit up to drink. The throbbing in her head lessened, but not much. Enough to make it home without wanting to collapse on the hillside, probably. As usual, she'd waited too long to take care of herself.

Charlotte tucked Gracie into her blankets and sank into a wingback armchair in the corner, pressing the heels of her hands to her eyes. The darkness offered slight relief from her migraine.

"Mama," Jonas said in a hushed voice, "do you think they're really cousins?"

Charlotte glanced at Jonas and immediately regretted it; the sudden movement made her head throb sharply. Given Jonas's unusual relationship with gender, she imagined they wouldn't find her suspicions as strange or unnatural as most of Seacliff would.

But her suspicions reflected things about herself that she preferred not to think of.

"Why do you ask, my love?"

Jonas shrugged, looking uncomfortable.

Charlotte hesitated. "Mrs. Livingston says they are."

Jonas's forehead crinkled, but they didn't ask again. God help her if Sasha ever took an interest in healing. Had Sasha asked, she wouldn't have let it go until Charlotte gave an answer she found acceptable.

"Let's find Mrs. Livingston," Charlotte said. "I'm afraid we can't give her good news, but sometimes that's how healing is."

Her headache jabbed at her as she stood. Thanks to the tea, it had retreated from the right side of her forehead back to the spot over her left eye, but it was as bad there as ever, as if to make up for its lack of territory. She winced, reaching for her cane.

"Mama?"

"I'm fine."

Jonas hovered at her side, their face scrunched with worry. "I can run get Uncle Arthur if—"

"I'm fine," Charlotte snapped, then drew a long breath. She attempted a smile that was contorted with pain. "Give me your arm, love, and I'll make it all right. Your uncle has his hands full with Sasha, I'm sure."

v. In which Arthur is made a proposition

Arthur took Sasha to the drawing room. Agnes's old deck of cards was on the mantel. She'd kept it there as long as Arthur could remember; seeing it comforted him. "How about a game of war?" he asked.

"Pirates is more fun."

Arthur smiled. "You don't have your sword, duck."

Sasha plopped down on the carpet, though the room boasted several cushy armchairs and a davenport to boot. "All right."

She quickly became more enthusiastic about the game, especially since she kept beating him. As with so many other things, Arthur was terrible at war. If the game had been called "romance," he might've been better at it. Then again, maybe not. He was good at reading romance, but when it came to real life, on the rare occasion potential romance presented itself, he mucked it up as he had with Mary Tierney.

Mucked it up was an understatement in this case. He'd thrown it away with both hands. He still wasn't entirely sure why, except that, while he'd grown fond of Mary, he hadn't been in love with her.

Partway through their third game, Agnes slipped into the room. She perched on the edge of the davenport, in her habitual spot but not her habitual pose. Usually, she sank into the cushions. She'd always been warm and easy. Even the death of her husband of fifty years hadn't ruffled her. Now, however, she looked shrunken, hands fidgeting in her lap.

Arthur got up from the floor with difficulty, putting a hand to his lower back as it spasmed in protest. That had been a fortieth birthday present from his body, the muscle spasm in his back. Usually, it hit at odd moments, but he had to admit that, in this case, sitting on the floor had been fair provocation.

"Hey," Sasha said. "We're not done yet. It's no fair to stop because you're losing."

His smile was more of a grimace this time. He rubbed his back. "We'll finish up, duck, I promise. Let me speak to Mrs. Livingston first."

Sighing dramatically, Sasha flopped back to gaze at the intricately painted (albeit flaking) ceiling. Arthur's grimace turned into a real smile as his pain faded. He used to come in from his work to find Agnes and Charlotte lying on the floor that way, head to head, their hands behind their heads as they pointed out fanciful shapes in the painted clouds to each other.

He wondered, briefly, whether Charlotte could be induced to do such a thing now with an aid in place, or some good pillows. These days, with her fatigue and aches, lying on the floor would be terrible, and getting up would be worse.

Arthur sank into the nearest armchair and reached for Agnes's hand. She chewed her lower lip. Usually, she stopped after a few seconds, laughed, and said perhaps she'd break the habit in another fifty years or so. Today, she merely went on mangling her lip.

"Mrs. Livingston," Arthur said, "you wanted to discuss something with me?"

"Yes," she said faintly, then more firmly: "Yes." Her posture relaxed; she stopped chewing her lip. "It's about a clock."

"What else?" Arthur said with a smile, but Agnes shook her head.

"Not one of my clocks, dear boy—not yet, at any rate. The last time Gracie and I were in Port Lorne, we saw this grandfather clock in an antique shop. The shopkeeper claimed it was over a hundred and fifty years old, but by God it was the ugliest clock I'd ever seen. All square edges, hardly any ornamentation . . . Gracie went to look at it every day, God knows why. It was absolutely hideous. I didn't buy it, of course."

"Of course," Arthur said in confusion.

Agnes drummed her fingers on her knee. "I want to buy it now."

"What does that have to do with me?"

"I want you to buy it for me. As my agent."

Arthur opened his mouth but closed it without saying anything.

"I can't leave Gracie," Agnes said, "not while she's like this. I simply must be with her. But I want that clock for her. If I had known when we were there that she'd— I've wired the seller, of course, to make sure it's available—someone else had their eye on it, but I convinced him I could pay more. It's dreadfully ironic. That clock will likely end up the most expensive piece in my collection once I have it—imagine! The ugliest clock you've ever seen, but—"

Arthur's tongue unstuck itself. "Mrs. Livingston . . . why do you want me to buy this clock for you?"

"It's for Gracie," she said wildly. Sasha glanced up from the floor, frowning, but resumed her painted-cloud gazing without interrupting. "I need to buy it. For Gracie. Don't you understand, dear boy? For all my riches, I can't do a thing for her. There's no cure in the world money can buy. I can't even give her relief without going to your sister or some doctor for help—but I can do this. I can buy a hideous old clock for her."

She sat gulping down air for several moments, eyes damp. Arthur fished a handkerchief from his pocket and handed it to her. She clenched it in her fist without using it, but when she spoke she sounded calm again.

"I would like you," she said, "to travel to Port Lorne on my behalf," and Arthur's heart leaped. "I'll provide you with a horse and cart. You'll have to go the direct route, through the wood, I mean—going around would take far too long. By the time you returned she might be— I'll provide money for any expenses you might incur, of course. You know clocks better than anyone in the village, certainly, and frankly better than half the so-called experts I've met in my travels. I want you to see the clock before I buy it. Make sure it's in working order and hasn't suffered any damage. If he tries to talk you up on price—well, let him, I suppose. I must have it as soon as possible, and the money is no matter . . ."

Arthur's hand clenched on the arm of his chair. Money was no matter to Agnes because she'd always had a great deal of it.

"I'll pay you handsomely," she concluded. "Half when you leave, plus expenses, and half when you return."

When she told him the sum, he rocketed out of his chair. Sasha popped up from the floor.

"Uncle Arthur?"

"I'm all right, duck."

He ran his hands through his hair. It was so much money. So much. Charlotte could live comfortably on the first half while he was gone. They could send for a doctor to care for her, to see if anything more could be done for her fatigue, her pain, her dizzy spells and bouts of brain fog. She could hire out one of the village girls to keep house, if she wanted. Not that she *would* want, because Charlotte eschewed all help, but perhaps if Arthur insisted . . .

Then—when he returned—with the rest of the money, they'd have enough to relocate to Port Lorne like he'd dreamed for so long, with some left over besides.

Here Agnes's cousin fell ill, and Agnes offered him everything he'd ever wanted, except a wife. But surely courting would go better if Arthur were a man of means, if not exactly of consequence, even if he was odd and not much to look at. With enough money, he could hire someone to fix up the house, as old Mr. Livingston used to do, instead of muddling through repairs himself. None of that would matter in Port Lorne anyway. Maybe, there, he could have a shop—make a living, a real one, not only repairing but designing, making, and selling timepieces.

He'd follow the same path through the forest his father had taken for so many years. He'd see the city, the clock shop (if it was still there), the ships coming in to port—the enchantment of the forest, perhaps even the Lord of the Wood—everything George had told him about. Everything he'd been holding so tightly to in the thirty years since his father's disappearance.

"Well?" Agnes said; he'd been pacing without responding.

The memory of George's last trip knifed through him. Arthur hadn't even said goodbye, too busy sulking.

He'd always wanted to travel through the forest. He'd always wanted to see Port Lorne. That was precisely *why* he'd been sulking that morning thirty years ago.

Yet now, instead of, *Yes, of course, I'd be delighted to go*, he said, "I shall have to discuss it with Lottie."

He forced himself to sit.

"Of course. I'd expect nothing else." Agnes leaned toward him, eyes wide. "But do decide soon, won't you, dear boy? Gracie hasn't much time."

His stomach clenched. He merely nodded, thinking of the

sickness. He'd always believed in the enchanted forest their father had told so many stories about, but now the enchantment seemed to have soured.

Even so, something small and deep inside him ached to go into the wood.

"You must convince him, Charlotte dear," Agnes said suddenly.

Charlotte had entered the room, leaning on Jonas. Arthur was on his feet instantly, forgetting Agnes's proposal at the sight of his sister. Her face crumpled in pain.

"What?"

"I've just made him the most wonderful proposal." Agnes sounded more like her cheerful self, but it had a forced quality. She rose, in a rustling of silk. "You must convince him to take it, and quickly, too. How is Gracie?"

Arthur gave Charlotte his arm. Her cane helped, but sometimes an arm was better. He relaxed as she clutched at him; her grip wasn't as tight as it could get when her pain and exhaustion were at their worst. The walk home would be long, but they'd make it all right.

Guilt surged through him. Sometimes, when he had extra money, he hired a cart to take them back uphill so she could ride instead of walk, but he'd given all his extra money to Mary.

"I did what I could for her," Charlotte said. "I'll leave you some tea, and a tincture to help her sleep. I'm afraid I can't do more."

Agnes pursed her lips, blinking rapidly. She pulled a pocketbook from her skirt, opened it, counted out money, and handed it to Charlotte. Arthur saw the thoughts warring on his sister's face: Their family could use the money, and Agnes could certainly afford it—unlike most of the villagers—but she hated to take so much for seeing a patient for whom she had done virtually nothing. Their father had been the same way. He could've made plenty of money as a doctor in Glenwhistle or Port Lorne or any number of other places, but he'd been determined to do right by the place he'd grown up.

Charlotte handed the money back. "It's too much, Mrs. Livingston."

"Nonsense."

"I couldn't do anything for her."

"I'm sure you did what you could."

"It's too much."

Agnes sighed, recounted the money, and removed some. She shoved the remainder back into Charlotte's hand.

"At least let me give you some of Theo's old shoes for your boy. He looks ready for new ones. I'm sure he's about the size Theo was at that age."

Jonas flushed but mumbled their thanks as Agnes found and gave them the shoes. *They* was only at home, no matter how much it chafed when the villagers said *he*. In a village where men were men and women were women, that had seemed safest, when they'd told their mother and uncle several months ago, in a trembling voice, that they were uncomfortable being called a boy. Arthur had always had a hard enough time being a failure of a man rather than something else entirely.

Charlotte gave a smile more like a grimace. Arthur put an arm around Jonas's shoulder, thanked Agnes more audibly, and steered the family outside.

"Think about my offer, Arthur," the old woman called after him, but he merely waved over his shoulder as the door shut behind them.

VI. In which Arthur makes a decision, which he may well come to regret

Charlotte's pain and exhaustion persisted. Arthur did what he could: brewed tea, brought heating pads and cold compresses by turn, sent the children outside to play and take care of the chickens and goat so the house would be quiet. He washed the bedclothes and hung them on the line, fed the children lunch, and even, when the time came, attempted to cook supper. The fish was overdone, the vegetables underdone, but Charlotte's migraine had never gone away and she couldn't stomach more than crackers anyway. Arthur ate with the children, poking at his fish so moodily that, had one of the children been doing it, he would've had the urge to suggest they not play with their food.

He couldn't stop thinking about Agnes's proposition. It was so much money. The adventure he'd always wanted.

But how could he leave Charlotte for so long, without anyone to look after her? How could he leave the children for so long? He'd never been apart from them a single night their entire lives.

He could ask one of the villagers to look in on the family, but such a request would likely come to naught. Not only because it was him asking, but because the villagers thought Charlotte, as a healer, ought to be able to heal herself and, more importantly, believed pain and exhaustion ought to be pushed past, not coddled.

Agnes might have agreed to it normally—all right, she might've sent a servant, normally—but he doubted she'd leave her cousin alone sick for so much as half an hour, and her servants were gone. Maybe one of the nuns would do it, though they rarely left the convent. The village school was their only connection to the outside world, and even that required their pupils to go into the convent.

Perhaps, instead of checking in, Agnes would let Charlotte and the children stay with her. Assuming Charlotte agreed to such an arrangement.

Jonas stole a sideways glance at him. "Are you okay, Uncle Arthur?"

He ran a hand through his hair. "Oh, I'm fine, duck. Just thinking. Check on Mother for me, won't you?"

Jonas obliged. Sasha was bribed into helping clean up, with a promise she could have three of yesterday's biscuits when she was done. With biscuits on the line, she whirled through the kitchen so quickly Arthur feared she might break rather than clean the dishes, but she was so enthusiastic that he couldn't bring himself to tell her to slow down.

Charlotte was still in her armchair when Arthur put the children to bed. As usual, Sasha tried to stall. But when Arthur turned to a kissing scene in his favorite novel and started reading it with relish, she decided bedtime was the lesser of two evils.

Pleased, Arthur filed "read kissing scene dramatically" away as a future solution to bedtime avoidance and went to check on his sister. Her head lolled onto her shoulder; she was asleep, for which Arthur was grateful. Half the time, when she sat down or went to her room for a nap, she failed to fall asleep, no matter how exhausted, and arose groggy and resentful.

He built up the fire in the grate, shook out the blanket on the settee, draped it over Charlotte, and tucked her in. To his dismay, her eyes cracked open before he had finished.

"What time is it?" she mumbled.

"Half nine."

"Are the children in bed?"

"Yes," Arthur said with a smile. "Sasha didn't want me to read about kissing, so she went to sleep."

Charlotte let out a soft huff of laughter, straightening in her chair. The bruises under her eyes, ever present, didn't seem as dark as they'd been earlier, though it was difficult to tell in the firelight.

Her laughter faded. "I lost the whole day. I hate it when I lose a whole day."

"You did manage Mass this morning. And taking care of Mrs. Livingston's cousin."

Her eyes flickered toward him and away. She sighed, rubbing her forehead.

"Yes, I took care of her . . . cousin, for all the good it did. The sickness—I can't do anything about it, Arthur. I can hardly treat the symptoms."

"I'm sure you do the best you can," Arthur said, but Charlotte shook her head.

"My best isn't good enough anymore. I can't help anyone."

"That's not true. Thomas Young would be out of work if you hadn't saved his arm after that accident at the cannery. Ada Brown would've died in childbirth if not for you, and probably the baby, too. I don't think her husband would say you can't help anyone."

Charlotte twisted her fingers together in her lap. "I couldn't help Gracie Buchanan this morning. I haven't been able to help anyone with wood sickness, and more cases each year."

"Lottie," Arthur said softly, because he knew what was coming, but too late.

"I couldn't save Mam." Her fingers clenched so hard her knuckles whitened. "I couldn't save John."

Arthur knelt beside her, untangled her hands. Her eyes were red rimmed and glassy.

"There wasn't anything you could have done," he started, but Charlotte said, "Please don't."

In silence, he squeezed her hands and retreated to his own chair. Charlotte had done what she could for their mother, but it had been too late. John had been dead by the time the other fishermen had hauled him out of the water that morning eight years ago. But he'd only lived so long in the first place because Charlotte had saved his life years before. When she was nineteen, he'd washed ashore unconscious and half drowned, the lone survivor—best they could figure afterward, since he remembered nothing—of a shipwreck. It had been the first time she'd saved someone's life. Missing memories aside, he'd lived happy and healthy until the sea had claimed him.

Charlotte looked at the ceiling, blinking back tears. She'd never cried much before, but since her illness she teared up at the drop of a hat. Yet another thing to add to her frustrations, Arthur knew. Their mother had been dreadfully weepy after their father's disappearance, not only at first but for the rest of her life, and Charlotte had resented it. Eileen had spent more time nurturing her grief than her children.

"What was that proposition Mrs. Livingston mentioned today?" Charlotte asked.

Arthur's skin prickled. He'd almost managed to forget it,

through the debacle of bedtime. "Oh—it's nothing. Something she wants me to do for her, that's all. It's not important."

Sometimes, when Charlotte had a bad day, she could be put off that way. Other times, she could be as persistent as Sasha.

Today, apparently, she was the latter. "What was it?"

Arthur explained Agnes's proposition. When he mentioned the money, Charlotte let out a low whistle.

"Not important! Arthur—"

"I know."

"Why didn't you agree at once?"

Why, indeed? Agnes Livingston had virtually handed him everything he'd ever wanted—but instead of accepting, he'd put her off.

"Well, as I said, she wants it quickly. Which means, you know—"

Unease crept across Charlotte's face. "You'd have to go through the wood."

"Precisely," Arthur said, relieved. "So you see why I can't . . . I can't take Mrs. Livingston up on her offer if it means entering the wood, can I?"

It came out more desperate than he'd intended. He just wanted Charlotte to tell him he couldn't go. If she said he couldn't go—he couldn't go; it was as simple as that. He wouldn't have to make the decision; he wouldn't have to live with more than mild disappointment in himself for not arguing harder in favor of going. He'd never learn whether or not the forest and the city beyond could stand up to the shining bubble of his long-held dreams.

"It is dangerous." Charlotte looked at him. "I know you don't think so—not really. But it is. If you'd seen as much of the sickness as I have . . . Supposing you came home with it? Or supposing you never came home at all?"

"You're right, of course. I don't know what I was thinking, even considering. Silly of me."

"Silly," Charlotte echoed. Her expression sobered. "But . . ."

Why was she saying *but*? Why wasn't she agreeing he couldn't possibly go?

"I don't . . . It's so much money. We could . . ."

"I know."

"You might inquire into housing while you're there. That is—you wouldn't have much time for that, I suppose, since you need to be back quickly, but if you placed an inquiry and had them wire the information . . ."

The prickling subsided. Arthur imagined finding a house with four separate bedrooms and a proper dining room (large enough for dinner parties) that was nonetheless reasonably priced, to which—upon taking possession—he could invite the many friends he was certain to have if he lived in Port Lorne.

"That is true. I hadn't thought of that."

Charlotte glanced at him. "I know you've always wanted to go."

His father's voice echoed distantly in his ears. *Not this year, son. When you're older.* He'd said it so many times.

"Yes," Arthur said wistfully. "Maybe the clock shop Dad told me about is still there."

"But you haven't said yes."

Arthur's thoughts ground to a halt. He'd hardly stopped thinking of all Agnes's offer could bring him. Not merely the money, but the chance to journey through the forest to Port Lorne.

But he hadn't said yes.

"Arthur," Charlotte said, "what is it you're afraid of? I know it isn't the forest," she added with a smile, "even if I wish it were."

Quite possibly he was afraid of getting everything he'd ever wanted. Far better to have been afraid of the wood, as was sensible. Alas, Arthur Throckmorton was not a sensible man.

"I'm afraid," he said in a low voice, "that I'll go, and it won't change anything."

"What do you mean?"

Arthur's fingers curled over the arms of his chair. "Well . . . what if I never make it? Not because of anything, I don't know, *eldritch* but simply because I'm a hopeless woodsman and a perfectly normal forest could kill me if it wanted? What if I make it but something happens to the clock on the way back and Mrs. Livingston never gives me the second payment? Or I make it back but I'm too late, and Mrs. Buchanan has died and can't enjoy the clock even a moment, and Mrs. Livingston is absolutely devastated and regrets sending me in the first place?"

Charlotte touched his hand, but now that he'd started, all the fears he'd spent the day suppressing surged over him like a tidal wave.

"What if I can't find a house in Port Lorne, even with all that money? Or I do, but when we move in it's falling apart, and I didn't notice beforehand because I know nothing about construction? Or the house is wonderful, but we can't find clients, and eventually our money from Mrs. Livingston runs out, and we have nothing left to fall back on and no way to get back here to start over? Or perhaps—" Arthur spoke faster than ever because if he didn't he'd never admit it "—perhaps everything in Port Lorne will be perfectly lovely, but I won't have any friends, or a wife, because I'm still *me*."

In the silence, his chest heaved. At his core, he'd always been afraid to make a change, because he'd always been afraid of finding that he—not Seacliff, not the loss of his father or brother-in-law or mother, not the lack of money—was the problem. It was so much easier to make believe, to pretend there were insurmountable obstacles to even attempting a change. That things would be perfect if only they ever happened, and it was simply a shame they never would.

After a long moment, Charlotte's fingers curled around his. "You don't believe that, do you? That you're . . ."

Arthur wasn't sure what he hoped she would say. Regardless, he was disappointed. After a pause in which he saw the gears turning in her head as clearly as if she'd been a clock he'd opened up, all she said was, "What are you going to do?"

It was the worst thing she could've asked.

"Don't you want to tell me what you think?"

She gave another small smile, squeezed his hand, and let go. "I've told you what I think."

"Yes, but—should I go or not?"

"You'll have to decide yourself. You're a grown man, Arthur. I'm not making the decision for you."

Arthur wiped his hands on his trousers. "But—but if you said—you could tell me the forest is too dangerous—that I have to stay—or—"

His sister shook her head. "I could, but I won't."

"What if you don't like the decision I make?"

"Then I guess I'll have to live with it."

Charlotte stood, too quickly. She clamped a hand down on his shoulder and swayed. He stood, too, but she said, as always, "I'm fine," and made her slow way to her bedroom alone, calling good-night as she went.

Arthur sat up alone for a long time.

Not this year, son, he heard his father saying, year after year. *When you're older.*

He remembered his father knocking on the door of the bedroom he'd shared with Charlotte, the same room his niblings shared now. The way he'd refused to answer, except for a *bye, Dad* so quiet George hadn't heard. His father vanishing within the trees by the time he'd run outside.

Arthur had regretted his momentary stubbornness for thirty years.

You think the forest is this beautiful place full of adventure and enchantment, he heard Charlotte saying yesterday, *but it's* dangerous, *Arthur.*

Dangerous it was. He knew that. Technically. He knew about the sickness, the disappearances. Their father's disappearance three decades ago.

Yet when Arthur thought of the forest now, all he remembered were his father's stories.

"It can't be *that* dangerous," he murmured, lost in images of a fairy prince in autumn finery and trees walking from place to place. "Not all of it, at any rate. Bess Little came from Port Lorne with that friend of hers just a few weeks ago."

Not this year, son. It occurred to him his father might have kept putting off bringing him along precisely because it had been dangerous. It was an enchanted forest, after all.

But even Charlotte must think the danger couldn't quite stand up to the money Agnes was offering, or she would have forbidden him to go. Begged him not to. But she hadn't.

He grabbed his novel off the side table and meandered up to the attic, mumbling about the forest all the way.

It was a small, cramped space, the attic, crammed with sacks of potatoes and carrots, old clothes, broken furniture they might repair or repurpose. Arthur's bed was there, too, shoved up against an exterior wall so cold that he was reluctant to relinquish the warmth of his quilt on chill autumn mornings. Just now, Freya was curled on his pillow.

Arthur stashed the book in a box under his bed, where he'd kept his romance novels since first hiding one from his mother.

She'd caught him with such a book at fifteen and given him an odd look.

Why would you be interested in a book like that? she'd asked, in a tone that had made him crimson with shame. He didn't remember how he'd responded, only that he'd mumbled *something.* After a long moment, Eileen had said, *I suppose it might teach you a thing or two about how to treat a lady.*

But she'd looked so uneasy every time she'd seen him with a romance novel that he'd gone back to hiding them. Biscuit baking had been much the same. When Charlotte was eight, their mother had taught her to bake biscuits. Arthur, fifteen, had asked whether she might teach him, too. Eileen had laughed and told him it wasn't something a young man needed to know. He'd been almost glad to make her laugh—she'd rarely laughed since their father's disappearance—except that it had been at his own expense, for reasons he didn't understand. Charlotte had taught him several years later.

Sometimes Arthur wondered how his father would have reacted to these things. George had always been so soft with him, so kind, so understanding of the ways in which Arthur was different from other boys. But perhaps he'd only been that way because Arthur had been so young: Eileen had been the same, until Arthur was a fifteen-year-old reading romance and asking how to bake biscuits.

His skin prickled. He'd been a failure all his life. He'd been afraid all his life, all the while pretending he had nothing to fear. He'd been afraid to tell his father who had broken his glasses. He'd been afraid to let his mother see his romance novels. He'd been so afraid to take the leap and move his family to Port Lorne that, the moment he had anything like enough saved up to manage it, he'd thrown his savings into the hands of the young woman he was supposed to be courting. For the romance of it all, was what he'd told himself—but wasn't it true he'd also done it as an excuse? So he could say, *Oh well, such is life, I'm sure I'll save enough someday*, and go peacefully about his dull, lonely existence in the comfort of knowing he couldn't do anything to change it?

The rising wind howled, rattling the tiny window over his bed. Outside, the dark mass of trees bent lazily in the coming rain. Their leaves rushed like ocean waves. Arthur sat on his bed, waking the cat, and gazed at the dark forest. *That* ought to have been what he feared. Instead he feared ridiculous, amorphous, almost nameless things.

No longer. He could do this. For God's sake, all Mrs. Livingston wanted him to do was buy a clock. He could buy a clock! He would love to buy a clock! Clocks were his whole thing! Surely he could do that for his family, even if he failed them in sundry other ways.

He fell asleep imagining a house in Port Lorne and all the friends he would have to fill it. In the morning, over coffee, he told Charlotte he'd decided to go, then went down into the village and told Agnes the same.

VII. In which Arthur learns to drive a cart

Arthur had not expected to set out immediately, but with the sun cresting the horizon he was in the driver's seat of a small cart hitched to a burly palomino gelding. The gelding tossed his head. He seemed to find Arthur's driving skills dubious before they'd even set out. Arthur didn't blame him. He'd never driven anywhere, never ridden a horse, barely interacted with a horse except to sometimes, surreptitiously, pet the nose of a cart horse after disembarking from the occasional hired cart on one of Charlotte's bad days.

Agnes had not seemed to think of this, probably because she'd always had a driver until now. Likely because he was Arthur, Arthur had not thought of it, either, until he was in the driver's seat, trying to get the driving lines in hand, and she'd already sailed back into the manor.

Arthur slapped the lines feebly. The horse snorted and pulled forward, but with Arthur's uncertainty and lack of guidance, he stopped.

Arthur climbed out of the cart, considering asking Agnes to show him how this worked, but she never drove. It was always her driver or, in recent years, Gracie. And Gracie was in no condition to teach him.

Foolishly, he led the horse along by the bridle. Thank God the fishermen were out to sea, the factory workers at their shifts, the women tending house since it wasn't market day, most of the shops shuttered for years. Ordinarily, the villagers ignored Arthur, but the few he passed now gawked and, when they thought he was out of earshot, laughed.

As he passed the Youngs' cottage, Cormac emerged, carrying a fishing net. He was one of the few fishermen of Arthur's generation who hadn't yet had to resort to the cannery.

Like the other villagers, Cormac stared. Unlike the others, he recovered, cleared his throat, and spoke.

"Trouble with your cart, there?"

Arthur flushed. Sometimes he'd forget how blue Cormac's eyes were; remembering flustered him. He never knew why.

"Well, er, Mrs. Livingston is sending me to Port Lorne on an errand, but I'm . . . I'm afraid I don't know how to, er . . ."

Cormac thumbed up his cap, gazing at him. Arthur had always wished Cormac would notice him; now that Cormac had, he found it overwhelming. He stared at the cobblestones, fingers tight on the driving lines. The gelding snorted at his shoulder.

"Easiest thing in the world," Cormac said at last. "I could show you, if you want. For a spell. Need to get back," he added, nodding in the direction of the sea. "Came in for a fresh net. Lost my best one first thing."

Arthur swallowed. "Yes, that would—that would be lovely."

They clambered into the cart, sitting so close their thighs pressed together. It was unbearably intimate.

This is what comes of having no friends, Arthur thought in a panic. *Anything at all starts to feel like intimacy.*

"I didn't know you knew horses," he said, attempting to make conversation. To his mortification, it came out as a squeak.

The corner of Cormac's mouth turned down. "Got an uncle who's a farmer a few miles inland. Da used to lend me out to him, when he needed me. Here, take the lines."

He talked Arthur around the perimeter of the village, correcting the way Arthur held the lines, telling him how to make the horse go faster or stop or change direction. The gelding's ears twitched toward them, but he was a placid beast and did whatever Arthur made him do (which wasn't always what Arthur had meant to make him do). Warm and strong, Cormac's hands made Arthur's stomach swoop whenever he touched Arthur to make some small correction, whether to the lines or Arthur's grip or posture. It would have been extremely distracting had Arthur not been determined to focus, to show Cormac he was worth the time and that they might be friends hereafter.

When Arthur knew enough not to pose a danger to anyone, they turned back into the village to practice driving through the narrow cobbled streets. Cormac had relaxed at Arthur's side. His thigh pressed closer than ever.

They stopped in the village square, chickens scattering around them. Though barely September, it was that brisk, sunny sort of morning that happens only in autumn. Fat white clouds hurled across the sky. Beyond them, the sky was blue; the sun shone strong one moment, weakly the next, as clouds raced one after the other. Damp from last night's rain, the cobblestones glistened. While many of the surrounding shops were dark, the windows of the fishery supply and general store (the latter of which was also the post office and telegraph office) glinted cheerfully, as if to draw attention to their wares. The old pub on the corner looked distinguished rather than rundown. Chickens clucked peaceably, golden brown and fluffy.

Seacliff had never been so beautiful. Arthur wasn't sure why it was beautiful now, but it made him loath to leave.

Cormac leaned back, linking his hands behind his head; his biceps swelled under his shirt. He glanced at Arthur. Dear

God, his eyes were blue. Arthur looked away, wiping his palms on his trousers.

"Not bad," Cormac said. Arthur warmed pathetically under the praise. "Mind, the wood'll be different. You are going through the wood, I expect?"

Arthur nodded. "Mrs. Livingston wants the clock quickly."

It seemed best not to mention why. Cormac was a sensible man, but so were most of the villagers, in most ways—yet they were a superstitious lot and never more so than when it came to the forest.

"It's a good cart for it. Small piece but good and sturdy, nice big wheels, should get you through without too much trouble—leastways without any trouble the wood don't make itself. Best take some rowan or yew, salt at least. I'd rub the cart with salt, too, and put some rue in the harness."

"Of course," Arthur said, though he hadn't considered these measures. The villagers had always taken such precautions, but his father never had. George had thought their superstitions just that: superstitions. He'd discouraged them in his children. They'd never gone farther into the forest than the edges when they were children, anyway, playing in sight of the cottage. Now, neither of them had entered the wood in years. The last time Arthur had done so, his brother-in-law had asked him to come along to chop firewood. Arthur had been hopeless, of course, but John had liked the company and having someone to carry half the haul back. Arthur could do *that* even if he'd grown winded and threatened to lop off his own limbs with each swing of the axe.

"Mind," Cormac said, "even with these wheels, odds are you'll have to dismount and unstick the thing now and again. The paths ain't what they used to be, so few folks drive through anymore. If you tell the horse go and it tries but don't get anywhere, could be you're stuck on a log or rock. Now, not meaning any offense—"

Arthur was prepared to be unoffended. Cormac's attention was worth that much.

"—but you're not a brawny fellow, probably be hard for you to move a rock or log without some leverage, especially with the cart over top of it. You'll want to have a shovel or suchlike on hand. If—"

He broke off. A knot of men had rounded a corner, seen them, and stopped. The men gawped, brows thunderous.

As an adult, Arthur was used to being ignored, but as a boy he'd been used to being gawped at, no matter how he'd shrunk himself down in a failed attempt to fit the villagers' expectations. He straightened in his seat, made sure his hands were right on the lines, and nodded at the men as he drove onward. The men's voices rumbled after them, too low to make out, but Cormac stiffened and slid away.

Arthur swallowed, aware something had changed between them in the last thirty seconds but not sure what. He ought to have known. The few hesitant attempts he'd made at forging friendships over the years had ended similarly, if they'd gotten anywhere in the first place.

He'd thought things were going well with Cormac. Why was it such a crime for another man to be seen being too friendly with Arthur?

"If?" he prompted, in a terrible attempt at sounding normal.

"What?"

Arthur cleared his throat. "You were going to say something, after you told me to bring a shovel."

"Don't recall."

Cormac's arms folded across his chest. When they approached his house, he snapped to attention. At the sight of them, his wife had frozen in the middle of sweeping the stoop, wearing the same expression the men had worn.

Cormac spoke without looking at Arthur. "I'll get out here."

Arthur stopped the horse.

"Thank you," he said helplessly, but Cormac had already leaped down. Arthur nodded at Mrs. Young, but she reddened and grabbed Cormac's arm the moment he was within reach. She muttered furiously at him. The only words Arthur caught, as he drove onward, were *with that sodomite.*

His stomach clenched. He'd never understood this sense of *difference* between him and the rest of Seacliff, but Mrs. Young's angry whisper made him wonder whether the villagers did. Whether they knew something about him that he didn't know about himself.

Clicking his tongue, Arthur urged the gelding faster. The cart bumped over cobbles now slimy instead of glistening. Fumes belched from the cannery and smudged the sky gray, smelling of fish guts. Arthur wrinkled his nose. He couldn't believe he'd thought Seacliff beautiful. It had always been ugly and had only grown uglier since his father's disappearance.

Thank God for Mrs. Livingston and her money. The first half was in his breast pocket.

Determined to put on a good face for his family, he sat ramrod straight in his seat and steered the gelding around the side of the hill, a less direct route to the cottage but less steep than the way the family always took. His driving practice hadn't involved hills, but the gelding threw himself into the harness and plowed upward without issue. Arthur plastered a smile on his face and sang out as the cottage came into view.

They made it to the top without getting stuck or tipping over. Despite the incident with Cormac, Arthur's smile stretched into the real thing. He'd done it. He'd driven a horse and cart for the first time, he hadn't died or destroyed anything, and now his family was coming outside to see his triumph.

With a shout, Sasha raced over before he'd stopped the cart.

"Careful, duck," he said, but the gelding stopped the cart itself to nose at the tiny human hugging its leg. Jonas hung back, clinging to Charlotte's hand. The goat slung her legs over the garden fence with a lusty *maaah*.

Charlotte's eyes were bruised as usual, but she smiled as Arthur looped the driving lines over the hook by his feet and clambered down.

"Did you teach yourself to drive a horse-cart?"

Arthur's smile faltered as he thought of Cormac, but he said archly, "I'm a man of many talents," even though he wasn't. Charlotte's eyes flickered over him. To his relief, she turned to the gelding and stroked his nose without further questions.

After tying the horse by the chicken coop, Arthur went inside and packed, nonsensically. He'd never been farther from Seacliff than some of the outlying farms, to which George had sometimes brought his children on house calls. Having filled a battered suitcase in the attic with clothes, food, tinctures, and toiletries, and a knapsack with a bottle of water, one more set of clothes, some herbs, his shaving kit, and no fewer than three books, Arthur was at a loss. What else might such a journey require?

He lugged the suitcase and knapsack through his workshop, slipping his old travel watch-repairing kit into his pocket for comfort. After a moment's thought, he grabbed his father's silver acorn from its peg, hung it around his neck, and tucked it into his shirt. It might not protect him on his way through, but it had come from the forest. His father had worn it constantly. That was a comfort, too.

Outside, Arthur stuck his suitcase in the back of the cart, set his knapsack on the driver's seat, remembered Cormac's words, and grabbed a shovel from the shed.

"What's that for?" Charlotte asked.

"In case the cart gets stuck."

Arthur blinked the sting from his eyes. He had a feeling Cormac wouldn't be speaking to him again.

Sasha stroked the gelding's nose, chattering to him about school starting next week, which lessons she was looking forward to, and which she found unbearably boring. She'd named him Maurice, since he didn't have a name (or Agnes hadn't told Arthur his name). Jonas reached out to touch Maurice's neck, relaxed when the beast didn't turn and trample them, and shifted closer. Freya wound around underfoot, threatening to trip everyone.

"Where are you going?" Jonas asked their uncle.

"Port Lorne," Sasha announced, before Arthur could respond. "He's going to buy a clock for Mrs. Livingston. Right, Uncle Arthur?"

Putting the shovel in the cart, Arthur swallowed a lump in his throat. "Right."

It wasn't for long. A week at most; Agnes was counting on him to return quickly. But now the time had come, he didn't want to leave the children.

"I suppose I should be going," he said reluctantly.

"Can I come with you?" Sasha asked.

I'll take you when you're older, Arthur heard his father saying. His fingers curled at his sides.

Predictably, however, before he could say anything, Charlotte said, "Absolutely not."

"What if Uncle Arthur gets lonely?"

"I'll be fine, duck."

Sasha opened her mouth to argue, but at a look from her mother, she turned back to the horse and cat with a huff.

Charlotte caught her brother's hand and drew him away from the children. Chickens scattered before them.

"Be careful."

"I will."

Her hand tightened on his. "I mean it, Arthur."

Arthur squeezed her hand.

"So do I," he said, though he'd said it automatically, but she shook her head.

"We've lost too much. I can't lose you, too. The forest is dangerous. Don't forget that. Please."

Her voice was tight. She blinked rapidly, like she was trying not to cry. Arthur gave a lopsided smile.

Reaching into his breast pocket, he gave her the money Mrs. Livingston had given him earlier that morning, except for the portion to cover the cost of the clock and his expenses on the trip. Charlotte inhaled sharply.

She thumbed through the bills but didn't smile as she stuffed them into her pocket. "It's no substitute for you, if you don't come back."

"I know. It's worth a good deal more."

"Arthur."

"Joking," he said, even though he wasn't. Gripping her hands, he kissed her forehead. "I'll come back, Lottie, I promise."

"In one piece."

"Yes."

"Without the sickness."

"I certainly hope so."

She was not amused.

"Yes," he said. "Perfectly well. Just the way I left. I promise."

"Wire me at the general store when you get there."

"Of course."

"And when you're coming back."

"Yes."

Charlotte pulled a tiny, roughly made cross of rowan from her pocket. "Don't laugh, but—I want you to take this."

"Where did it come from?"

She worried her lip with her teeth. "It was with Dad's

things. It's . . . I've had it for years. Like you've had the acorn in your workshop. I don't know where he got it. He always said the rowan crosses, the salt, all of it—it was all . . ."

"Superstition."

Charlotte nodded. "But it was in his things."

Arthur's skin prickled. The rowan cross threatened to unsettle something about his long-held memories of his father, but probably it had been nothing more than a curiosity. Though he hadn't believed them, George had always been interested in the villagers' superstitions.

"Why haven't you shown this to me before?"

Charlotte gave a tight smile. "I barely remember him. You've always had more of him, you were so much older than I was when he disappeared. I wanted to have a piece of him to myself."

So she said, but here she was, giving the rowan cross to Arthur because she was worried about him entering the wood.

She cleared her throat, pressing the cross into his hand. "I don't believe in it, of course. It's not that I think it will protect you, I just—"

Arthur hugged her. Charlotte hugged him back, burying her face in his chest in a way she hadn't done since they were children.

"I'll come back," he repeated. "I will. I promise I will."

She nodded, pulling away to dab at her eyes with the corner of her apron. Arthur slipped the cross into his pocket with the watch-repairing kit.

"Children," Charlotte called, her voice wobbly, "your uncle is leaving. Come say goodbye."

The children hugged him. The goat lipped at the legs of his trousers. Arthur tried to push her away, but it was difficult with the children in his arms.

"If I can't come with you," Sasha said, "will you bring me a present?"

"What kind of present, duck?"

"A sword." Sasha's eyes gleamed in anticipation. "A real one instead of a big stick."

"*Don't* get her a sword," Jonas said. Their mother laughed wetly.

Arthur laughed, too, but there was a sting in it. "I don't know that I can find a sword, duck, but I'll tell you what I've found when I come back. Perhaps," he said, trying to will it into being, "we shall all go to Port Lorne together one day, and you can choose your own sword. I'm sure you'd prefer that, anyway."

Jonas groaned. Arthur kissed the top of their head. He barely had to bend to do it anymore; they were almost as tall as Charlotte.

"Take care of your mother," he murmured in their ear.

They nodded, clung tight to him, and let go. "Be careful," they whispered.

"I will," Arthur said, and meant it.

He shooed the goat away, led Maurice through the gate, and clambered into the cart. The wind tussled his hair and tugged at his coat. Heather undulated around him. Waves crashed at the bottom of the cliff.

"Well," he said, as stoutly as he could manage, "I'm off."

He saluted, clicked his tongue at the horse, and rumbled into motion. The trailhead yawned before him.

Determined not to look scared in front of his family, Arthur focused on the image he'd had of entering the wood. It was like a scene in a book: The intrepid hero, a normal man who would no doubt discover there was more to him than anyone—himself included—had ever imagined, drove toward the trees, gazing fearfully at the forest before breaching its depths anyway. He'd slap the driving lines, and man, horse, and cart would vanish, like the trees had swallowed them up. A terrifying image in the end, to be sure, but dreadfully romantic and heroic. The victory of the human spirit over the insurmountable power of nature and all that.

Instead, branches whacked him in the face.

"Ow," Arthur mumbled.

His forehead stung. When he touched it, his fingers came away clean. He wasn't bleeding: just hurt. His face *and* his dignity, not that he had much dignity anyway, so the less said about that the better. He hunched in his seat, avoiding the trees' grasping fingers.

Maurice plodded along without concern. Arthur hoped that was a good sign; animals had a sense for danger, didn't they?

Something black and furry popped up beside him. Arthur yelped, nearly falling from the cart. Snorting at the disturbance, the gelding broke into a trot and veered off the path.

"Mrowr," a familiar voice said.

The cat. Freya had climbed into the cart. She sat beside him, fluffy tail curled around her, and turned her serious golden gaze on him.

Breathing hard, Arthur turned the horse back toward the path and straightened his glasses.

"Not that I'm not glad of the company," he told the cat, "but don't you think you ought to stay home with Lottie and the children?"

She gave him a look that said quite plainly, *You need more watching than they do.*

Arthur sighed. "True, I suppose. Well, I fancy I need less watching than Sasha, since I'm less likely to run headlong into danger just because it looks exciting—my present venture excluded. But it doesn't look dangerous, does it?"

Leaves trembled in the canopy. Here on the forest floor, all was close and quiet. The path at the horse's feet, barely wide enough for a single carriage, was the same path his father had taken so many times. The trees were turning crimson, though it was only the first of September, and the dim light was green-gold. The fish-gut smell that hung over Seacliff's narrow streets vanished a short way into the forest; the air smelled like turning leaves and birds flying south and autumn storms.

Arthur breathed deeply. He'd never gotten used to the fish-gut smell, though the cannery had been open for years and the stench had come along with it. The disappointments of August and Cormac Young and Seacliff and his own failings faded in the distance, shut out by the surrounding leaves and trunks.

"I'm on an adventure at last," Arthur told the cat. She licked a paw without responding.

His father had trodden this same trail. Arthur almost clambered out of the cart and walked, to follow in George's footsteps if only in a literal sense. But Agnes needed him to return quickly—Charlotte needed him to return quickly—he wanted to return to his family quickly, so he stayed in the cart and flapped the lines. Maurice's ears twitched, but he increased the pace from a plod to a trot. Arthur whistled, really glad, for the first time, to have agreed to Mrs. Livingston's proposal.

VIII. In which Arthur narrowly avoids falling into a pit, but his luggage, alas, does not

By early afternoon, some of the shine had worn off the adventure. Arthur's back ached from sitting the same way for so long; it was a matter of time until his spasm returned. With a horse and cart, Cormac had told him, three or four days would see him to the other side of the forest, if no harm befell him and he didn't stop much, but he'd already stopped twice: once to stretch his legs and piss behind a tree, once to rifle in the suitcase for the heating pad Charlotte had packed him. He didn't need it yet, but he stuffed it inside his knapsack, preferring to have it close by.

An hour later, the cart bumped hard over something in the path, jolting Arthur from his seat. Cursing, he clung on and pulled Maurice to a stop.

At his side, Freya opened her eyes, annoyed at the disturbance. Arthur massaged his chest, breathing hard. He'd been daydreaming about Port Lorne, hardly paying attention to where they were going since they had not yet come to a fork or turn. Now he was paying for it with a strained back.

Maurice threw himself into the harness, but the cart didn't

move. Dismounting with a grimace, Arthur patted the gelding's neck.

"All right, old fellow, no need for that. Let me take a look. I'm sure our wheels have gotten stuck."

He retrieved the shovel and knelt beside the front driver's-side wheel with a groan. His knees ached in protest, but he gazed under the cart.

A human hand flopped out.

Arthur yelped. He scrambled away, wielding the shovel like a sword. His chest heaved.

The fingers curled in the dirt, pale and still. Trembling, Arthur stuck the shovel back in the cart and dug through his suitcase for a torch, trying not to imagine the fingers wrapping around his ankle while he wasn't looking.

Kneeling back beside the hand, he turned on the torch and followed its thin beam of light along the fingers and wrist, beneath the cart, to the arm they were attached to. Freya settled at his side; it made him feel marginally better.

"Hello?"

A low groan. Christ. Had he killed someone? He'd certainly run them over.

Arthur rocketed to his feet and reached for Maurice's bridle, so jittery the gelding tossed his head and snorted uneasily. Stroking his neck, Arthur focused on his own breathing, *in for four, hold for four, out for four*: a cycle Charlotte had taught him in her earliest days as a healer, to help him calm down when he panicked. Freya twisted around his legs, mewling.

"Watch out, Freya," Arthur said. "All right, Maurice. Let's—let's see if we can get the cart off them, hmm?"

It took some maneuvering, but Maurice was a patient horse. Freya oversaw their efforts from the driver's seat.

Arthur's neck kept prickling as if someone other than the cat were watching. He would've been almost grateful, desperate for help with a situation he hadn't foreseen and felt unequal to, but no one was there. He had the uncomfortable feeling it might've been the trees.

When the cart was safely off to the side of the path, Arthur got a clear view of the hand's owner.

It was a boy, seventeen or so, buried in the path up to his shoulders. His flaxen hair was brown with mud. His face and arms were scratched, his shirt more dirt than cloth. No wonder Arthur hadn't seen him; so much moss blanketed him it might've grown there.

His face was white and waxen, veined in black—and unfortunately familiar. A village boy. Hamish, Arthur thought his name was.

Arthur let out a breath. The boy's eyes opened, blue and filmy and threaded thinly with black veins. Arthur shrank back, but the boy gasped something that might've been a word.

Heart pounding, Arthur bent close. "What?"

Hamish reached for him. Hesitantly, Arthur took his hand. The boy coughed black ooze, his grip crushing Arthur's fingers. Arthur resisted the urge to pull away, but his spine tingled.

"Brigid," the boy croaked.

Arthur's stomach clenched. *Ma's convinced she's eloped like Mary did, but we're afraid she's gone into the wood.* Perhaps Brigid Tierney had done both, or tried to.

Before Arthur could decide what to say, Hamish's cheek dropped to the leaf litter. His fingers went slack.

Arthur skittered away as if death were a contagion. He turned to Maurice and rested his forehead against the horse's neck, breathing deeply, *in for four, hold for four, out for four.*

When he turned around, a stunted, twisted tree stood where Hamish had been.

Arthur's mouth went dry. "Hamish?"

No response. Not even the rustle of leaves or the call of a

bird. Arthur reached for his shovel, holding it up like a bat, and approached the tree. Its roots bumped out of the earth, angled like Hamish's arms had been.

"Hamish?"

Dirt shifted beneath Arthur's feet. A tangle of root bent like fingers.

Arthur backed hastily away, dumped the shovel into the cart, and vaulted into the driver's seat, sticking the torch in his knapsack.

"Let's get out of here."

Maurice started forward without waiting for Arthur's command. Arthur grasped the lines, then froze. The gelding seemed certain of where he was going, but the path had moved. Before Arthur had stopped the cart, it had run straight ahead the short distance he could see through the trees. Now it veered left.

The forest had shifted, just like in his father's stories.

He swallowed. He'd always wondered why, in those stories, nobody noticed the paths shifting before their eyes. Now he didn't have to wonder. The forest had waited until his back was turned.

"Do you think it still leads to Port Lorne?" he asked the cat in a hushed voice. She rested a paw on his thigh as if to make sure the forest didn't do away with him as it had Hamish.

The farther the cart bumped onward, the more Arthur saw to unsettle him. They passed a beech carved with the ghostly scars of decades of lovers' initials, the freshest of which were *BT + HM*. Brigid and Hamish. They'd passed by together, perhaps planning to start a new life in Port Lorne as Brigid's older sister had in Glenwhistle. Thinking the forest so beautiful until it swallowed them.

Swallowed Hamish. Arthur hoped Brigid had found her way back to the village. Black ooze dripped from their initials, staining the beech's smooth, gray bark. Arthur's stomach flipped. He rubbed the rowan cross in his pocket like a good luck charm.

Occasionally, he noticed black ooze dripping from another tree. Arthur didn't want to touch any tree, but the black ooze made him stay particularly far from the ones it stained.

The underbrush rustled. Arthur halted the cart.

"Who's there?"

He grabbed the shovel, planning to whack whatever came at him at least as hard as Sasha whacked him while playing pirates.

"I warn you I'm armed!"

The rustling reached a peak. Arthur stood in his seat, swinging the shovel before him in what he hoped was a threatening manner.

Freya slipped from the cart, gazing at the underbrush with a twitching tail. She pounced. The rustling stopped.

Arthur lowered the shovel. "Freya?"

She trotted back with a dead squirrel clutched in her mouth, hopped into the cart, and deposited her prize at his feet.

"Er . . . thank you." At least it wasn't something worse. "You can have it. I'm . . . not hungry."

The cart rumbled onward. Freya brought the squirrel with her. Arthur wished she hadn't.

The romantic notions he'd had about the wood dwindled as afternoon wore on and evening shadows crept in. The beautiful golden light of an autumn afternoon faded into menacing grays and blacks. More and more trees dripped black ooze the farther he ventured. Some took on strange forms, branches bent into uncomfortable angles like broken limbs. The path shifted again and again, never when he was looking. At last, it disappeared.

Not knowing what else to do, Arthur drove onward. His muscles ached; without the path, the cart jolted constantly over rough ground. Maurice's ears twitched back and forth. His gait had slowed to a creep, as if he hoped the forest wouldn't notice him. Freya had slipped from the driver's seat into the space between Arthur's suitcase and the shovel, where she hunkered down until only her golden eyes were distinguishable from the shadows. Arthur pulled his knapsack into his lap like a shield.

The earth rumbled. Arthur shot upright, his back spasming, but he clutched the lines with one hand and his knapsack with the other.

"What was that?"

The cat hunkered farther down in her space. Maurice twisted his neck to look about, ears twitching. He stamped uneasily.

Another rumble.

The forest floor opened behind them.

The horse screamed. The cart backed into the maw of the sudden pit. A rear wheel slipped over the edge.

Arthur swore, stumbled down, threw his knapsack as far from the pit as he could, and grabbed Maurice's bridle. The cat streaked past and up a tree.

Maurice would not calm down. He reared, wrenching Arthur's arm.

"Come on, come *on*," Arthur moaned, but the cart slipped backward. Terrified of losing the horse, Arthur fumbled with the harness, then gave up and lunged for the shovel. His suitcase slid to the back of the cart, but he left it. He stabbed at the traces, striking repeatedly until they frayed and broke and slithered free. The cart slid into the pit and vanished, taking Arthur's suitcase with it.

Maurice shot forward, but Arthur grabbed his bridle. Trembling, he garbled out, "It's all right, you're all right, it's all right," over and over.

With a final rumble, the earth closed. A tree sprouted, grew, and died, dripping with the same black ooze as so many others.

Arthur's chest heaved. He looped the driving lines over a

healthy branch and crept toward the tree, shovel in hand. He tested each step, afraid the ground would give way beneath him, but it was as solid as ground should be.

The ooze smelled faintly mechanical. Arthur reached out but withdrew without touching it. He touched the shovel's blade to it instead.

With a faint hiss, the metal corroded. Arthur flung the shovel aside and skittered back to the horse. Freya slunk down from her tree.

No cart. No way of getting Mrs. Livingston's clock back from Port Lorne, if indeed he made it there. He had a horse but no saddle and didn't know how to ride; he didn't know if Maurice was saddle-broken anyway. The path had moved, he didn't know where it was, and it had shifted about so much he couldn't be sure of reaching either Port Lorne or home even if he found it. He had no luggage except for his knapsack with its single change of clothing, heating pad, three romance novels, shaving kit, torch, water bottle (half empty), and a few herbs he wasn't sure he remembered how to use.

He couldn't even use the heating pad, because he had no way to heat it, because he was Arthur and hadn't thought to pack a firelighter or matches, though he'd known he'd spend more than one night camping in the forest.

"This is very bad."

His voice was insignificant in the expectant silence of the wood. Freya brushed against his legs, but her company was paltry comfort now.

Figuring he was far closer to home than Port Lorne, Arthur turned reluctantly back the way he'd come. The way he thought he'd come. He could no longer tell.

IX. In which Charlotte has an unexpected visitor

Charlotte may have made her brother promise to return safely, but she was mortified to learn how much she'd come to rely on him in the last six months. He'd only left this morning; already she felt like everything was falling apart without him.

She'd been all right initially, except for the worry needling her insides. She'd made the children an early lunch and gone down to the village alone with her cane and her medical kit. That had been quite bad enough: People stopped talking abruptly when they saw her.

At first, she'd thought they were talking about her, not that she knew why they'd have cause to; she'd always worked hard to make sure they didn't. Then she'd heard her brother's name and Cormac Young's—together. She didn't know why that should be, either, since Cormac had never paid Arthur much mind. She'd turned her attention toward today's patients, but the whispers persisted.

A village like Seacliff, small as it was, always had plenty of patients. Someone pregnant, someone ill, someone who'd sprained or broken or lost a limb. No one ever stopped to let their various injuries and illnesses heal properly. *Grit your teeth and press on.* That was what the villagers believed. They'd gossiped about Charlotte's mother for that very reason; she'd descended into grief rather than pushing through it. If one didn't press on through whatever ills life threw at them, one would never get on at all. Who would pay the bills, mend the nets, cook the supper, repair the roof?

Although she knew bodies needed rest, Charlotte struggled not to feel that way herself. She knew of at least three medical crises she likely could've helped with had she not been laid up with her own illness for weeks. At the time, she'd barely cared, so sick she wasn't sure she'd recover. Now she couldn't stop thinking of them.

The sea was a violent provider. The cannery possibly even more so, as Charlotte was reminded late this afternoon by a factory worker whose hand was so lacerated as to be unsavable. He was fourteen and had smaller hands than the grown workers, so when a gang knives machine jammed up, he'd been told to stick his hand into it to fix the jam. The bosses had been loath to shut production down to examine the machine properly.

Anger simmered in Charlotte's gut. The injury had been entirely preventable.

The hand had to come off. The boy's work would slow, and probably he'd lose his job. He was unbearably cheerful about it, although she sensed an undercurrent of tension as she worked up toward telling him he would lose the hand. Seacliff hadn't yet beaten him into the gruff, grim village man he would one day be, as all the village men were. All of them but Arthur, because he spent more time buried in books and his own head than reality.

Perhaps that was one of the reasons the villagers disliked him; he didn't push through life's ills so much as ignore them. Nonetheless, Charlotte sometimes envied him. Her best semblance of a defense against the realities of their lives was determined practicality. It only worked until life wrenched control from her hands, reminding her that practicality could never overcome things like bosses who cared more for profit than people or the slow poisoning of the sea at the hands of the cannery and the distant, wealthy men who had built it.

Daydreaming couldn't overcome those things, either, but it might have given her an occasional respite.

She did what needed to be done, bandaged the boy's stump, and gave his mother instructions for his care, promising to return in the next few days to make sure it was healing. Then she headed home. She'd intended to make more house calls but couldn't bear it after that one.

Leaning on her cane, she limped back through the village. Her father's bone saw weighed heavy in her bag. Early evening sunlight unspooled in thin strands, weak, but it hurt her eyes. The hill loomed before her. The steps seemed impossibly steep.

Charlotte's vision swam. She sat on a stump and cried, angry at the bosses, angry at herself for not being able to climb the hill alone, angry at Arthur for leaving her to her own devices. Angry at herself all over again, because she'd refused to tell him to stay, though he'd given her ample opportunity, and because she ought not to have needed him so deeply in the first place.

"You all right?"

A short, stocky person stood over her, dressed in a working man's clothes: shirt, trousers, braces, and boots, with a cloak under their arm and knives at their belt. But it was a woman around Charlotte's age, with tawny skin, black hair slung in a braid over her shoulder, and serious dark eyes.

"I'm fine." Charlotte wiped her eyes on her apron. "I was taking a rest before heading uphill. That's all."

The woman rubbed her chin. "Sure of that, are you? Looked to me like you were weepin'."

Charlotte's fists clenched in her skirt. "I wasn't."

"No matter." The woman shrugged. "C'mon, give me your arm."

Charlotte glared at her.

"Need help getting uphill, don't you?" the woman asked. "Must be your cottage I passed back there. Give me your arm. I'll help you home."

Charlotte flushed but begrudgingly allowed herself to be pulled to her feet. The woman took her medical bag over one arm and offered Charlotte the other.

Breathing hard, Charlotte leaned against the woman with her cane in her other hand. Despite the weak sunlight, the warmth made her dizzy and winded.

"All right?" the woman repeated, but Charlotte couldn't respond until she'd caught her breath.

"Fine," she gasped. "Let's go."

They made their way uphill. Although her cane helped, Charlotte was grateful for the support. Her father hadn't thought to build handrails alongside the stairs all those years ago. She hadn't thought about it, either, until her illness.

At the door of the cottage, the woman turned to go, but Charlotte said, "Half a moment."

"Need help getting in?"

"No, but if you're going down to the village, let me grab you a hat."

"The sun ain't so bad."

"It isn't that." Charlotte considered the woman's clothes, thinking uncomfortably of Agnes and her supposed cousin. When hunting, Gracie Buchanan might've gotten away with trousers by virtue of her riches, but this woman didn't look rich. "Seacliff isn't likely to take kindly to a woman running about in trousers. It'll do you better to disguise yourself as a man, if you can. If you won't be here long."

The woman looked her up and down, like she was trying

to decide or communicate something, but Charlotte couldn't imagine what.

Seeming satisfied, the woman nodded and followed her into the cottage. "I won't be here long. Two, three days at most."

The children's voices trailed from the kitchen as Charlotte led the woman into the sitting room.

". . . going to see if she's on her way back," Jonas was saying anxiously. They relaxed when they caught sight of their mother, but their brow furrowed at the stranger by her side.

Sasha, on the other hand, delighted in their unexpected visitor.

"Why are you wearing trousers?" she asked, eyeing them enviously.

The woman chuckled. "Because I don't much care for frocks."

"Me neither," Sasha said, "but Mama and Uncle Arthur make me."

Charlotte started up the attic stairs. "Please don't encourage my children."

Head spinning, she paused with her hand on the wall. The stairs were open on one side, and she had a sudden, horrible vision of herself falling off of them and breaking her neck.

Jonas appeared at her side. "What do you need, Mama?"

"That old flat cap, love. The one your uncle never wears."

Jonas nodded, scrambled up to the attic, and returned with cap in hand. It was a hideous brown thing Charlotte's mother had bought for her brother when he turned seventeen because, as she'd said, *every young man needs a cap.* Arthur had tried it on, thanked her politely, hung it on a peg in the attic, and never worn it. Their mother hadn't noticed.

Charlotte handed the cap to the woman. "Here."

"Awful ugly," the woman said, but she set Charlotte's

medical bag on the floor, coiled her braid on her head, and jammed the cap on over it.

Charlotte's chest stabbed with annoyance, though she and Arthur had always thought it ugly, too. "All the more likely to do the trick, then. The village men don't choose their hats for looks."

The woman tugged at her clothing, pulled the cap low over her eyes, and adjusted her stance. When she had finished, her figure was more or less hidden in folds of fabric, and what was visible of her face might've belonged to a boy.

Her voice dropped half an octave. "Thanks."

Sasha giggled. The woman tugged one of her pigtails with a grin. Despite herself, Charlotte liked that grin.

Her mouth twitched. "I'm not sure that will fool anyone for long. You might want to avoid talking too much."

The woman shrugged and said, in her normal voice, "Too bad. I'll be asking plenty questions."

Charlotte escorted her back to the stoop. "Why?"

"I'm looking for someone."

The woman thumbed the cap farther up her forehead, contemplating the slate roofs of the village. The setting sun reflected in her gaze.

Charlotte's breath caught at the sight of those serious dark eyes. Good thing the woman had said she wouldn't be here long. Otherwise, lonely as she was without her brother, Charlotte might have invited her to supper to get to know her.

Not for the first time, she wished she didn't need Arthur so much. Needing people was how one got hurt. She'd learned that first from her mother, then her husband. She didn't intend to learn the lesson again.

The woman pulled the cap off, turning to Charlotte. "The name Maggie McIntire mean anything to you?"

Charlotte was taken aback. "Bess Little's friend, isn't she? The one who was visiting from Port Lorne."

The woman nodded. She turned the cap over in her hands. "You know by any chance what happened to her?"

"She went home, didn't she? That's what I've heard."

"You see her go?"

Charlotte's skin prickled. She thought uneasily of the dark trees into which her brother had vanished only this morning. "No."

The woman didn't seem to share her unease.

"Shame. Thought you might've seen her, if she headed that way, what with your house practically right up against the trees." She jammed the cap back on and started downhill. "Thanks again."

Charlotte didn't respond. She stood on the stoop, chest heaving, until the ugly brown cap vanished downslope, lost amidst the rolling heather.

She stepped inside and slammed the door.

"Mama?" Jonas slipped to her side, Sasha hot on their heels. "Who was that?"

Charlotte closed her eyes. "No one. She helped me up the hill, that's all."

"I liked her," Sasha said. "And I liked her trousers."

Charlotte said nothing. She staggered to the sitting room, shrugging Jonas off when they tried to help, sank into her armchair, and didn't get up again the rest of the day.

x. In which Arthur loses his horse

They didn't make it much farther before stopping for the night. The spasm in Arthur's back persisted, probably because he'd pushed through it to prevent the horse from falling into that horrible pit. He longed for something with which to warm his heating pad but was grateful he'd managed to keep it. He might have to make it another day or two, but once he got home, he could sit in his armchair and doze off with the heating pad at his back. The forest would be nothing more than a horrible dream.

He wished Charlotte had talked him out of coming here; he would've stayed home if she'd insisted. Then he wished he'd had enough gumption to decide to stay home without her insistence. *Thank you for the opportunity, Mrs. Livingston, but I'm afraid I can't take it on at this time.* Would that have been so hard to say?

Since they no longer had a cart, Arthur removed Maurice's harness. He inspected the nearest tree with his torch to make sure it was ooze-free and looped the driving lines around a branch. He sighed. If he made it back, it would be without the clock. He could set out again, but by the time he reached Port Lorne—if he reached Port Lorne—it would be too late.

He wasn't sure he could've said no. He couldn't have turned the money down, not when his family could use it so much.

It didn't matter that he'd accepted. He was lost in the forest; all he knew was that home was closer than Fort Lorne. He would return in defeat, if at all.

Don't think that. Of course he'd make it home. He had to. He'd promised.

Arthur slipped a hand into his pocket, rubbing the rowan cross Charlotte had given him. A piece of their father she'd kept just to have one. Arthur didn't quite believe it would protect him, but he didn't quite not believe it, either. It was a piece of his sister as much as a piece of their father now. He couldn't help thinking it would somehow ensure he'd make it back to her.

Settling in for the night, Arthur was faced again with his own ineptitude: He'd failed to pack anything that might make sleeping on the ground more comfortable. Admittedly, he hadn't thought of sleeping on the ground but in the cart. He threw his coat down, close enough to the horse for comfort but not so close the horse might trample him in his sleep, and curled up with a shiver that rattled his back. He used his knapsack as an extremely bulky, lumpy pillow. The cat settled on top of him, purring.

Unsettling sounds filled the forest. Arthur had always fallen asleep to the ocean crashing against the cliffside, but here the noises were all wrong: clicks, grunts, rattles, a groan that made him shoot upright (to the cat's disgruntlement) and listen until he was certain he'd been imagining it. Maurice tossed his head uneasily. Arthur inched closer, deciding being trampled in his sleep was less of a danger than whatever had happened to Hamish.

It was the worst sleep of his life. The best that could be said was that his back no longer hurt when he awoke, far too early and to a gloomy gray light rather than the fabulous golden light he'd left in.

Arthur's stomach grumbled almost before he'd awoken, but all his food had been in the suitcase. He remembered little of the foraging his father had taught him at the edges of the forest long ago, and the plants farther in were different. Those he recognized were threaded with black veins or disintegrating under ooze dripping from trees above. And his father's lessons had focused first and foremost on medicinal plants, not necessarily edible ones.

On a yellowed bush, Arthur found a scant handful of late-season bilberries, dark and soft with age. They left him utterly unsatisfied.

The gray light did not brighten as morning wore on, depressing Arthur's spirits further. He led Maurice by the bridle, on foot; since he couldn't ride, he didn't know what else to do. The driving reins were so long that, without a cart, he wrapped them around his arm like a length of rope.

At midmorning, they came upon a stream. It was a small, clear, gravelly thing burbling so merrily over rocks and down dips that it seemed out of place. Arthur stumbled toward it, dropped his knapsack, and threw himself down to slurp water until his teeth ached with cold. He refilled his water bottle, which he'd emptied the day before, and lay back.

"That's better," he sighed, though his stomach sloshed.

A number of silvery fish darted to and fro. Freya wetted her paws in pursuit. The fish were small but normal; the trees lining the banks were healthy. If Arthur could devise a way to catch fish without line or net, he could build a fire and have fish for his supper. Notwithstanding the fact that he was a hopeless angler even in Seacliff, where there were lines and nets aplenty.

Perhaps the cat would catch something. Perhaps she'd deign to share it with him. Perhaps he'd manage to build a fire. Surely rubbing sticks together or something of that nature would work. The sky was overcast, but he could see it for the first time since entering the wood, thanks to the break in the canopy afforded by the stream. That was something.

Maurice shook his mane, grazing along the stream's edge. Arthur gathered sticks and twigs and sat beside him to make a fire. He failed miserably. The cat didn't catch a single fish.

"At least I'm no worse at fishing than you are," Arthur said to her. She glared.

The sight of the sky improved his mood. The trees didn't feel so oppressively close.

Arthur considered the nearest trunks. Didn't moss grow on the north side of trees? Moss seemed to grow any which way it wanted, but that was all he had to go on, directionally speaking. Perhaps north was where the moss grew thickest, in which case, the stream ran more or less southward. For now. If it curved aside, he'd have to figure out another way to get his bearings. Assuming his bearings were correct in the first place.

"We might as well move on. Let's see if we can follow the stream home. Homeward. Home-ish."

Freya headbutted his ankle and trotted downstream, turning back with a soft *mrrf* to make sure he followed. He did, once he'd dragged Maurice away from his grazing.

After a couple of hours, the bank grew rocky and difficult. Reluctant to leave the stream's steady burble, Arthur followed the slope of the land downward beside it, slipping over increasingly large stones. Maurice's ears twitched. He skidded and tossed his head. Freya leaped from rock to rock.

"Do slow down," Arthur puffed at her. "It's not as easy for us as it is for you, you know."

The stream fell down rocky steps into a shallow pool. Small, scanty trout flicked back and forth, silver in the trembling water.

The canopy opened wider, but the clouds above had thickened and darkened.

Arthur reached for a tree to steady himself but recoiled; the tree oozed black. He slipped on a stone, skidded, and slid the rest of the way down the slope. Maurice snorted as the driving lines tightened then slackened.

Breathing hard, Arthur rolled up his sleeves and crawled to the pool's edge; he'd scraped his palms on the rocks. Despite the sick tree nearby, the water was clean and cool. Arthur dipped his hands into it to soothe the sting.

Cat and horse joined him. Freya cleaned his hair sympathetically, but Maurice stood snorting on the stream bank, his ears swiveling back and forth.

Arthur sat back, shaking his hands dry. Freya stood on her hind legs to continue cleaning his hair. He petted her, gazing at the surrounding trees. With his overactive imagination, many of them looked like people.

Like that one there. The trunk was knobby, twisted into a shape not unlike a human face. There was the nose. There a pucker like an eye, and a knot like another. There a jagged hole like a mouth. There a branch with a twiggy end like an arm reaching, a hand grasping. Black ooze dripped from the mouthlike hole in the trunk. Arthur shuddered, standing to shift away from it.

It was a hazel tree, its branches thick with nuts, but he didn't even think of harvesting any. On a branch, a butcherbird speared a mouse on a twig. Arthur looked away, feeling sick.

A sharp bark sounded through the trees. He whirled around.

Three roe deer bounded toward the pool. Like the villagers struck down by wood sickness, all three were veined with black.

Arthur's stomach turned. Not only were the deer veined—

they were translucent in places, bones and musculature visible beneath skin and fur. The ribs of one. The jawbone of another. The vertebrae of the third.

Heedless of the pool, they splashed toward him. Freya scrambled out of their way. Maurice stiffened, quivering, and bolted.

Arthur's mouth went dry. "Maurice!"

The deer bounded right into him. He stumbled, fell, and hit his head on the rocky bank. Stars rang in his eyes. The deer's hooves bruised as they bounded over him. Then they were past, without giving any sign they'd noticed him or Maurice or the cat.

Wincing, Arthur sat on a rock and touched his forehead. His fingers came away bloody.

His head spun. "That's not good."

Freya slunk along the edge of the pool to sit at his side.

"The bandages were in my suitcase. Why did I think I could do this? I should've listened to Lottie. She told me it was dangerous, and I thought I'd be fine because—I don't know why I thought that. We don't even have the horse anymore."

The horse hadn't been any use without the cart, but having a big, bulky beast at his shoulder all morning had been a comfort. He scooped Freya up and buried his face in her fur.

"You can't leave me, all right?"

She made a face, disgruntled at the sudden hug, but didn't wriggle free. Letting out a breath, Arthur set her back down. She put a paw on his thigh and purred at him. He focused on the purring instead of the blood trickling down the side of his face. Not for the first time, he wished he were more like Charlotte. She would've known what to do.

Untucking his shirt, he tried to tear a strip of fabric away with his teeth. All he got was an aching jaw and a damp hem.

He splashed water onto the wound and pressed his hem to his forehead, hoping the injury was small enough for a little pressure and time to stop the bleeding.

Arthur sighed. The loss of the horse had sucked any hope from the day. His one remaining comfort was the stream. It gave him something to follow, hopefully something that wouldn't shift or vanish on him. The cat would've been a comfort, too, if he hadn't been afraid she'd run off or get eaten.

The ground trembled. So faintly at first that Arthur thought he'd imagined it.

"Do you feel that?" he asked Freya.

She tensed, her golden eyes fixed on the underbrush across the stream.

"Freya?"

She scrambled up his shoulder and clung to him, claws digging into his skin.

"Ow— What—"

More deer burst from the trees. A whole herd of red deer this time, hinds barking in alarm as they raced through the forest. Birds flew with them, whistling or cawing or crying. A raven seemed to turn to Arthur as it passed, croaking in warning. Like the roe deer that had knocked him over, many of the creatures were partially translucent, affording a glimpse of their skulls, their vertebrae, their ribs.

Arthur cowered until they'd passed. He got slowly to his feet, checking his forehead. The blood was already tacky. Not too bad of an injury, probably.

"That's something," he mumbled. "What d'you suppose . . . ?"

A high, soft whistle shrilled. The hair on the back of his neck stood up. Wind burst through the undergrowth, so strong it buffeted him.

"What . . . ?"

Then he saw them.

A pair of massive—eagles, he might've called them, if they hadn't been all wrong. Black as the storm clouds out to sea each autumn. Eyes that flashed like lightning. They winged along as though they weren't far too large for a forest understory. Each time they called out—that high, soft whistle rather than the terrible screech Arthur would've imagined—a gust of wind whirled through the trees, growing stronger and colder. Trees cracked and groaned. Branches broke and smashed to the ground.

Freya yowled in his ear. Arthur swore, shouldered his knapsack, and started running.

XI. In which the children find a corpse

Charlotte had slept fitfully in her chair and awoken at dawn, exhausted. There had been chores to do, so she'd shuffled to the kitchen to make tea. That roused her some. *So that's something*, she imagined Arthur saying, as he so often did, and she sighed. With a horse and cart, he could be to Port Lorne and back in a little over a week, if all went well, but already the time since he'd left felt interminable.

Throughout the day, Jonas slipped into the role left vacant by their uncle's absence. Distracting Sasha so Charlotte could have some quiet and get things done. Tidying the house, less erratically than Arthur usually did. Noticing when Charlotte had a stab of pain or a dizzy spell, bringing her an ointment or stool or whatever else they thought she needed.

At lunchtime, Jonas was making sandwiches when Charlotte entered the kitchen. A piece of ham dropped on the floor; they called for the cat, but she failed to appear.

Their brow wrinkled. "Where's Freya?"

Where indeed? Freya's habitual place at any meal was on the table (if Charlotte wasn't around) or under the table (if she was), waiting for an opportune moment—but Charlotte hadn't seen the cat since yesterday morning.

Sasha had been drawing, but she looked suddenly shifty.

Charlotte sighed. "Dearest, have you done something with the cat?"

"No."

Charlotte's head throbbed. "Sasha—"

Sasha jutted her chin. "I didn't want Uncle Arthur to be lonely, but you wouldn't let me go!"

"So you sent the cat?" Jonas said in exasperation.

Rubbing her forehead, Charlotte reached for the piece of ham. When she straightened, her heart palpitated. She dropped into her chair, breathing hard, and Jonas hovered over her. She couldn't bear it anymore.

"I'm fine," she snapped.

A flush crept across Jonas's cheeks. Nodding, they returned to making sandwiches. Charlotte opened her mouth to apologize, but that snap had been all she could manage. She sat shamefaced at the table, waiting for her heart to calm down. By the time it had, Jonas had finished making lunch, served the family silently, and disappeared into their room.

Sasha negotiated cleaning up in return for a whole handful of biscuits. Charlotte agreed to it without argument, pushed out of her seat, and went after Jonas.

She hesitated outside the children's bedroom, her hand poised to knock. Inside, she heard sniffling.

She didn't know what to say. She lowered her hand.

Feeling guilty, she returned to her chores.

Early that afternoon, the clouds outside thickened and darkened. Charlotte's joints ached as they did with oncoming rain. She worked through the pain, since no one suggested she shouldn't, until it grew so bad that she was near tears. Grabbing painkillers, she settled in her armchair by the fire.

The relief was instant. Not total—not even significant. But dear God, just to sit and close her eyes and do nothing . . .

The fire crackled. Outside, distant thunder rolled. The windows in the kitchen rattled, but in the sitting room Charlotte drifted, warm and comfortable, not asleep but not quite awake, either. Her fingers twitched on the arm of her chair; she missed the rowan cross. She hadn't kept it on her the way she did John's wedding ring, but it had been a comfort to know it was in her bedside table whenever she wanted it. To know she had a piece of her father that was *hers*, to sit and fiddle with it—to remember what little she could of George Throckmorton—without anyone knowing.

The house was silent except for the rattling windows in the other room. How nice, she thought, that Arthur had kept the children quiet so she could rest.

Then she remembered Arthur was somewhere in Shiftleaf with Agnes Livingston's horse and cart.

Her eyes snapped open. Without Arthur to keep them so, why on earth were her children (all right, why was Sasha) so quiet?

"Children?" she called, unwilling to relinquish the support of the armchair.

They didn't answer. Guilt prickled at her once more. She called again, louder, then rose stiffly. Her joints still ached, but the painkillers had put the ache back into its rightful place as tolerable.

The door to her brother's workshop was cracked. Beyond, the children were having a whispered argument, the subject of which Charlotte already did not want to know.

"Children?" She nudged the door wider. "What's going on?"

"There's a dead girl outside!" Sasha sang out.

Mud spattered up her legs to the hem of her skirt, and her stockings were falling down. Jonas was in similar disarray.

"I told her not to touch!"

Charlotte's stomach clenched. "Show me."

Sasha dragged her outside, pulling her along so fast she stumbled. Lightning flashed on the horizon. Jonas shivered.

They reached for their mother's hand, their earlier contention forgotten. Guilt needled Charlotte like thorns.

"Not so fast," Jonas told Sasha.

Their sister stuck her tongue out but did as she was told, to Charlotte's relief.

The dead girl was yards from Shiftleaf's edge. The trees shivered in the breeze off the sea. The first raindrops plopped onto Charlotte's nose. She clutched the children's hands tighter. Thunder rumbled, low and much closer than it had been before.

Charlotte's stomach turned.

Brigid Tierney.

She lay supine on the ground, like she was sleeping: arms neatly at her sides, eyes closed peacefully, long lashes sweeping over pallid cheeks, dark hair fanned out around her.

But there was the growth.

Moss and heather carpeted her legs, her arms, her belly. Not merely covering her, but growing from her skin and clothes. White flowers dotted her hair like stars. Only her face, neck, and half her collarbone were bare of greenery.

Charlotte's skin crawled. Wood sickness was bad enough. This was worse. This, Charlotte had never seen.

She stumbled back, her chest tight with fear. Breathing came hard. Clutching her heart, she sucked down air until the tightness went away.

"Mama?" Jonas said. Cautiously, like they expected her to snap again.

Charlotte swallowed. "I'm all right, my love."

Tiny toadstools sprouted in a ring around the girl. Sasha reached for one, but Jonas jerked her away.

Gritting her teeth, Charlotte knelt at Brigid's side to check for a pulse. The neck, not the wrist. She didn't want to touch the wrist, with that greenery sprouting from it.

No pulse. Of course not. Not with that growth. Charlotte's

lips thinned, but she checked Brigid's nostrils, too, to see if there was any breath.

"Sasha, run get me a spoon."

Sasha did so. Charlotte held the spoon to Brigid's nose. Nothing.

Slowly, Charlotte sat back on her haunches and gazed into the forest's depths. She didn't know what had happened to Brigid—but she knew it had happened in Shiftleaf. It was as if the forest, after swallowing her, had spat her back out.

"What do we do?" Jonas whispered.

What indeed. Charlotte liked to think herself mistress of most medical situations—which this wasn't, admittedly. Mortuary rather than medical. Dead bodies rarely discomfited her. This one, however . . .

Thunder cracked overhead. Jonas jumped like a cannon had gone off. The sky broke open, drenching them all.

Charlotte stood with difficulty, her joints groaning. She'd pay for being out in the rain later, but for now she had to get word to the Tierneys, one way or another.

"Come along, children." Her voice wobbled. Silly. "Let's get out of this wet."

Jonas bit their lip, eyes fixed on Brigid. "What about . . . ?"

Charlotte's stomach twisted.

"She'll keep." She hoped she was right. Perhaps Shiftleaf would swallow Brigid back up. "Come along."

The children sprinted into the cottage. Charlotte staggered after them, wishing she'd thought to grab her cane until Jonas doubled back with it. She took it gratefully and pressed their hand. Water matted their curls.

Charlotte's fringe plastered to her forehead, dripping water into her eyes. She sent the children to the washroom to change into dry clothes, then sat alone in the kitchen, cold, wet, and in pain, with dread creeping through her.

Arthur was in the forest somewhere. Charlotte had worried enough about him going. Wood sickness, the eldritch beings said to live there—for heaven's sake, the idea of Arthur in a forest! Charlotte loved her brother, but he was no woodsman. Had this been a perfectly ordinary forest, she would've worried about him traversing its depths. Everything that made Shiftleaf what it was had honed that worry to a sharp point.

Now this. Whatever had happened to Brigid might well happen to Arthur, and Charlotte didn't even know what that was.

She ought to have told him not to go. He'd practically begged her to, but she hadn't. She hadn't wanted to urge him, afraid it would be her own fault if he didn't come back—but she hadn't wanted to forbid him, either. The money had been too good to pass up. Now . . .

She dropped her head into her hands, letting out a long breath, and steadied herself. Her joints ached, she was exhausted, there was a body out back that needed tending to, and her brother was undefended somewhere in the same forest that had spat said body out, but she could handle it. No need to worry the children, nor to think anything might have happened to Arthur, until she had proof. Probably he was fine. He had their father's silver acorn and the rowan cross. Charlotte didn't believe they'd protect him, but she didn't quite not believe it, either, silly as that was.

She mopped off with a kitchen towel. Rain pounded against the window, but through it came a knock at the front door. Wearily, Charlotte went to answer.

It was Kitty Tierney, looking half drowned despite her bumbershoot. Charlotte's sense of mastery over the situation faltered. She'd intended to inform the family; she had not expected the family to come to her, not realizing she had horrible news to bear them.

"Sorry to bother you, Mrs. Prentice," Kitty shouted over

the downpour, "especially in light of Ma's behavior the other day, but this rain has her gout acting up, and we was wondering if you might come to town and take a look."

Charlotte steeled herself. "We've found Miss Brigid."

Kitty whitened. "Where?"

Briefly, Charlotte explained. When she'd finished, Kitty was silent for several moments. A muscle worked in her jaw; she blinked too much. To Charlotte's surprise, she said, sounding like she had a cold, "Law, Mrs. Prentice, you're soaked through. Must be cold as anything. You get yourself some dry clothes and sit by the fire while I send for Pa."

Charlotte objected, but Kitty fussed over her so that she was soon seated by the fire in a dry shirtwaist and skirt. Arthur's fussing she could often ignore, if she wanted. He nudged and suggested, brought her a stool or gave her his arm without being asked, but if she insisted hard enough that she was fine, he'd back down. Kitty, however, had the advantage of a firmer personality combined with a sudden personal tragedy that made Charlotte more pliable than she was otherwise inclined to be.

Kitty strode down to the nearest inhabitance and paid its owners' oldest son a dime to run to the Tierneys' house and tell her father what had happened, then returned to wait out back by her sister's body. Jonas enticed Sasha to stay in the kitchen with the promise of biscuits and a game. Despite Kitty's insistence she remain in her chair, Charlotte put on her coat, took a bumbershoot from the stand by the front door, and went outside to wait with her.

By now, the moss and heather had stretched and grown until it had sewn itself into the ground. Brigid looked like she'd grown from the earth. The growth had crept halfway up her neck. Charlotte shivered, as much from that growth as the cold.

Her knees ached. She shifted from foot to foot, but the ache persisted.

Kitty's jaw was tight. She dashed a palm across her eyes. She was so young, Charlotte thought. Brigid had been even younger: barely sixteen, dark haired and pink cheeked, a cheerful girl if prone to flights of fancy. Now she was dead, grown over with so much greenery she might've been a stone in a long-abandoned churchyard.

"I'm sorry," Charlotte said.

Kitty shrugged, apparently trying, as was Seacliff's way, to act as though grief was nothing. Her eyes were red rimmed.

"Ma's been talking about her like she's dead, figuring she run off with some boy or another like Mary." Her voice cracked. "I wish she'd run off like Mary. I don't care how ill a match it was, neither."

By the time the Tierneys arrived—in a trap that got stuck in the mud partway up the hill and had to be freed by what looked like half of Seacliff's population, who had followed despite the rain—only half of Brigid's forehead and one dark-lashed eye were visible.

Mrs. Tierney wailed at the sight. Her remaining three daughters tried to convince her to wait in the trap, but she stumbled after her husband.

Her wails sounded like the cries of a banshee. Charlotte shivered, then clenched her fists until her nails dug into her palms. Silly to think such a thing. She was uneasy at the death, and the growth, and the proximity of the forest; that was all. The horse hitched to the trap pranced uneasily in its traces.

Determined to be useful, Charlotte opened the shed for Mr. Tierney. He hauled an armful of shovels and spades outside, but the villagers drew back.

"Well?" he said.

"Begging your pardon, Chuck," one of the fishermen said gruffly, "but it's bad luck to touch someone what's been claimed by the wood. Best leave her here. She'll put the devil in us."

"Heaven's sakes," Charlotte said. "She'll do no such thing. Dig her up this instant."

She did not add, *Do you think I want a corpse in my backyard*, but it was there at the edge of her mind. Brigid's body felt like an omen.

Ridiculous, Charlotte kept telling herself. Undoubtedly a trick of the mind, the kind of thing she thought when her body gave way to pain and fatigue and a fog descended upon her brain until she lost all rationality.

Mr. Tierney leaned on a shovel. He was pink cheeked like his daughters but considerably shorter, worn and gray like the other men but less weatherbeaten because he owned the pub.

"We can't well burn her in all this wet," he said wearily. "Come on, lads, we'll be done in a jiff."

No one responded or moved any closer.

"Please," Kitty said through gritted teeth, "we just want to bury her."

Her mother started wailing again. Feeling Kitty and her father might get farther with the villagers if her mother were not there, Charlotte touched Mrs. Tierney's shoulder.

"Come inside, Mrs. Tierney. You'll catch your death out here. Kitty said—"

"I may as well," the old woman croaked. "One daughter dead, another quite as good as, what with her no-good husband who'll surely ruin her—"

Charlotte sighed. With Brigid dead on the ground before her, Mrs. Tierney found breath to bemoan Mary's elopement to Glenwhistle. Perhaps that tragedy was easier to face.

"Kitty said your gout's been acting up," Charlotte continued, as if Mrs. Tierney hadn't interrupted. "Standing in the rain will make it worse. Let's have a spot of tea, shall we?"

To her relief, Mrs. Tierney nodded. The howling wind blew rain sideways under Charlotte's bumbershoot, not that it mattered since they were both soaked anyway.

A sudden scream behind them. Charlotte twisted around so fast she slipped in the wet grass, but Mrs. Tierney kept hold of her. Clutching each other, they gazed toward the forest, where Kitty and Mr. Tierney had convinced the villagers to dig Brigid free.

The Tierneys' horse squealed and kicked, trying to free itself from the trap. Mr. Tierney snatched its bridle, whispering soothing things to it. The villagers backed away as another scream sounded. Kitty snatched a shovel off the ground and brandished it before her, whiter than ever.

A horse burst through the trees, a burly palomino creature wearing nothing but a bridle. It screamed a third time, its eyes wild. Claw marks raked across its haunches.

"See there!" a cannery worker said. "A devil upon us already, and we ain't hardly touched her yet!"

Charlotte staggered toward the creature, her heart in her throat. The horse tossed its head but stood quivering and silent when she caught hold of its bridle. Stamped in the cheekpiece were the initials *TL* for Theodore Livingston, Agnes's deceased husband. It was one of Agnes's carriage horses. The same gelding that had disappeared into the shadows of the forest not two days ago, harnessed to Agnes's cart, with Arthur taking the lines cheerfully. Arthur could not get to Port Lorne without it.

"Mrs. Prentice?" Kitty gripped her elbow. "What's wrong?"

"Arthur," Charlotte gasped, and the rain and chill and ache caught up with her. She collapsed, her legs jellylike.

"Mrs. Prentice!" Kitty looked over her shoulder. "Someone help me get her inside."

Someone gripped Charlotte's arms, someone took her bumbershoot, someone steered her into the cottage. Jonas ran to put water on for tea. Sasha wanted to know what had happened, but Charlotte could only sit in her armchair, soaked and shivering, wondering how to tell the children their uncle was in trouble.

XII. In which Arthur ill-advisedly crosses a bridge

Arthur sprinted alongside the stream, afraid to leave it. With each of the eagles' whistles, cold air blasted behind him, closer than before. But the stream was all he had. If he lost sight of that, he feared it wouldn't matter what the eagles did to him.

The water dove thundering into a ravine. Arthur stumbled, avoiding the chasm. Freya's claws dug into his chest.

Winging along behind him, the eagles caught sight of him. One opened its terrible beak and let out another whistle. A burst of wind cut through him like a knife.

Arthur fell to his knees, numb with cold. The blood froze on his forehead. Frost spread over leaves and flowers, rocks and bark. Ice crackled across the waterfall.

Breathing hard, Arthur struggled to his feet. He staggered along, the cat at his side, with one eagle following. Its mate winged onward without it, vanishing in the trees.

Arthur skidded to a halt. A swinging bridge swayed over the ravine.

Its ends were speared into massive trees whose bark had grown around them, or perhaps the bridge had grown *from* the trees. Its rails were not rope but long, thin twists of bark and wood. Moss and lichens stained them gray-green. The planks were raw and soft with age; several were missing. At the bridge's far end, brambles grew so thickly in the shadow of tall black pines that there seemed no way past.

Arthur swallowed. The bridge looked treacherous. He didn't know what lay beyond the brambles, or if he could get through them in the first place.

The eagle whistled behind him. Arthur rubbed his arms with numb fingers. Gritting his teeth, he started across the bridge.

"Oh, I don't like this," he moaned.

The cat raced past, her fluffy tail waving in his face. He watched her closely, certain she had a special animal sense for which planks were safe.

Then he stopped watching, because the eagle was closing in. He stumbled along. Planks creaked. Frost crackled. A plank cracked underfoot, and Arthur lunged for the bridge's sides.

The plank gave way. Arthur's leg slipped six inches. The straps of his knapsack dug into his shoulders.

The eagle cried out, closer now, the frost thickened to ice with a sharp crack, the cat bounded back across the bridge as if to help—

The eagle was upon him.

Arthur yanked his leg up. Freya launched herself at the raptor, clawing into one massive wing. Snapping its beak angrily, the eagle rammed the bridge, buffeting Arthur against its sides.

"Freya," he croaked.

The cat yowled. The eagle shook her off; she hurtled toward Arthur's head. He tried to catch her in his arms, caught her with his face instead, and yelped in pain.

With a crack and a roar, the sides split, the far end came unmoored, and the bridge collapsed.

"Freya, jump!" Arthur yelped.

She pushed off his back and skidded with a yowl into the brambles.

Arthur leaped after her. The knapsack weighed like an anchor.

His fingers scraped stone, not enough. He clung to the bridge as it fell, slamming into the side of the ravine.

The eagle whistled once and winged away. Little comfort, now that Arthur clung to a crackling length of bark slick with frost.

He tried to pull himself up. Rose an inch, slipped back down. He clung tighter.

"Freya?"

A disgruntled, furry head peered into the ravine.

"Help me," he moaned. His hands slipped. Pieces of the bridge cracked apart and fell away, splashing into the stream far below. His breath hitched. *In for four, hold for four, out for four, in for oh dear* his hands were slipping farther—

The bark split. Arms straining, Arthur renewed his grip and pulled himself up—up—up. He dug his feet into the side of the ravine and pushed off, hurtling upward into thorns.

The remains of the bridge buckled and dropped, landing with a distant splash at the bottom of the ravine.

Arthur struggled away from the thorns with a whimper, so desperate to be free of them he nearly fell after the bridge. Heart pounding, he sat on the narrow strip of earth between the ravine and the brambles with his head in his hands. His face was scratched. His arms and shoulders ached.

"Mrrf," Freya said, twisting around him. He let out a breath, comforted by her soft, warm *aliveness.*

Arthur staggered to his feet, taking stock. He was alive. He wasn't frozen into a block of ice; his fingers were stiff but not blue. That was something. He had the cat, who wound around his ankles with a purr. Charlotte's rowan cross and his watch-repairing kit were in his pocket. His father's silver acorn hung from his neck. Miraculously, he hadn't lost his knapsack. He shrugged it off, afraid it might have come open during the encounter and lost his books.

All three were in place, alongside the paltry other items he'd had in his knapsack instead of his suitcase. He sat back with a sigh. That was something, too.

But there was a sharp drop before him, thick brambles behind him, and massive eagles who knew where. He shuddered. If they returned, he'd be a sitting duck. He was alone except for the cat. His forehead wasn't bleeding anymore because the blood had frozen, but it would surely resume bleeding once he warmed up. His fingers were so stiff he doubted he could've done anything about that even if he'd had more medical knowledge.

"Come on, Freya. Let's get off this ledge."

Whatever was beyond the brambles, it had to be better than here. The cat picked her way through them without so much as a scratch.

"Show off," Arthur said.

He plucked at the nearest cane, careful not to catch his fingers on the thorns. To his astonishment, at his first touch, the brambles pulled aside, creating a narrow trail.

Arthur peered through. All he could see was Freya's furry form and darkness.

She *mrowred* at him.

"If you think it's safe."

He clutched his knapsack to his chest and sidled sideways through the brambles. They closed behind him as he went. He swallowed, feeling like he'd stepped into the cup of a carnivorous plant.

The brambles opened into a thicket of pine trees, through

which was whiteness. The pines enveloped Arthur in their spicy scent but, like the brambles, gave way before him and closed behind him. He wasn't sure why they'd let him through. Whether that was good or not.

"Thank you," he said, just in case.

Neither trees nor brambles responded. Probably for the best.

Arthur turned around and dropped his knapsack.

It was snowing.

Not just snowing—fat, fluffy snowflakes drifting in the soft gray twilight—but *snowy*. Snow blanketed the ground and iced branches like gingerbread. It was the second of September, but in this little woodland vale, it was firmly winter. The doing of the terrible, cold-bringing eagles, perhaps.

The vale looked lived-in. The snowy clearing had a firepit, a stone oven and well, a clothesline, and a low table with several crates jumbled beneath it. Rough-hewn stools scattered in the midst of everything else. An arched wooden door stood in the face of a bulbous wooden house to the left.

None of the trees was stained black. A blue tit hopped along the branches of a nearby fir, singing and perfectly opaque. It was almost hard to believe Arthur hadn't imagined the skeletal animals and oozing trees.

Nonetheless, he advanced into the clearing cautiously, hugging his knapsack to his chest. "Hello?"

No one answered. Everything was well-kept, but the falling snow had obscured any recent footprints.

Arthur bit his lip. It seemed strange the forest would offer a haven after putting him through so much, but the vale seemed safe enough. Safer than where they'd been, at any rate, but whose home was it? Whoever lived here might jump out and attack, or challenge him to a series of riddles, of which he'd get the last wrong and be turned to stone, or eaten, or perhaps they'd skip the formalities and eat him right off the bat.

Well, no good standing here.

He knocked on the door of the oddly shaped house. "Hello?"

Not a house: a tree. Rather, it *was* a house, but a house built into—or growing from—an oak tree with an impossibly distended belly. Instead of a roof, the crown of the tree branched up and out, extending past the surrounding evergreens in both directions. Arthur gaped, recollected himself, and knocked again.

"I don't mean to intrude, but . . ."

The door creaked open. Arthur swallowed. Notwithstanding their helpfulness, he didn't like the way things kept responding to him—as if someone were watching.

He peered into the tree-house. "Hello?"

It was unlike any house he'd ever seen, all wooden curves and smooth edges. The door and windows curved into funny, fairy-tale shapes. Greenery draped the walls and stairs, but he couldn't tell whether it grew from them or had been hung there. The thin light of a winter evening filtered through the windows and, somehow, the ceiling. Craning his neck, Arthur found the ceiling wasn't a ceiling so much as the dense and tangled canopy of a tree, except that no cold or snow came through. Odds and ends dangled from the branches: dried bunches of herbs, coils of rope, bags of roots and apples, and a curious silver basin.

For all its wonder, the house was tiny. By the door was a small round table with a single chair tucked under it. Beyond were a woodstove and two armchairs, one shabby, the other barely touched. A double bed with a curved headboard and a patchwork quilt squeezed into the far corner alongside a small side table and a chest of drawers. An icebox and counter were along the front wall. A short, low staircase curved around the wall behind the stove and disappeared, perhaps to a washroom. That was it.

The house was warm and dry, however, which was all Arthur

could wish for. A fire crackled within the stove; a pot of stew simmered on its surface. Arthur's mouth watered. Someone must have been here recently, to have left the fire going, but he stepped farther into the house without thinking. His extremities stung in the sudden warmth. No longer did he wonder whether the vale was safe, what eldritch creature might live here, why the forest might have led him to safety after all the tricks it had played. His whole concern was for his immediate needs, all of which the house promised to meet.

Freya had already wandered as far as the armchairs, nosing at them as if to determine which was more comfortable.

"By all means," Arthur said. "Make yourself at home."

He staggered toward the woodstove, but his legs wobbled and gave way. Now that he seemed safe, his body had given up on, well, everything.

Not sure what else to do, he kicked his shoes off and dragged himself to the bed. He collapsed on the patchwork quilt, too exhausted to bother getting under it. The cat curled into a fluffy black ball at his side. Within minutes, they were both asleep.

They hadn't been asleep long when they awoke to a figure standing over the bed.

The cat hissed and streaked across the room, darting under one of the armchairs.

Arthur's heart hammered, but he sat up slowly. The figure was a man, mostly. Shorter than Arthur by several inches, with pallid skin, as if he hadn't seen the sun in a long time, and dark hair in a knot. A scar ran from his left brow to his cheek, his eye milky and faded; his other eye was hazel, dark and mossy in the dim light of the woodstove. He wore old furs and a knee brace, put his weight on his left leg.

The man had antlers. Autumn leaves, crimson and gold, wound around them. A tangle of greenery curled over his shoulders and around his throat as if it had grown there.

Arthur's breath caught. The man was like something from a fairy tale.

Or he was, until he growled, "This is too much."

Arthur scrunched his shirt in his fists. "I'm sorry. I didn't mean to intrude, I—"

"Is it not enough for men to destroy the forest? Must you penetrate my very home?"

Gripping Arthur by the shoulder, the man dragged him from the bed. Arthur's mouth went dry. The man's fingers dug into him, hard and hurting.

He threw Arthur into the snow. Arthur landed hard on his elbows, socks damp and skin stinging with cold. The man stood over him, chest heaving. Breath curled from his nose like steam. A tendril of greenery lifted from his shoulder as if looking over it.

Freya slipped past and stood over Arthur, her fur standing on end.

"Get out," the man said, his voice low and hoarse, "and if the forest lets you live, tell the rest of your kind to stay away."

Arthur rolled shakily to his knees. He noticed, with a shiver, that the man had a wolf's paws instead of human feet.

"All right," Arthur gasped, "all right, I'm going—let me grab my shoes and I'll—"

The man lunged. Arthur flinched, but the man merely grabbed the silver acorn hanging from his neck and glinting in the winter twilight. Freya hissed; he ignored her. The green tendril shot toward her, bobbing about her ears. She batted it away.

"Where did you get this?" the man asked.

"It was my father's," Arthur squeaked.

The man's grip tightened, knuckles against his throat. Arthur swallowed.

The man's eyes flickered over his face. "Your father?"

"George Throckmorton."

The man's anger drained away, leaving his expression unreadable. The greenery at his shoulders swayed confusedly.

"George Throckmorton," he repeated under his breath.

He let out a huff of something like laughter. His breath fogged Arthur's glasses.

He released the acorn, hand dropping to his side. For the first time, he considered Arthur. Arthur shrank under his gaze, wondering what he was looking for. What he saw.

"You must be Arthur," the man said.

Arthur's skin prickled. He hadn't known what to expect when he'd found the vale, when he'd entered the tree-house, but it wasn't this. He didn't know what to make of this angry little man with his antlers and paws, his scar and knee brace, who was unknown to Arthur but knew his name.

"How do you— I don't—" Arthur got to his feet, hugging the cat. She twisted in his arms to glare at the man and his greenery. "Who are you?"

The man dragged a hand over his face.

"The Lord of the Wood," he said.

XIII. In which Arthur meets the Lord of the Wood

Arthur's heart sank. This? This was the Lord of the Wood? In his many daydreams over the years, Arthur hadn't imagined this. He'd imagined a benevolent fairy prince, girt in autumn finery, who would welcome him as he'd once welcomed George Throckmorton.

The Lord of the Wood gave a crooked, bitter sort of smile. "I don't look it, do I?"

Arthur flushed. He'd been staring, trying to recapture a piece of his father in the other man's face. The eyes like sunlight, the hair like shadows. His inky hair in its knot was the only thing about him that Arthur recognized from George's stories.

The cat squirmed out of Arthur's arms. She wound around his ankles, glaring unceasingly at the Lord of the Wood.

"Dad didn't—" Arthur ran a hand through his hair. "I'm sorry. You're not what I expected."

The Lord of the Wood knew his name. He didn't know why that should be. George had met him long before he'd married Arthur's mother.

"You're bleeding."

Arthur touched his forehead. The blood had mostly congealed, but a small wet spot crept down his face. He shuddered.

"Yes, those—those awful eagles."

The Lord of the Wood squinted into the twilit sky as if he might see them winging overhead. "Stormwings. They bring storms in from the sea every year. Earlier than they used to."

"Is that why it's winter here?"

"It's always winter here." The Lord of the Wood nodded toward the open door of the tree-house. "You'd better come inside. I'll patch you up."

He turned toward the door. Those wolf paws left massive clawed prints in the snow. Freya sniffed at them and growled.

Arthur hugged himself, shivering. "My lord—"

"Don't call me that."

Arthur faltered. "Then what do I call you?"

The Lord of the Wood's shoulders hunched. For a long moment, Arthur thought he wouldn't answer, and Arthur would have to resort to an awkward *um, excuse me* whenever he wanted to address the other man. Being. Beast. Whatever exactly he was, with his antlers and his paws and his human face with its angry eyes and beautiful hair.

At last the Lord of the Wood said, "Ira. My name is Ira."

Arthur twisted his fingers together, wondering whether his father had known the name. Why his father had never mentioned the scar or knee brace—though many fishermen in Seacliff had something like them—or the antlers or paws. "Why are you letting me in?"

"Because you're bleeding."

"But . . ." Arthur took a step forward. A tendril shot up from the Lord of the Wood's shoulders; he hastily stepped back. "A moment ago you were ready to throw me out. Now you want to take care of me. I don't understand."

Glancing back at him, the Lord of the Wood raised an eyebrow. "Do you want to stay here in the snow with your forehead bloody?"

"No."

"Then come inside."

Arthur tried, but the tangle of greenery slipped from the Lord of the Wood's shoulders. It rose up right in his path, clicking faintly. Vine, leaf, branch, and flower grew until it loomed over him, *creature-like.* It swayed threateningly. Arthur swallowed.

The Lord of the Wood—Ira—turned. "Enough, Calyx."

The plant creature reached for Arthur with a tendril.

"Calyx."

Calyx shrank, until it was the size and roughly the shape of a small dog, and trotted past him into the house.

"What the hell is that?" Arthur croaked.

"My guardian," Ira said in distaste. "It should leave you be now."

Arthur wasn't reassured by that *should*, but he traipsed into the tree-house with the cat mewling disapproval at his heels.

He stood in the doorway until Ira nodded him toward the unused armchair. Calyx sprawled beside the woodstove like a dog, though its shape had gone vague. Arthur gave it a wide berth.

His glasses fogged up; he wiped them on his shirt and put them back on. The cat leaped into his lap. His socks were squishy with melting snow, which made him wish he didn't have feet, but he couldn't bring himself to take them off.

Ira shed his furs and hung them on a row of pegs by the door. Without them, he was small and lean, wearing mended trousers and a linen shirt with toggles sewn on. He limped through the room for a rag and water, then sat in the other armchair to remove the knee brace from his twisted right leg.

Arthur tried and failed not to stare at his paws, reddened when Ira caught him.

Ira's mouth pressed into a grim line, but he didn't comment. "Let me see."

Arthur scooted his chair closer. The cat growled as Ira touched him. Tendrils shot from Calyx's strange, lumpy amalgam of plant anatomy, turning toward Freya. Arthur ran a hand through her long fur until she quieted. He was grateful to have his own self-appointed guardian, given the circumstances, but he wished she wouldn't set the plant creature off.

Ira dabbed blood from Arthur's forehead. Arthur studied him. The scar over his left eye. The long, dark lashes. The curve of his nose, lips, and chin. The gentle expression he wore, though he'd been so angry to find Arthur in his home in the first place.

Ira's eyes met Arthur's. Arthur flushed. Eye contact felt too intimate at the best of times. Far more so now, when the Lord of the Wood was inches away, tending his wound, and it didn't matter that the left eye was milky and unseeing. But he couldn't turn away as Ira's gaze flickered over him.

"I see him in you," Ira said. "George. You have kind eyes like he did."

Arthur's skin prickled. No one had ever said they'd seen George in him, except occasionally his mother when she was trying to make him feel better about himself. Now someone had, he felt his father had been keeping secrets. Like the rowan cross in Arthur's pocket that Charlotte had found in their father's things.

Arthur's hand clenched in the cat's fur. "What was he to you?"

"He was my friend."

Looking away, Ira opened his hand. Arthur was both relieved and disappointed to no longer endure the Lord of the Wood's gaze, but he didn't think about it long: A single leaf grew from Ira's palm.

Arthur's breath hitched, but Ira plucked the leaf and smoothed it over his forehead like a gauze pad as if it had been nothing.

"He talked about you all the time," he continued. "You and your sister. How tall you'd gotten. The latest trouble you'd been into."

His eyes flashed once more across Arthur's face. Arthur reddened. The only trouble he'd ever gotten up to was being pushed around by the other boys. Nothing to have made him seem bold and intrepid.

"He was terribly proud of you both," Ira said, and Arthur couldn't take it anymore.

"He always told us he just met you once."

His voice rang in sudden silence. Calyx clicked ominously, but Arthur hardly noticed.

Ira's brow furrowed. Swallowing, Arthur lowered his voice.

"He said you saved his life, and he never saw you again."

Ira's hand lingered on Arthur's forehead. Freya swatted at his fingers. Calyx surged up from its spot by the stove, but Ira smacked the tendril that reached for the cat. The plant creature curled up with an angry rustle.

"Would you like to see?" Ira asked.

"See?"

Ira reached for the silver basin hanging from the branches overhead. He filled it with water from a pitcher and handed it to Arthur. Nudging the cat from his lap, Arthur placed the basin there instead.

It was shallow, of dimpled silver, with a leather strap at one end. Arthur's reflection peered up at him.

Ira plucked a strand of long, dark hair from his own head and dropped it into the water.

The basin glowed; the water rippled. When the ripples stilled, Arthur was looking at his father.

He was younger than Arthur had ever seen him, with thick black hair kept longer than he'd worn it in later years. He sat leaning against a tree, shivering, his skin ashen with illness.

A stag approached. Larger than most red deer, with a glorious golden mane and antlers twined in autumn leaves. The Lord of the Wood. Ira.

The air shivered around him, and he was a man—but different than he was now. No antlers grew from his head; his boot-shod feet were human rather than canine. His eye was unscarred, his leg untwisted. He crouched beside George and felt his forehead, giving a small, reassuring smile when George's brown eyes cracked open, fever bright.

The image shifted. George Throckmorton was well, his color better, eyes no longer glazed with sickness. He sat in an armchair—the same armchair Arthur sat in now, Arthur realized with a jolt—drinking from a mug and laughing. His laughter echoed, shivering through Arthur. He'd never thought he'd hear his father's laugh again.

Ira sat across from him, also laughing, and perhaps that was even more surprising than the way he'd transformed from stag to man. He rose to refill George's mug.

Arthur's heart thumped painfully. "I don't understand. How . . . ?"

A new image. George and Ira hiking the forest together. Trees turning gold and crimson bent as if in greeting. A hare rabbited across the path, whole and healthy. Not one tree dripped ooze. Birds sang in the branches; none was translucent or veined with black.

Pausing, George pointed at fleshy, pinkish fungi growing out of reach on an elder.

Jelly ear, he said, his voice echoing as his laughter had, and Arthur wanted to cry, hearing his voice. *I could use some for the spate of flu going around the village, if I could get at it.*

You can get at it.

Ira touched the tree. The fungi slid down the trunk and stopped within easy reach.

You are a wonder. Smiling, George harvested several fleshy fruits. *Someday you'll have to tell me how you do that.*

"Wood and water hold memories," Ira said now, standing at Arthur's side. "These are mine."

Arthur ran a finger along the basin's lip. "This isn't wood."

"In the same way this is—" Ira reached for the acorn hanging from Arthur's neck, his fingertips brushing the hollow of Arthur's throat "—the basin is. They both come from the same tree."

Arthur's skin twitched at his touch. Hard to reconcile Ira-of-memory with the Ira before him now. Not merely because of the physical differences, but because it was difficult to imagine Ira-of-now smiling as he had in the memories.

"It's a real acorn, then?" Arthur asked. "We always thought it was a carven trinket."

The image in the basin shifted once more. A stag dragged itself through the forest on a shot leg. Men shouted somewhere behind him.

Ira yanked the basin from Arthur's lap, sloshing him with water. The cat hissed as water splashed over her.

Arthur stared, but Ira emptied the basin and spoke as if there had been no interruption.

"The acorn came from the heart of the wood. It is—it was—a silver oak tree, the first tree that ever grew here and the source of all Shiftleaf's magic. All that's left now is a stump." He dried the basin and hung it back on its branch. "That's why the forest is dying."

Arthur's heartbeat quickened as he thought of the sickness. The trees oozing black. The skeletal animals roaming the forest.

Ira dropped into his armchair, running a hand through his hair. Several strands came loose from his knot, falling about his face or tangling around his antlers. Calyx crept from its place by the stove to wind around his feet.

"If not for George," Ira said, "it would be dead already."

Arthur's fingers dug into his knees. "What do you mean?"

Ira looked sideways at him, his eyes flickering over Arthur's face. Arthur wondered whether he was trying to find more of George.

"He really told you so little of me?"

Arthur nodded. "How many times did he see you, really?"

Ira's fingers drummed on the arm of his chair. "Many. He stopped by whenever he traveled between Seacliff and Port Lorne. Sometimes he'd stay a day or two to keep me company."

He stood abruptly, swearing as he tripped over Calyx.

"Accursed thing," he growled, kicking it away. The tangle of plants slung itself back toward the stove. Muttering to himself, Ira grabbed two bowls from a cupboard, ducking to avoid catching his antlers in the items hanging from the ceiling.

Arthur's head spun with questions, but they whirled through him so quickly he couldn't grab hold of one. George Throckmorton had always been the one solid thing in his life. Even in memory—despite the space he'd left behind when he'd gone—George had felt dependable and real. Steady. Someone Arthur could look back on for comfort when life shook him, again and again. Now the very memories shook. How much of what his father had told him through the years was untrue? Why would he not have told his children the Lord of the Wood was his friend?

Unbidden, Charlotte's criticism of Arthur's own bedtime stories came to mind.

You never mention the sickness. Or the disappearances. You don't even tell the children about Dad's *disappearance.*

He told the stories as his father had told them, preferring to remember George's stories to the realities of the forest. Had his father edited his tales for similar reasons, or had there been something else to it?

He could certainly see why George might not have mentioned Calyx.

Ira shoved a bowl of stew into his hands. "Eat."

His brow furrowed as Arthur picked up a spoonful of stew only to let it plop back into the bowl. Freya purred at Arthur's feet, stopping occasionally to glare at the Lord of the Wood or his chlorophyllous companion.

After a long while, Ira took the bowl and spoon away. Washing them, he nodded toward the corner of the room. "You can take the bed."

"What?"

"The bed," Ira repeated. "You can have it. I'll be fine in my armchair."

Arthur dragged a hand over his face. "Oh. Yes. Thank you. I suppose there's no point leaving until morning."

A long silence as Ira dried the dishes.

Then he said, "You're not leaving."

"Well," Arthur said, taken aback, "no—not now, of course, but—"

"Not ever."

Arthur had misheard. He thought Ira had said "not ever," as if he expected Arthur to remain in this wintry vale for the rest of his life.

Before he could ask Ira to repeat himself, however, Ira said, "This is your home now."

Arthur twisted around. Ira's shoulders hunched, but when he turned from the counter his expression was firm. A pit gnawed at Arthur's stomach.

"No, but—but—" He floundered, his mouth dry. "Lottie—the children—for heaven's sake, Mrs. Livingston, she's counting on me to go to Port Lorne and—"

Ira gave a sardonic smile. "How do you propose leaving with the bridge out?"

Arthur's heart sank. He'd forgotten the bridge. "Surely there's another way?"

"There isn't," Ira said bluntly, "and if there were, the forest would kill you before you made it halfway home."

"But—you could take me. If you showed me the way—"

"I don't leave the vale."

"You showed Dad the way out."

Ira's jaw tightened. "That was long ago."

Arthur tried to rein in his panic. "Please. Please, I— Surely it wouldn't take long, I only traveled a couple of days to get this far. If you could just—"

Eyes smoldering, Ira lunged across the tiny space and grabbed Arthur's collar.

"I don't leave the vale," he growled.

His fingers clenched at Arthur's throat. Arthur swallowed with difficulty. His eyes stung.

Ira released him, backed away. He closed his eyes and let out a breath, dropping into his chair. Calyx climbed up behind him.

Arthur pressed into his own chair, his heart rabbiting. The pit gnawing at his stomach widened.

Ira's voice was hoarser than ever. "I'm sorry."

Arthur didn't know whether he meant for the situation or for grabbing him like that. After a moment, Ira jerked his head back toward the corner.

"Take the bed. You'll be more comfortable."

Mechanically, Arthur drifted toward the bed. Freya followed, winding about his legs. He lifted her onto the bed after him. Outside, branches clattered in the breeze, but the windows didn't rattle. He missed the rattling of his window in the attic. The windows in the kitchen.

He peeled off his socks. Across the room, in the dim red light of the stove, Ira seemed an ancient, immovable figure, splayed in his chair, gazing silently into the coals with greenery draped around his shoulders. A stoic god instead of the amiable fairy prince Arthur had always imagined. His antlers gleamed faintly gold, illuminating their curves and pointed tips.

Arthur crawled beneath the patchwork quilt, turned toward the wall, and buried his face in the cat's fur, thinking of home.

XIV. In which Arthur visits a grave

The cottage was bright and clean. Arthur sat in his faded floral armchair, reading a romance novel with earplugs in because Charlotte, in her armchair and embroidering a handkerchief, was listening to her favorite radio program. A fire crackled in the grate. The children played war on the rug at their mother's and uncle's feet. Sasha was winning, of course; Jonas was losing with good grace, which Sasha hadn't learned to do yet.

Then Sasha asked Arthur if he'd read his book aloud. That should've been his first clue things were amiss, because Sasha never asked him to read his books aloud, lest she hear a kissing scene. But Arthur, delighted, obliged. It seemed a perfectly sensible thing to do.

Waking was a slow business. The images faded, but the ease and comfort of an evening spent by the fire with his family remained. Arthur was exceptionally warm, the cat purring on his chest. The window wasn't even rattling. Any moment, Charlotte would call him down for breakfast, if she was up. Since her illness, she sometimes slept late.

With that thought, Arthur decided to get up. If she was asleep, he could make her breakfast in bed. Or, well, he could ask Jonas to help him make her breakfast, since Arthur needed supervision in the kitchen for anything other than baking. Even toast eluded him: It either burned or turned out closer to stale bread.

He opened his eyes, squinting. How odd. The attic was never so bright, no matter the time of day; the window over his bed was small, and the attic was all unwhitewashed beams and planks. He felt around the windowsill for his glasses, but the sill wasn't wide enough and his glasses weren't there.

Arthur found them on a bedside table on his other side. He frowned. He didn't have a bedside table.

When he put his glasses on, his heart sank. The bed was not his own.

He let out a long breath. The Lord of the Wood. He was in the Lord of the Wood's house—in his bed—in a wintry vale in the middle of the forest. By the looks of it, Ira had tucked him into extra blankets while he'd slept. Good thing, too. As Arthur shoved them aside and swung his legs over the bed, he shivered. The frigid floorboards stung his feet.

A dream. Arthur had dreamed he was home. It had felt so real—

He turned over and squeezed his eyes shut, wishing he *were* home. If the Lord of the Wood was to be believed, Arthur would never go home again.

He should've known. Stumbling into the relative safety of the vale had seemed too good to be true, but he'd been too exhausted to worry about it.

What would Charlotte think? The children? He'd promised to return. He'd thought he'd bring back the clock, and Agnes would give him the rest of the money, and they'd all be better off.

Instead, he'd spend the rest of his life in this eternal winter. His family would never know what had happened to him, the same as when his father had vanished.

He wished George had found his way to the vale. If he had, surely he'd be here now. Older, grayer, likely less cheerful, after three decades in a sunless, snowy vale far from his wife and children, but alive and well. It would almost have been worth being trapped here.

Arthur sat up slowly. "Ira?"

A movement overhead caught his gaze. Calyx dropped to the floor and swayed over him. Gasping, Arthur scrambled farther back onto the bed.

Freya darted between them. Her ears flattened, but she made no noise as she glared at the plant creature.

Arthur's voice quivered. "It's all right."

He hardly knew which of them he was talking to. Fronds shifted in his direction. Anything further he might've said died in his throat.

Calyx turned away and slid across the floor, its leaves and vines and branches and flowers shifting and weaving until it was dog-shaped. It pushed the door open and vanished outside.

Letting out a breath, Arthur patted Freya's side. "I don't like that thing, either."

A pair of lumpy woolen socks had been left on the bedside table. Like the extra blankets, they had not been there when Arthur had gone to bed. He softened at the sight. Ira had left them out for him.

He pulled the socks on and braved the frigid floorboards to stir up the coals in the woodstove. No spare logs to be found, but stirring the coals did something, at any rate. Arthur warmed his hands. He found his shoes, shrugged on his coat, and crept outside. Following him to the door, Freya put one delicate paw in the snow and sat in the doorway with a disgruntled meow.

The Lord of the Wood was nowhere to be seen. Thankfully, neither was his plantish guardian.

Arthur's breath fogged before him. His coat was inadequate for this kind of cold, but he snuck toward the brambles. He glanced over his shoulder, expecting Ira or Calyx to pop up and stop him.

The brambles were thicker and pricklier than he remembered. He thought they would part before him as they had yesterday, but they didn't.

"Open up, please."

Nothing happened. Arthur's hands clenched and unclenched at his sides.

"Please?"

Nothing.

"I just want to go home. Let me go. Please."

Determined to escape, he tugged thorny canes apart. The forest was enchanted; surely the bridge had magically repaired itself since yesterday. If he could just get through these damn brambles, he could cross the bridge and go home.

He lost his grip on a cane. It smacked him in the face. He stumbled back, clutching a cheek scratched so deeply it bled. His throat closed up; he wanted to cry.

"Please," he whispered.

Freya braved the snow to wind around his legs comfortingly. He sat, heedless of the damp and cold, and rested his chin on his knees. He'd get home. He'd find another way out of here, no matter what Ira said. Somehow.

"It won't have grown back, you know."

Arthur's head jerked up. Ira stood before him with a cord of wood in his arms. His antlers gleamed in the gray morning light, as did the claws on his massive wolf's paws. Calyx trailed behind him, shrinking and morphing into a shape not unlike a cat. Freya glared, unamused.

"What?"

Ira stowed all but a couple logs beneath the table. "The bridge. The forest could regrow it, but it won't."

"Why not?"

"The better to keep me here."

Arthur got to his feet. "So when you said you don't leave the vale . . ."

Ira gave a slantwise smile. A wolfish smile. Arthur shuddered.

"The forest makes it difficult." The smile vanished. "You must be cold. Come inside. Let's take care of that scratch."

Arthur glanced back at the brambles. He'd only hoped the bridge had grown back, but he'd been certain the brambles would let him through. Now they seemed determined to keep him here.

Inside, Ira wiped blood from his cheek and dotted a salve on the scratch. Calyx stood guard beside him.

"No harm done. It'll heal before you know it."

Ira stirred up the coals in the stove. To Arthur's relief, Calyx turned away. It dragged itself into Ira's empty armchair and draped itself over the whole thing.

"It's trying to protect me," Ira said suddenly. "The forest."

Huddled in his own chair, Arthur said nothing. Freya jumped into his lap.

"It thinks I'll be safe as long as I'm in the vale," Ira continued. "As long as nothing changes. That's why it's always winter here. Nothing changes in winter, the forest thinks. It's right, a bit. That's why the wood's sickness hasn't infected the vale yet."

He crouched beside the stove with a log.

"Of course, it won't work." The log went into the stove. "One day, the sickness will spread here as it has everywhere else. I'll die, and the forest will die with me."

He didn't sound upset by this, merely resigned.

Despite himself, Arthur felt a kinship with the Lord of the Wood. As Seacliff had been dying a slow death since the draining of the fishing grounds, Ira's home was dying a slow death from wood sickness.

"Is all this because the heart of the wood was chopped down?"

Ira stiffened but said, after a long moment, "There's something I should show you."

He rose with a soft groan, rubbing his knee, and glanced at Arthur.

"Have you eaten yet?"

Arthur shook his head. Ira pulled a fur from the pegs by the door and tossed it at him.

"Eat. Stew is in the icebox. Then put that on and come find me."

"Come find—"

Ira had already stalked outside. Calyx scrambled off the armchair to follow.

Arthur lifted Freya onto the floor. "Not very chatty, is he?"

He ate the stew cold, straight from the icebox. Freya begged for bits of meat. Had they been home, he would've resisted the begging (or tried to), but the cat had to eat.

When they'd finished, he wrapped the fur around himself. It was thick and warm and smelled, faintly but surprisingly, of spring flowers. Arthur closed his eyes, breathing in the scent and trying to pretend he was home, on a bright May morning, hanging laundry with Charlotte. But there was the scent from the woodstove, too, and the sting on his cheek where the brambles had struck him. With a sigh, he headed outside.

Ira had left clawed pawprints, bordered on one side by odd drag marks that must have been made by his guardian. Arthur followed them.

Around the side of the house, Ira had returned to chopping wood. Despite the cold, he'd shed his furs and shirt. His back was corded with muscle—and his shoulders were feathered. Glossy black feathers like those of a raven winged from shoulder to shoulder across his upper back.

Arthur inhaled sharply. The paws and antlers had been quite enough.

Calyx huddled at the base of a nearby tree, smaller than usual. It shuddered at each chop of the axe, tendrils sliding over itself as if shielding nonexistent ears.

Wiping his brow, Ira turned and threw down the axe. The feathers were less noticeable from the front, barely rounding the tops of his shoulders. Instead, Arthur was confronted with his chest and the trail of fine, dark hair running down his stomach and into his trousers. The sight threatened to do funny things to him, like make him blush for unclear reasons. Arthur tended not to give his own body much thought—although he knew the village girls didn't find him much to look at—but suddenly he was more conscious than usual of his love handles, his hairy chest and belly. Ira was so lean and muscular.

With the axe no longer working, Calyx relaxed, its vines and tendrils loosening.

"Sorry," Ira grunted. "Thought I'd get a little more done before you got out here. How's the fur?"

Missing, Arthur thought in a panic, averting his gaze from Ira's chest.

"Fine." His throat was dry. How odd. "Er, I mean, much warmer than my coat in all this snow, thank you."

Ira nodded, turning away. To Arthur's relief, he shrugged his shirt back on, redid the toggles, and pulled on his furs.

"This way."

Arthur left a good distance between himself and Ira. Every time he strayed too close, Calyx grew, clicking at him.

The snow curved around behind the house, where bare winter trees closed in. Before them stood a half-buried hunk of rock like a single headstone. Rather than a name or dates or *in remembrance of* or any of the usual things, it was carved with an image of yarrow in bloom.

Despite the frigid air, woodland flowers grew in a slab before the stone. Arthur recognized some of them. Five-petaled yellow flowers on a small shrub. Star-shaped blooms giving off a strong scent of garlic. Frothy white ones Arthur was certain Charlotte kept in stock in her medical kit as a matter of course. Good for pain, he thought, but he couldn't remember their name. Not heal-all, although he saw that, too, with its tiny, two-lipped purple flowers. Similar blossoms in blue—or perhaps that was heal-all, and the purple ones were something else.

Mints, Arthur thought. He'd never get the hang of mints.

He bent and touched the leaves of the nearest mint, whichever kind it was, confused by this garden blossoming in the middle of the snow. "What is this?"

Ira gave a smile that didn't reach his eyes. "Your father."

He kicked at the snow. Calyx wrapped a single tendril around his leg, but he shook it off.

"The ground wasn't so hard back then. Otherwise I couldn't have given him a proper burial."

It took several moments for Arthur to understand. His father's headstone. His father's grave. Of course the Throckmorton-Prentices had grieved him, but thirty years of grieving a man who had vanished was different than being presented with his resting place.

Arthur touched the top of the headstone. His eyes stung with tears, but the cold air threatened to freeze them. He swallowed.

He didn't know what to say, but thinking of his father, he laughed wetly. Seacliff had found George so high-and-mighty when he'd returned from Port Lorne, because learning healing from the likes of them had been (as they thought) beneath him. Because, while he'd respected their superstitions, he hadn't believed them.

Yet he'd been friends with the Lord of the Wood. He'd never eschewed telling his children stories in which magic figured. He'd accepted magic if he'd seen it, would've wondered about the workings of the magic keeping the flowers at his snowy grave alive instead of insisting on a nonmagical explanation.

"Hi, Dad," Arthur whispered, his voice wobbling, and he sat in the snow and cried.

Standing behind him, Ira touched the top of his head. Calyx swayed nearby, but since Ira rather than Arthur had closed the distance between them, it contented itself with standing guard.

At last Ira said, "He died saving me."

Arthur wiped his tears on his sleeve. Avoiding his gaze, Ira settled in the snow beside him. He stretched out his right leg, rubbing his knee. It seemed like he was avoiding looking at the grave, too.

"Thirty years ago, when woodsmen were felling the heart of the wood, hunters tried to kill me at the same time."

"Why?"

"My life is bound to the forest. If one of us dies, so does the other. They wanted the land." Ira's fingers tightened on his knee. "I couldn't get away. They'd already got a bullet in me."

He dragged his hands through his hair. A strand came loose from his knot, hanging around his face. Arthur's fingers twitched with the urge to tuck it back into place. He twisted his hands in his lap instead.

"They caught me," Ira said. "Bound me. And then George came running and pulled them off. He'd been passing by." His jaw clenched, voice blunt. "He held them off long enough for me to get away. That's the only reason the forest is still standing. But the bastards were so angry at his interference that they killed him."

Arthur's breath hitched. Thirty years. Thirty years spent wondering what, exactly, had happened to his father. At first, of course, folks had whispered that he must have abandoned the family—finally decided he was too good for them, or for Seacliff. Eileen had refused to believe it. Charlotte, five, had merely asked, again and again, when her daddy was coming back with her new doll.

Arthur, twelve, had refused to believe, then quietly started to doubt, then come to think that George had not only left but left because of him. He was too soft, too dreamy, more interested in cogs and gears than the workings of the human body. He'd driven his father away, he'd thought.

When he'd said as much to his mother, she'd told him, *Your father couldn't love you more if you'd passed the Triple yesterday. I know what it's like to have a man leave you, sweetheart, and it's not like this. He didn't leave. I know he didn't.*

Not long afterward, another village man had gone into the wood and never come out. Then a young couple. A child. Then more. The Throckmorton-Prentices came to know, in a general sense, what had happened to George. He'd been a victim of the forest, like the others. It had been as true to Arthur as the stories George had told about the Lord of the Wood.

Now, seeing his grave, learning how he had died—it was too much. A closure and a bigger question all at once. The Lord of the Wood had not only been George's friend, but a friend so precious George had risked his life for him. Died for him. And it had not been Shiftleaf but ordinary men who had killed him.

Ira glanced over. "I'm sorry. I . . . Maybe I shouldn't have told you—"

Arthur shook his head. "It's all right. We've always wondered . . ."

Hesitantly, Ira touched his back. Arthur leaned into him without thought, squeezing his eyes shut. Calyx clicked fretfully but did not interfere.

After a moment of stiffness, Ira slipped an arm around him. It was ludicrous. This was the Lord of the Wood. An eldritch being, a shape-shifter, the stuff of lore and legend. Antlers and autumn leaves crowned his head. Beneath his furs, his shoulders were feathered. Where his feet should have been were wolf paws. A sentient ball of plant life followed him wherever he went.

But he was also a small, grim man, sitting in the snow with his arm around Arthur. He was warm and wiry, soft with all the furs he wore.

After a while, Ira stood. Arthur clambered to his feet, missing the heat of him. His trousers chafed, wet from melted snow.

Reaching into the trees, Ira pulled a bronze pocket watch from a branch. "You should have this."

Arthur let out a breath. The case was engraved with his father's initials.

"It hasn't worked in decades, I'm afraid," Ira said.

No matter. Arthur could fix it.

He clutched the watch to his chest. "You don't know what this means to me. Thank you."

Ira kicked at the snow. "It's nothing."

Arthur felt lighter than he had all morning. He had the case of watch-repairing tools with him. He'd have the watch working by the time he found a way home. He *would* find a way home. Anything seemed possible, with his father's watch in his hands. Even his damp trousers—even Calyx swaying nearby, waist-high—didn't bother him.

He smiled at Ira. It was the first time he'd smiled since losing Agnes's cart. "It really isn't."

The tips of Ira's ears pinkened, but he turned away. "More chores to do yet."

Arthur slipped his father's watch into his pocket. "Can I help with anything?"

"You're a guest."

"I don't know about that." Arthur followed him back around the bend toward the stump where he'd been chopping wood. "If I'm going to be here forever like you seem to think, surely I'm something other than a guest. I might as well help how I can—though I admit I'm likely to muck things up. That was my greatest source of help at home, mucking things up. I daresay I'm even better at it than the children."

Ira let out a huff of laughter. That was something, Arthur thought. He'd made this grim man-beast-person laugh, however little.

He hoped he'd be able to make Charlotte laugh like that again someday. Soon. One way or another, he'd get home, no matter what the Lord of the Wood said.

"All right," Ira said. "But first things first. Let's get you out of those trousers."

"What?" Arthur said.

XV. In which Charlotte tries to form a search party, to no avail

In the two days since Agnes Livingston's horse had returned without her brother, Charlotte had tried to organize a search party. Her joints ached in the aftermath of the storm. She was fatigued, too, and could barely think straight, except for that single clear, terrible thought: *Arthur is in trouble.*

What kind of trouble, she didn't know. But he certainly hadn't sent the horse home alone. She didn't like to think what might have separated them. Perhaps whatever had left the claw marks in Maurice's flanks.

With each of the family's losses, Charlotte had thought it was the worst thing they could face. Now, with her brother gone, she knew: This was the worst. All those times before, she and Arthur had lost—but they'd had each other.

Leaning on her cane, she went to house after house, and the few open shops, asking anyone she'd ever helped with an ailment or injury, however slight, to please, *please*, help find her brother.

No one would do it. Long suspicious of Shiftleaf, Seacliff was spooked worse than ever by the appearance of Brigid Tierney's body. People who had, a week ago, risked the forest's edge for food or firewood, with prayers or rowan or yellow flowers for protection, would now not risk it at all. Even the reward Agnes set at Charlotte's request was not enough to entice the villagers into the wood.

By Thursday afternoon, Charlotte was filled with a sense of dread. No one would help find her brother.

Numb, she stopped in at Agnes's to check on Gracie. Her condition hadn't changed, which was only a comfort because any change would be for the worse. Charlotte once more gave her tea and a tincture and sat in the drawing room with Agnes. She'd run herself ragged, going all over town, but she couldn't bear to stay home. If she stopped moving for too long, she feared, the knowledge her brother was lost in the wood would overwhelm her.

Agnes was in her habitual spot on the davenport, thumbing through her old deck of cards. "Any change?"

"No."

"Any word from Arthur?"

Charlotte rubbed her fingers. Her joints were stiff. "No."

Agnes nodded, looking like she hadn't heard. Charlotte had never seen her so distracted.

"I'll be by again tomorrow," Charlotte said, and stood.

A wave of dizziness swept over her. She swayed, gripping her cane.

Agnes glanced up for the first time, with a faint frown. "Charlotte dear? Are you quite all right?"

"Yes, of course. Good day, Mrs. Livingston."

"Good day, Charlotte."

Charlotte took it as a bad sign that Agnes hadn't corrected her. Not that Charlotte planned to stop addressing her as such, but Agnes never failed to correct her. Gracie's illness had her reeling.

Charlotte slipped briefly into the stable to examine Maurice's claw marks. Her nose wrinkled; the straw smelled as if it hadn't been changed in days. The carriage horses and a single mule whinnied as she entered. She patted each of them, but her lips pressed into a line at the sight of their dry water buckets. With her servants run off, Agnes evidently wasn't taking care of them.

Rubbing her forehead, deeply annoyed, Charlotte went searching for the spigot and feed. This wasn't her job. Surely Agnes could pay someone enough to look after her stables, though no one would enter the manor. Charlotte didn't feel up to mucking out stalls, but she could feed and water the horses. This time. She'd bring the issue up with Agnes when she stopped by tomorrow.

The feeding done, she lingered in Maurice's stall. Maybe the claw marks could provide a clue to whatever had happened to Arthur—but no. Charlotte didn't know what had made them, or whether it had separated Arthur from his horse or sunk its claws into the horse after he'd run off. At least they hadn't shown any sign of wood sickness. Charlotte tried to tell herself that was something, but it was paltry comfort when claws could do quite enough damage.

She made her slow way through the village until she reached the McGills'. Young Dougal McGill's stump was healing well after the incident in the cannery. His mother had changed the dressing for him frequently and prevented him from doing overmuch while he convalesced. Often, the villagers ignored Charlotte's instructions to rest and let themselves heal after illness or injury, so she was grateful his mother had taken her orders seriously.

But the boy was considerably less cheery than he'd been Monday, spooked by phantom pains in a hand he no longer had.

"That's quite common, I'm afraid," Charlotte told him wearily. "It should lessen over time."

She was certain she knew of treatments for phantom limb

pain, but she couldn't think what. So she didn't mention them. She left dissatisfied, feeling like she'd accomplished nothing.

Old fishwives populated the village square, having their afternoon gossip. They nodded at Charlotte; she nodded back. Hardly had she passed them before they huddled together, whispering—in the way of old women who were trying to be discreet but were also half deaf—about her brother's disappearance. And, worse, mortifyingly, about *her.*

". . . no denying he's an odd one, but I do feel for the family."

"Yes, of course—can't imagine he's much of a provider, but her having to take care of the children all on her own . . ."

"I've always wondered why some nice widower hasn't snatched her up. She might've had a decent provider if she'd remarried."

"Too late now. With how sick she's been, she probably can't handle a cannery worker's passel of brats when she's got two of her own already, I shouldn't wonder . . ."

"Nonsense. She could handle that and more if she'd try harder."

Charlotte reddened, her skin prickling, and hurried to escape their overloud whispers. Perhaps it didn't matter what she did, how respectable she was. How hard she worked, even at her own expense. She'd given Seacliff no reason to talk about her through the years, but here the old gossips were, talking about her anyway, for things beyond her control.

She could manage on her own. She could. She *could.* And Arthur—well, wanting him back had nothing to do with how useful he might be. She wanted him back because he was her brother. As for a nice widower, she'd known for a long time a new husband might've made life easier. She'd been courted briefly several years back, by an unmarried man around Arthur's age. But she'd caught him shaking Jonas, for some minor offense the nature of which she didn't know to this day, and frostily told him he needn't come around again. She'd had no offers since, but that was a relief. A new husband, even a kind one, would've been another ball to juggle. The family had made do so far. Somehow, they'd keep going.

That was what she'd thought, until Arthur's horse had come back without him.

There was a hand at her back. Charlotte jumped, jarring her aching joints.

"Sorry," a familiar voice murmured in her ear. "Didn't meant to scare you none."

It was the woman who'd helped her home Monday afternoon, in shirt and trousers, with Arthur's ugly old flat cap jammed on her head.

Charlotte rubbed her chest, letting out a breath. "You're still here."

The woman nodded.

"Need to restock before heading back through the wood. They told me there was no market till Friday." Her voice soured with annoyance. "Back in Port Lorne, there's a market every day."

"Yes, well," Charlotte said irritably. "We're not as big as Port Lorne, as I'm sure you've noticed."

The woman took her arm like they were old friends. Charlotte wanted to snap at her and shake her off, but she didn't. To her surprise, the woman led her on a circuitous path through deserted alleyways and side streets.

"Why are we going this way?"

"The better to talk private-like." In sight of the fishwives, the woman's voice had been deepened; now she let it return to normal. "Besides, you said they'd not like a woman in trousers. With those kids of yours, figured you're married, or used to be. Didn't think folks'd like it if you was walking arm in arm with a stranger, neither, especially one what's been upsetting 'em with a bunch of questions. Figured they might talk."

Charlotte huffed a bitter laugh. "They certainly would talk, even if we were merely taking a turn about the square together. What did you want to discuss?"

"I've had my ear to the ground, I'll own to it. Your brother's vanished in the forest, and your neighbors won't look for him. That right?"

Charlotte's throat tightened. She nodded.

The woman squeezed her arm. "All right, so we're in the same boat. My sister, Maggie, visited a while back. Friend of that Bess Little what lives in Port Lorne now, but she come home when her sister had her baby, and she asked Maggie to go with her. Well, Maggie was supposed to be back two weeks ago, only she never showed. I tried wiring to see if maybe she'd stayed longer without telling us, must've sent dozens of telegrams in two, three days, but I never got a response."

She thumbed the flat cap higher up her forehead.

"I would've come sooner, but with Gran and Granddad half laid up with age it's my work in the textile mill what keeps us fed anymore. Thought it'd make matters worse if I left Gran and Granddad alone—all right, not *alone*, there's all my cousins hanging around making a nuisance of themselves, but if I could trust 'em to take care of Gran and Granddad we'd not be so hard up as we are in the first place.

"Well, Gran come to talk to me a few days after I sent all those messages and told me if I wanted to come see about Maggie, I might as well do it. Said she had a feeling, and I'd best listen to it and go. And I said to myself, if no one in Seacliff'll wire me back, I guess I'll go there myself, and I'll give my cousins a good earful first about checking on Gran and Granddad while I'm gone.

"I found this—" she fished a silver acorn on a chain from her shirt "—in the wood."

Charlotte's heart stuttered. "Where—how—"

"It's Maggie's. Found it hanging on a branch back by the first tree. Figure she left it as an offering for safe passage through the wood like Gran says folks used to. She's the one what gave it to Maggie. Maggie always liked her stories about the old ways and the Lord of the Wood. Believed in 'em, too."

Examining the acorn, Charlotte calmed. The chain was thinner than the chain on the acorn Arthur had worn into the forest.

The woman tucked the acorn back into her shirt, catching Charlotte's gaze. "You seen one before?"

"My father's." Charlotte's eyes prickled. "The Lord of the Wood saved his life and gave him that to remember him by. My brother had it when he left."

The woman's lips twisted. "All right, so you know something about the Lord of the Wood. Good. Thought folks on this side of the forest'd know more about him than we do in Port Lorne, seeing as how he's supposed to live closer out this way, but not a person I could find who'd tell me anything."

"Seacliff is a superstitious place. It's bad luck to so much as speak the wood's name—so people say." Charlotte had come to believe it over the years, despite her best intentions, but she didn't want this city woman to think her a superstitious backwater hick. "You'd be lucky to get anyone to tell you a single thing about the wood that wasn't how to protect yourself from its evils. What's your interest in the Lord of the Wood?"

"That comes to my point." The woman nodded back toward the square. "Maggie made it safe to Seacliff, that's certain. Bess said she left when she meant to. That's certain, too. But she never made it home. It's a sure bet something happened to her in the wood, but I didn't see hide nor hair of her on my way here. I figure, if I can find the Lord of the Wood—if anyone can tell me what happened to Maggie in that forest, it's him. Maybe he can tell you what happened to your brother, too."

Charlotte's breath hitched. She hardly believed in the Lord of the Wood anymore. Arthur was either alive alone in the forest, scratched and dirty and trying to find his way home, or he was dead beneath a tree—perhaps grown over with moss like Brigid Tierney. She shuddered.

"Since I heard about your brother," the woman said, "I been thinking, the two of us could look for the Lord of the Wood together."

"Together? What could you want with me?"

"Word around town is you're a healer, and a damn good one. God knows I could use one. I do all right, but—"

She pulled her collar down. A line of rough stitches sat below her collarbone on the right side. The skin had barely started scarring, pink and puckered. Its edges were an angry red that concerned Charlotte; it might've been infected.

She stopped walking, tugging her arm free of the woman's to yank her collar farther down and examine the wound.

"You do move fast," the woman drawled, "we ain't even introduced ourselves yet," but Charlotte barely heard her.

"Didn't you use any antiseptic?" she asked in exasperation.

The woman shrugged, batting her hands away. "Didn't think to bring any. Not making that mistake again. I'm fine, all right, no fever or anything—I'd have a fever by now if it had got infected, aye?"

"How long since you got it?"

"Guess they were right about you being a healer." The woman tugged her collar back into place. "Don't rightly remember. Early. I'd found the acorn, so must've been three, four days afore I got here."

Charlotte frowned. "It should've healed better than this by now."

"See?" The woman gripped her shoulder. "We could help each other. You got the healer's touch, I got the woodsman's skills—we could find the Lord of the Wood. Find out what happened to our siblings. Together."

Charlotte faltered. She'd been so focused on the woman's injury that she'd hardly processed her offer. *The two of us could look for the Lord of the Wood together.*

She swallowed. "I don't even know your name."

Releasing her, the woman held out a hand. "Elspeth McIntire."

"Charlotte Prentice."

"There," Elspeth said. "Now you know my name. How about it, Lottie?"

Just as she'd taken Charlotte's arm to walk through the village, there she went, calling Charlotte *Lottie* as if they'd known each other for ages. No one but Arthur had called Charlotte that in years. She bristled.

"I can't. I have children. Without . . ." Her throat closed around Arthur's name. "They've already lost their father. I'm all they have. If I never came back . . ."

Her voice wobbled. She cleared her throat.

"Besides," she said, "you saw how I needed help getting up the hill the other day. I wouldn't last ten minutes in the wood."

"Alone, maybe not. It's a fair thought about your weans. But I was thinking, bound to be safer with two. Maggie and Bess made it through together all right coming here. It was going back alone that Maggie disappeared."

"You made it safely here alone."

Elspeth grinned.

"I'm just that good. Anyway, you're forgetting this." She pulled her collar down to reveal the scar again. Charlotte flushed. "Point is, both of us together, maybe we'd have a chance."

They'd reached the edge of the village.

"Need help getting home the rest of the way?" Elspeth asked.

The fog clinging to the edges of Charlotte's mind, always ready to rush in after an emotional upset or with pain or a change in the weather, thickened and threatened to spread. Nonetheless, she shook her head, thinking of the old gossip in the square saying, *She could handle that and more if she'd try harder.*

"I'm leaving first thing Saturday," Elspeth said, "if you want to go. If you want to talk it through some more, I have a room at the pub."

Charlotte wrinkled her nose. "The convent might've given you shelter, if you wanted someplace less rough."

"I like rough." Elspeth's eyes glinted. "Besides, I don't hold no truck with nuns, and they don't hold none with me, neither."

"Why not?"

As she had on the stoop the other day, Elspeth considered Charlotte, searching for Charlotte knew not what. Then she said, in a low voice that made Charlotte shiver, "Ran away with one once. They don't take kindly to it when you do that."

XVI. In which Arthur fixes a watch

Between helping Ira with chores, Arthur explored the vale for another way out, despite Ira's insistence there wasn't one. To his astonishment, there was hardly more to the vale than what he'd seen. The funny little tree-house with the clearing curving around three sides of it, the firepit, stone oven, well, clothesline, table, crates, stools, headstone, and flowers. The pines and brambles surrounding them, so thick and dark.

This afternoon, as Ira darned shirts with Calyx at his feet, Arthur said, "I'll get more kindling," and scurried outside before Ira could tell him they didn't need more. Arthur examined the brambles for an opening through which he could slip. His cheek throbbed where they had scratched him yesterday morning.

"Mrowr?"

Freya picked her way toward him, her nose wrinkled in distaste for the snow. Arthur scooped her up and buried his face in her fur.

"We'll get home, won't we?"

She leaped down and wound into the thorns.

Arthur's heart skipped a beat. "Careful!"

Only her golden eyes were visible. She chirped at him.

They're only brambles, she seemed to say, but he was so much bigger than she, and already with that scratch throbbing unnaturally on his cheek.

There. A gap in the canes. Arthur stepped into it, but the brambles tightened, grasping at him with thorny fingers. He hastily backed away, rubbing his arms with a shudder. His imagination conjured canes wrapping around him, thorns puncturing his skin.

"I can't," he said shrilly. "They won't let me through."

Freya emerged and twisted around his ankles. He scooped her up again. She settled against his shoulder, purring.

"All right. All right. There must be another way."

He followed the brambles around until he reached his father's grave. He touched the top of the headstone, as he'd taken to doing whenever he tramped around the clearing. Already the vale's size wearied him; he couldn't believe he'd ever thought the village small, with the open sea stretching to the west. Here, the only openness was the sky above. Even that felt constricting, framed in bare, black branches, eternally overcast.

Guilt plucked at him. Ira had been stuck here far longer than he had.

Still. Arthur had his family to get back to. And if he found his way out of the vale, surely Ira could leave, too.

Behind George's grave were trees rather than brambles. Arthur stepped into their midst. He held his breath, anxious despite their lack of black ooze.

He picked his way through with the cat clutched to his chest. If they went far enough, these trees had to give way to those of the surrounding forest. Yes, those trees would drip black with strange, unsettling sap. Yes, skeletal birds would inhabit them. But they'd mean he'd escaped the vale—the first step to going home.

Arthur hadn't gotten far, however, when the trees thickened.

A few yards later, they took on menacing shapes. This one twisted like a man looking over his shoulder. That one had a cavity open in a silent scream. A third reached for him with fingerlike branches. He skittered away, but another clawed into his back.

He yelped, trying to break free. Everywhere he turned were more horrible, humanlike trees, each frozen in an aspect of terror. His heart hammered. Branches grabbed at his coat, dragging him deeper into their midst. Whispers sounded in his ears. Arthur slapped branches away, but they smacked him in the face. His cheeks and forehead stung.

Snow crunched nearby. "Arthur!"

"Over here!"

Arthur's breathing was ragged. Trees groaned. His eyes played tricks on him; he caught a glimpse of Charlotte's face in a trunk. He squeezed his eyes shut, clutching the cat so tightly she hissed.

"Sorry."

She headbutted his face.

Ira's steps slowed as he neared. Arthur had grown used to their sound in the last day and a half, the softness of his paws' padded steps, the limp that increased if Ira had been on his feet too long. Arthur had never heard his steps so fast as they'd just been, however. When Ira drew up beside him, he was breathing hard. Calyx slithered after him, winding into a nearby tree.

"Are you all right?" Arthur asked.

"I couldn't find you," Ira snapped.

Arthur flinched but said, "There's nowhere for me to go, apparently."

He glanced at Calyx as if it might lash out at him for speaking to its lord that way. Perhaps he should have worried more about the Lord of the Wood himself. Ira's face was white, his jaw tense. His eyes blazed.

"What were you doing back here?"

"Trying to find a way out."

"I told you," Ira growled, "there is no way out."

He dragged Arthur back through the trees, the same way he'd hauled him out of the house the night they'd met. Calyx followed, slinging itself from tree to tree.

Arthur twisted. Ira's fingers clawed into his shoulder. Freya swatted him. Ira didn't seem to notice, but Calyx clicked at her.

"Let me go," Arthur squeaked, but Ira didn't. Yanking free, Arthur stumbled back. He was grateful to be clear of the twisted trees, but the Lord of the Wood's white face and angry eyes scared him.

Ira's gaze flickered over him. Chest heaving, he turned away, dragging a hand through his hair. Calyx crept out of the trees and wound up his body, draping over his shoulders like a cape.

After a long moment, Ira's posture loosened. He turned back to Arthur, calmer and less pale, but Arthur stayed where he was.

"I was afraid," Ira said evenly, "the forest had done something to you."

Arthur hugged the cat gently. "I thought I was safe here."

"You are. I think you are." Ira let out a breath. "It let you into the vale. It wouldn't have let you in if it had thought you were a threat. But . . ."

His eyes flickered toward the trees. Thinking of Hamish, Arthur felt sick.

"Were they . . ." he asked, not sure he wanted to know. "Were they people? Did it do something to them?"

"They were hunters who tried to get at me here. The forest didn't let them."

Arthur shivered. He was glad Ira had not been killed, but the idea of the forest doing whatever it had done to them . . .

"It hardly recognizes friend from foe anymore," Ira said. "But you have the acorn. It knew that as part of itself. I think that's why it let you in. You should be safe here, but . . . Don't take it off. Ever."

Arthur repressed an urge to make sure the acorn was around his neck, though he'd worn it continuously since leaving the cottage.

He glanced at Calyx. "It hasn't seemed to stop your companion from watching me."

The plant creature turned fronds in his direction.

"Calyx is . . . different." Ira grasped at the creature, but it leaped from his shoulders to his antlers. He grimaced but let it be. "Come on."

He reached for Arthur's shoulder, but Arthur recoiled. Ira's hand dropped back to his side. He nodded Arthur toward the tree-house, avoiding his gaze, and left distance between them as they trudged through the snow. Calyx stretched between his antlers.

"I'm sorry," Ira said quietly.

"What for?"

"Frightening you."

They paused at the door. Ira's gaze lingered on the brambles.

"The forest shouldn't do anything to you, if I don't let it. But it doesn't listen to me anymore."

Freya squirmed to be let down. Arthur tried to set her in the snow, but she sprang from his grasp clear through the tree-house door. Undoubtedly, her least favorite part of being stuck here was the eternal snow.

"I don't see why it worries you," Arthur said. "I've only been here a couple of days. I'm nothing. To you, I mean. You could've been well rid of me."

Ira's eyes flickered over his face. "You're not . . ."

He stood aside so Arthur could go in. Slipping from his antlers, Calyx balled up in its spot by the stove.

"Your father saved my life," Ira said. "Letting you die seems a poor way to repay him."

Arthur watched him stump around the room, befuddled. He'd thought Ira was angry he'd tried to leave again; maybe he'd been wrong.

He still felt the trees and brambles grasping at him. With a shudder, he sat at the table with his tool kit and his father's pocket watch. Repairing the watch would provide a welcome distraction from the memories and his repeated failure to escape the vale. Freya jumped up beside him, loafing on the table.

To his surprise, he was able to wind the watch. The winding mechanism and mainspring were likely fine, then. Hearing the watch tick, after days without hearing a single clock, cheered him.

The ticking stopped. Arthur sighed, but it wasn't unexpected. He'd open the watch up, clean all its parts, and see which ones weren't working.

Ira pulled up his armchair and sat, a basket of clothing and a sewing kit at his feet. Arthur had only two sets of clothes, including the ones he wore now, and kept tearing them in his repeated escape attempts. Ira had repaired them and offered to let out some of his own clothes so Arthur would have spares. Freya glared at him, evidently unimpressed.

For a while, they worked in silence. Arthur disassembled the watch, laying each part out as he removed and cleaned it. Freya cocked her head, gazing at the doodads around her, perfect for batting off a table.

"Don't you dare," Arthur said.

She continued gazing at the watch's parts but didn't touch them. In a moment, Arthur had forgotten her.

"I am sorry," Ira said, "that there isn't a way out of here."

Preoccupied with his work, Arthur said nothing.

been prouder of it, either, thought it gave the place some distinction since none of the other shops had clocks. But that day, it'd stopped working, and he had it opened up on the counter when I walked in."

Arthur rubbed the engraving on his father's watch.

"I don't know what it was. The cogs and gears, the way it all fit together just so, the ticking when he'd gotten it working—I fell in love with everything about it. I still love it. The ticking is so—" He flushed, smiled ruefully. "Sorry, I—that was a lot."

Ira's brow furrowed. "It wasn't."

"I didn't mean to talk so much, I know you don't care about clocks, probably, I just—"

Setting the shirt aside, Ira touched Arthur's wrist. Arthur shut up. His skin prickled with embarrassment. It had been a long time since he'd rambled at someone outside the family that way; he'd learned decades ago to keep himself contained around everyone else. He'd known since boyhood that it annoyed people.

"Sorry," he mumbled. "You didn't want to know all that."

Ira's hand was still on his wrist, warm and gentle. Arthur didn't know what to do with that; in his experience, men didn't touch each other this way. Once, on an impromptu house call with his father, he'd gone to the home of an old fisherman whose friend was languishing in bed. The fisherman had touched his friend's hand, but so briefly and secretively—when George's back was turned—that Arthur almost thought he'd imagined it. And even their thighs pressed together had been too much for Cormac.

Yet Ira seemed to think nothing of it.

"It's all right," he said. "I like that you love clocks that much. That you love anything that much." He let go of Arthur's wrist, to Arthur's simultaneous relief and disappointment. "What is it, about the ticking?"

Arthur gave a small smile, his embarrassment fading. "Don't get me started. You'll regret it."

"I don't think I will. I've been alone a long time, except for Calyx."

Arthur ran a hand through his hair. "You're not what I expected. From Dad's stories."

"What did you expect?"

"I don't know." Not quite true, but Arthur was unwilling to admit to the romance-novel-cover fairy prince he'd been carrying in his head for more than thirty years. "Something more mythic, I suppose. But you're just a person. Antlers and paws and plant-guardian-pet thing notwithstanding."

The corner of Ira's mouth twitched, but he said earnestly, "All I've ever wanted to be was a person."

"What do you mean?"

Ira busied himself with his sewing. He'd cut one shirt apart to add fabric to another.

"I don't . . . fit in here, the way everything else does. It doesn't matter what form I take—the beasts, the plants, they all know I'm not one of them. But I've never fit in with humans, either, because I'm not human. I'm always the Lord of the Wood. I'm never just Ira."

He'd gone pink.

Arthur hesitated. Their situations weren't the same, but his way of being a person had always seemed wrong, somehow.

"Well," he said lightly, "now I've seen you wake up in your chair with your neck sore and your eyes crusty. I can't say I see you much as Lord of the Wood myself."

Ira let out a huff of laughter.

"Anyway," Arthur continued, "I've never fit in, either. The villagers think I'm odd."

"Why?"

Arthur smiled ruefully. "I've never quite known. Because

I like the wrong things, I suppose, and because I'm bad at everything, and . . ."

Because of everything about me, because that was the case as far as he could tell.

He buried the thought without voicing it. "Well, I appreciate that you had to ask, anyway."

Ira huffed another laugh. Arthur's smile turned into the real thing.

"Here," Ira said, "let's see whether this shirt fits."

He tried to stand but dropped right back into his chair because Calyx was wound around his feet. He kicked it away with a beleaguered sigh, stood, handed Arthur the altered shirt, and turned away so Arthur could change.

Arthur did the toggles, thinking of his parents talking about him in their bedroom before George's last trip to Port Lorne.

He's so . . . You know what he's like.

To this day, Arthur didn't know what his father had meant.

He hadn't quite finished doing up his toggles, but he said, "Ira?"

Ira turned around, his gaze dipping over the sliver of Arthur's chest where the shirt was open. "How is it?"

"The shirt's fine. I just wanted . . . What did Dad tell you about me? Did he ever . . . ?"

He wasn't sure what he wanted to ask. Whether he wanted to ask. He could go on believing his father had loved him as he'd been, would've loved him as he was, and never thought him strange.

"Did he what?"

Arthur squeezed his eyes shut.

"Nothing. Never mind." His cheek throbbed. He cleared his throat. "How does my scratch look? It feels . . ."

Ira stepped closer, Calyx trailing him like a shadow, and touched Arthur's cheek. Arthur winced.

Ira's hand dropped to his side. "You'll have a scar, I expect, but it's healing well."

Arthur nodded. When he'd finished with the toggles, Ira had him move his arms to check his range of motion.

"He never said you were odd," Ira said suddenly. "George. If that's what you were wondering." He fiddled with the collar of the shirt, his fingers brushing against Arthur's skin. "He worried you were lonely."

Arthur avoided his gaze. He certainly had been lonely, as a boy. If he thought about it, he might realize he was lonely still, so it was better left unthought about. He had Charlotte and the children. They were all he needed.

Not that he had them now. Nor would he, unless he managed to escape the vale.

Ira stepped back, releasing Arthur's collar. "I have a salve that will help with your scratch. Use it whenever you need."

Arthur touched his cheek gingerly. The scratch didn't feel any bigger, but it hurt like a much worse injury. Something about the brambles, no doubt. Something magical and terrible to keep Ira in the vale by making any injury incurred in attempted escape worse than it ought to be, which now kept Arthur in the vale, too.

"For what it's worth," Ira said, "I think—I think you're lovely. I'm sorry you can't leave, but . . . I like your company."

Arthur's chest bloomed with faint warmth, like the first spring flower poking through the snow. He still wanted to leave, if he could—but if he couldn't, at least he was stuck forever with someone who didn't think he was odd. Someone who understood loneliness probably better than he did, since Ira lived alone—unless one counted a sentient tangle of greenery—and had, it seemed, for decades.

"It's a small consolation," Arthur said, "but thanks for saying it all the same. I've— Of course I want to go home, and

I'm, er, well—" with a glance at Calyx, whose fronds turned in his direction "—I'd feel better if your guardian weren't always glaring at me—not *glaring*, it doesn't have eyes, but—"

Ira's lips twitched.

"The point is—" Arthur wasn't sure how to express what Ira's words meant to him. "Well, I'm glad we're friends."

He blanched; maybe he shouldn't have said that. Were they friends, when he'd been here barely more than two days and spent much of it doing chores in companionable silence? So little of the silence in his life had been companionable that it felt like more than enough to him, but he suspected most people would've disagreed. Regardless, he wasn't sure one was supposed to *announce* one was friends with someone.

But Ira gave a small smile—a real one, not slanted or sidewise or wolfish—and said, "So am I," and Arthur relaxed. Smiling that way, he thought, Ira was really quite striking.

Ira turned away.

"I'll do a couple more shirts tomorrow. Then I'll start on some trousers for you."

XVII. In which Charlotte makes a promise she might not be able to keep

By Friday, Charlotte was desperate. She stopped at the general store to see whether any telegrams had arrived for her. None had. Of course. Without the horse, Arthur couldn't have reached Port Lorne yet, if indeed he reached it at all.

Friday was market day. Shopping and trading for seafood, meat, and produce in the village square, villagers and visiting farmers crowded into the general store for goods they couldn't get from each other. Busier than usual, Mrs. Armstrong, the wife of the owner, had been annoyed at Charlotte's insistence on checking for a telegram that couldn't have come.

"Perhaps it's for the best," she said now, unpacking a shipment lately arrived from Glenwhistle.

Charlotte stiffened. "I beg your pardon?"

Sasha and Jonas clung to her hands. Sasha had been uncharacteristically quiet since Maurice's return without her uncle.

"Not meaning any offense—" Mrs. Armstrong slotted new bolts of fabric into place on the shelves behind the counter "—and Mr. Throckmorton was nice enough in his way—"

Anger boiled in Charlotte's blood. Sasha's hand tightened on hers.

"—but you've got two mouths to feed as is, and it's not as if he was much help, was he? If he'd been a half-decent fisherman, or any good in the cannery, it would've put you in an awful spot, his being gone, but—"

She broke off, turning aside to help a farmer's wife who wanted some thread.

Charlotte's jaw clenched. That was all they'd ever thought of Arthur. *He's an odd one*, the villagers said, when they said anything. After childhoods in which they'd bullied him, they'd spent adulthood ignoring him—until whatever had happened with Cormac Young. She was almost angry at herself for having expected them to help find him in the first place.

"Not that it isn't a tragedy." Mrs. Armstrong returned to her bolts of fabric. "And your weans without their father all these years—"

Charlotte's eyes prickled at the unexpected mention of John. The second Mrs. Armstrong drew breath, she'd take the children and go home with their shopping undone. She couldn't bear any more of the villagers' heartless sympathies.

"—I understand what a loss it is to you as a personal matter, of course, but you can't expect our men to go risking their lives for the likes of *him*."

"Don't talk about my uncle that way," Sasha said, far too loudly. A hush fell over the shop.

Mrs. Armstrong peered down at her. "Not meaning any offense, lassie, but—"

"You're mean." Tears welled in Sasha's eyes. "All of you! You won't even look for him!"

"Dearest," Charlotte said, reaching for her, but Sasha broke away, hands balling into fists.

"I hate you!" she cried at Mrs. Armstrong, the surrounding villagers, the visiting farmers, every adult in the shop. "I hate all of you! I hope *you* get lost in the forest!"

"Sasha," Jonas said, sounding panicked, but Sasha shoved past an old woman and ran off. The bell over the door jingled in her wake. Charlotte's heart twisted.

"Go after her, love, will you?" she said to Jonas. "Make sure she gets home all right. I'll catch up."

They nodded and went. With the children gone, everyone stared at Charlotte instead. Her skin prickled, but she drew herself up and gazed icily at Mrs. Armstrong.

"Thank you for checking on that telegram for me. Good day."

Mrs. Armstrong looked surprised. "Don't you want your kerosene?"

Charlotte left without responding. She'd meant to buy several things, and she'd have to come crawling back later to get them. Right now, she couldn't stand people staring or take another casually cruel comment.

She wanted to shout at them and cry as her daughter had. All that kept her from doing it was the fact that she was thirty-six years old and a mother. Suddenly, being a grown-up felt intolerable. No wonder Arthur spent so much time daydreaming.

Outside, in the square, temporary stalls and carts offered mollusks, small and scanty fish, minimal squid, apples, lamb, grouse, and berries. Charlotte staggered past without stopping, grateful for her cane.

A man with a flat cap raised his hand in greeting; she blinked, not recognizing him, then realized it was Elspeth McIntire. She nodded back but was relieved when Elspeth returned to her shopping.

Since she no longer had the children with her, Charlotte stopped to check on Jean Crawford, a skittish newlywed expecting her first, then Rosie Young. Mrs. Young was out front, tending the chickens and weeding around the stoop.

"Reckon she's all right now," she said, when Charlotte asked after Rosie, "but I'd not say no to you taking a look. That cough did linger something fierce. I never seen anything like it, leastways not in a hearty girl like our Rosie."

Charlotte had; her own illness back in February had been like that. Mrs. Young nodded her inside. Charlotte thanked her and went, hoping she wouldn't find Rosie laid up in bed like she'd been for so long.

She needn't have worried. Rosie was at her father's feet in the sitting room, with a fluffy chick asleep in her arms, nattering on about what her mother had brought back from the market and what the chick might look like when it grew up. In his chair, repairing a fishing net, Cormac nodded at her periodically. His lips twitched.

At six, Rosie talked more and faster than anyone Charlotte had ever met; she hardly drew breath between words. Her color was better than it had been in church on Sunday.

Charlotte smiled. "Feeling better, I see," and what a relief that was, in a week during which nothing had gone right.

Scrambling to her feet, Rosie presented the chick, which peeped sleepily at the disturbance. One of its feet was deformed.

"This is Pippin," Rosie said proudly.

"She's lovely."

"He."

"Rosie, lass," Cormac said, "take Pippin and help the boys out back, eh?"

"Nuh-uh. They're mean to him."

"Help Mam out front, then. He ought to be around other chickens anyhow."

"Okay."

Rosie skipped from the room, hugging her chick.

Cormac huffed a laugh. "Back to her old self, as you see."

"I'm glad of it. She seems fond of her new pet."

Cormac's smile faded. "It'll be a trick getting that chick

away from her. We would've culled it, its foot being how it is, but she's hardly let it go since it hatched. One of these days she'll have to learn."

Charlotte's eyes prickled foolishly; it wasn't as if she weren't used to such things. The episode at the general store thorned at her, making her emotional. That was all.

She cleared her throat. "She's not short of breath? Doesn't tire easily?"

Cormac shook his head. "Just as you seen her. She's about driving her brothers up a wall. But her mam and I sure are grateful, Mrs. Prentice."

He fiddled with his net. Glanced toward the window, where his wife, in apparent exasperation, tried to stop Rosie from telling a passing couple all about her chick.

"You've not heard from your brother?" Cormac asked.

Charlotte's breath hitched. "No."

"How're you holding up?"

Charlotte twisted a hand in her apron. No one had asked. Everyone expected her to carry on—she'd expected it herself—because that was what one did, through grief or pain or any upset at all.

Her lip trembled. "I'll be better when he's home."

If he came home. She dabbed at her eyes.

Cormac avoided her gaze. "Hope he'll be all right."

Charlotte staggered toward him. "Would you go? Would you look for him? If people knew you were going, others might—"

He shook his head. "I can't."

"Please. I'd go myself, but there's my—" Charlotte ground it out, unused to drawing attention to it "—my condition, and my children—"

Cormac was on his feet. "And my own children? How d'you think my Anna'd manage without me? Besides—" he raised his voice as Charlotte tried to object "—if I went looking for him . . . I can't have folks thinking—"

"Thinking what?" Charlotte's fist clenched on her cane. "What happened between you and my brother?"

Cormac's ears pinkened. "Nothing."

"I know that," Charlotte snapped. "I mean, what happened that's made the villagers talk as if something happened between you and my brother?"

"*Nothing.*" Cormac dropped back into his chair. "I taught him his way around a horse-cart, is all. Folks saw us driving together and thought there was something to it."

Like what? Charlotte wanted to ask, but she didn't. She wanted to tell him how kind he'd been, teaching Arthur to drive the cart, to ask him, again, to look for Arthur and convince others, but Mrs. Young stepped in.

"Mr. Neely's outside," she said to Cormac. "Wants a word. I told him you were engaged, but he's awful keen if—"

"Mrs. Prentice was just leaving," Cormac said, with a terrible air of finality. "See her out, would you?"

He stalked outside. Charlotte papered over her distress, told Mrs. Young Rosie seemed right as rain but to come up to the cottage if her symptoms reemerged, and left. The journey uphill was slow and painful, and Charlotte collapsed into her armchair the moment she made it home.

Sasha was shut away in the children's bedroom. Jonas had put away the laundry Charlotte had left by her armchair the day before, intending to sit for only a moment. Now she was home, Jonas made her tea and brought a salve for her joints without being asked. Charlotte wanted to cry.

Jonas turned on the radio and tuned it to her favorite program. If romance novels were Arthur's guilty pleasure, *Tales of Terror from the Radio Waves* was Charlotte's. She liked knowing that, however bad life got, at least she wasn't trapped in a

Gothic mansion with a man she was both attracted to and afraid of or a becoming young woman who was secretly a hungry supernatural monster.

After the day she'd had, such things didn't comfort her nearly as much as usual.

She wondered if this was how it would be if Arthur never returned: Jonas growing up too soon because she spent so much time exhausted and in pain that her children would have to take care of her. The way Eileen had gone after George's death, Charlotte had been determined not to do that to her own children. But now—

Words echoed in her head, dismissive, disdainful. *She could handle that and more if she'd try harder.*

Her jaw clenched. She gripped Jonas's hand.

"You take such good care of me. You're very good to me. And I . . . I appreciate it."

They reddened but nodded. "I promised Uncle Arthur."

Charlotte pressed her hands to her face. "You shouldn't have to."

Jonas settled in their uncle's armchair, which had become their habitual seat in the last two days. Seeing them there hurt, made Charlotte sharply aware of how much they missed Arthur, though they hadn't said as much.

"I don't mind."

"That's not the point." Charlotte took a deep, steadying breath. "I'm your mother. You and your sister aren't supposed to take care of me. I'm supposed to take care of you."

"You do take care of us."

Not like she used to, she thought. Not like she ought to.

The radio played a jingle. Jonas picked at the faded floral upholstery.

"Do you think Uncle Arthur's okay?"

Had the situation been reversed, Arthur would've instantly

assured Jonas their mother was fine and would be home before they knew it. He might've even believed it, or told himself he did.

Charlotte was too pragmatic for such optimism. "I don't know. I hope so."

Jonas hugged a throw pillow.

"If he doesn't come back," they said softly, and Charlotte's fingers tightened on the arms of her chair, "can we talk about him?"

She looked at them in surprise. "Of course, my love. What do you mean?"

They fidgeted. "It's just, you never talk about Papa. Or Granddad. Or Nan. Uncle Arthur says it makes you sad to talk about them."

Her throat tightened. Damn Arthur. Damn him. She'd never said as much. Why did he have to know her so well, when she worked so hard not to let anyone know her? When she tried not to let anyone see the cracks in her armor?

She swallowed hard. "I'm sure it won't come to that."

Her radio program came on; they listened to it together. Jonas held the throw pillow against themself like a shield, fingers tightening whenever anything scary happened. Charlotte was too distracted to enjoy the thrill of fear the program normally gave her. She tuned in and out, kept thinking of Cormac. She'd been so hopeful, when he'd unexpectedly asked after Arthur, that she'd found someone who would help—but he'd refused, same as everyone else. He'd been more concerned with what people might think than a man's life.

Partway through the program, Sasha emerged from the bedroom with swollen eyes. Charlotte stood so quickly her head swam. Recovering, she asked, "Are you hungry, dearest?"

Sasha nodded. She said nothing through supper, nothing in the sitting room afterward, nothing when Charlotte told the children to go to bed.

The latter put Charlotte on her guard. Sasha always objected to bedtime. Charlotte settled back in her armchair, listening.

She sat for so long with no sound but the fire crackling in the grate that she almost gave up. God, she was tired. The chair was so comfortable. Perhaps she'd been wrong—misinterpreted Sasha's uncustomary silence—perhaps she could close her eyes like she so desperately wanted to and comfort her daughter in the morning.

Then a door creaked open. The floorboards in the hall groaned.

Charlotte waited to get up until a second door creaked. The workshop door, opening and shutting. She hurried toward it.

Sasha was closing the garden gate when her mother made it outside. The gate squeaked. Sasha flinched, paused, and closed it carefully the rest of the way. Over her shoulder was a pillowcase, tied off and bulging, and her rag doll was under her arm. She wore her coat and boots and a look of determination that made Charlotte want to cry, or hug her, or both.

"Sasha."

Sasha flinched but turned around.

"I'm going to find Uncle Arthur," she said mulishly, "since no one else will."

Charlotte rubbed her forehead with her knuckles. "Come inside, love."

"I'm going to find Uncle Arthur."

"I heard you." Charlotte nodded at the pillowcase. "What are you taking?"

Sasha considered her, as if trying to figure out how much of a trick this was.

"The last of the biscuits. And bandages in case he's hurt. And a clean frock for me in case I get dirty."

Charlotte's mouth tilted into a tired smile. "You do always manage that."

Sasha did not dignify this with a reply. "And a blanket for when I sleep, and one of Uncle Arthur's books, in case he's scared."

Charlotte's chest tightened. "Please come inside, dearest. Perhaps in the morning—"

"You won't do anything. He's lost and you haven't done anything at all!"

Charlotte was so tired. "Yes, I have. Of course I have. Come inside. Please."

"You won't even try to find him!" Sasha stomped her foot. Charlotte reached for her, but she pulled away. "You don't even care!"

She burst out crying, angrily, and collapsed on the ground, sobbing into her pillowcase.

I do care, Charlotte wanted to say, *I miss him, too, I'm scared, too*, but she didn't. Nothing short of searching for Arthur herself would convince Sasha she was just as desperate to have him back.

Elspeth McIntire's voice echoed in her head. *Both of us together, maybe we'd have a chance.*

Maybe she *could* find him. Maybe, in the wood, there was even a chance of curing the sickness. It was an eldritch disease, a magical disease. Surely any potential cure must be magical, too.

Of course, if Charlotte went, she might never return. She couldn't risk orphaning her children.

But if she didn't go, she feared it was a matter of time before Sasha successfully snuck off alone. Charlotte would be out, or incapacitated by pain and fatigue. One way or another, Sasha would manage it. Jonas would probably try to stop her, but Sasha never listened to them.

The forest rustled, feeling more alive than usual in the darkness. Charlotte gazed at it warily as she stroked the top of her daughter's head. Unsettlingly, the forest seemed to gaze back.

Being silly, Charlotte thought, but she couldn't shake it.

At last, Sasha cried herself out and sat hiccuping on the ground. Charlotte pulled her daughter to her feet and dried her eyes.

Sasha leaned against her, feeling fragile. Charlotte had never thought of her as fragile before. Then again, Sasha was too young to have experienced the losses the rest of the family had. Only Eileen had died since she'd been old enough to remember such a thing, and Eileen had been, to Sasha, mostly a weepy older woman who pinched her cheeks too much and was better avoided unless baking biscuits. She had not been precisely relieved by her grandmother's death, but she hadn't grieved the way Arthur and Charlotte had—though their grief had been complicated by their resentment.

"Let's go to bed, dearest," Charlotte said.

Sasha nodded. Charlotte kissed the top of her head, waited for her to collect her doll and pillowcase, and led her back toward the house. The moon threw their elongated shadows across the garden plots.

"He'll come back, won't he?" Sasha asked in a stuffy voice, and this time Charlotte couldn't bring herself to hedge the way she had with Jonas.

"Of course, dearest."

"Promise?"

The two of us could look for the Lord of the Wood together, Charlotte heard Elspeth McIntire saying. *I'm leaving first thing Saturday, if you want to go.*

She glanced at the dark maw of the forest, having a horrible feeling she would soon disappear inside it herself. Thinking how inevitable it was she should someday enter it, after the way it had shaped her whole life.

"I promise."

XVIII. In which Charlotte goes after her brother, because no one else will

If I'm not back in two days," Charlotte said, "Miss Tierney will take you to the convent. The sisters will take care of you."

"I don't *want* nuns to take care of me," Sasha wailed. "I want to come with you."

"You can't, dearest. I need to know you're safe."

Charlotte sorted through her bags once more. A change of clothing, her travel medical kit—fully restocked, with extra items added—a bottle of water, a heating pad, a knife, firelighters, a torch, matches, a cooking pot, a kettle, and dried fruit.

Standing beside her, Elspeth grabbed her wrist. "You're stalling, Lottie. You been through your bags three times this morning."

"It won't hurt to check again," Charlotte snapped, shaking her off, "and stop calling me Lottie."

She already regretted taking Elspeth's offer, but if she entered the forest, better not to go alone. Besides her own supplies, she'd have Elspeth's, including the knives at her belt.

Kitty Tierney sat across from them, chewing her lip but saying nothing. Apart from Agnes and the children, she was the only one Charlotte and Elspeth had told about their plans. Charlotte hadn't wanted to leave the children alone for two days.

And in case she didn't return . . . Well, someone had to make sure they went to the convent.

Not for the first time, she wondered if this was a mistake. She'd told Elspeth she couldn't go, told Cormac Young she couldn't go, because of her children, but here she was, leaving them anyway. Safer with Elspeth she may have been, but there was a good chance the forest would swallow Charlotte whole, never to be seen again. Or that she would only leave its depths veined in black, another victim of wood sickness. She resented her mother for all but abandoning her and Arthur after their father's disappearance; could she risk actually orphaning her children?

But no one else would search for her brother. Sasha would never forgive her if she didn't do everything within her power to bring him home. And part of Charlotte—possibly a nonsensical part—believed she might find a cure for the sickness if only she saw where it came from.

It was easier to focus on all that than on her own despair should Arthur never return.

Compulsively, she checked her travel medical kit to make sure she'd added glass vials to it like she'd intended. She had an idea of taking samples in the forest. Samples of what, exactly, she couldn't say. The vials were right where she'd nestled them, wrapped in a pair of gloves.

"*You* won't be safe," Sasha insisted. "I could protect you."

Unbidden, an image of Sasha yelling and hitting a bear with a stick sprang to Charlotte's mind. Her lips twitched despite herself.

"I'm sure you could, but I'd much rather you stayed here with Miss Tierney. Please, love."

Grumpily, Sasha banged her feet against the legs of her chair.

"Wheest, my little bug." Elspeth tweaked Sasha's pigtails and crouched beside her. "Think I'll let your mam get ate up? She'll come back all right."

"Tell her to let me come! She'd have to say yes if you said."

Elspeth laughed. "Oh, aye, I reckon she'd do anything I asked. She scowls at me so sweet."

Charlotte flushed but didn't dignify the comment with response. She resented how quickly her daughter had taken to Elspeth McIntire (and her trousers) and was trying not to because there was enough resentment in her life already.

Kitty touched the girl's wrist. "Your mam tells me you like a good bedtime story. Times were I used to tell my sisters stories after Ma sent us to bed. I'll tell you one tonight, if you like."

"Every night," Sasha mumbled, sounding less enthused than she usually did when negotiating such things.

Elspeth chuckled. Kitty frowned at her but merely agreed, "Every night," and withdrew her hand.

Rain pattered, but when Jonas took Charlotte's bags outside, everyone trailed out with them. Elspeth strode on ahead. At her insistence, Charlotte had borrowed a mule and gig from Agnes.

The gig was a good idea. Charlotte didn't know how to ride, but Elspeth knew how to drive, and riding or walking for long periods would be hard on Charlotte. Sitting in the gig would likely be uncomfortable, too, but she'd last longer in a vehicle than on foot.

On their way through the cobbled streets, the villagers had stared. Cormac Young had raised a hand briefly before turning away. All her life, Charlotte had avoided giving the villagers a reason to talk about her, except when she'd married John. Then, the villagers had shrugged and said, *What can you expect from a silly young girl but to marry a stranger whose family is unknown?* They'd blamed her mother instead, for shirking her parental duties and allowing it.

Now, however, Charlotte was doing something truly impractical, and this time she wasn't a nineteen-year-old whose whims might be excused as youthful foolishness. Moreover, she'd given Seacliff a good reason for gossip, riding through town in a borrowed gig with a stranger who was, as far as the villagers knew, a single man.

Let them talk, Charlotte thought angrily. She had plenty to say about them, with how they'd always treated her family and her brother in particular.

Elspeth stowed their bags under the cross-seat. Charlotte stroked the mule's nose, asking, "What shall we name him, Sasha?"

Sasha kicked at a garden plot. When Charlotte held out a hand, Sasha ran to her and buried her face in her mother's apron. Charlotte's eyes stung. She kissed her daughter's forehead.

"Be good for Miss Tierney," she said, and added, as a kind of prayer, "I hope to see you all soon. Thank you for keeping an eye on them, Miss Tierney."

Kitty nodded. As Elspeth rearranged the bags to fit better, Kitty grabbed Charlotte's hand. Raindrops frizzed her fringe and dripped on her nose and cheeks, but she didn't wipe them away.

"You sure about this, Mrs. Prentice?" she asked in a low voice. "Mr. Throckmorton's nice enough, but you got children. You really think you can find him? With that—that *woman*?"

Charlotte's skin prickled. Elspeth had kept the disguise on through the village, but she hadn't bothered in the cottage. Kitty had been astonished to find her sitting in Charlotte's kitchen and had not warmed to her, eyes lingering with disapproval on Elspeth's trousers and braces.

Sasha sidled over to listen. As with Jonas the other night, Charlotte couldn't bring herself to spout false hopes with no reasoning. But she couldn't bring herself to admit she wasn't certain at all, either.

"I don't know." She left the comment about Elspeth unacknowledged. "But I can't leave him out there, not if there's a chance of bringing him home."

Kitty bit her lip. "I hope you come back all right, Mrs. Prentice."

She backed away, grasping the children's hands and glancing suspiciously at Elspeth. Sasha's eyes were liquid. The sight made Charlotte want to go back inside, sit on the settee with her children tucked on either side of her, and tell them a story as Arthur did while she worked on her needlepoint.

She swallowed. "Two days. Don't forget."

Jonas nodded. Sasha merely clung tighter to Kitty's hand.

"Lottie!" Elspeth had finished with the bags. "You coming or not?"

"Don't call me Lottie."

Charlotte clambered into the gig, wedging her cane beside her. Elspeth vaulted into the other seat and clicked her tongue at the mule. The trees rustled in the breeze off the sea. Charlotte held her breath as they closed around her, ducking to avoid the branches reaching across the path like fingers.

The wind seemed suddenly quiet and distant. Leaves rustled overhead, but no wind breached the undergrowth. Though the rain continued, few raindrops made it past the thick canopy.

Charlotte's skin crawled at the silence. She reached for the wedding ring hanging on its chain from her neck, rubbing it for comfort. John had ventured into the wood occasionally for firewood, or to hunt, never straying far because she'd worried about him, and he'd always returned. She tried to believe his ring would bring her luck as she journeyed through the forest, but she didn't believe in luck. Each new storm life hurled at her weathered away the little she dared believe. Despite herself, she'd believed the rowan cross would protect her brother. Now his horse had come back without him. She'd been foolish to think anything could keep him safe. If the wood wanted to take him, it would.

She bit her lip. "Should we be doing this?"

"Too late for that. We're in the forest, and I ain't turning this mule around because you're having second thoughts."

Charlotte regretted, again, taking Elspeth up on her offer. She wondered how many more times she'd regret it before they were done. However it ended. With their siblings found, alive and well, or dead, or—more likely—Charlotte and Elspeth lost to the wood, too.

In the dirt before them, wheel tracks. Light impressions, as might be made by a cart weighed down with nothing more than a man, a cat, a knapsack, and a suitcase, but unmistakably wheel tracks.

"Arthur?"

Charlotte's voice fell short. In the forest, she felt more insignificant than she ever had in her life.

"Sure, he'll answer right off if you call," Elspeth said. "Just off the path, I shouldn't wonder. Not far from home at all."

Charlotte scowled.

Glancing at her, Elspeth added, "Probably lost the path."

"How would you know?" Charlotte snapped, though losing the path sounded exactly like something Arthur would do.

Elspeth smirked. None of Charlotte's barbs ever seemed to land. Charlotte wasn't sure whether that annoyed her. Every time she snapped, she remembered how Elspeth had helped her home Monday, without even knowing who she was.

"Been all through here before, remember?" Elspeth nodded at the trees. "The path don't like to stay underfoot. I don't know what kinda stories your village tells about the forest, Lottie, but it's named like it is for a reason."

Charlotte noted the way Elspeth dodged saying the forest's name, the same as any villager in Seacliff. She wasn't what Charlotte expected from a city slicker, except that she was so scandalously familiar in such a short amount of time. It was well-known in Seacliff that folks from Port Lorne and Glenwhistle didn't behave right.

"Don't call me Lottie. How'd you find your way to Seacliff, then?"

Elspeth snorted. "What d'you expect me to call you the whole way through this godforsaken forest? 'Mrs. Prentice'? Sure, must be the trees care just as much for that horseshit as your villagers."

Charlotte colored at the language, but Elspeth ignored her.

"I'll leave you right here to be devoured by whatever eldritch beastie wants you the first time you call me 'Miss McIntire,' I swear to God, and I don't care if I do need stitches again and don't have a healer to do 'em for me."

"How'd you find your way to Seacliff?" Charlotte repeated in annoyance. "If the path kept shifting, how'd you get here?"

"The acorn. It's . . . like a compass. Concentrate on it, and you can feel where the first tree is. That don't move. If you know about how far you're supposed to go, and where the place is compared to where the first tree is, you can find it right enough."

"What's the first tree?"

Elspeth raised an eyebrow. "Well'n'all, here I thought the villagers wouldn't tell me anything about the forest on account of their superstitions, but I guess you all just don't know the first thing about it, do you?"

Charlotte's head throbbed, whether from the close forest air or this irritating, betrousered woman.

"I know plenty. I've lived in the forest's shadow my whole life."

"Me, too. Green Streets, that's what our neighborhood's called, backs right up to the trees. Or it used to, afore they started cutting 'em down. The first tree's just what it says on the tin. It's the first tree that ever grew here. The start of the whole forest. Ain't a normal tree, either, it's a big old silver oak—*silver* silver, I mean, you'd think it a sculpture if you didn't know better—and it's massive and it's ancient."

"Where did it come from?"

Elspeth shrugged.

"It's the Oak King's tree, Gran always said, and the Lord of the Wood is supposed to be his son. I seen it once. Gran took Maggie'n'me to it, God, more'n thirty years ago now. I was barely knee-high to a grasshopper, and Maggie was younger'n that, don't know that she even remembers. Great silver tree it was, with branches spreading overhead and offerings piled at its foot. All that's there now is a stump. Tree was cut down three decades ago. The factories were expanding, owners wanted the land, figured no one'd much care if the forest came down because it'd make travel easier. Green Streets cared, God knows. It used to shade our streets, keep us from the worst of the weather, but no one ever asks what we want. Anyway, that's where I found Maggie's acorn." Elspeth sounded wistful. "That's almost the first thing I remember, Gran taking us to see that tree."

Something black dripped onto the path before them. The mule wavered, snorting uneasily. Charlotte clutched Elspeth, her heart pounding at the sudden disturbance.

The gig swayed, but Elspeth stopped it, tripped down, and took the mule's halter, stroking his nose.

"Enough of that, now," she murmured. He stopped prancing, but his flanks quivered.

Charlotte clambered out. In the middle of the path was a black puddle, viscous and smelling faintly mechanical. Another drop plopped into it from the end of a branch overhead.

Charlotte swallowed. "What is that?"

Elspeth shrugged, but her eyes were troubled. "Don't rightly know. There's trees all over like that. Like the forest is sick."

The black trailed from branch to trunk. Black veins ran the entire length of the tree, so much like those streaking the victims of wood sickness.

Charlotte shuddered, but she was a healer before she was anything. She approached cautiously.

"Lottie—"

Elspeth's voice was tight, but Charlotte waved a hand at her.

She peered at the veins. They told her nothing except that something in the forest was wrong. She didn't need a tree to tell her that. Not when villagers were vanishing in the forest or emerging with wood sickness.

Still, she returned to the gig and dug her gloves and one of the glass vials from her medical kit. Another black drip plopped into the puddle. Small enough to drip into the vial, if she was careful. She rolled back her sleeves, tugged the gloves on, and circumvented the puddle to hold the vial to the end of the branch.

"Lottie, what're you doing?"

Being silly, probably. The tree seemed infected, not as if it were a source of the sickness, and she couldn't ask what had happened or whether it felt any pain—as if a tree felt pain anyway.

"Like you said, it's like the forest is sick. This might teach us something about the sickness. How to cure it, or . . ."

"Lost a foreman to it a year back, and his brother's a doctor. Ain't no cure."

"I know," Charlotte said churlishly. "That's why I'd like one."

She corked the vial, peeled off her gloves, and wrapped them inside out around the vial.

"Careful with that," Elspeth said sharply. "Mind you keep it away from everything else."

"There's nowhere else to keep it, unless you'd like me to hold on to it the whole way through the forest."

Elspeth scowled. "Well, keep it away from us. Already had a run-in with a sick wee beastie my first time through."

Charlotte stowed the vial. "Is that where you got your scar?"

"Aye. A sparrowhawk come right at me—creepy-looking thing it was, all veiny like folks with the sickness, but parts of it was see-through, too. I could see its skull in its head clear as day. Never seen anything like it. Never seen a sparrowhawk fly right at a body and attack 'em, neither, but there it is. Wasn't afraid of me at all. Like it'd got rabies, but I never seen a bird with rabies afore."

Charlotte shuddered but plucked at Elspeth's sleeve. "Come here. I want another look at your scar."

"Can't wait to get this shirt off me, more like," Elspeth said, but she obliged.

Ignoring that comment, Charlotte pulled Elspeth's collar down as she had in the village on Thursday. The wound by her collarbone wasn't any worse, nor any better, pink and puckered with angry red edges.

But there was no sign of wood sickness.

"I don't understand," Charlotte murmured, running her fingers over the scar. Elspeth's breath hitched, but she paid no heed.

"Understand what?"

Charlotte met her gaze. "You've seen the sickness. Takes on fast. Kills fast, as often as not. Maybe half the patients I've seen with it have injuries like this—or not like this—all sorts of injuries. They could've been attacked, like you, but by different animals. If the animals were infected, that could be how they contracted the sickness. But you don't have it. And this happened—when? About a week ago?"

Elspeth nodded.

"You should've already shown signs of infection," Charlotte said, "based on what I've seen. But you haven't."

"Ain't that unusual, is it?" Elspeth tugged her collar back into place. "Constitution of an ox. Plenty of times Gran or Granddad or Maggie's got the flu or suchlike, and I've never gotten it even after playing nursemaid for a week or more."

"I suppose." Charlotte rubbed between her eyes. Her headache wasn't bad enough to lay her up for the day, thank God, but enough to irritate her and make the day stretch out longer than it had any right to. "I suppose other villagers could have come back with minor injuries but not fallen ill, and I'd know nothing about it. It's so different from anything else I've seen. It almost seems too much to hope that some people are simply immune. And I've not seen anyone with an injury behaving this way. By now it either should've healed or become infected, but it hasn't."

"I'm alive at any rate." Elspeth grinned. "You are a damn good healer, aren't you?"

Charlotte flushed at the language but said mildly, "I try to be. On that note," she added, as Elspeth helped her back into the gig, "I've been wondering something. I doubt my being a healer is the talk of the village. My neighbors wouldn't have started spouting off at a stranger about what a great healer I am for no reason."

Elspeth said nothing.

"I suspect you asked around about me," Charlotte said.

Elspeth flushed. "Might've."

"Why?"

Elspeth's eyes flickered toward her. She bit her lip. Charlotte's stomach dipped.

"When you give me that cap," Elspeth said in a low voice, "I knew you were like me."

Charlotte froze. "Like you . . . how?"

Elspeth opened her mouth, but Charlotte turned away, afraid of what she might say. She thought of a young woman who had once pushed her up against the side of the church, the words the villagers had whispered about Arthur and Cormac, and the words they would've whispered about her if they'd known. Kitty spitting out "that *woman*" like an insult.

"I don't know what you're implying," Charlotte said in a shaking voice, "but whatever it is, you're wrong."

Elspeth's brow furrowed. Charlotte trembled, her insides prickling with fear. Ever since she'd discovered this about herself, she'd been afraid of anyone else finding out. Falling in love with John had been a relief; she'd thought she couldn't be caught, might even be cured, if she'd fallen so hard and fast for a man. Then there'd been that woman outside the church, and now Elspeth, with her trousers and her history of running off with nuns.

"My mistake," Elspeth said, making Charlotte at once relieved and regretful. "Kind of you, was all. To give me that cap. Warn me about the villagers. That's all."

Charlotte's chest heaved. Elspeth clambered back up beside her, careful to leave space between them, took the driving lines, and clicked her tongue at the mule. Charlotte burned with shame and guilt.

Her only comfort was the continued presence of the wheel tracks, which made her feel hopeful of finding Arthur soon. Never mind that Elspeth's plan was to find the Lord of the Wood instead.

If Charlotte found Arthur first, she'd turn around and head right back to Seacliff, and Elspeth McIntire could do as she liked.

XIX. In which Arthur sees his family, but not the way he expects

Arthur's last attempt at escaping the vale had been yesterday morning.

Too nervous to reapproach the brambles, he'd tried to climb over the tree-house. He should've known he'd fail; Arthur had never been much of a tree climber. Sasha was much better.

He'd fallen, landed on his back with a yelp, and winded himself. Ira had found him sprawled in the snow. As when he'd discovered Arthur amidst the trees the day prior, he'd been pale and tight-jawed. But he hadn't growled or snarled or lunged at Arthur and grabbed him. He'd merely asked, in a strained voice, what had happened, and made Arthur wiggle his fingers and toes and move his arms and legs to make sure he hadn't been paralyzed in the fall.

(He had not.)

Despite Calyx's objections, Ira had helped Arthur to his armchair (when had Arthur started thinking of it as his? he wasn't sure), warmed the heating pad for him, and checked periodically to make sure he could still move his limbs. Eventually, Ira had regained his color and lost the tension in his jaw. And

Arthur had realized, in astonishment, that he'd been frightened. Even though the forest, this time, could not be blamed for anything that might've happened. The fall had been entirely Arthur's own fault, the climb his own ridiculous idea.

For the rest of the day, Arthur sat in his chair, nursing a strained back and reading a novel. By Saturday afternoon, between chair, heating pad, and a pain-killing ointment, Arthur's back felt better except for the occasional twinge. His mood, however, had taken a sharp dive. He tried to read, but he couldn't help thinking what a long life it would be, with only three books and one watch and no Sasha to run in and interrupt his reading.

Freya purred in his lap. That didn't help, either. He kept wondering whether the children missed her.

For a while, he sank into the story, but at last—realizing he'd read the same paragraph several times without absorbing it—he closed his book with a sigh. To his surprise, he found Ira turned toward him at a sharper angle than usual, like he wanted to get the best look he could at Arthur with his one functional eye.

"What?" Arthur asked.

Ears pinkening, Ira turned hastily away. "Nothing."

There was a stick of charcoal in his hand and a yellow block of paper in his lap. He often had something in his hands in the evening hours they whiled away by the stove, but usually it was work. Laundry to fold. Torn clothes to mend, or clothing he was altering for Arthur. Garlic to jar. Root vegetables he'd taken down from the ceiling to peel for tomorrow's supper. A knife and a block of wood to make a new foot for the bedside table when it wobbled. Pruning shears, because Calyx needed periodic pruning like the cat needed brushing.

This didn't seem like that.

"What are you doing?" Arthur asked.

"Drawing."

Arthur's interest was piqued. "I didn't know you could draw."

"It's been a long time. I haven't . . . Being here, without even the seasons changing—I ran out of new things to draw ages ago."

Arthur leaned over. "Can I see?"

Ira's ears were pinker than ever. Biting his lip, he handed Arthur the yellowed paper.

It was covered in sketches of Arthur. Arthur reading in his chair, sitting one way, then another, because sitting properly in chairs was another on the long list of things he was bad at. Arthur frowning, or smiling, or with eyes close to the page as he got lost in a particularly tense scene. The sketches were quick and simple, lines layered over lines without erasure, but it gave them softness.

Arthur caught Ira's gaze, not sure what to say. The sketches, the sharing of them, felt like a gift.

Ira cleared his throat.

"You're very expressive." He took the block back, set it aside. "I wanted to sketch you the other day—you made so many faces while you were repairing the watch—but it's been so long, and there was the shirt to alter for you . . ."

"Are there more?" Arthur asked. "If you don't mind showing me?"

Ira went to the chest of drawers by the bed, returning with a sheaf of yellowed papers. Calyx nosed at him; Ira leaned into its fronds and vines.

"I used to draw George a lot. I liked drawing people, but I saw so little of anyone but him. Think it got on his nerves sometimes."

He handed the papers to Arthur and perched in his chair, drumming his fingers on his thighs.

Arthur's eyes prickled, but he smiled. There was a portrait, George wearing a grin so like Charlotte's.

"It looks just like him. You're very good."

"Thanks."

Arthur sifted through the drawings, drinking them in as if a rain of new images might deepen the pool of memory. The portrait was the most detailed, like George had sat for it, but the rest were sketches like those Ira had done of Arthur. Profiles in various moods. George reading or sorting plants. One of George looking over his shoulder, annoyed, as if Ira's incessant drawing of him had indeed gotten on his nerves.

Arthur chuckled, but a lump swelled in his throat.

"Lottie certainly does look like him," he said, tracing his father's brow with a finger. He missed Charlotte telling him about the latest development in her favorite radio program. Sasha running to show him a bug she'd found. Jonas asking questions about their father.

He wanted to cry, but he handed the drawings back and sat blinking in his chair. Ira deposited Calyx in its spot by the stove and put the drawings, charcoal stick, and block of paper away.

Returning to his seat, he touched Arthur's shoulder briefly. "Are you all right?"

Arthur swallowed. "It's just, I promised them I'd come back."

"Your family?"

Arthur nodded. "You seem to expect me to accept that this is my home now. But I can't bear the thought I might never see them again."

Ira hesitated. "There is a way. It isn't . . . It won't . . . You won't be able to speak to them. I want you to know that. But you could see them."

"How?"

Ira nodded him toward the table. Careful to avoid tangling

his antlers in the items hanging from the ceiling, he took down the silver basin, filled it with water, and set it before Arthur.

"In my memories?" Arthur said in disappointment.

Ira shook his head. "It can do that, if you wish. But it can show them to you now, too. Wherever they are, whatever they're doing. For memories, hair. For this . . ."

Taking Arthur's hand, he produced a pocketknife. Arthur recoiled. Ira released him.

"Do you want to see them?"

Arthur's hand tingled at the prospect of making contact with the blade, but he nodded.

Ira opened the knife and held it to Arthur's fingertip. He paused.

"It may disorient you. It's not like seeing the memories."

Arthur let out a breath. The blade flashed, his finger stung, and a drop of blood fell into the basin.

He stood inside his cottage kitchen, gazing out at the heathery cliffside, the dark and turbulent sea beyond. His heart pounded at the change. The windows rattled in their panes.

"Ira?" Arthur said, but he could no longer see or hear the Lord of the Wood. He felt a pang, imagining Ira in the vale alone.

Until he turned and saw the children.

To his surprise, they sat at the table not with Charlotte but with Kitty Tierney. His worry softened: Charlotte had asked for help in his absence! He'd hoped she might but hadn't actually expected her to.

The thought didn't last long. Sasha slumped, her head on her arms. Jonas picked at their lower lip, a habit they'd mostly grown out of but sometimes fell into when stressed. Each of them had a plate of fresh biscuits, but neither had eaten any. Sasha's plate was shoved off to the side.

"Children?"

They didn't respond. Arthur moved toward them, feeling oddly like he was in a dream.

Kitty's eyes flickered between the two children. She broke a biscuit into pieces and said, in a voice of forced cheer, "Well! Time yet before bed. What about that story, then, Sasha?"

Sasha sniffled. To Arthur's astonishment, fat tears slid down her cheeks and dripped from her nose.

"Sasha," he said weakly. "Duckling, don't cry. Everything's all right—"

Kitty touched Sasha's elbow.

"There now," she said soothingly, but her brow furrowed. "Your mam's smart as anything, and besides, she's got that—that Miss McIntire with her. She'll come back all right."

Arthur's blood ran cold. "Come back from where?"

Kitty didn't answer.

"What if she doesn't?" Jonas asked, picking at their lip. "What if Uncle Arthur never comes back, and she doesn't either?"

"Jonas," Arthur croaked. "I'm right here. Where's Lottie? Jonas—"

None of them noticed him. A trick, that's all it was. A trick of a silver basin and a knife and his own blood, and a man with antlers who'd told him he could see his family.

He reached for Sasha. His hand passed through her, as if he were a ghost—as if she were.

"I'm sure she will," Kitty said. "With your uncle in tow, I shouldn't wonder. If anyone can come out of that forest alive, she can. Come now, children, let's have a story and I'm sure we'll all feel much better for it."

Arthur tore from the kitchen. The forest? Charlotte wouldn't have gone into the forest—no, not even to look for him. It was foolishness, and Charlotte was not a fool. She was in the house. She had to be.

"Lottie!"

The sitting room was empty. Her bedroom, too, and her boots and cane were not in their habitual place beside her bed, nor her coat on its hook. Still Arthur searched, thundering up to the attic as if he might find her sorting through old clothes or broken furniture.

"Lottie!"

Into the washroom without even knocking. Through his workshop, out into the garden, as if she might've been hanging laundry by moonlight.

All deserted.

"Lottie," he whispered.

The small stretch of heather between the fence and the forest's edge was empty. Flattened by wheels the way it had been flattened by his father's feet thirty years before, when Arthur had run outside this same way, too late.

He threw the gate open and sprinted into the trees, but no sooner had they closed around him than he was sitting in a chair at a tiny table in a funny wooden house. He gasped for breath, glancing around wildly in confusion.

"I did warn you," Ira said quietly beside him.

Blood congealed at Arthur's fingertip. He pictured the slump of Sasha's shoulders, Jonas picking their lip, the missing boots and coat and cane, and the same empty yard he'd run outside to three decades ago.

"Arthur?"

Arthur shoved back from the table, bolted to his feet, and ran outside.

"Arthur—"

He didn't make it far. Yards from the door, Ira caught his hand, tugged him to a stop. His eyes went over Arthur's face in alarm.

"What's wrong? What did you see?"

Arthur yanked his hand from Ira's. His voice was high with panic. "It's Lottie—she's come after me—she's in the forest—"

Snow soaked into his socks, but he didn't care. Ira blocked his path.

"Let me pass," Arthur said.

In the doorway, Calyx unraveled, clicking. Ira held his hands up, talking to Arthur as if he were a spooked horse. "Come inside. I'm sure we can—"

"I have to find my sister!"

"Arthur—"

Arthur pushed past. Ira grabbed his wrist, but Arthur whirled around, wrenched away, and shoved him.

"Let go of me!"

Calyx slammed into him.

Vines squeezed around his stomach and ribs, spiraling down his legs and binding them. Clawing at the creature, Arthur collapsed in the snow.

"Don't," Ira said, his hoarse voice laced with panic for the first time since Arthur had met him. "Calyx, stop!"

Vines shackled Arthur's wrists. Calyx wrenched his head back—then tendrils slithered *into* him. His nose. His mouth. His ears. Ira was shouting, but it was distant, muted.

Arthur screamed, tried to, but he choked on plant matter. Leaves sealed over his face, vines wrapped around his neck—he gasped for breath, couldn't breathe—stars burst behind his eyelids—

He was free. Sucking down air, he scrambled away from where he'd been, afraid he'd find himself trapped again.

"Arthur?"

Several yards away, Ira wrestled Calyx under control. It had grown bigger than Arthur had ever seen, spilling vines and fronds over Ira's arms and shoulders. Tendrils swayed in Arthur's direction. He backed away.

Ira's face was pale, his eyes wide and horrified. "Arthur—"

A vine shot in Arthur's direction. Arthur turned and ran.

"Arthur!"

He sprinted blindly across the vale, launched himself at the brambles, and clawed his way into them. They smacked him, stinging his cheeks and neck and hands.

"Arthur!"

He was buried in brambles. They yanked on his clothes and arms. A thorn pierced the fleshy part of his hand.

Somewhere behind him, Ira swore. With an unpleasant dragging sound, a vine wrapped around Arthur's ankle. He kicked at it, made contact.

"Calyx, *stop*—"

Angry clicking, a growl, and Calyx let go.

The brambles grew thicker and thornier, scratching Arthur's face, catching on his hair, snaking around a wrist, more thorns piercing his skin. He kicked forward inch by inch.

A *mrowr* sounded in his ear. Freya crept past, winding through the canes with ease. Arthur gritted his teeth and followed. Thorns tore his shirt and skin.

Then he fell forward. With a splash, he landed face-first in frigid water and sat up sputtering. Behind him, Ira called his name with increasing desperation.

Arthur squeezed his eyes shut. He still felt Calyx forcing vines down his throat, into his nose and ears.

He still saw the wheel tracks in the heather behind the garden back home.

"I'm sorry," he said, and he splashed away from the vale.

xx. In which leaving the vale does not go well

The air was so much warmer than it had been in the vale that Arthur's head throbbed at the change. Downstream the water carved into the landscape deeper and deeper, heading into the ravine, but here it only came up to Arthur's knees.

Arthur tore a thorn from his hand and splashed clumsily through, forgetful of the knapsack and watch and novels and shoes he'd left behind. Forgetful of his wet socks, his many scratches, his torn shirt, his throbbing hand, the blood beading on his palm—even Calyx wrapping itself around his body. All he could think of were the wheel tracks in the heather, and Charlotte coming into the forest after him.

Unconcerned with such things, Freya jumped from rock to rock. She made a face when water splashed her toes but otherwise seemed pleased to be leaving the eternal winter of the vale.

Arthur hadn't reached the opposite shore when the water upstream bubbled. He froze. Wide-eyed, Freya leaped from a final rock and landed on the opposite bank. She glared, tail twitching.

A maiden arose from depths the stream did not have. She stood forlornly with water trailing from her white frock and golden hair and ashen skin. Arthur didn't know what she was, but he knew enough about fairy stories to take a step back. His chest heaved. Back beyond the brambles, Ira was still calling for him.

The maiden's voice burbled like water running over rocks. "Help me."

"How?" Arthur asked cautiously.

She held out her arms. "Carry me across."

That seemed an odd request, given her circumstances, but it also seemed like a bad idea to refuse.

"Why?"

"Carry me across."

The cat hissed. Arthur felt she probably had the right idea of things.

"With all due respect—"

The maiden stepped closer without a splash. Arthur didn't like that.

"Carry me across."

"I'm—I'm likely to drop you." One could not be rude to fairies, or things like fairies, but by God he didn't want to find out what would happen if he touched her. "I'm not very strong."

She closed the gap between them, much less sickly than her ashen skin had made her appear. She wore a forlorn expression, but her dark, sad eyes gleamed hungrily.

Her voice shifted, no longer burbling but thundering like water over a cliffside, sudden and deadly. "Carry me across."

"No—no, that's all right, you don't want me to—"

Her eyes flashed red. "Carry me across!"

She plunged a hand to his chest, her fingernails sharp as talons. Arthur cried out, struggling, but her nails clawed into him.

Freya launched herself at the maiden. The maiden stumbled, releasing Arthur, but she threw the cat off. Her red eyes glinted.

"Oh no." Arthur splashed away from her, but the bank didn't seem any closer. "Oh no, oh no, oh no, oh no, oh—"

She yanked him back. He fell with a splash, sputtering, with water up his nose. Baring too many, too sharp teeth, she grabbed his collar, pulled him to his knees—

A raven burst over the brambles. It swooped at the maiden, grabbing her hair in its talons. Shrieking, she released Arthur.

The raven pulled away, circled briefly, and dove. Its talons raked the maiden's face, drawing greenish blood. She screeched.

With a splash, the raven shivered into an antlered man. Ira stumbled as he landed, leg buckling, but he righted himself and shoved Arthur toward the bank.

"Get to shore."

The maiden lunged toward Ira. He shivered into a wolf and stood, growling, between her and Arthur.

Arthur stared. Knowing Ira could shape-shift was one thing; seeing it was another. George had only said he turned into a stag.

And despite his refusal to leave the vale before, Ira was here. Just because Arthur needed him.

Something tugged at Arthur's trousers. He flinched, then saw the cat on the nearest rock, batting at his leg.

"Quite right."

The maiden flew at Ira. Snarling, the wolf leaped to meet her. Arthur stumbled onto dry land.

Behind him, the wolf yelped. Arthur found a stick half as long as he was and so heavy he almost couldn't lift it. He dragged it back toward the stream. It scraped against his injured hands.

The maiden swayed toward Ira. He panted, ears flat against his head. Blood trickled into his scarred eye. His sides heaved, but he bared his teeth.

Arthur splashed into the water, wielding his stick. He

smacked the maiden in the shoulder—hardly enough to do more than anger her, but it distracted her. She turned angry red eyes on him.

The wolf hurled himself at her. They landed in the water together, thrashing; then they went still.

Arthur's mouth was dry. "Ira?"

The wolf heaved. Arthur gripped his stick tight, unsure whether Ira was getting up or if the maiden had proven triumphant and was pushing him off. No—the wolf rose shakily, coughed once, and turned toward him. The maiden's pallid body drifted away, spilling into the ravine.

"Ira?"

The wolf shivered into a man, but he collapsed. The maiden's greenish blood rimmed his lips. His own blood stained the left side of his face.

Arthur shivered. He was safe, or seemed to be. If he left now, he could search for Charlotte, not that he knew where to start. Freya wove back and forth on the bank, mewling as if to say, *Come on, let's go.*

But Ira had saved his life. Ira had left the vale, even though Arthur had shouted at him and shoved him. Even though the forest made it difficult to leave, and Ira so desperately hadn't wanted to.

Setting the stick down, Arthur approached him. "Let me help you up."

Ira nodded wearily. His eyes raked over Arthur's face and bloody hand. "You're injured."

Arthur laughed, a little hysterically. "Have you seen yourself?"

Ira's forehead and upper arm bled. Arthur's stomach clenched, but he pulled Ira to his feet and supported him. Together, they made their way toward the brambles. With a grumble, Freya followed.

To Arthur's annoyance, the brambles opened before them. He couldn't help saying accusingly, "You said there was no way out, with the bridge gone."

"Yes, well," Ira said, his voice even hoarser than usual, "I wouldn't call a hungry glaistig's stretch of water a way out."

Arthur didn't argue the point. Instead he asked, "Should I have carried her across, after all?"

"She would've killed you either way."

The brambles closed behind them. Arthur's hand throbbed where a thorn had pierced it. He swallowed back a lump in his throat. He'd escaped the vale only to come right back.

XXI. In which flowers grow somewhere unexpected

Back in the vale, Calyx was waiting. It was smaller than ever, vaguely dog-shaped, but Arthur tensed as it crept toward them. Freya hissed.

"Are you happy now?" Ira snapped at the plant creature.

It rubbed against his legs, but he kicked it away—lost his balance, but Arthur kept him upright. Calyx crawled up a nearby tree to mope.

Arthur glanced at it as they passed, neck prickling. "You're sure it won't follow us inside?"

Ira shook his head. "Its whole purpose is to protect me. I got hurt because it scared you away."

"I thought the forest was protecting you."

"Calyx came from the forest." Ira's blood dripped a red trail in the snow the whole way inside. He collapsed in his armchair. "The last time a human was in the vale, I thought he was a traveler who'd gotten lost, that he needed my care, but he . . ."

He touched his scarred eye. Arthur's stomach heaved at the thought of someone scarring him that way on purpose. It was bloody now, the scar, the same as Ira's forehead and arm. Arthur closed his eyes and breathed deep, *in for four, hold for four, out for four.*

"I thought he was going to kill me," Ira said, "but the forest sent Calyx. It handled the problem."

Arthur shivered but focused on rooting through the kitchen for rags, bandages, and scissors. Unable to stand his wet socks any longer, he replaced them with a fresh pair. Things were quite bad enough without wet socks.

"I should've realized," Ira went on. "It's been clinging to me like a shadow for so long, I forgot how dangerous it can be. I was afraid I wouldn't be able to stop it. I thought . . ."

Arthur filled a bowl with water. "It wasn't your fault."

Ira looked unconvinced. Apparently deciding the rescue had gone some way toward making amends for his behavior the day they'd met, the cat allowed Arthur to attend to him without interruption. She curled on the bed, barely glaring.

Antiseptic, Arthur thought. He needed to disinfect the wounds.

"Do you have any—" what was that plant? Charlotte always had a paste or ointment of it with her medical things "—sweet amber?"

"I can."

Ira waved a hand. A shrub with oval leaves and cupped yellow flowers sprouted beside his chair. Arthur's breath hitched, but Ira slumped, like that small act of magic had drained his energy.

Biting his lip, Arthur cut away Ira's shirtsleeve and pressed a towel to his upper arm. "Hold that, will you?"

Ira did so. Arthur touched the shrub's foliage, considering. The leaves, not the flowers. For this, anyway. Sweet amber had many uses, not that he could remember most of them. He plucked leaves from the shrub, wishing he'd asked Charlotte to teach him more about herbalism over the years. Most of what he'd learned had been in the past six months, so he could help her on bad days.

Arthur's heart stuttered. Assuming he managed to leave again, what, exactly, was his plan? To wander the forest at random, hoping he found her?

Ira leaned back with his eyes closed and the towel, rusty with blood, against his arm. His forehead bled freely. Arthur bit his lip so hard it hurt. He found a mortar and pestle in a cabinet and ground the leaves, hoping for the best.

Head wounds bleed a lot, he heard Charlotte saying in clipped tones, over a year ago, as she cleaned Sasha's forehead while he panicked beside her. Sasha had somehow climbed onto and fallen off of the cottage roof.

A little water and the ground leaves made a paste, though one runnier than Arthur had been hoping for. He set the mortar and pestle down, wet a towel and wrung it out.

As Arthur cleaned the blood from Ira's upper arm, he couldn't help glancing at the door, like Calyx might burst in. But it was as Ira had said: Chastened, the plant creature remained outside, wrapped moodily around a tree.

Ira's nostrils flared. Arthur worried something might've happened to his eye: Odd little bloody clumps lined his scar. Arthur wasn't sure he wanted to know what they were. His stomach clenched, but he breathed deeply and focused on his work. Ira wouldn't look so bad if not for him.

In a small voice, he said, "Thank you. For what you did. You didn't have to."

Ira cracked an eye open. "You could've been killed."

"So could you." Arthur reached for the mortar. "This might sting. Sorry."

He dabbed the sweet amber mixture onto Ira's arm. Some of it dribbled down his bicep, staining his skin green, but most of the mixture stayed where Arthur wanted. Ira winced, but his eyes flickered over Arthur's face.

"I wouldn't let anything happen to you. Not if I could stop it."

Arthur looked away. He couldn't stand that serious hazel gaze, even as gentle as it was now. He wasn't sure why, except for his usual thing about eye contact, whatever the reason for that. Thank God Ira never demanded it as so many people did.

"What did you see?" Ira asked.

Arthur paled but focused on bandaging his arm. He explained what he'd seen in the basin and added, as he finished with the bandage, "I don't know what to do. I don't even know when she left! It might've been an hour ago—a day—I've no idea. She could be anywhere by now. How am I supposed to find her? With the paths shifting—the stormwings—the sickness—"

His vision swam as he imagined what could've happened to Charlotte by now. Charlotte like Hamish, black-veined and covered in moss and vanishing when Arthur's back was turned.

Arthur dropped his head to his knees and breathed through the cycle Charlotte had taught him. He'd never imagined *this*. Dying in the forest or being trapped in the vale forever: yes. Charlotte coming after him, as if she had any hope of finding him: absolutely not.

A hand on his head, gentle and comforting. Arthur focused on it, grateful that Ira did not have the same hang-ups about physical touch between men that Seacliff did. At home, Arthur was used to the weight and warmth of someone's hand on his. Sasha would bowl into him for a hug, just because, or snuggle against him as he told a bedtime story, or demand a piggyback ride around the garden, even though she was getting big for that sort of thing and it often triggered his back spasm. At twelve, Jonas still sought him out to cuddle on the settee together after a bad day at school. Even Charlotte, despite her reserve, often squeezed his arm or touched his shoulder when he was upset or sunk so deep in his work that there was no other way to get his attention.

"Perhaps she'll find her way here," Ira said.

Then they'd both be trapped. Wonderful.

A couple more breathing cycles, and Arthur had calmed enough to examine Ira's forehead. The bleeding had slowed, but blood congealed at his hairline, in his scar with its strange bloody clumps, on his cheek and temple. Arthur tried to channel the calm Charlotte radiated whenever she cared for a patient.

Cupping Ira's face in his hand, Arthur dabbed blood from his forehead. Ira's eyes fluttered closed, but his breathing wasn't as labored as it had been. With the blood cleaned up, the wound didn't look as bad. Arthur applied the sweet amber to it, taped gauze over it, and turned his attention to cleaning the blood off Ira's face.

As he wiped blood from the scar, something emerged he had not expected. He'd thought—feared—that the clumps had been oddly shaped bubbles of blood, that the scar had opened up in the altercation.

Instead, Ira's scar was dotted with flowers.

White flowers stained pink. Five-petaled and tiny. Arthur swallowed, touching a fingertip to the scar.

Ira jerked away. "Don't. Please."

"But . . . your scar." Arthur's heart fluttered in panic. "It's growing flowers."

Ira's brow furrowed. He reached for the scar but lowered his hand without touching it.

"That's new," he said wearily, but Arthur, more panicked, caught his hand. His nails had lengthened into claws. Gray hair furred his fingers. Like his hands were turning into paws the way his feet had.

"What's happening to you?" Arthur whispered.

Ira's thumb brushed across his knuckles. "I told you. The forest is trying to protect me."

"But—this—how does this—"

"It makes it harder for me to leave the vale."

Ira slumped in his chair, letting out a breath. Arthur squeezed his hand.

"The first time I left the vale after your father died," Ira said, "I changed to a stag. Always liked being a stag, when I'm not in human form instead. Sometimes I liked it better. But when I changed back . . ."

He gestured at his antlers. They gleamed in the low light.

"The second time, it was the paws. The third time, the feathers. The more time I spend transformed outside the vale, the less of me changes back. And I start to lose myself. To feel like a real beast, instead of just looking like one. It was never like that before."

He gazed absently at their linked hands.

"I used to change for the fun of it. Now I never know whether I'll be able to change back."

A lump formed in Arthur's throat. The forest made it so difficult for Ira to leave the vale, yet he'd done so for Arthur. He'd transformed for Arthur, too, to face the glaistig, not knowing whether or to what extent he'd become a man again.

Arthur swallowed. "Is there nothing that can be done?"

Ira leaned forward, reaching for the silver acorn. His new claws scraped over Arthur's throat but didn't break the skin. Arthur shivered. On the bed, Freya raised her head, eyes narrowed, but she curled back up when it became apparent Arthur wasn't in mortal danger.

"With this . . ." Ira's fingers curled around the acorn. "If the heart of the wood were replanted, it would heal the forest. Calyx might calm down. And I think . . . I think it'd put me back the way I was."

"Then—why haven't you done it?"

Ira shook his head.

"It's not a matter of stepping outside and planting the acorn wherever you want. It has to be planted where the tree is. Was. In the stump." He dragged a hand over his face. "I tried. I ran out of acorns, planting them in the vale, or just outside it. Some of them took, but it didn't work."

"How do you know?"

Ira smiled humorlessly.

"Because the forest has grown sicker since." He squeezed Arthur's hand and let go. Arthur hadn't realized their hands were still linked. "Besides, you'd know if it worked. I've had to do it once before, centuries ago. The tree had been struck by lightning. It grew back the second I replanted it."

He ran a hand through his hair, making a face when it tangled in his new claws.

"I was so scared when I saw it like that, blackened and split and broken, half of it fallen over. When I replanted it, and it grew . . . I thought I could protect the forest forever. And now I can't even get to the heart of the wood."

His fingers drummed on the arm of his chair. "Let me see your hand."

Arthur gazed at Ira as he cleaned and bandaged Arthur's hand. At the flowers in his scar, there because Arthur had needed him.

Arthur fiddled with the silver acorn, thinking about all Ira had said about it. "How far is it to the heart of the wood?"

Ira shrugged. "Three days on foot. Maybe less, if you travel hard and don't stop much."

"What if we went there?"

Ira frowned. "What if—"

Arthur knelt at his feet, touching his knees.

"What if we went to the heart of the wood?" Arthur shifted closer. "What if we replanted it? What if we healed the forest? Then it would be safe, wouldn't it, like it used to be when

Dad came through every year? And nothing would happen to Lottie—I could find her, no matter how long it took, we could go home—and you could—"

"I can't leave the vale."

"You did, just now."

Ira opened his mouth but closed it without saying anything, as if that hadn't occurred to him.

"I did," he said slowly.

Arthur nodded, fingers tightening on Ira's knees.

"We could do it—I'm sure we could. You could keep me safe, and I could . . ." Arthur faltered, not sure what he might lend to the venture, but he recovered quickly. "Well, if you don't transform, there's no problem, right?"

Ira touched his scar uneasily. "I'm not sure about this. I might sprout more flowers just for leaving."

"We'll figure something out if it comes to that."

"Maybe."

Ira pried Arthur's fingers from his knees. Blushing, Arthur skittered away and flung himself into his armchair.

"If I ordered the forest to regrow the bridge," Ira said, "if it knew why we were leaving . . ."

"It might let us go?"

Ira's brow furrowed. "It's safer here."

"For now. Isn't that what you told me? That the sickness will spread here eventually?"

Ira's fingers curled over the arms of his chair.

"Ira," Arthur said gently, "I can't stay."

"Don't you like it here?"

"I—well, I hadn't thought about it," Arthur said in astonishment. "It's— That's not the point. I promised my family I'd come home, but I haven't, and now Lottie's come to find me. I can't let her die out here. Not if I can help it."

A little hesitantly, he reached for Ira's hand. There had been so much touch between them, but Ira had initiated most of it. Ira threaded his fingers through Arthur's; Arthur relaxed.

"And it could help you, too," he said, "replanting the tree. You said so."

"I said I thought it could." Ira avoided his gaze. "I wasn't like this, last time. What if . . ."

His jaw tightened. He swallowed.

"What if," he said, "what if we go, and we plant the tree, and the forest is healed, and I'm still like this?"

Arthur's heart clenched; he understood that feeling. He squeezed Ira's hand.

"We have to try, don't you think? You're my friend. I'd hate to see you stuck like this forever when there was something we could do about it. But I can't make it myself. Even if the forest didn't try to kill me—" he laughed ruefully "—I'm sure I couldn't make it anyway. I'm useless. But together—please, Ira. I need you."

Ira's gaze latched on to their hands, then flickered over Arthur's face. His right eye was dark in the dim glow of the stove. The scar over his other eye gleamed white with flowers.

Shaking Arthur off, he leaned forward with his forearms on his knees. Arthur's heart sank, but Ira said, in clipped tones, "We don't leave till morning."

Arthur would have to hope his sister would be all right in the meantime. "Yes. Of course."

"You'll do exactly as I say."

"Well—all right."

"The whole way there."

"Yes."

Letting out a long breath, Ira sat back. Errant strands of hair fell around his face. Without thinking, Arthur tucked one behind his ear.

"We'll leave Calyx here." Ira's eyes met his. "You're sure about this?"

"Not at all." Arthur gave a small smile. "But we have to try."

His hand lingered on Ira's face. Ira laid a hand clawed and gray with fur over his.

"All right. We set out at first light."

XXII. In which Arthur crosses a bridge again, to worse results

Arthur had been eager to set out, but his body had complaints when he awoke the next morning. He was sore from his haphazard flight through the brambles; his scratches stung; his hand still throbbed where a thorn had pierced it. A purplish bruise circled his wrist like a cuff. Similar bruises, from Calyx, colored his throat and torso.

Besides, Arthur had never been an early riser. When he arose before Charlotte, it was only because she frequently slept late since her illness. Before, no matter how early he'd awoken, she'd beaten him to it. Once, some fifteen years ago, he'd spent the night in the sitting room, determined not to sleep, so he could be up first. Instead, he'd awoken in his armchair by the fire, a knitted blanket tucked around him, to the sounds of Charlotte making coffee.

Now, he shuddered with yawn after yawn as he dressed, slipped the rowan cross into his pocket, and checked his knapsack for the all-important novels. He thumbed through them, comforted by the softness of the well-read pages. Freya twisted about him, mewling for her breakfast as she did every morning though Ira always gave it to her.

(That had not improved her opinion of him.)

"All set?" Ira asked behind him.

Arthur jumped, embarrassed to be caught with three novels instead of more useful provisions. He flushed as Ira leafed through a book.

"Your books?" Ira asked, more in curiosity than judgment. "I don't think you'll have much time for reading."

Arthur pinkened.

"If you must know," he said, "they're, er, they're romance novels," as if that weren't obvious from the women swooning into the arms of shirtless, flowing-haired men on the covers. Or, in the case of the novel he'd been telling Charlotte about, into the arms of a shirtless creature with lots of fur and fangs and horns and burl but also, somehow, perfect humanoid abs. "And I know there won't be time for reading. That's not why I brought them out here in the first place."

"Then why?"

Why indeed. Not merely one, but three. He'd nearly brought more when he'd set out from the cottage, though he hadn't been going on a pleasure trip. He'd brought the books for the same reason he'd brought his watch-repairing kit and his father's acorn: They were a comfort.

(Had he repacked the kit? He'd had it on the bedside table since fixing his father's watch, but he couldn't bring himself to check whether he'd added it to his bag while Ira stared at him for packing something equally silly.)

"Romance novels," he said, still very pink, "promise happy endings no matter the dangers and difficulties. I thought if everything seemed hopeless, they might remind me it's not. That we'll restore the heart of the wood, and you won't be half a beast anymore, and Lottie will be safe, and I'll find her and make it to Port Lorne and buy Mrs. Livingston's clock, and Mrs. Livingston's cousin will get well, somehow, and we'll have all this money, and we'll all live happily ever after. Except for the romance bit, I suppose, not much hope of finding the right girl in the forest—"

Ira's brow creased, but he didn't interrupt.

"—after forty years of finding wrong ones in town, but, well, that's not a priority just now anyway."

Arthur paused, his words echoing in his own ears. He'd said rather too much.

"They bring me hope. That's all."

Ira considered him, his expression strange and soft. After a long moment, he closed the book and slipped it into Arthur's knapsack. "Come on."

Feeling less foolish than he might have, Arthur closed his knapsack, shrugged on the furs Ira had lent him, and followed. Freya gave a disheartened meow that suggested she was wasting away due to their neglect, but she followed, too.

Outside, snow was falling. Arthur shivered, grateful to leave the vale's endless winter. The snow filled in his footprints and Ira's pawprints as if they'd never been there.

Calyx unwound from its tree and dragged itself after them. Ira rounded on it.

"Absolutely not. Stay here."

It clicked despondently. Despite himself, Arthur pitied it. It only wanted to protect Ira, after all, even if its way of protecting him was deeply unhelpful and had almost gotten Arthur killed.

"Someone has to watch over the vale," he said to it, "don't you think?"

He shivered as it turned fronds toward him, feeling, as usual, like it was glaring at him.

"I was only trying to help."

Ira nudged the plant creature with a clawed foot. "Away with you."

Calyx moped back up its tree.

They halted before the brambles. Ira's fingers curled into fists. He paled, his face strained. The delicate white flowers blooming in the valley of his scar were at odds with his expression. Arthur bit his lip, but he touched the back of Ira's hand. Carefully, barely, in case Calyx came racing down the tree to choke him for it.

Ira cleared his throat, but his voice was hoarse as usual when he spoke.

"Open up."

The brambles quivered. Thorned canes peeled back, more slowly than they had when they'd let Arthur into the vale. Freya trotted through them with a chirp. Arthur let out a breath but smiled encouragingly and followed. Ira kept close behind him.

They stood at the ravine's edge, gazing at the water below. Across from them, frost from the stormwings' passage edged the autumnal flora.

Ira's fists tightened. "Regrow the bridge."

Nothing happened. Ira's nostrils flared.

"It's not going to listen to me," he growled.

"Not with that attitude."

"The forest has hardly listened to me in three decades."

"We can't give up after one try."

Ira gritted his teeth. "Regrow the bridge."

The forest was silent except for the small, secret rustlings of unseen creatures in the underbrush and canopy. Ira rubbed his forehead. Before he could say anything more, Arthur unfastened the acorn from his neck and held it up.

"I know you want to protect him. And maybe this, too. But we're going to the heart of the wood—we want to, if you'll let us cross. We're trying to help you."

Silence. Stillness.

Then, a low rumble. Arthur stumbled. Ira grabbed the back

of his shirt and yanked him from the ravine's edge. Freya hissed, darting behind them.

With a crack, new limbs burst from the trees on either side. They thinned and lengthened, slinging across and braiding together. Vines slithered over them, wove together into sides. With another rumble, logs rolled down the length of the vines, which sheared them into planks.

When the forest stilled, a new swinging bridge hung across the ravine, green with moss and lichens and smelling of fresh wood. Breath catching at the sudden construction, Arthur hung the acorn back around his neck.

Beside him, Ira had gone white, jaw clenched, fists tighter than ever. A few days ago, that expression would have scared Arthur. Now he recognized it for what it was. Ira wasn't angry; he was afraid.

Arthur touched one of his fists. "It'll be all right."

Ira shook his head. "I can't do this."

"Yes you can."

"I haven't left the vale in more than twenty years."

Arthur gave a small smile. "You left just yesterday to save me."

Ira's fists unclenched slightly. "You keep bringing that up."

"You keep forgetting."

Arthur waited, but Ira stared rigidly out at the forest without speaking.

"Let's breathe a moment, shall we?" Arthur said.

"What?"

"Breathe with me. Just for a minute. Four counts in, hold for four counts, four counts out, then hold again and start the whole thing over."

"Arthur—"

"Trust me."

Ira's mouth twisted, but he nodded. Arthur caught his gaze, despite his own discomfort with eye contact, because Charlotte had kept them breathing together that way when she'd taught him this. He took them through three cycles. By the end, Ira's fists had uncurled and jaw unclenched.

He let out a breath, running a hand through his hair. "Thanks."

A strand had come loose from his knot. Arthur tucked it back into place.

"Come on. I'll be right beside you. Let's go, Freya."

The cat *mrowred* and trotted onto the bridge, pleased to leave their snowy prison behind.

Arthur started across, but Ira caught his hand, so tightly it hurt. Arthur's injured palm throbbed, but he waited. For a long moment, Ira stood like that, hands tight on Arthur's, eyes squeezed shut. Then, nodding, he opened his eyes. When Arthur took his first step onto the bridge, Ira followed, clinging to him.

Crossing was easier this time, except for Ira clutching Arthur's hand. Freshly grown, the bridge was not half frozen from stormwings, nor did it crack and creak underfoot—though it did bounce with each step, so much that Arthur had to stop in the middle to fight back a wave of nausea. They reached the other side without event.

Ira slipped one paw off the bridge and onto the forest floor.

Where he stepped, greenery unfurled. Sprouts unwound, then, as if excited to see him, exploded into bitter vetch or heal-all or wild garlic. Toadstools burst through the leaf litter, blue violet, brownish gold, blush pink.

"*Oh*," Arthur breathed.

The plants wilted and blackened. The toadstools liquefied.

A muscle tightened in Ira's neck.

"What happened?" Arthur asked in a hushed voice.

The muscle ticked, but all Ira said was, "Come on."

They set off in silence. Ira's jaw was so tight it hurt Arthur's teeth to look at him. The muscle kept ticking, with greater frequency as the swinging bridge vanished behind them.

It should've been magical, traveling the forest with the Lord of the Wood. Near the vale, the trees were in their autumnal finery, crimson and gold with silvery trunks. Unseen birds called. Intermittent sunlight filtered green-gold through the canopy; the unseasonable frost vanished farther from the vale. Autumn greenery sprouted on the forest floor with every step Ira took.

But it wilted each time he stepped away, leaving a trail of limp, blackened stalks and leaves behind. Like the forest's sickness was following them. Arthur imagined it trailing his sister through the forest like this—catching up to her, leaving her frail and cold and veined in black. Shuddering, he drew closer to Ira.

Their elbows bumped. Ira flinched.

"Walk on my other side."

"What?"

"Walk on my other side," Ira snapped. "I can't see you on this side. You startled me."

Arthur flushed. "Right, sorry."

He'd been walking on Ira's left without thinking, glancing at the white flowers blooming in Ira's scar. Perhaps he was imagining it, but moss furred the scar now, too, half hidden beneath the blossoms. Probably he *was* imagining it. He moved to Ira's right without mentioning it.

Ira scrubbed a hand over his face. "Sorry. Being out here again is . . ."

"It's all right."

The sickness became more evident the deeper into the forest they went. On Arthur's initial journey, infected trees had been frequent, but so had trees that looked perfectly fine. In the vale, there had been no infection; immediately beyond, only the plants wilting at Ira's feet had signaled anything wrong. But as they walked farther, an increasing number of trees oozed black or had leaves withered gray instead of red or gold or green.

Ira swallowed.

"I didn't know," he said, after an hour in which not a word had passed between them. "I didn't realize it had gotten so bad."

Arthur wanted to say something reassuring, but Ira bent, clutching his heart.

"Are you all right?" Arthur asked in alarm.

No mistaking it now. Moss thickened along his scar, spread to his ear. Arthur reached for him, panicking, but Ira straightened. He breathed hard through his nose.

"S'all right," he said. "The tarnish is spreading. The stump is dying. I don't feel it when I'm in the vale."

"Perhaps you should go back. I can go on alone, I'm sure I could—"

Ira shook his head before Arthur could decide how to end the sentence.

"We go together or not at all." He grimaced, but his breathing evened out. "I'm all right. Come on."

They walked onward, but their pace lagged. Arthur kept glancing at Ira, worried about his breathing and the moss creeping across his face. Three days. They only had to make it three days. Surely the growth couldn't take over too much of Ira's body in so short a time.

Ira shoved him suddenly aside.

"What—"

Something with a mouthful of sharp, mossy teeth glided from the trees like a flying squirrel. Arthur yelped, but Ira transformed into a stag, catching the creature on his antlers. Snorting, he shook it off, and it landed on a trunk.

Freya darted up the tree after it.

"Don't," Arthur said in a panic.

Before the cat could get at it, the creature leaped at Arthur. Those sharp, mossy teeth flashed.

The creature plunged its teeth into his neck.

Arthur fell to his knees, gurgling. He scrabbled for the creature but was unable to get a grip on its body, which lengthened into something slithering and winding, shaggy with lichens.

With a roar, the stag shivered into a wolf. He lunged at Arthur—Arthur moved his hands aside with a muffled squeak—the wolf's jaws closed around the creature's body.

For a long moment, the three of them were locked together: the wolf holding fast to the creature, the creature holding fast to Arthur's neck, Arthur's fingers at the creature's mouth. The wolf growled. Arthur reached for him, a hand clenching in Ira's fur. He couldn't breathe.

The creature's hold slackened. Gasping, Arthur pried the creature off. The wolf shook it between his teeth and flung it away. It crumbled into dust.

Arthur's heartbeat pounded in his ears; his breathing was harsh. He pressed a hand to his mangled flesh, fingers slick with blood. He retched into the soil. Nothing came up.

Freya crept down from the tree and wound around him, mewling anxiously.

Ira was a man again. He knelt at Arthur's side, pulled his hand from his neck. His mouth twisted.

Arthur tried to ask how bad it was, couldn't. He gurgled.

Ira swore. "Can you stand?"

Arthur nodded but stumbled. Ira steadied him.

"I know somewhere safe we can take care of this. Come on."

Arthur took a step and crumpled. Cursing, Ira hefted Arthur over his shoulder and limped through the forest, flowers blooming and dying behind him.

XXIII. In which Charlotte and Elspeth escape a muddy ending

They found the shovel at the foot of a tree.

The tree drooped, veined in black and dripping. The shovel's tip was corroded, but Charlotte recognized it nonetheless; it had come from her garden shed.

She stumbled from the gig in a daze.

"Lottie," Elspeth said, but Charlotte grabbed the shovel.

"Arthur?"

The forest was silent.

"Arthur!"

Charlotte reached for the tree, like it might provide a clue to where her brother had gone, but Elspeth's fingers closed around her wrist. She yanked Charlotte back. The shovel clanged on the ground.

"For the love of God," Elspeth said, "don't touch it."

Charlotte lunged at the shovel, but Elspeth held her back. "It's ours."

"What're you on about?"

"The shovel. It's ours." Charlotte tried and failed to wrestle free. "From our shed. Arthur took it with him. To unstick the cart, he said."

She swallowed.

"The wheel tracks end here, don't you see? And here's our shovel at the foot of this tree."

Elspeth's grip didn't loosen until Charlotte stopped fighting her. "Then we know he passed by, don't we? Leave it, Lottie, there's a good lass."

Silly to cry over a shovel, but Charlotte wanted to. She wanted to cry at the nickname, too. It reminded her so much of Arthur because he was the only one left who called her that.

She wiped her eyes and left the shovel, but she wouldn't let them move on until she'd dug the vial of black ooze from her medical bag. To her relief, the glass was undamaged. The shovel's corroded tip had made her worry the vial might've been damaged, too, but it seemed the ooze had different effects on different materials.

By the time she'd clambered back into the gig, the path had vanished. Charlotte gasped, but Elspeth shrugged.

"Happens. Told you. S'all right. We've got the acorn."

"That might help if we were going to the first tree. I don't see how it'll help us find the Lord of the Wood."

Elspeth smiled crookedly. That was the only way she'd smiled since yesterday, crookedly. Charlotte missed the easy grin she'd worn back in Seacliff.

"Never you mind. It'll save us getting lost, and that's all you need bother about."

Not long after that, the temperature dropped, cold and sharp. Unseasonable frost limned the foliage around them. Elspeth whistled, wrapping her cloak around herself.

Charlotte had no cloak. She had an old coat that would have protected her from an autumn chill but not the sudden winter that had befallen. The cold knifed into her.

Ahead of them, a fox slunk across the path. Charlotte

shuddered, drawing closer to Elspeth. The fox's skull showed through its fur.

Spooked by the forest, Charlotte wanted to believe she was imagining it, but she remembered Elspeth's description of the sparrowhawk that had attacked her. The fox gazed at them with eyes blank and black. It should've been more skittish, Charlotte thought.

The fox regarded them then slunk onward, vanishing into the underbrush.

Elspeth shook her head and clucked at the mule. His ears twitched as they continued onward.

Realizing how close she'd gotten to Elspeth, Charlotte shifted away. She missed the warmth immediately. Her fingers were stiff, her joints aching, but it was hard to say, just now, what bothered her more: the pain or the memory of the fox's skull showing through its fur. She curled in on herself, shivering.

Wordlessly, Elspeth removed her cloak and offered it to Charlotte.

Charlotte hesitated. "You'll be cold."

"Not as cold as you, I reckon."

Charlotte took the cloak gratefully. She meant to say *thank you*, but what came out was, "Why is it so cold?"

Elspeth shrugged but offered no answer.

Charlotte curled away from her. Elspeth's kindness made her burn with shame. They'd hardly spoken a word to each other after her outburst yesterday, but Elspeth had built a fire, cooked them supper, and seen that Charlotte was comfortable when they'd bedded down for the night.

Charlotte hadn't even known what Elspeth was going to say. How she thought they were alike. It could've been anything, not that Charlotte could think of many ways they were similar and fewer still that might be signaled by the giving of a cap. But she'd thought so much lately of feelings she'd suppressed for decades that she'd jumped to conclusions.

She snuggled into the cloak, squeezing her eyes shut. "I'm sorry."

"What for?"

"For . . . for yesterday. For . . ."

She sputtered into silence. Elspeth shrugged again, but her brow puckered.

Then she straightened, tense as a bowstring. "Maggie?"

Charlotte glanced at her. "What?"

Elspeth's dark eyes snapped, but she spoke in a hushed voice. "It's *Maggie*."

Charlotte's heart sank. She tried not to picture what Maggie McIntire might look like, grown over like Brigid. "I'm—"

Elspeth slapped the driving lines with a laugh. "Maggie!"

Charlotte clutched at the seat. "What—"

"Just there." Elspeth pointed through the gloom. "Don't you see her?"

Charlotte squinted. Through the trees, a figure in white materialized. It looked in their direction, or appeared to. At this distance, in the frigid gloom, it seemed to have no face.

"Maggie," Elspeth called. "Christ. Couldn't've come home and eased us afore you come back out here?"

"Elspeth," Charlotte said, "I don't think that's Maggie."

"'Course it is. Always did like to wander the forest, never mind how dangerous it's got."

Elspeth urged the mule faster. Charlotte shrank into her seat. Facial features failed to materialize as they approached.

Here I am, a voice seemed to say, but the figure had no mouth with which to say it. The voice was layered; Charlotte jolted upright, certain she'd heard Arthur's tones.

The trees were too tight for the gig. Impatient, Elspeth

yanked the mule to a stop, vaulted from her seat, and sprinted toward the figure.

"Maggie!"

"Elspeth, don't."

Charlotte shrugged off the cloak and clambered down. She slipped, feet hitting the ground too hard. Pain spiked up her shins and jolted her knees.

The figure vanished.

Elspeth skidded to a stop. "Maggie?"

An unseen bird called overhead.

"Elspeth," Charlotte said through gritted teeth. "Come back to the gig."

"But—" Elspeth's fingers twisted in her shirt. "I saw Maggie. I swear I saw her."

"It was a trick. The forest trying to take you. Come back to the gig before it succeeds."

Elspeth let out a breath, but when she tried to turn back, she didn't move.

"Lottie?"

Charlotte retrieved her cane and limped as fast as she could toward Elspeth, gritting her teeth so hard her jaw ached.

"Lottie!"

"I'm coming." Charlotte meant to sound soothing but didn't manage it. "Hold on. What's—"

Through the undergrowth, she saw: Mud had Elspeth ankle-deep. It dragged her deeper before Charlotte's eyes. It was up to her shins. Her knees. The muddy pit bubbled like boiling water. The harder she struggled, the faster she sank.

Fingers crept from the mud, all in different states of decay. Mummified, some of them, others half rotted or skeletal.

Elspeth lunged for a nearby branch, but it broke under her weight. She thrashed, grasping for any vine, bough, or stone she could see, all out of reach.

"Lottie," she said, sounding panicked.

Charlotte had never expected her to panic, but those fingers, dozens of them, grasped at her, pulling her deeper. She was up to her hips in mud, twisting away from the fingers all around.

Charlotte swallowed but said firmly, "Stop struggling. You're making it worse."

"Sure, it was a picnic before," Elspeth ground out, but she did as she was told. Her fists clenched and unclenched at her sides. The fingers curled around her wrists. She wrenched away. "Help me!"

Charlotte nodded, hoping she could pull Elspeth free despite the sucking mud, the dead fingers, though every movement ached.

She held her cane out but hunched, almost dropping it, before it had gone far from the ground. All right. Not her cane. A branch—there were fallen branches all around. She picked one up, but it was so heavy she could barely lift it.

She wanted to cry. Six months ago, she might've been able to do something about this. She blinked back angry tears.

Think, she told herself. The mule. The mule could pull Elspeth free.

"Stay here," she said, hurrying back to the gig.

"Oh, aye, I was just about to run off," Elspeth snarled.

Charlotte's fingers were so stiff they hurt, but she fumbled with the gig's traces until they'd been loosed. She led the mule by the bridle back to Elspeth. It tossed its head, but Charlotte tugged it forward.

"Come *on*."

Elspeth was waist-deep now, panting. The fingers had vanished, but mud crept up her stomach and chest like it was alive. It turned aside when it reached the silver acorn on its chain, creeping around Elspeth's ribs like bands instead.

Charlotte flung the traces toward her. "Catch hold of these."

Elspeth lunged, grabbed them. She nodded, pale and shaking. "Hurry. They're still grabbing at me."

Charlotte slapped the mule's rump. The mule threw itself forward.

The traces slipped from Elspeth's grasp. Gasping, she looped them around her hands.

"It's all right," Charlotte said. This was just like a medical emergency, she told herself, even though it was nothing like a medical emergency at all.

A hand crawled from the mud and grasped the hem of her skirt. She yelped, beating the hand off with her cane.

"Leave go," Elspeth said through gritted teeth. "No point both of us getting pulled under."

"Don't be ridiculous," Charlotte snapped. "If you let go of those lines, I'll kill you myself."

Elspeth scowled but redoubled her grip, grunting and trying to twist free. Charlotte grabbed the mule's bridle. She kept whacking her shoes with her cane, felt that hand grabbing her again, though she was now out of reach.

Slowly, they pulled Elspeth free. Her waist appeared. Her hips. Her thighs. Her knees. Fingers came with her, grasping at her ankles. She kicked them. A nasty crack, and the fingers retreated.

With a horrible sucking sound, the mud released her. She went flying, crashing into the undergrowth.

The mule stamped and pranced, braying in alarm. Charlotte looped the driving lines around a nearby branch and stumbled in Elspeth's direction.

"Elspeth!"

She was on her back, breathing hard. Mud was crusted into her clothes, daubed onto her arms, splotched on her cheek and forehead. Charlotte wanted to kneel beside her and clean her off, but her knees protested. Instead, she leaned over Elspeth, hands gripping her cane so tight it hurt.

"Are you all right?"

Elspeth squinted at her. "Think I might've dislocated my shoulder."

Her voice shook. She sat up, arms around her legs, looking small.

"Can you," she started, and stopped. Charlotte reached for her, but Elspeth shook her head. "Don't say anything. Don't—You told me it was the forest, I should've known it was the forest, so don't say 'I told you so.'"

I wasn't going to sounded insincere even if true, so Charlotte said nothing. Elspeth sounded near tears.

Charlotte helped her up. They leaned against each other, exhausted and in pain. Charlotte unlooped the driving lines from their branch. In silence, the women returned to the gig, where Elspeth reattached the traces.

"Let me take a look at you," Charlotte said.

Elspeth shook her head. "Let's move, first. Feels like . . . like those hands are gonna come crawling out of the mud after me."

Charlotte glanced over her shoulder. The mud looked like nothing more than an innocent puddle in the midst of the undergrowth. She shuddered.

They clambered back into the gig and went on their way. The mule's ears twitched constantly. Charlotte made Elspeth wrap back up in her cloak, worrying over her; she was ashen, clammy.

After a long while, Elspeth rasped, "I thought it was Maggie."

"I know."

"Don't know why I thought it. Daft of me."

"It wasn't—"

"It was. You know it was." A pause. "Do you think she's alive?"

Charlotte fidgeted with John's ring. Maggie had gone missing over two weeks ago. Hard enough to believe Arthur might have survived, and he'd entered the forest so much more recently.

Elspeth glanced at her. Dried mud crusted her trousers and shirt. "You don't think so."

"I don't know."

Elspeth turned away. "That means you don't think so."

Charlotte bit back the urge to snap. "It means I don't know."

They drove on in silence. Elspeth shuddered periodically, batting nothing from her trousers. Charlotte resisted batting, because it was foolish. The fingers weren't there. She curled her toes in her shoes, focusing on that feeling instead of phantom hands reaching for her.

The gig bumped over a dip, and pain shot through her. Charlotte wished the forest floor were smoother. She rubbed John's wedding ring.

Elspeth glanced over, eyes lingering on the ring, and cleared her throat.

"Thanks. For that. Back there."

"It was nothing."

"They tried to get you, too. Could've left me."

"No I couldn't."

Elspeth bit her lip. "Well, thanks."

Warmth fizzed under Charlotte's skin. Foolishness. They grated on each other, she and Elspeth, and they'd known each other only a few days. Anyone with any decency would've done the same in Charlotte's place.

The trees opened up, the land fell away, and they were on a bluff overlooking the sea. Late afternoon sunlight stabbed orangely across the sky.

Charlotte's breath hitched at the sight. The forest was so close, so dim. Suffocating. The sea may have stolen Charlotte's husband, but she'd never lived out of its sight. She knew how dangerous it could be, but it was steady, too, predictable in its tides. It was the warp and woof of her life. She'd never slept without the roar of it outside her window as waves crashed at the bottom of the cliff.

The trees on the cliffside were stunted but mercifully free of black veins. A rowan with fernlike leaves turning orange and clusters of bright red berries clung to the rocks. The air was more seasonable here, not the biting cold of winter but chilly as a wind swept in off the sea. Charlotte breathed deeply, glorying in the wild, salty air.

"Missed the sea breezes more'n I thought," Elspeth said.

"Me, too."

"Might as well stop here a spell. Could use a rest, after . . . all that." Elspeth climbed out of the gig, unhitched the mule, and pulled a bag from under the cross-seat. "I don't know about you, but I'd rather take my chances out here than in there while we eat anyhow."

"Amen," Charlotte said fervently.

Elspeth yanked clean clothes from her bag. Pulling her muddy shirt off, she turned away, but not before Charlotte glimpsed the curve of a breast. Reddening, she turned resolutely the other way.

After they'd eaten, Charlotte examined Elspeth's shoulder. Since she'd unhitched the mule easily, Charlotte had already decided her shoulder probably wasn't dislocated, but she checked anyway. It wasn't displaced or swollen.

"Strained, I think, not dislocated."

"Hurts like balls."

Charlotte flushed at the language but said evenly, "I have an ointment that can help with the pain."

Elspeth lay face down on her cloak—sat up, made a face, and removed the silver acorn on its chain before lying down again—so Charlotte could pull her shirt up and massage ointment into her shoulder. She was wiry and muscular. No matter how Charlotte reminded herself Elspeth was another patient who needed help, she couldn't stop remembering that flash of breast she'd glimpsed.

She was relieved when she finished with the ointment. Surely because Elspeth's color and breathing had gone back to normal, and Elspeth had shown no other signs of shock.

Tugging her shirt back into place, Elspeth froze. "Lottie?"

"What?"

Elspeth turned around, jaw tight. She pulled her collar down, revealing her scar with its stitches.

Its edges were feathered in black.

Sucking in a breath, Charlotte pulled her closer to examine it. The thin blackness unfurled outward into veins before her eyes. Her heart stuttered. What had caused it? Elspeth had undoubtedly been infected by the sparrowhawk that had left her scar—but why had symptoms appeared after almost two weeks of nothing?

"It's just now?" she asked.

Elspeth nodded. "I'd swear to it nothin' was there before I lay down."

"Before you lay down . . ." Charlotte murmured. "Where's your acorn?"

"My . . . ?"

The acorn was on the cloak where Elspeth had left it. Charlotte considered it, remembering how the mud winding around Elspeth's body had avoided it.

"Have you taken it off since finding it? Until now, I mean?"

"Nay, sleep in it and everything. Wouldn't've taken it off just now if it hadn't been so uncomfortable lying on it that way."

"Here. Let me—"

Charlotte clasped the chain back around Elspeth's neck. The moment she'd done so, the black veins stopped spreading.

Charlotte let out a breath. "It worked."

"Veins're still there."

"They're not getting any worse." That wasn't much, but it was something. "I think the acorn has been protecting you, somehow, and that's why you haven't had any symptoms until now."

The wind picked up, colder now. Charlotte shivered, wishing she'd brought a heavier coat. She hadn't expected it to be so cold in early September, nor to end up on a bluff while wandering the wood.

"Here." Elspeth wrapped her cloak around Charlotte. "If you want it."

Charlotte snuggled into the cloak gratefully. "Thanks."

Elspeth nodded. She turned away to hitch the mule back up, but she kept pausing to touch her scar uneasily.

Perhaps the acorns were the answer. The sickness was magical, eldritch. Charlotte was certain the cure had to be magical, too.

One way or another, she'd figure it out. She wasn't about to lose Elspeth to the sickness as she'd lost so many others.

XXIV. In which Arthur takes a dunking

Arthur was no longer a person; he was a throbbing mass with a mangled neck. He drifted in and out of awareness. Ira's breathing, harsh. His own bones jolting with each step. Freya skittering, her cries. Ira swearing as she got underfoot, almost tripping him.

A new sound, a creaky voice like a tree that had learned to talk.

"Oho!" The voice twinkled. "My young lord! And with a human. How long's it been since the last one? Must be near as long since last I saw you."

"Not now, Maud. He needs in the pool."

The throbbing sharpened as Ira shifted Arthur in his arms.

Then, a strange sort of *nothing.*

Arthur opened his eyes.

He was surprised to find he could. He hadn't been able to do much of anything since the attack except gurgle and cough blood.

As far as he could tell, he was underwater, but it didn't feel like water. It was neither warm nor cool. It had permeated his clothing but didn't *feel* wet. It was silent but not in the usual way, where water pressed upon the ears, where the silence might be broken by movement or bubbles.

Small, smooth pebbles in green and blue and purple—like sea glass, though it could not be sea glass in this motionless water—layered the bottom of the strange pool. Its walls, or sides, or edges, Arthur couldn't see. He might've been alone in the middle of a great ocean, except that there were no fish, no seaweed, no anything. Just the sea glass, and the water, and his arms making no ripples as they windmilled.

That surprised him, too. He could move his arms. His legs. He no longer throbbed with pain, but thick redness ribboned lazily from his neck.

Panicked at the sight of his own blood, he sucked in a breath, panicked harder—then stopped, heart hammering, because no water had entered his lungs. He could breathe, in fact. His breath whooshed harsh and quick, matching his heartbeat.

Ghostly figures materialized. The faces of woodsmen, some with axes in hand; villagers, some of whom Arthur recognized, or thought he did, sour and pinch-faced. Blood pounded in his ears.

One figure pushed through the rest. The bottom dropped out of Arthur's stomach.

Dad? he said soundlessly.

George Throckmorton smiled, translucent and wavering. Arthur thought he'd remembered his father perfectly, but it seemed George's tip-tilted eyes were warmer brown than he'd pictured, his black hair thicker, his belly rounder. In a trance, Arthur swam toward him, arms and legs pinwheeling, the wound in his neck forgotten. He barreled into his father, gripping him tight in a hug that wasn't quite there.

Dad, he said.

George rubbed his back then pulled away. If he'd heard Arthur at all, he didn't acknowledge it. Just turned his son's head, wearing the same calm, serious expression he'd worn whenever Arthur had come home with a black eye and broken glasses as a boy.

He pressed a hand to Arthur's neck. Light spilled from his palm, so bright Arthur's eyes squeezed shut. When his father withdrew, he opened them. George nodded at him.

Arthur touched his neck but couldn't find where the creature had clung to him. His fingers came away clean, although he couldn't tell if that was because he was underwater or because he was no longer bleeding.

His eyes prickled. Dead for thirty years, in the middle of an enchanted pool in the forest, his father was caring for him. Arthur reached for him. The spirits faded away, one at a time, until, with a small smile, George faded, too.

Dad, Arthur said, but his father was gone.

Hands gripped his shoulders. Someone wrenched him from the pool. As his head broke the surface, his lungs flooded. He landed on his knees on a pebbled shore, spewing water.

"Arthur." As it had when Calyx had attacked, panic laced Ira's hoarse voice. "*Arthur.*"

He clutched Arthur's shoulders, but Arthur shook his head and coughed up more water.

"He's fine," the creaky voice said dismissively.

"He was down there for almost ten minutes. He's *human*, Maud."

"He's not bleeding anymore, is he?"

At the words, Arthur reached for his neck. It was uninjured.

Ira crouched before him, a hand tight on one shoulder. He touched Arthur's face carefully—so carefully, his touch a whisper like he feared he'd break Arthur open. With a pang, Arthur realized the fur on his hands had thickened and spread.

"Are you all right?" Ira asked. "Can you say anything?"

Arthur opened his mouth but merely wheezed. He coughed several more times, swallowed, and managed to rasp, "Dad."

Ira let out a breath. He released Arthur, rather to Arthur's disappointment, and examined his neck, his hands, and his face. The thin white scar on his cheek from his first morning in the vale was still there, but the pool had healed his more recent injuries from the brambles and the bruises Calyx had left. Freya conducted her own inspection before vigorously cleaning Arthur's wet hair.

Ira rounded on a tiny old woman who looked as if she'd grown from a tree. "You might have warned me."

She shrugged. "You wanted him healed. He's healed."

Arthur stared. Standing no higher than his knees, she had skin as brown and wrinkled as the bark of the yews behind her, a shock of white hair, and deep-set eyes as silver as the acorn around his neck. Her apron was stained green with moss. Several ravens hopped back and forth, looking up when she spoke.

She prodded Arthur with a stick. "So it was his cat that almost ate me, was it? I can't say I like him as much as the last one."

"The last . . . what?" Arthur asked.

"Human," Ira said. "George, she means."

"That's the one," the woman said.

Arthur bit his lip. How much better than him had the forest known his father? The sight of George in the pool had been a comfort, but he'd been no more than a ghost. None of the questions Arthur had had about him since setting out had been answered; it seemed they never would be.

"This is Maud." Ira nodded at their surroundings. "She's the guardian of the pool."

Trees with yellow-edged, fernlike leaves ringed banks pebbled with the same colorful stones as the pool's bottom. More ravens perched in their branches, preening or watching the proceedings of the four figures below with bright eyes.

The water's surface was silver and unnaturally still. Arthur shuddered, remembering how *nothing* it had felt.

Before him loomed a tangle of ancient yews. Their branches dipped to the ground, groaning like old men. Their mossy boughs formed a rough circle like the entrance to a fairy realm.

Arthur wasn't convinced they weren't. Maud and the still, silver water certainly seemed folkish.

"When we get out of here," he rasped, "I'm not going to find fifty years have passed without me getting any older, am I?"

Ira let out a huff of laughter. "No."

Maud prodded at his paws with her stick. "Do I get a proper greeting, now your friend is safe?"

"Sorry." Ira's expression softened as she pulled his face down to her level, pressing her forehead to his. "I've missed you."

"Long time," she said. "Long, long time."

Ira pulled away, gripped her hands, and peered into her eyes. "You're sure you're all right?"

She patted his cheek like a grandmother. A raven hopped onto his knee, nudging his hand until he stroked its feathers.

"If the sickness had come here, you'd know." She nodded at Arthur. "For one thing, your friend would still look like a fuath's chew toy."

Wet from the pool, Arthur shivered. Water dripped from his hair into his eyes and ears, his trousers chafed uncomfortably, and his socks—well, wet socks were basically the worst thing ever, evil spirits with horrible teeth aside.

Dislodging the raven, Ira knelt before him and pressed his hands to Arthur's cheeks. He swore.

He reached for the buttons of Arthur's shirt.

"What are you doing?" Arthur squeaked, with a strange thrill of panic.

"We need to get you out of these wet clothes." Ira's voice was a low growl, angry in a way Arthur had grown to recognize meant he was worried. "Maud, a fire."

She had one crackling within moments. *Magic*, Arthur thought.

Then he stopped thinking, because Ira yanked the shirt from his shoulders and reached for the button of his trousers.

With another odd thrill, redder than ever, Arthur pulled away. "I'm perfectly capable of that, thank you anyway."

Maud wheezed with laughter, a susurration like wind in the leaves. The ravens laughed with her; their laughter was unsettlingly human.

Nodding tightly, Ira went to retrieve their furs and bags. His limp was more pronounced than usual, now he'd carried Arthur through the forest.

Arthur peeled his wet socks and trousers off, racked with shivers. Maud dropped his knapsack at his side. He flushed, turning away; she laughed.

"Good heavens. Humans are silly about nudity. You've spare clothes in that, he told me. And a heating pad, which might do you some good once I warm it. Here."

She handed him a towel. Arthur mumbled a thanks and dried hastily. He yanked a spare set of clothes out of his knapsack; he'd packed two, his own and a set Ira had altered for him.

He re-dressed, picturing Ira on his knees, reaching for Arthur's trousers. He reddened again and tried to stop picturing it.

When he turned, fully clothed, Ira wrapped several furs around him. Their spring-flower scent enveloped him alongside their warmth.

"Thanks."

Arthur's teeth chattered. Underwater, the water had felt like nothing. On shore, it felt like *water* in all the worst ways.

"Sit here a spell." Maud dragged over a log larger than she

was so Arthur could sit by the fire. "You warm yourself till the soup's done."

She nudged him toward the log with her stick, then disappeared with his heating pad into a wizened stump nearby. A bit of bark like a tiny chimney smoked at the stump's top. White-spotted red toadstools grew around the door like a garden.

Freya crawled into the stump but came flying out followed by tiny kitchen implements and a string of what were unmistakably curses, albeit in a language with the same creaky quality as Maud's voice. Ravens went flying and settled back in the surrounding trees.

The fire stung Arthur's nose and cheeks, but the furs helped. Freya settled on his lap, purring deeply. That helped, too.

"I saw Dad," Arthur said in a hushed voice. "In the water. I saw Dad."

Ira sat beside him, removing his knee brace. "All the spirits of those who die in the forest end up here."

Arthur's stomach clenched. He huddled over the cat, stroking her fur, and reassured himself that he hadn't seen his sister in the pool. Surely that meant Charlotte was alive, wherever she was.

Ira massaged his knee, letting out a sharp breath. Arthur glanced at him.

"If you went into the water," he began, but Ira interrupted.

"It won't work on me."

"Not even . . ." Arthur gestured at his paws.

Ira smiled humorlessly. "Shall I show you?"

"I don't see how it would hurt to try. I suppose you can turn into a fish and not come out gasping."

Laughing softly, Ira undid the first toggle of his shirt, the second, but Arthur said hastily, "Never mind, no need to show me, if you say it won't work I believe you."

To his simultaneous relief and disappointment, Ira shrugged

and quit undoing his shirt. He didn't redo the toggles, though, and Arthur couldn't stop staring at his collarbones.

"Would it do anything for chronic pain?" he asked. "A human's, I mean."

Ira's eyes went over his body like he'd find pain mapped there. Arthur smiled faintly.

"Not me. Lottie's been . . . She took sick back in February. I've never seen her so ill. She coughed all the time, she was exhausted, hardly left her bed for weeks—when she did, she could barely make it across the room without getting short of breath—and that was on top of the aches and fever and all the usual things you'd expect. She's been so tired ever since, and in pain more often than not, so I just wondered . . ."

Ira shook his head. He looked calmer now than he had when he'd pulled Arthur from the pool.

"I asked Maud, once. Ages ago. I brought a sick human to her, hoping the water could cure him. I'd done everything I knew to do, but he kept getting worse. I wouldn't believe her when she said it wouldn't help. He died a few hours after I pulled him out of the water."

Arthur shivered, imagining Charlotte wet and cold and sicker than ever.

"Maud likes to say," Ira added, "that it's like expecting surgery to cure the common cold."

They fell silent.

Arthur's neck throbbed. He touched it, yelped when his hand throbbed, too. He examined his palm, expecting the injury from the brambles to have reappeared.

"I thought I was healed," he said anxiously. "Why does it still hurt?"

Ira dragged a hand through his hair. "It'll do that. You're healed, but you're not unchanged."

Maud emerged from her stump with Arthur's heating pad

and two bowls of a smoky vegetable soup. The scent tickled Arthur's nose. He took his heating pad and, when his neck stopped throbbing, downed the soup, starving after the trek through the forest and the fuath's attack.

The sun started to set; golden rays sliced through the trees. Their shadows dimmed the pool's silver glow, but Arthur gazed upward, grateful for a brief sight of blue after so many days in the vale with its snow and clouds. The first star appeared deep in the vault of the sky.

Maud brought him a second bowl of soup. Arthur ate more slowly this time.

"Eat up." Ira had finished eating and was now on his back on the ground, doing a series of knee exercises. Stubble shadowed his cheek. "We have a ways to go yet tonight."

"Ought to stay." Maud nudged his paw with her stick. He swatted her away. "It's safe here. You head out now, who knows where you'll end up sleeping."

Shaking his head, Ira returned to his exercises. "We can't afford the daylight. The faster we get to the heart of the wood, the better."

Arthur said nothing. He knew they needed to hurry, but he was cold and damp and sore. The pool had healed his wounds, but his hand and neck throbbed with phantom pain, his muscles ached from the day's walk, and something deeper in him ached from what he'd seen in the water. He pulled his father's watch from the pocket of his damp, discarded trousers and was relieved to find it ticking.

When Arthur had finished his second bowl, Ira put his knee brace back on and shouldered his pack. Arthur reluctantly shouldered his own. Freya wound between his legs until he bent and scratched behind her ears.

"Here." Maud thrust a vial of silver water into Ira's hand. "Might as well take some. That'un seems likely to need it

"Nothing to be done about it."

"No, surely there's—" Arthur cast his mind around. "You might shave it off?"

"I didn't pack a shaving kit."

"I did," Arthur cried, nearly tripping over himself in his eagerness to be useful.

He dug through his knapsack, throwing things aside. Freya glared as his heating pad narrowly avoided beaning her in the head.

"I— Oh, I've forgotten a mirror."

"Doesn't matter. I'm used to shaving without one."

Arthur produced the shaving kit with an air of triumph. "I know it wasn't strictly necessary, but I'm, er, well, it bothers me. The stubble coming in, I mean. Every time I've tried to grow a beard, it's come in all patchy and horrible anyway. Just another thing I'm bad at."

Ira sat on the ground, removing his knee brace. "What do you mean?"

"Oh, you know." Arthur gestured at nothing in particular. "I'm bad at all the things I'm supposed to be good at, that's all. The things men are supposed to be good at. I can't fish, or hunt, or chop wood, or repair the roof in such a way that the shingles don't go flying off the second there's another storm . . . I can't even grow a beard properly, and for that matter I don't shave very well, either. I always miss a spot. Or cut myself."

Arthur handed Ira the shaving kit. "The things I *can* do are things I'm not supposed to do, or not supposed to want to do, and all the rest I can't do. I'm really quite useless."

He said it matter-of-factly because it had so long been a fact of his life, but Ira frowned.

"You don't think much of yourself, do you?"

"That's not—I don't—" Arthur's skin prickled. "What makes you say that?"

Ira spread a fur on the ground and laid the items in the shaving kit out in a line. "That's the third time you've told me how useless you are."

"Well—I am."

Arthur tried to smile, to make light of it, but Ira, gazing at him earnestly, said, "You've been good company to me, you know."

Arthur pinkened. "I'm not sure being good company counts."

Ira ran a hand over his face, grimacing at the moss growing from below his eye to halfway down his neck. Glancing at Arthur, he added, "I wouldn't have left the vale if not for you. I wouldn't call that useless."

Arthur opened his mouth to respond, had no idea what to say, and closed it. He wasn't sure that counted, either. Freya lay at his side, close to the fire.

Ira settled into shaving uncertainly. What he was shaving was moss, not hair; it hadn't grown in the shape of a beard, and the new claws and fur made holding the razor awkward. He grunted as he nicked himself. A clump of moss dropped to the ground.

Arthur opened a book, but he couldn't help staring. Watching moss fall from Ira's face, as he held the blade with a hand that had become more like a paw, was oddly fascinating.

Nicking himself again, Ira swore: The cut bled this time. He set the razor aside, opened his hand, and sprouted a small leaf. He plucked it and smoothed it over the cut with a growl.

"This would be easier if my fingers were *fingers*."

"Would you like some help?" Arthur asked.

Ira held out the razor. Arthur sat beside him but rethought it immediately. The angle was terrible. And with Arthur sitting on Ira's left, every stroke of the blade would come as a surprise.

"Can I . . . ?" He shifted. "I think it will be easier if I'm . . ."

"Whatever you need."

Arthur straddled him. Ira swallowed as he settled into place.

Of course, Arthur thought. *I have just told him I always cut myself shaving.*

"I won't cut you," he said gently. "I promise."

Ira nodded. Arthur lathered him in shaving soap from his neck to his left cheekbone; he'd save the bit below the eye for last. He worked up one side of the cheek and down the other.

Closing his eyes, Ira tilted his head back. Wisps of hair had dislodged from his knot. Arthur tucked them behind his ear.

Along the jaw with short strokes to avoid nicks, because it was usually along the jaw that Arthur nicked himself, then on to the neck. Tilting Ira's head back farther, Arthur pulled his collar aside. To his astonishment, Ira's pulse thundered. When Arthur brushed his fingers against it, Ira's head snapped up so fast that Arthur almost fell off him. Ira steadied him, a hand at his waist.

Arthur swallowed; his mouth was dry, for unclear reasons. The chill autumn air, perhaps, although why it shouldn't have struck him until now he didn't know. Ira caught his wrist, gazing at him intently.

Arthur's breath hitched. He thought of his romance novels—of the heroine's first brush against the hero's skin, of moments of help and care more intimate than they'd been meant to be. Like the heroine with the love interest who was (anatomically) a monster, tending his wounds after a run-in with a monster hunter.

Anatomically? Arthur heard Charlotte saying, and he blushed. Perhaps Ira's wolfish anatomy extended up his legs, to his nether regions—

Arthur's blush deepened. He wasn't sure why he'd thought that.

He cleared his throat. "I have to get around your eye."

Ira released him. Cupping his chin, Arthur bent his head to the side. He liked the press of Ira's body against his, the way Ira did whatever he indicated. Something fluttered frantically in Arthur's chest.

He let out a soft breath. *Focus*. Examining Ira's scar, he bit his lip, the fluttering in his chest fading.

"Hold very still."

"All right."

Ira's voice was lower and hoarser than ever. Arthur's stomach dipped at the sound.

Focus, he told himself as sternly as he could (not very). He lathered fresh soap as close to Ira's eye as he dared. Getting shaving soap in one's eye surely hurt whether it was blind or not, and Arthur was afraid of reopening his scar, or expanding it.

More carefully than ever, he scraped moss away with the shortest strokes possible. The scar he left. Its white flowers had closed up in the darkness.

Arthur ran his hands along Ira's jaw, neck, cheek. Feeling for any moss he might've missed, he told himself, but Ira was gazing at him again and that made him want to keep doing it. Stomach swooping, he grabbed a towel and cradled Ira's head in his hand to wipe the remaining soap away.

Ira leaned into his touch. Face upturned, throat exposed. For one wild moment, Arthur pictured the women in nearly this pose on the covers of his novels and the flowing-haired, muscled men leaning over them, ready to kiss them.

His ears pinkened. What a silly thing to think of.

What was it about the simple act of shaving that made his brain run amok with silly thoughts tonight? Now he was remembering the old fisherman whose shack he had visited with his father on that impromptu house call. Not merely the fisherman touching his sick friend's hand, but the questions Arthur had asked his father about the two men afterward.

Why do they live with each other? Aren't either of them married?

George had hesitated. *They're old bachelors, son. Neither of them is likely to marry at this point. Cheaper to keep one house instead of two, so they live together.*

Arthur had been satisfied with that answer—though he'd wondered, later, why there had been only one bed in the shack. By then, his parents had gone to bed together, and he knew better than to disturb them. When everyone awoke in the morning, he'd forgotten about it.

He wasn't sure why he remembered it now, except that his brain had been doing funny things since Ira had handed him the razor.

He tossed the towel aside and scrambled away. "Done."

Feeling foolish, he wiped the razor clean and packed everything back into the kit. Behind him, Ira ran a hand over his skin with a sigh.

"Thanks."

Arthur's ears were pinker than ever. "It was nothing."

Ira lay back on his fur, clasping his hands behind his head. He grimaced as his antlers touched the ground, leaving space between his skull and the forest floor. Turning onto his side instead, he propped his cheek on a fist. His lips twitched.

"It was useful."

Arthur's face burned. "If you're making fun of me—"

"I'm not." Ira snagged his hand as he passed. "I'm not. Really. It was helpful. Thank you."

Arthur nodded. Ira let go, but his gaze lingered as Arthur put the shaving kit away.

"I don't like you because you're of use," he said.

"Then why?" Arthur asked, because he couldn't imagine another reason someone outside his family might like him. That was, in large part, the reason he tried so hard to be useful. The reason he felt so defeated by his uselessness. Surely, if only he were useful, people would see how worthwhile he was—surely he would *be* worthwhile—and he would have friends.

"I spent thirty years in winter." The moss was gone, but Ira's skin, where it had been, was faintly green. "When you came, it felt like spring. Like you woke me up."

Arthur opened his mouth but closed it again without saying anything. At every turn, he half expected Ira to stop speaking to him. Like he would suddenly realize what a crime it was for other men to be friends with Arthur.

Instead, Ira said things like that, as if they were obvious. As if Arthur was worth something to *him*, never mind what anyone else thought.

Arthur settled carefully on the fur, facing Ira but leaving plenty of space between them. Ira gave a small smile. It was really something, Arthur thought, how such a smile could light up his grim face that way.

"I feel like," Ira said, "when I'm with you, I'm . . . me again. Like the drawing. I'd almost forgotten how much I used to enjoy it, it's been so long since I had anything new to draw. But then there was you, making all those faces when you fixed the watch, and then while you were reading, and I just—it had been so long since I felt like I *had* to draw, but suddenly I had to."

Arthur prickled with embarrassment, imagining the expressions he might've made without being aware of it, but Ira's face was still illuminated with that small, soft smile. Ira, it seemed, not only didn't mind the way he sank into his work, or a book, but liked it. Arthur's embarrassment faded.

"But since it seems so important to you," Ira continued, "you *have* been useful. Like I said, I wouldn't have left the vale, if not for you. I . . ."

His smile faded. He picked at the fur.

"Seeing Maud . . . It's been a long time. If the sickness had taken her . . ."

He picked harder, digging into the fur with a claw. Arthur scooched closer and laid a hand over his wrist.

Ira stopped picking. "I just wonder what might have happened to her if I'd stayed away any longer. What's happened to all the rest of the forest. I've been so afraid to leave the vale, and now it's all . . ."

His fingers clenched. Arthur squeezed his hand.

"I'm the Lord of the Wood." Ira sounded bitter, whether because he preferred to be, as he'd said in the vale, *just Ira*, or because he felt like he no longer lived up to his title, Arthur didn't know. "I'm supposed to protect the forest. Instead I hid away in the vale telling myself I couldn't leave if the forest wouldn't let me. If you want to talk about uselessness . . ."

Arthur touched his cheek. Letting out a breath, Ira relaxed into his hand. That frantic fluttering was back, but Arthur ignored it, stroking Ira's cheek with his thumb. Before, Ira had seemed to want to make him feel better about himself; now he hoped he could return the favor.

"You're doing something now. That's all that matters."

Ira hesitated. "What if we don't make it?"

Sitting up, Arthur laughed ruefully.

"The only certainty is that nothing will change if we don't do anything. I know that much too well. Do you know, I've always dreamed of change—always. I spend so much time daydreaming about what our lives could look like if we moved to Port Lorne, or if I were a different man. But I never do anything about it. I always hope a change will drop into my lap—even that something dreadful will happen, and I'll be *forced* to change. Anything rather than do it myself."

He sighed, running a hand through his hair. A blond lock tumbled over his forehead. Settling beside him, Ira brushed it back into place.

"I'm always so afraid that whatever I do won't make a difference," Arthur said, "that I never do anything. When Mrs. Livingston offered to send me to Port Lorne . . . I should've said yes right away, but I didn't because I was so afraid. That's no way to make a change, is it?"

"Why now?" Ira's hand lingered at Arthur's temple. "Why this?"

"I'm planting a tree." Arthur smiled faintly. "I may not be able to do much, but surely I can do that."

"There's all the forest to get through first."

Arthur's smile faded.

"Yes. That is a concern, I admit, but—that's what I have you for, isn't it? Besides, it's not just me this time. At home, I told myself—well, I didn't tell myself anything, really. I pretended everything was fine. But if I thought about it, it really only made *me* unhappy. Moving to Port Lorne might have been good for the family, but I told myself it was too expensive to be worthwhile. At least in Seacliff we knew what our problems were. This . . ." Arthur let out a breath. "Lottie's in the forest, and I haven't the slightest idea how to go about finding her. But if I do this—I can make sure she's safe, wherever she is. And . . ."

He met Ira's gaze, briefly, with a smile.

"If I can help you, too, so much the better."

Ira's hand was warm against his temple. Arthur pinkened, thinking again of his romance novels and wondering why all of this felt so much like something out of one, except that they were both men.

He remembered driving through the village, how he'd felt with Cormac's thigh pressed against his. Perhaps that had something to do with it. But if so, Mrs. Young's angrily muttered words might, too. Arthur swallowed, trying to forget them.

Ira's hand trailed from Arthur's temple, down his cheek, to his jaw. His fingers curled in to keep his claws from Arthur's skin.

"Arthur, I . . ."

The fluttering in Arthur's chest pulsed like wings against his rib cage, more frantic than ever. He leaned closer, desperate to know what Ira might say. Afraid to know what he might say. Mrs. Young's words whispered at the back of his mind.

In the distance, a mournful howl sounded. Ira wrenched away. He rose stiffly and raised his head, animal-like, listening. His jaw tightened; his clawed hands clenched.

Whatever had been fluttering in Arthur's chest sank, weighing in his stomach. He sat up, drawing closer to the fire. Freya peered into the darkness with wide, golden eyes. Her tail lashed.

Another howl. Several. Ira swiped a hand through the air.

The earth rumbled. Trees burst from the ground. They bent toward each other, forming a protective ring around the fire. Freya growled at the disturbance but didn't seem to mind it as much as the howling.

Arthur, on the other hand, minded very much. With the earth quaking underfoot, he nearly fell into the fire. Yelping, he scrambled close to Ira, in the hopes the sudden trees wouldn't touch him, and sat trembling against his leg.

Ira touched the top of his head, but his eyes fixed on the trees. They grew together, trunk melting into trunk, branch weaving through branch, leaving a single opening overhead through which smoke could escape. When the howling sounded again, it was closer—but muted.

Arthur let out a breath.

Ira glanced at him, antlers gilded in the firelight. "Wasn't sure that'd work."

"I'm glad it did." Despite the apparent safety of their new shelter, Arthur pressed closer and dragged the cat into his lap. She grumbled in protest. "Do I want to know what's out there?"

Ira sat beside him. "They can't get at us, now. Get some sleep."

Arthur curled up uneasily with the cat in his arms. Did Charlotte have shelter for the night? Or was she out in the open, where any manner of eldritch creature might gobble her up?

Beyond the mass of trunks and boughs, the howling grew closer. Freya's ears swiveled in its direction, intent, which did not make Arthur feel any better. With Ira at his side, staring into the fire, Arthur drifted into dreams in which shadowy beasts clawed at their shelter, trying to get in.

XXVI. In which Charlotte discusses grief, even though she'd rather not

It was after dark when Charlotte and Elspeth stopped for the night, but the cliffside was brighter than the wood. They hadn't discussed their mutual desire to avoid the depths of the forest as long as possible, but Elspeth hadn't turned the mule in toward the trees, and Charlotte hadn't asked her to. It was colder out here, with the sea breezes blowing, but she had Elspeth's cloak. The stars seemed close enough to touch.

They made camp in a spot where the trees were farther back from the ledge, leaving a comfortable amount of room for the mule, the gig, a fire, and themselves. Two silver saplings stood nearby, which had been the deciding factor; Elspeth thought a sapling of the same kind as the first tree might lend them some safety.

One of the trees wasn't fruiting. In fact, it was tarnished, no different than the silver in Agnes Livingston's manor when it went too long without polishing. The other, however, was thick with acorns. Charlotte harvested a handful, hoping their magic could cure the sickness.

Before supper, she gave Elspeth a once-over to be safe. The hands in the mud had left fingerprint bruises on Elspeth's ankles and calves. Elspeth avoided the sight but told Charlotte not to bother about them; they didn't hurt. Her shoulder was sore but hadn't bruised or swollen. Her scar and stitches were still black, which made both women uneasy—though neither said anything about it—but the veins had spread no farther. So far, it seemed, Elspeth's acorn was protecting her from worsening symptoms.

Charlotte dug the glass vials from her medical kit, plucked several blades of grass, and sat by the fire. Besides the vial of black ooze, she now had one of bark she'd scraped from an infected tree and another of sickly gray leaves she'd picked out of the leaf litter. An animal sample would've been useful, but she didn't relish getting bitten or clawed by an infected beast, and she was unwilling to test anything on Elspeth until she'd tested it elsewhere.

Carefully, she uncorked the black ooze and dropped a blade of grass into it. She did the same to the vials of bark and leaves, then examined them all.

Black veins shot through the grass in the ooze. Did the ooze always infect things so quickly, or was the blade simply sucking it up like water? Charlotte wasn't sure. Either way, the grass looked infected now.

In the other vials, nothing happened. She leaned forward, holding them closer to the fire to make sure she wasn't missing anything. John's wedding ring glinted in the firelight.

Beside her, removing her boots, Elspeth nodded at it. "That was your husband's, then, aye?"

Charlotte reached for it automatically. With Elspeth watching, she tried not to rub the ring, but no sooner had she forced her hand away than it slipped right back.

"How long ago?" Elspeth asked.

Charlotte's eyes stung. "Eight years. Sasha doesn't remember him."

"You must miss him."

Charlotte's hand closed over the ring. "I try not to."

"Why not?"

Elspeth's gaze was unbearable. Charlotte busied herself putting the vials away, planning to reexamine them in the morning. Once her samples were fully infected, she'd think how to test the acorns' efficacy against the sickness.

"My father vanished in the wood thirty years ago," she blurted, resuming her seat, "and my mother was never the same after. Arthur carted me around the village, begging for jobs or money so we could eat. When John died . . ."

Her throat tightened. She'd talked about him so little in the past eight years.

She swallowed with difficulty. "For the first week afterward, it was all I could do to get out of bed. And Mam was so weepy about it, you would've thought it was her husband dead all over, instead of mine, and I thought about how little she'd been there for us after Dad vanished. My children weren't even as old as I'd been. I had to be there for them. But I couldn't be if I thought too hard about John, because every time I thought about him I missed him, and every time I missed him I fell apart, so I . . ."

God help her. If Elspeth asked what he'd been like, Charlotte wouldn't be able to stand it. She was already constantly close to tears since her illness.

Her chest ached like it might shatter. She remembered the first words he'd ever said to her, after three days in which he'd drifted in and out of consciousness while she'd tried to save his life, this beautiful stranger. *So you're real. Thought you might be an angel.* He used to bring her sea pinks when he came home after a long day of fishing. He used to ask Charlotte to teach him what she could about healing, because sometimes accidents happened on the boats and there wasn't time to get back to land for help. He used to whittle; he'd whittled her favorite whistle.

He used to sit up half the night wondering why he couldn't remember more of his life as a sailor. When he'd first come to, he'd had no idea where he'd been or how he'd gotten there; he'd thought he was nineteen, living back home with his mother. He didn't remember what ship he'd manned, what port he'd sailed from. He didn't remember leaving home, in fact, though he knew he'd always wanted to be a sailor. When he wrote home to his mother and received a letter back from a neighbor instead, they discovered he was twenty-five. He'd left home six years prior, shortly after his mother's death.

That had been the worst part, John learning his mother was dead. Or rather relearning, because he'd been there for it. He'd arranged for her burial. But after whatever had happened at sea, he'd forgotten it. Everything from that point in his life onward was gone.

Sasha, his mother's name had been. He'd asked if they could name the baby after her. Around the same time, they'd planted a rosebush at the corner of the cottage because his mother had always kept a sachet of rose petals in her pocket. Unable to remember his sailing days, John had tried to recreate as much of the life he could remember as possible. All knowledge of his life at sea came from letters exchanged with a friend back home, accepted as fact but never really remembered except in bits and pieces: the way he could work a boat almost instinctively; half the tune and lyrics to a shanty one of the crew had taught him.

Sometimes, Charlotte wondered how much more he might have eventually remembered if he'd lived longer. If one day he might've told the children stories about his days at sea the way her own father had once told her and Arthur about his travels through the forest.

She blinked, but tears dripped down her cheeks.

"Sorry," she said thickly.

Elspeth thumbed away her tears, then seemed to realize what she was doing and pulled away. "What for? Does a body good to weep now and then."

Charlotte laughed snottily, made a face, and accepted the handkerchief Elspeth offered. "I'm not sure about that. It doesn't feel good."

She wiped her eyes, blew her nose.

"You got more options, you know," Elspeth said. "It ain't a choice between letting your grief swallow you whole and never spit you back out, or refusing to feel it at all."

Charlotte's skin prickled. Between her mother and the rest of Seacliff, those had always felt like the only options. Just as it felt her only option regarding her pain and fatigue was to push through them, no matter how disabling they were.

Behind them, in the forest, something screamed.

Elspeth scrambled to her feet, bootless. The mule snorted and tugged at its line. Charlotte's heart pounded at the unexpected noise. She reached for the kettle, the nearest item that might do as a makeshift weapon.

Another scream. Elspeth's brow furrowed. "That sound like a horse to you?"

Charlotte stood slowly, clutching the kettle. "Yes."

A horse burst through the trees, wearing a bridle and the remains of a harness. Driving lines and traces trailed behind it.

It galloped right past them, toward the edge of the cliff. Charlotte gasped, but it pulled up short. It reared, still screaming. She stumbled back.

Elspeth approached the creature cautiously.

"Don't," Charlotte said, but Elspeth said in a low, soothing voice, "S'all right."

She raised her hands, like the horse was a constable who

might arrest her, and kept speaking in that low, soothing tone.

"There now, me beauty. S'all right. Let's have a look at you, eh?"

The horse shook its mane. Its eyes rolled, but it stopped screaming, and all four feet went back on the ground, to Charlotte's relief. Getting stepped on barefoot by a horse was hardly the worst thing that could happen to Elspeth, especially now they knew she had the sickness, but a broken foot in Shiftleaf was quite bad enough.

The horse quivered, jerked away as Elspeth reached for it.

"S'all right, now. C'mon." She stroked its neck. Its sides heaved, but it stayed put. "Good lad. Let's see whether we can't get all this nonsense off you."

She frowned as she removed the tattered remains of the harness.

"Looks like he come from a work camp," she said to Charlotte. "Probably been running around the forest for weeks on his own."

Charlotte's skin prickled. "Then what happened to the rest of the work camp?"

"By the looks of this harness, nothing good." Elspeth tied the horse beside the mule; they nosed at each other. "Around the time Maggie was supposed to've come home, a whole camp vanished in the forest. They were meant to pull up what's left of the first tree, but that's what we thought, they'd vanished. Well, when I come upon the first tree and Maggie's necklace—I found 'em. The workers didn't vanish. The forest ate 'em up. Turned 'em into trees, and other things. Could be the horse escaped all right, 'cept he's good'n'shook up."

Charlotte shuddered, thinking of Brigid Tierney. Her stomach turned. A whole work camp taken by the forest, turned into trees and who knew what else—

She squeezed her eyes shut, but she could picture them, an army of trees with branches like human limbs and knots like faces.

"Do you think," she croaked, "the tree where we found Arthur's shovel—what if—"

Elspeth shook her head. "You'd know it, if that tree'd been a person. Trust me."

Elspeth would know; she'd seen people-become-trees. But the images persisted. Charlotte breathed in and out slowly, in counts of four, the way she'd taught Arthur long ago to help him through bouts of anxiety.

"Lottie?"

Charlotte finished her breathing exercise. "I'm all right."

She glanced at the forest, half expecting another horse—or something nastier—to come tearing out and run them all over the cliffside. Elspeth examined the horse for injuries.

"Bit scratched up. Awful thin. No sign of the sickness, thank the Lord for that. One of us is enough."

She murmured in the horse's ear and kissed his nose. He nuzzled into her with a whicker. Elspeth scratched behind his ears, did the same to the mule, and resumed her seat by the fire.

"How did you do that?" Charlotte asked. "Calm him down like that?"

Elspeth yanked one of her bags toward her and went digging through it for nothing. To Charlotte's astonishment, she seemed almost embarrassed.

Clearing her throat, Elspeth said, "It's the horseman's word. So Gran says. She comes from travelling folk, though she never saw much of her kin after settling down since Granddad ain't a traveller. Don't know if you ever seen any travelling folk. I never heard of any campsites out this way, and no wonder, Seacliff being how it is. Reckon the villagers'd run 'em right off."

"The horseman's word?"

Elspeth reddened. "Aye. Always had an affinity for the beasts, even when I was little. Horses, mules, donkeys, anything equine, I've got a way with 'em. Gran says it's one of the travellers' gifts. Granddad says he's met plenty other travellers and didn't none of 'em have gifts except their skill as craftsmen, but Gran insists it's so. She gets a feeling about things, herself, and usually it turns out her feeling was right. Oh, Maggie used to get so jealous, she did, asking why she didn't have a gift . . . 'Course, that was afore she grew up and we all saw what a green thumb she had, but she always says it's nothing but time spent with green things, learning the way of 'em. Not the way I took to horses like a fish takin' to water."

"It sounds wonderful."

"Never did me much good. We never had so much as a donkey, and outside the family folks thought I was a freak. Gran, too, they used to say she was a witch, what with her intuition. She says she heard worse growing up, but—well, it wears on you, you hear it often enough."

"Is it magic, then?"

Elspeth shrugged. She fiddled with a spare shirt she'd pulled from her bag, shoulders hunched like she was remembering names that had been hurled at her long ago. Charlotte softened, wanting to make her feel better. She hadn't imagined Elspeth caring what people thought of her.

"My brother used to get plenty of that, too. He's . . . Well, he's Arthur. He's . . . he's so . . ." Charlotte hardly knew how to describe him, especially to someone not from Seacliff. "He's soft, I suppose. Not like the other village men at all. They've always disliked him. They used to say such awful things about him."

Elspeth stuffed her shirt back in the bag. "They don't anymore?"

Charlotte thought of the whispers the day Arthur had left,

the words about him that hadn't been *freak* but might as well have been.

"Not as much. Not to his face."

Elspeth scowled. "Might as well be to his face, if they're going to say it. Can't deck a man if he's only insulting you behind your back. Then folks think he's right, because what'd you get so upset about?"

"I admit it's difficult to imagine Arthur 'decking' anyone."

"What about you?"

"I should think it obvious that I've never 'decked' anyone, either."

"Not that. The villagers never talked about you that way?"

Her dark eyes were curious. Charlotte resisted the urge to look away.

"I made sure they didn't."

Elspeth nodded. "Explains a lot."

"About what?"

"You. How proper you are. That's it, ain't it? You think folks won't talk if you play by their rules."

Charlotte flushed, mortified. Bad enough, Arthur knowing it saddened her to talk about the family's losses, but he'd known Charlotte all her life. Elspeth clocking the reasons for her strict adherence to propriety barely a week after meeting was worse.

She opened her mouth but couldn't think of anything to say.

Elspeth grinned. "Speechless, are you? Never thought I'd see the day."

Charlotte glared at her, propriety be damned. "You—you absolute—"

"C'mon, Lottie. I'm sure there's a nasty name in there somewhere."

Nothing rude enough to satisfy Charlotte's annoyance would agree to come out of her mouth.

"Numpty'd do," Elspeth suggested.

Charlotte expelled a breath, angry to need a suggestion, but she took it. "You *numpty*."

It did make her feel better.

"Bravo," Elspeth said with a smile. "Maybe next time you can reach for the big guns, if'n you know any worse words than that."

She was quite the most annoying person Charlotte had ever met.

XXVII. In which Arthur runs afoul of the wild hunt

Arthur's neck and hand ached. That was the first thing that was wrong.

The second was that morning light spilled through a split in the tree trunks.

The third was that Ira was gone.

Arthur scrambled to his feet. "Ira?"

Silly to call out like that. He could see the entirety of the shelter Ira had grown for them last night, a ring of wood with a smoke hole overhead—and a thin, splintered gap in one side.

Arthur scooped up the cat, who had been curled into a sleepy ball by the remains of the fire. She grumbled, but he clutched her to his chest, afraid to be alone with that gap in their shelter. He remembered hearing—dreaming about?—claws scraping, something trying to get in.

"Ira?" he called, slightly louder.

No response.

Arthur examined the shelter for a groove or any indication of a door. He prodded at the wood around the gap. It opened, leaving a wider hole through which he stepped out into the forest.

Sunlight stabbed into his eyes as leaves shifted overhead.

His foot caught on something; he righted himself against the shelter.

Glancing down, Arthur gasped. A massive arrow was lodged at the base of a tree. Long, ragged claw marks dug into the shelter's sides, all around the splintered wood.

Panic welled in his chest. "Ira?"

No one answered, but the surrounding greenery was flattened. Clumps of limp, blackened flora trailed around their campsite and away.

Arthur buried his face in Freya's fur, focusing on her weight and warmth. On his own breathing, *in for four, hold for four, out for four.*

"All right. We can find him. We'll just follow his trail. Then . . ."

Then, he didn't know. Ira might have gone anywhere. Even back to the vale, despite his talk last night.

A small part of Arthur hoped he had. If Ira had returned to the vale, Arthur had no choice but to retrieve him. Of course it would mean restarting their journey, but the vale was safe.

Stop it. They had to replant the tree. For Ira. For Charlotte. Arthur couldn't give up and go back to the vale, no matter how tempting. No matter how difficult it was to *choose* to do something, how much easier it was to go on doing nothing. To tell oneself there was nothing to be done.

Arthur let out a breath, rubbed the rowan cross in his pocket for comfort, and set Freya down. Crawling back into the shelter, he stuffed the fur they'd slept on into Ira's pack and shouldered it, hefted his own (significantly lighter) knapsack in his arms, and said, in a voice meant to be firm and determined but not quite either, "Come on, Freya."

They set off, following the trail of dying flowers. A horrible, sibilant sound that reminded Arthur uncomfortably of whispers accompanied them, seeming to come from the trees.

He reached again for the rowan cross. It had become a habit in the last few days, the same way Charlotte so often fiddled with John's wedding ring.

In the distance, howling.

Arthur stopped in his tracks, heart hammering. Not howling. Baying. Somewhere ahead, a pack of hunting dogs, like the hounds Agnes's husband used to keep. Arthur had never liked that sound; to him it meant some innocent rabbit or fox was about to be killed for nothing more than a rich man's leisure.

This was worse. The baying had strange, ragged edges, laid over with screams and the moaning of a great wind.

Arthur swallowed. That sound raised the hair on his neck, made him want to run as fast as he could in the other direction. Ira's trail of dying greenery led straight toward it.

Freya twisted around Arthur's legs. He picked up the nearest stick and held it like a sword. Just in case.

"Let's go," he said in a strangled voice.

The baying grew louder with every step. Arthur's legs shook, but he pressed on until Freya's fur stood on end and his ears rang. His hands itched to cover them, but he didn't.

Through the trees, by a stream rushing white and loud, a dozen hounds circled. They were sleek and black, the size of cart horses, with gleaming red eyes. Their strange, ghostly forms melted and reformed each time they lunged toward their prey.

It was a stag. A glorious red deer with a golden mane and autumn leaves twined in his antlers, and a scarred eye and a twisted leg. A hunting knife was lodged in his right shoulder.

Arthur's mouth went dry. He flung himself around the back of a tree, trying to quiet his breathing. Freya hunkered down in the underbrush.

"Easy, boys," a gruff voice called. Arthur shivered. Like the baying, the voice had an edge to it. "He got me, sure enough, but I'll live."

Arthur set the packs down, gripped his stick, and edged around the tree. The speaker was a man, more or less. The way Ira normally was, both man and not. He was tanned and weatherbeaten, like Seacliff's fishermen, in fine hunting clothes like old Mr. Livingston used to wear—but they were the color of storm clouds. So was his hair; so were his eyes, which fixed on Ira hard and flinty. When he moved, no matter how little, it was sudden and forceful, the way storms appeared out to sea in autumn.

A bow and quiver were slung over his shoulder, or Arthur thought so, but they *glimmered.* One moment there, the next gone. Arthur couldn't be sure he wasn't imagining them.

"Been a long time, *lord*," the huntsman said, flinging the title at Ira like an insult, in that same howling voice.

His cheek was scratched. Instead of blood, silvery-white fluid dribbled from it, looking like nothing so much as light. Ira gazed at him warily, flanks heaving.

"Felt your power waning, so I have. Once you kept my hunt muzzled, but no longer."

The huntsman reached over his shoulder, and now it was certain: A great black bow was in his hands, with a massive arrow—like that at the campsite—nocked to the bowstring.

Arthur sucked in a breath. The nearest hound cocked an ear, but Arthur focused on its master. The huntsman raised the bow, drew the string to the corner of his mouth—

Arthur leaped out from behind the tree with a yell, striking a hound with his stick. It yelped but wrenched the stick from his hands. Arthur went flying and crashed to the ground at the huntsman's feet.

The huntsman lowered his bow in surprise. "What's this, now?"

Arthur got to his feet shakily, grabbed his stick, spent a pathetic moment wrestling the hound for it, and gave up. He stood between stag and huntsman, though one arrow for him and one for Ira would finish them both. The stag snorted, his breath hot at Arthur's shoulder.

"I'm his friend." Arthur's voice trembled. "And I'm not going to let you kill him."

The huntsman snorted. "Friend? Pet, more like. He's always had a soft spot for humans, the devil take it. Wouldn't let the wild hunt run in these parts for hundreds of years. Now . . ."

He fingered his bow.

Arthur swallowed. "If you kill him, the forest will die. There won't be any hunting left."

The huntsman thundered laughter. Arthur shuddered.

"There's always hunting to be done," the huntsman said, in a soft voice even worse than that wind-like howl. "There's always prey to be found."

He gripped Arthur by the throat, his hand cold and hard as iron.

"What a fine specimen you'll make."

Arthur scrabbled at his fingers, but the huntsman lifted him into the air like it was nothing, until Arthur's toes barely scraped the forest floor.

With a screech, Freya darted past the hounds. She sank her claws and teeth into the huntsman's arm.

Swearing, he dropped Arthur and tried to shake her off. Arthur collapsed on the ground. He massaged his throat, wheezing.

The hounds rushed their master. They yelped and barked and bayed, leaped and snapped at the cat crawling all over the huntsman's body.

"Go!" Arthur gasped at Ira, but the stag flinched when Arthur reached for him. His nostrils flared, his ears twitched, so *deerlike* that Arthur's heart sank.

I start to lose myself, he remembered Ira saying. *To feel like a real beast, instead of just looking like one.*

"Not now," Arthur moaned.

"*Enough!*" the huntsman roared.

Freya went flying. The hounds scattered, zigzagging back and forth. The stag's sides quivered, but he was frozen with fear.

Arthur snatched at the leaf litter for another stick—a stone—anything that might help, however little. His fingers curled around a rock the size of a gull's egg.

The huntsman straightened, breathing heavily. He looked less like the fishermen in Seacliff now. The storm cloud color of his hair and eyes and clothes seemed to have bled into his skin. More silvery-white light seeped through the claw marks Freya had left.

Arthur threw the rock at him. It missed wildly.

With another thunderclap laugh, the huntsman raised his bow and trained it on Arthur. "What was that supposed to have done?"

He stepped closer, his arrow jabbing the hollow of Arthur's throat. Arthur whimpered.

The stag gored the huntsman with his antlers.

The laughter died on the huntsman's face. His mouth fell open, but no sound came out. Light spilled from his stomach.

His hounds yelped, vanishing one after another as if they'd never been. Light spilled faster and faster, blazing until it enveloped the body in a white sheen. When the light faded, the huntsman was gone. Silvery-white ribbons dripped from the stag's antlers, vanishing before they hit the ground.

Arthur's chest heaved, but he reached for the stag. "Ira?"

The stag gazed at him warily, ears twitching. Arthur withdrew, uncertain. He'd hoped Ira had remembered himself when he'd killed the huntsman, but if he had it had been short-lived.

"Ira. It's all right. It's me."

Was it the magic? The forest not understanding that the ways it tried to protect him hurt him instead? The hunting knife in his shoulder? Whatever it was, Arthur had to remind Ira of himself and dress his wound.

His stomach turned. Blood. There would be blood. More than what was already smudged into the stag's mane.

Arthur took a step forward. The stag tensed, and he stopped.

"Ira, please."

The stag eyed him. Letting out a breath, Arthur sank onto his haunches.

"What now?" he asked Freya.

XXVIII. In which Arthur faces several things he'd rather not, including a stab wound and feelings

After a long, long while, the stag lay down beside the cat. She didn't seem to bother him, but he eyed Arthur warily. Progress nonetheless, until the stag started worrying the knife. Arthur gritted his teeth. His neck was throbbing, and Ira nudging the knife in his own shoulder made it hurt worse.

Arthur's thighs burned from squatting there for so long before the stag's ears stopped twitching at him. A while later, Arthur's legs numbed. His back spasmed; he shot his hands out, narrowly avoiding toppling over.

The stag's ears twitched again, but his head dropped to the ground. Taking a bath beside him, Freya was unconcerned. She seemed to mind Ira considerably less in this form.

Arthur was not unconcerned. He crawled toward the stag and stroked his neck. The stag's nostrils flared, but he didn't kick or bite or try to escape.

"That's it. It's me. Please, Ira. You've got to remember."

Arthur lifted the stag's massive head into his lap. He didn't know what to do. It had taken so long just to get Ira to let him approach.

"Please. Please remember."

The stag snorted. Eyes brimming, Arthur laughed, kissed his nose, and pressed their foreheads together.

A moment later, his forehead was resting against Ira's.

Arthur laughed once more and burst into tears. Ira kissed his brow and lay back in his lap. His hand went to his shoulder. The knife. Bile rose in Arthur's throat.

"How long's it been?" Ira asked.

Arthur wiped his eyes. "Too long. I thought I'd lost you."

Ira scrubbed a hand over his face. His ears had not changed back with the rest of him; they were a deer's.

"I don't . . ." Ira's brow furrowed. "I don't remember what happened. The hunt ran last night, the wild hunt. It was the dogs we heard. The Huntsman collects human souls."

Arthur shivered and held him tighter.

"I was afraid he'd find you. But I don't . . ." Ira's voice was uncertain. "I remember feeling scared and mixed-up. That's it. I don't remember changing. It's a haze until you kissed me. I don't remember the rest."

Arthur stroked his forehead.

"You're all right now." His voice trembled. "That's all that matters. What do we do about . . ."

He touched the hilt of the knife gingerly. Ira let out a sharp breath, then, to Arthur's horror, yanked the storm cloud blade from his shoulder.

"What are you doing?" Arthur cried. He didn't know much about stab wounds, but he was reasonably certain one ought not to yank objects out of them like that.

The knife vanished in a wisp of light. Blood reddened Ira's shirt. Arthur wanted to throw up.

"Had to come out eventually," Ira said. "Where's my pack?"

Arthur's head spun. "You're lucky I thought to bring it, you muppet! Why didn't you ask before you pulled a knife out of your shoulder?"

Ira's mouth twitched.

"It's not funny! Where's that water?"

"What water?"

Arthur pulled Ira's pack toward him and dug through it. "*The* water. From Maud's pool."

"I told you, it won't work."

"It might."

"It won't."

Arthur ignored him. The water had healed him; it would heal Ira. It had to heal Ira, because otherwise Arthur would have to patch him up, and Arthur was the worst possible person to have to do so.

He found the vial and uncorked it with shaking fingers.

"Arthur. Don't waste it."

Arthur tilted the vial, letting half the water splash onto Ira's shoulder before Ira touched his wrist.

"Don't waste it."

Too late, Arthur wondered if he ought to have wiped the blood away first—removed Ira's shirt—done something in preparation. He corked the vial.

Freya settled on Ira's stomach, purring. Ira let a clawed hand rest in her fur. Arthur's chest tightened: The hand was hardly a hand anymore. It was entirely covered in fur now, except for the palm, which had thickened and darkened into a metacarpal pad.

Arthur tore his eyes away and waited, clenching the vial of water. Blood seeped through Ira's shirt.

"Why isn't it working?" Arthur fought with the cork. "Maybe if I use the rest—"

Ira closed his eyes. "Don't. It won't work."

The cork popped. Arthur almost dropped the vial; water

sloshed onto the ground. He swore and spilled the rest over Ira's wound.

"Arthur—"

Arthur had used up the last of it. Nothing.

"No—"

"I told you."

"But—" Arthur's voice pitched upward "—what do I do?"

"Needs cleaning first."

Ira sat up, grimacing, and clawed at the toggles of his shirt.

"Don't do that," Arthur said. "I'll cut it away."

The worst injury he'd ever dealt with had been a broken arm, when Sasha had fallen from a tree in the churchyard. There had been no blood, though seeing Sasha's arm at that angle had made his stomach turn, and of course Charlotte had taken care of it. She'd simply had him hand her things, tell Sasha stories to keep her calm, and hold the girl's arm in place so she could splint it.

Arthur undid the toggles of Ira's shirt, then sawed across its shoulder with a knife from Ira's pack. The bloody fabric was at once damp and tacky. His head spun, but he clenched his jaw. Peeling the shirt away, he had to stop. The injury was neat, not torn or jagged, but that was little comfort with Ira's blood welling beneath his fingers.

Arthur swallowed, closed his eyes, and breathed deeply until the wave of dizziness passed. Ira needed him. It would be like caring for Charlotte on her worst days. Except for the blood.

As he thought of his sister, Arthur's skin prickled. She might be having a bad day this very moment. What if she lay down, weary and aching, and the forest swallowed her up?

He focused back on his breathing. He couldn't do anything for Charlotte right now, but he could do something for Ira. And once Ira was taken care of, they could continue on toward the heart of the wood—they could replant the tree—they could make sure Charlotte was safe, wherever she was.

Arthur reached for Ira's canteen, thought better of it, and found a small bottle of gin amidst the bandages and ointments in the pack. The sight of them calmed him. They reminded him of Charlotte, the composed way she went about binding wounds and treating illnesses and birthing babies, no matter how dire the situation. Surely Arthur could channel her now. Her surety and calm, if not her knowledge. Not this knowledge—though afterward, if he didn't muck it up, he could use the knowledge he'd gained in the last six months to alleviate the pain.

Arthur splashed gin on the wound. Ira winced.

Wadding the ruined shirt up, Arthur pressed it to Ira's shoulder. Ira's nostrils flared, so reminding Arthur of how he'd been as a stag that he was relieved all over by Ira's transformation back.

"Isn't there anything that can prevent you from becoming so . . . deerlike?"

"I can stay in the vale."

Arthur bit his lip. "Perhaps you should go back."

Ira covered Arthur's hands with one of his own. "Perhaps we should."

"Not *we*. You. If the tree isn't replanted—not that I suppose I'll get very far on my own, but—"

A small V formed between Ira's brows. Arthur wanted to smooth it away, but he focused on keeping pressure on the wound.

"I'm supposed to protect you," Ira said.

"Protecting me isn't worth your life."

Ira's eyes flickered over his face. "Maybe it is."

Something small and soft bloomed in Arthur's chest. His own life wasn't worth much at all; Ira's was far more valuable.

Suddenly, he wondered if there was a reason he'd never found the right girl.

Ira's shoulder had stopped bleeding. That was something. Letting out a breath, Arthur dabbed dried blood away, packed the wound clumsily, and bandaged it. Freya cleaned Ira's hair as if for moral support.

"I'm afraid it's not done well," Arthur said, but Ira nudged the cat away, sat up, and brushed a lock of hair back from Arthur's forehead. Arthur shut up, the tips of his ears pinkening.

"I'm practically as good as new."

Ira got to his feet, grimacing. He leaned more heavily on his left leg than usual. Whatever exactly had happened last night, it had been hard on him.

"We should move on. The wild hunt has gotten us off track."

Arthur's heart sank. "How do you know?"

"I feel it. The forest's magic. Like a map in my bones. You could tell, too, though, with the acorn. Here."

He held out a hand—almost a paw. Arthur pulled the acorn over his head. Ira curled Arthur's fingers closed over it.

"The acorn knows where it came from. It's attuned to the heart of the wood, what's left of it, and with it you can feel the stump. That doesn't move, no matter how much the other trees do."

His fingers tightened on Arthur's.

"Can you feel it?"

For a long moment, there was only the warmth of Ira's hand on his. Then, concentrating on the silver acorn, Arthur felt it, like a bright ball of light to the north. A snarl of magic like the tangle of greenery in a wood at the height of summer. The acorn was *alive* with it in a way Arthur hadn't noticed until now.

"Oh."

The corner of Ira's mouth turned up. "As long as you have the acorn, you can find your way through the forest."

He doubled over. Freya twined around his legs, mewling.

"Ira?"

Ira breathed hard through his nose, straightening slowly. "M'all right. The tarnish."

His jaw tightened with pain. Moss spread across his face.

"It's growing back." As Arthur watched, white flowers burst into bloom in Ira's hair. Moss crept down his throat and toward his collarbone. "It's growing faster."

Ira shrugged, but a muscle tightened in his neck, from the pain or the growth Arthur didn't know. "It'll get worse the farther we go."

Arthur lurched closer, scraping moss away with his fingers. Freya scrambled out from underfoot.

"How can you be so calm about it?"

Ira flinched and placed a clawed hand over Arthur's, stilling his frantic scraping.

"We're two days from the heart of the wood, and with the detour, we're almost as far from the vale, too. I'm sunk no matter what we do. It doesn't matter."

"It matters to me. Surely there's some way to . . ."

Arthur's fist clenched tight around the acorn. Something so small, yet it could save the whole forest if only they brought it to the place it had come from.

"I wonder . . ." He unfastened the chain. "May I?"

"It's the only thing protecting you."

Arthur gave a small smile. "I thought you were doing that."

Ira bit his lip but nodded. Arthur fastened the chain around Ira's neck, fingertips brushing against his skin.

The moss stopped growing. Ira's jaw relaxed. He ran a hand over his face with a sigh.

Letting out a breath, Arthur smiled. "It worked."

Ira's brow creased. Arthur didn't understand why; surely he ought to have been happy, or relieved.

"What's wrong?"

"Nothing, I just . . ."

Ira's gaze roved over Arthur's face, up to his eyes, down to his mouth, in a way that made Arthur's stomach swoop. He touched the hollow of Arthur's throat, fingers curled to keep his claws away. Arthur shivered pleasantly.

He wondered whether Ira felt the things he did. The things he thought he did. It was so much like the things the heroines in his books felt for the strange, exciting men who rescued *them* from danger, but he wasn't sure he was meant to feel this way about another man. He'd never known it to be like this, either in books or real life, could remember nothing like it in any story his father had ever told or any romance he'd ever read.

He touched Ira's cheek with a finger, thinking again of the old fisherman and his friend. In three decades, he'd never wondered what had become of them.

Now he wondered a great deal. About himself. About things about which he'd never thought to wonder, because he'd thought his parents and his novels had taught him everything he needed to know about the way love was supposed to be.

Arthur traced a finger along Ira's scar, down his cheek, to his jaw. Eyes fluttering closed, Ira slipped a hand through Arthur's hair to the back of his neck, drawing him closer until their foreheads rested against each other. Until they shared the same air.

"Arthur," he breathed.

His breath was warm in Arthur's face, sweet with the scent of flowers. Arthur was seized with a wild urge to kiss him.

Mrs. Young's muttered words sounded in his head. He pictured the expressions on the faces of the other men as he and Cormac drove through Seacliff together. Cormac stiffening beside him, creating space so their thighs no longer touched.

Flushing, Arthur pulled away.

"Arthur?"

Arthur shouldered his knapsack with such force he almost knocked himself over. "We should go. You said we're off track."

"Yes. Of course."

Ira shouldered his own pack. He gazed at Arthur, impassive. Then he said, "This way," and headed into the trees. Arthur let out a breath and followed, hoping he could leave all the confusing things he was feeling there beside the stream.

XXIX. In which Charlotte and Elspeth get into a scuffle with some trees

The glass vials, like Elspeth's scar, were unchanged by morning. Charlotte examined them as Elspeth packed up camp, hitched up the mule, and tied the horse to the back of the gig. The grass in the vial of ooze was still veined; the grass with the infected bark and leaves was still healthy. Touching infected plant matter—being closed in with it overnight—had not transferred the sickness to a healthy plant.

Charlotte packed the vials away with a frown. That was information, she supposed, but not much, since she'd never seen the sickness pass between people anyway. She suspected the grass in those vials would go on uninfected.

The next step was seeing whether she could coax the sickly blade back to health with the silver acorns she'd harvested. But how? Plant matter could not ingest medication. Creating a topical might work, but she thought that dubious—more likely to heal an injury than cure an illness. As they trundled along the cliffside, she was deep in thought, turning over possibilities.

Elspeth glanced at her occasionally but said nothing until afternoon. After a warm and golden morning, clouds had drawn in dark and gray. Out to sea, the sky was black. The promise of a coming storm etched itself into Charlotte's bones. The pain distracted her from her thoughts about curing the sickness, not that she'd been getting anywhere with that anyway.

"Think we're getting close," Elspeth said.

"How do you know?"

"The acorn. It feels . . ." Elspeth sucked in her cheeks, considering. "I don't know. More alive. It likes this place. The Lord of the Wood must be nearby. Aside from the first tree, I don't know what else in the forest'd make it feel this way."

The forest was to their right, but only a few scraggly trees, like the rowan they'd camped by last night, appeared in their path. As they went on, those trees distorted into fantastical shapes. Here was one with roots high and bent like knees. Here one twisted like a man looking over his shoulder. Here one with a knot open in a silent scream.

Shuddering, Charlotte drew closer to Elspeth. They were sharing the cloak this morning. Elspeth had offered it to Charlotte, but she'd been shivering herself. Remembering how Agnes had described the progression of Gracie's sickness, Charlotte worried. Elspeth had been all right, despite the forest's unseasonable cold, until her sickness had shown up. Rather than mention that, however, Charlotte insisted they share. Sea breezes could flay a body to the bone, this time of year. The sickness need not have anything to do with it.

The misshapen trees increased in number the farther they went. Elspeth's mouth pressed into a grim line.

"'Member how I told you you'd know it if that tree was a person?"

Feeling sick, Charlotte nodded. Elspeth jerked her head at the surrounding trees.

"Who do you think they were?" Charlotte asked in a hushed voice.

Elspeth shrugged, but her brow puckered. The mule halted, stamping a foot. His ears twitched frantically, swiveling in every direction. At the back of the gig, the horse snorted and tossed his head.

Elspeth threw off the cloak, climbed down, and stroked the mule's nose, murmuring in his ear. Slowly, his ears stopped twitching, but he shook his head. She sighed.

"What is it?" Charlotte asked.

"He don't want to go any farther. Spooked by them trees." Elspeth patted his neck. She was shivering again; Charlotte handed the cloak down to her, but Elspeth waved it away. "No matter. I'll lead him on foot. C'mon now, there's a good lad. I'll be right alongside you the whole way."

She led the mule by the bridle. The strange trees closed around them.

The gig kept sticking, lodged between trunks or caught on roots. Each time, Charlotte feared it would remain stuck. Elspeth seemed afraid of the same thing; she went from muttering curses as she freed it the first three times to working in silence, glancing around shiftily.

Wind hissed through the leaves. Charlotte's skin prickled. The hissing seemed almost to form words. Incomprehensible at first. Then—voices. They might have been coming from the trees, but they sounded unsettlingly familiar. Like Arthur. The children. John.

Find me.

Help us.

You didn't save me.

She swallowed, her stomach twisting. Silly; obviously she was imagining things. It was no different than the evil spirit that had lured Elspeth into the muddy pit yesterday. She held on to that thought, but now she saw faces, too, the half-imagined features of everyone she'd ever loved.

They're not real. She clenched her fists until her nails dug into her palms. *It's the forest's trickery.*

The gig paused, but Elspeth made no move to unstick it. She shrank into the mule's side, eyes squeezed shut.

Breathing deep, Charlotte climbed down with the cloak tight around her and her cane in hand. The voices whispered in her head.

You can't save us. Why did you let me drown? You'll never find me. You should've saved them.

Clenching her jaw, she touched Elspeth's shoulder. Elspeth jumped.

"Elspeth?"

Elspeth shook her head.

"Not real," she muttered. "Not real, not real, not real."

"No," Charlotte agreed. "No, they're not real. Come, now."

She'd never seen Elspeth like this. Even when mummified fingers had been dragging her into the mud, Elspeth had been sarcastic. Realizing she had the sickness had made her uneasy, but she'd gone about her business anyway. Now she pressed against the mule like she hoped to melt into him. At the back of the gig, the horse whinnied.

"Elspeth."

Charlotte gripped her shoulder, but Elspeth shrank away. Charlotte let go.

Voices crowded her head. She barely heard herself when she spoke, but she fought to keep her tone calm and gentle.

"Elspeth, it's all right. It's me. I'm here."

Elspeth eyed her warily. "Are you—are you real?"

"Of course I'm real," Charlotte snapped.

You should've saved them, the voices taunted her. *You can't save them.*

Faces melted in and out of trunks, but Charlotte focused on Elspeth. Elspeth who was flesh and blood, Elspeth who annoyed her, Elspeth who had plenty reason not to like her but looked after her anyway.

Charlotte touched her back. "Of course I'm real. You feel that, don't you?"

Elspeth swallowed but nodded.

"I don't know what you're hearing," Charlotte said, "or what you're seeing, but it's the forest playing tricks on us. That's all. That's not real. I'm real, Elspeth."

John's face appeared in a nearby tree. Charlotte's heart stuttered. The long lashes, the high cheekbones, the chin and nose like Sasha's—

You left our children, he said mournfully, and he faded away.

Charlotte squeezed her eyes shut, her grip tightening on her cane. *In for four, hold for four, out for four.*

"It's not real," she repeated irritably. "It's a trick. Of course it's not real."

Elspeth's fingers curled around hers. "You're real."

Charlotte let out a breath, forced her eyes open. "That's right. Come on, now. Let's take a step forward, all right? That's it. Now another one. And once more."

A step at a time, she walked Elspeth through the trees. Elspeth kept one hand clenched tight on hers and the other on the mule's bridle. The mule snorted but, to Charlotte's relief, neither he nor the horse seemed subject to the same trickery as the women. Voices sounded in Charlotte's head, but focusing on her own voice—"Next step, that's right, now another"—and helping Elspeth dampened them. Whenever another face appeared before her—Sasha, Jonas, Arthur, her mother, her father, her husband, a patient she had failed to save—she squeezed her eyes shut, tightened her grip on Elspeth's hand, breathed *in hold out*, and snapped, "It's not real."

The spot over her left eye jabbed her, threatening a migraine, but she gritted her teeth and squeezed Elspeth's hand

and limped onward. Her joints ached with the coming storm. Normally, Charlotte ignored her pain, until she couldn't; now, she focused on that, too, because the pain at least was real.

Through the trees, she glimpsed indistinct whiteness. She sucked in a breath, hoping it wasn't some new danger.

"Just a few more steps."

Elspeth clenched her hand so tight it hurt.

They stumbled. Then, as if the trees had spat them out, they were free. The whispers silenced. The faces vanished.

The unpleasantly human trees had gone still. Elspeth let go of the mule, dragging a hand through her braid. The horse and mule pranced a short distance away from the trees, the gig swaying between them, but she didn't seem to notice.

"Are you all right?" Charlotte asked.

Elspeth was pale and gasping, eyes fixed on the trees like she still saw faces in them. Setting her cane aside, Charlotte draped the cloak around Elspeth and took her hands.

"Elspeth."

Elspeth's gaze snapped to her.

Charlotte squeezed her hands. "Breathe with me a minute."

Elspeth swallowed, but she followed Charlotte's breathing through several cycles. By the time they finished, her body had relaxed. She sighed.

"Thanks," she whispered.

"Are you all right? You seemed . . ."

Elspeth shook her head. "It was awful. Them faces."

"Voices, too, I suppose."

"You heard 'em?"

Charlotte smiled faintly, unwilling to admit it had been real. "Well, I heard something."

Elspeth let out a long breath. "But you got us out of it. You didn't let 'em get to you. I was . . ."

Charlotte's skin prickled. Elspeth's hands were tight on

hers, her voice soft, but Charlotte didn't see how she'd done anything special. She was practical and stubborn and could sometimes put those qualities to good use; that was all.

She pulled away, reaching for her cane. "It was very upsetting. I hope you don't think less of yourself for reacting like anyone would."

Elspeth smiled crookedly.

"That's about the nicest thing you've yet said to me." She caught the mule by the bridle and stroked his neck. "Animals seem all right, anyway. Where are we?"

They turned to survey their surroundings.

It was a little woodland vale, caked in snow—except for flowers blooming in a slab at the foot of a headstone before them. The headstone was carved with yarrow instead of the usual things. Charlotte touched it, wondering whether it was the Lord of the Wood's and, if so, who had buried him.

She hoped not. If the Lord of the Wood was dead, there was no hope of finding their siblings. They could either wander the wood until their dying day or go home defeated and pretend Arthur and Maggie might one day emerge unharmed.

Her forehead throbbed. Now the danger was past, the memory of the faces and voices tumbled through her head.

Nonsense, she told herself, but the voices sounded discordantly.

"Come on," Elspeth said. "Let's see what's what."

xxx. In which Charlotte gains a new pet

The snow was up to Charlotte's ankles, dampening her socks. She was colder than she'd been all day, but the bite of snow distracted her from the memory of the faces and voices.

Nearby, a blue tit alit on a branch and burst into song. Elspeth laughed, running a hand through her hair. Charlotte let out a breath; the forest had been so silent. Whatever this place was, the sickness hadn't touched it.

A tangle of greenery dropped into the snow before them, startling the mule. Elspeth quieted him but drew closer to Charlotte. The greenery stretched over them menacingly.

Almost menacingly. It wobbled as it grew, half frozen, the tips of its leaves and vines black with cold.

Then it sneezed: curled in on itself, shivered violently, and exploded. Vines, leaves, and flowers unspooled around it. Elspeth dragged Charlotte back with a curse, but the plant thing flopped in the snow. It clicked miserably, so softly Charlotte almost thought she was imagining it.

Handing Elspeth her cane, she approached.

"Lottie," Elspeth said sharply, but Charlotte crouched in the snow with difficulty.

A tendril shot up, swaying in her direction. It curled back in a moment later, shivering. The plant creature reminded her of Freya. Not as she was now, but as she'd been three years ago: a scrawny kitten hiding under the Throckmorton-Prentices' chicken coop, hissing when Charlotte found her.

Charlotte held out a hand. "It's all right. We won't hurt you."

"What're you doing?" Elspeth said incredulously.

"I think it's cold."

The tendril uncurled, reaching for Charlotte's hand, and made contact. It wrapped around her wrist.

"That's right," Charlotte said soothingly.

"*We're* cold, Lottie. Leave it be. It's some sort of eldritch—something."

Various appendages dragged themselves toward Charlotte, seeking warmth. The plant creature pulled itself into her arms and snuggled into her. Charlotte wasn't sure what it was, exactly, but it seemed harmless now.

"Why, it's nothing but a houseplant. Let's take it with us."

She rose on joints stiff with cold. The plant creature slung down several vines; the extra support stabilized her.

Elspeth stared.

"What?" Charlotte said.

"Who *are* you?"

Charlotte flushed, but she cradled the greenery in her arms. It had been the same with Freya. The children had been over the moon about their new pet but seemed to have expected her to turn it out of the house because she wouldn't let the cat sit on the table. Arthur had been astonished she'd brought a cat inside in the first place. Did people think she was heartless?

"Let's get on with it, shall we?"

Elspeth shook her head but handed Charlotte's cane back without further objection. As they rounded a bend in the snow, the unmistakable signs of habitation distracted her entirely from Charlotte's new pet.

Everything was half buried, like no one had been here in some time. The little stone well and matching oven. The table with crates jumbled beneath it. The laundry line. Scattered stools not unlike one Arthur had made for Charlotte in recent months, albeit more soundly constructed.

In the face of a massive, bulbous oak tree ahead was a door.

"We made it," Elspeth breathed. "We're here."

"How do you know?"

"It's like Gran's stories. 'Cept for all the snow, I guess."

Releasing the mule's bridle, Elspeth stumbled toward the door as if in a trance. Charlotte hesitated, wondering whether she should see to the animals, but went after her. Tendrils unfurled from the greenery to telescope in the direction of the tree.

Elspeth wrenched the door open.

"Elspeth—"

She'd already disappeared inside. Charlotte heard her clomping around, calling *hello*, so it seemed she hadn't met an untimely end. Nonetheless, Charlotte was cautious as she ducked inside.

The house was tiny, a single room except for whatever might be up the low set of stairs curving around the back, and disappointingly empty. But no dust had accumulated. The coals in the woodstove, though dark and cold, had been burning recently.

Elspeth disappeared up the stairs. Charlotte staggered toward the bed in the corner and sank onto it, stroking the greenery's fronds. The throbbing over her left eye jabbed at her. She winced.

Then she saw the tool kit.

It lay on the bedside table, so familiar that Charlotte forgot where she was and what they were doing. She opened the kit and took stock. A collection of miniature screwdrivers. A case opener. A cleaning cloth. A straight, nickel-plated brass bar with a thick middle and thinner, notched ends, one smaller and one larger. She could never remember the name of the latter, but it was undoubtedly Arthur's: The drip of paint on it had been there for years.

A tendril reached for the tool kit and poked at it. The plant creature clicked faintly.

"Lottie?"

She blinked. Elspeth had come back from wherever the stairs led and was frowning at her.

"All right?"

Charlotte closed the tool kit. Her chest buzzed. "Arthur's been here."

"How do you know?"

"This tool kit. Watch-repairing tools. They're his." Charlotte clutched the kit to her chest, half expecting him to pop out of nowhere. The plant creature curled over her arm. "I'd know them anywhere. He's been here."

Elspeth examined the stove. "Can't've been gone long. Someone's been here within the last couple days, that's sure enough."

Charlotte's hope at finding the tools faded.

"He was here. He must have been safe—" if he'd had his tool kit out, though she couldn't imagine how he would've come by a watch to fix in the middle of the forest "—so why did he leave?"

The only reasons Charlotte could imagine Arthur would have left a safe place, after running into danger in the forest, were bad ones. Something, or someone, had chased him out. Or killed him. Turned him into a tree. There had been so many of those twisted, terribly human trees. Would Charlotte even recognize her brother, if he had joined their ranks?

You'll never find me, his voice whispered in her head.

Her fingers dug into the tool kit. She breathed deeply, *in for four, hold for four, out for four.* The plant creature crept over her shoulder, shivering, and draped around her like a cloak.

"Hey, now," Elspeth said. "You know he was here. That's something."

Charlotte laughed wetly.

"I mean it." Elspeth crouched beside her. Her eyes flickered toward the plant creature, but she let it alone. "Maybe he's headed back to Seacliff. Lord of the Wood might've gone to take him home, same as he did for my gran and your da all them years ago."

"Maybe." Charlotte wanted to cry. "But I could have found him here and gone home myself. Or I could've trusted he'd make it back and stayed home in the first place." Realizing what she'd said, she flushed. "That is—"

Elspeth smiled crookedly. "S'all right. You could've been home and I could be looking on my own. Looking on my own was the plan anyhow, till I met you."

"I didn't mean—"

"S'all right." Elspeth dropped into one of the armchairs by the stove, wrapping herself tightly in her cloak. "Know you're none too fond of me. We're working together, that's all."

She seemed morose, and no wonder. Charlotte had been so astonished to find a positive sign of her brother that she'd forgotten all about Elspeth's sister. Now she'd implied she'd rather not be traveling through the forest with Elspeth at all. Not that she wouldn't rather—but that was because of the forest, not Elspeth, though Elspeth was irritating and sarcastic and dreadfully informal. She was kind, too, in her deeds if not always in her words, and among the trees she'd been . . . Charlotte didn't know what to term it. Scared. Vulnerable.

Charlotte abandoned the tool kit and joined Elspeth by the stove, the greenery swaying on her shoulders. The armchair she sank into offered a small amount of comfort. After three days in a gig, over bumpy forest paths, a proper chair was a relief.

The plant creature slid from Charlotte's shoulder, formed into a ball, and rolled toward the stove. Finding the coals cold, it clicked fretfully.

"Maybe your sister was here, too," Charlotte said.

Elspeth let out a long breath, gazing into the dark stove. "Don't have to tell me lies to make me feel better. She's been gone for weeks. I know it's just as likely I'm looking for a corpse."

Her face twisted. Maybe she'd heard her sister's voice in the trees. Taunting, telling her, *You'll never find me*, the way Arthur's voice had taunted Charlotte.

Charlotte wanted to comfort her, but that one sentence had been her attempt. Silly to have said it. It was the sort of thing Arthur might have said, and that was well enough for him.

She didn't like to sugarcoat things, though. If that's what he did, she couldn't do the same. If he believed the pleasant things he said, she wasn't sure how he managed it. Denial, maybe, and that certainly didn't do anyone any good.

Maybe not, then, seemed a worse thing to say. And if Charlotte had already considered that Maggie might have been here but taken everything with her when she left, Elspeth must have considered it, too.

She drummed her fingers on the arm of the chair. "I don't dislike you, you know."

"Sure, it's a fact I'm just about your favorite person."

"Don't . . ." Charlotte turned toward her. "It's true that . . . Well, you do annoy me often enough."

"There you are."

"And we're very different," Charlotte said, ignoring her. "And goodness knows you have no sense of propriety."

Elspeth snorted, but it seemed an improvement over the way she'd been staring into the stove. Charlotte heartened.

"But you've been good to me," she continued. "Helping me home when we met, even though you didn't have a clue who I was, and I know I was rather belligerent about it. You've been sharing your cloak with me for two days. I know you've been freezing today, but you wouldn't take it unless we shared."

"Right," Elspeth said—acknowledging the borrowed cloak, Charlotte thought, but Elspeth crouched beside the stove to build a fire.

The greenery, sitting nearby in a tight ball, loosened slightly. Tendrils trailed toward Elspeth, turning between her and the stove.

"Don't eat me or nothin'," Elspeth said to it.

Charlotte's lips twitched. Despite herself, she was, in fact, fond of Elspeth.

"I'm not sure what to make of you, I suppose. That's all."

Elspeth paused in the middle of sticking a log in the stove. "Gran and Granddad, neither. Must've been fifteen the first time they caught me with a girl."

That hadn't been what Charlotte meant, but she didn't respond.

"They've come around pretty well in the last twenty years," Elspeth continued, returning to the stove. "But times are it happens Granddad tells me about some nice man he's met who'd provide for me good if I ever wanted to settle down, or Gran asks if she can use me to pin up a dress she's taking in or letting out for someone, and once I'm all pinned in she makes a big deal about how beautiful I am."

Charlotte resisted the urge to speak, because what had threatened to come out, foolishly, was, *You* are *beautiful.*

"They're all right, most times, but then I got all them cousins hanging around, and God Almighty, the way they bang on about me being an old maid, or how I could find a nice widower if I wanted one, or how I'm giving menfolk dirty thoughts on account of my trousers showing off the shape of my legs—"

Charlotte flushed. She hadn't noticed that herself, when they'd met. Now that it had been said, however—as Elspeth bent forward to light the stove—

Less her legs and more her buttocks, which certainly were shapely.

Of all the ridiculous things to think.

"Maggie's about the only one who's ever known what to make of me." The fire flickered to life. The tangle of greenery relaxed, its tendrils turning toward the warmth. Elspeth shut the door, adjusted the damper, and sat on the floor. "Or she don't care if she hasn't. She was twelve when she made me my first pair of trousers. Gran wouldn't then, and Granddad wouldn't give me any of his old ones. It's mostly his, what I wear now. Wore 'em down eventually. But that was my first pair, the pair Maggie made."

"She's older?"

Elspeth shook her head. She wrapped her arms around her knees.

"That's the thing. She's always taken care of me, Maggie has, never mind she's the younger. Think I got it into my head over the years she don't need taking care of, but I worried about her going to Seacliff with Bess—tried to talk her out of it, if you can believe it. Must've been the first time in my life me and Gran and Granddad were all right alongside each other agreeing on something. Oh, she was mad. She's always spent plenty time in the wood, ever since we was girls. Said she'd be fine if anyone would, and why didn't we trust her, and she was going with Bess anyhow, not by her lonesome. Didn't much like it when I said she'd be coming home alone, the way they planned it."

Elspeth rested her chin on her knees.

"Think that made her maddest of all. She thought for sure I'd be on her side when she told Gran and Granddad she was going, and I wasn't. I was working when she left with Bess, but I figured when she come back I'd make it up to her. Only she didn't come back. And now we're here and she ain't, and the Lord of the Wood ain't, neither."

She let out a long breath. "I don't know what to do."

Charlotte bit her lip. She didn't know what to do, either, certainly not about finding either Arthur or Maggie, or the Lord of the Wood, for that matter. She knew she ought to comfort Elspeth, but she didn't know how to go about it. Comforting anyone older than her children always seemed impossible. In medical scenarios, she was more likely to provide a sense of calm and surety than comfort, unless there was good news—but then it wasn't her, was it, but the news itself that was comforting.

Well, if she could only offer a sense of calm and surety, that was what she'd do.

"We wait," she said firmly. "You said it looks like someone was here within the last couple of days. It must be the Lord of the Wood who lives here—this is the only place we've been where the trees aren't infected. Perhaps that—whatever it is—" with a nod at the tangle of greenery "—is his pet."

She longed to sit beside Elspeth, but if she sat on the floor she wouldn't be able to get up.

"I think we're safe here. We can catch our breath, rest for a couple of days. The Lord of the Wood has to come back sometime. We'll give it a day or two. If he's not back by then, we'll consider our options."

Elspeth ran a hand through her hair. Strands came loose

from her braid, falling messily around her face. "Guess a rest'd not be so bad."

"Of course not. It'll give us time to recover from . . . from whatever happened back there," Charlotte said, unwilling to mention the trees, "and I can keep an eye on your symptoms, and the animals can have a rest, too."

Swearing, Elspeth rocketed to her feet and stalked out, probably to take care of the horse and mule. They'd left the creatures tethered to the gig outside.

The room warmed with the fire flickering in the stove. Charlotte sank deeper into her armchair, grateful for a break from the gig and its jolts, the forest and its dangers. The plant creature crept into her lap and sprawled across it like a cat, leaving blackened vines and fronds on the floor behind it. New anatomy grew from it, green and fresh.

Charlotte stroked a tendril, her mind drifting back to her brother's tools. Her head dropped into her hands. It was better than what Elspeth had; Charlotte had *some* proof Arthur had been here, alive and safe.

Her eyes stung anyway. She couldn't stop thinking how close she might have come to finding him here. How close he might have been to coming home when she left.

Elspeth stumbled back inside in a whirl of cold.

"Snowing like anything," she grunted, kicking her boots off. Her teeth chattered. Finding a lone fur hanging on a hook by the door, she tugged it on over her cloak. "Couldn't find a shed or anywhere to put the animals, but around the side of the house was more sheltered, so I guess that'll have to do."

Charlotte didn't respond. She'd meant to boil water for tea and dig her painkillers from her medical kit, but, as usual, she'd waited too long to take care of herself. Now she wanted nothing more than to fall asleep in the chair, if she could, with the pleasant weight of the plant creature in her lap. But her thoughts kept cycling between how recently Arthur must have been here, what might have happened to him by now, and the terrible echo of his voice in the trees. Her head and joints ached so badly she couldn't have fallen asleep anyway.

"All right, Lottie?"

Charlotte pressed her palms to her eyes. "It's this weather. It's wreaking havoc on me."

"Had you in its grips all day, hasn't it?" Elspeth considered her. "You was all kinds of quiet this morning. Pain, was it?"

"Yes."

"Why didn't you take anything for it?"

Charlotte didn't answer. Because they'd been traveling, and she hadn't wanted to stop just to find her painkillers, let alone long enough to light a fire for tea. Because she'd been too busy fighting her brain, considering ways to administer silver acorns to infected plant matter, so caught up in treating the sickness that her own pain had gone untreated.

Because she felt like she ought to be able to handle the pain, push through it, even though that was, frankly, a ridiculous and unrealistic expectation.

Shaking her head, Elspeth brought Charlotte her medical kit. "You got something in here for it, I trust. You best take it before you feel any worse."

Charlotte dug two tablets from her kit and downed them.

Elspeth nodded, satisfied. "Good girl."

Charlotte flushed without quite knowing why. She cleared her throat. "I have a tea in here that can help, too, and it might warm you up. Boil some water, won't you?"

Elspeth did so. While the water boiled, she swept up the blackened plant matter the creature had left on the floor and threw it into the fire.

By the time the tea was ready, the tablets had softened the edges of Charlotte's headache. She picked at the leftover stew

Elspeth had found in the icebox, aware she needed to eat but unequal to it. *Better than nothing*, she told herself, and imagined Elspeth telling her *good girl* for each spoonful she managed to swallow. Then she stopped imagining it, because doing so made her flush again.

Out the windows, snow swirled thick and white. But the armchairs were comfortable and the stew was delicious and the air had warmed and the tea had lessened the ache in Charlotte's joints, though the spot above her left eye jabbed at her periodically. In her lap, the plant creature hummed, apparently asleep. Wrapped in the cloak and fur, with her hands around a second mug of tea, Elspeth had stopped shivering so much.

It wasn't home, but all things considered, it wasn't terrible.

"Getting late." Elspeth got up to wash the supper things. "You can take the bed. I'm gonna sit up anyhow. Think about things."

Charlotte hesitated. Elspeth seemed all right now, but she'd been so cold all day. Even if she hadn't been—after three days on a gig jolting through the forest, the incident with the mummified hands, and the one with the twisted trees—Charlotte thought they'd both be better off in a bed than in an armchair or (God forbid) on the floor.

Rising, she deposited the plant creature beside the stove. The humming broke off; the creature curled into a ball, and the humming resumed.

"We could share," Charlotte said.

The corner of Elspeth's mouth turned up. Charlotte regretted offering.

"Share, could we?" Elspeth said. "I don't know. Sounds mighty improper."

Charlotte was mortified.

"Fine," she snapped. A tendril unspooled from the plant

creature, turned in her direction. "Sleep in an armchair and wake up with a crooked neck for all I care."

"I didn't say no."

Scowling, Charlotte turned away. She stroked the tendril with one finger, hurried across the room, and quickly changed into her nightclothes and braided her hair. She curled up in bed, as close to the wall and as far from Elspeth as possible. Chuckling, Elspeth adjusted the fire. The plant creature clicked at her.

"None of that, now. I'm the one keeping the fire going, so you best be nice if you want to stay warm."

The clicking subsided—almost. It didn't stop but quieted, the way Sasha muttered when Charlotte caught her doing something she wasn't supposed to.

Charlotte lay awake for a long time, listening to Elspeth putter about the room doing she knew not what. She nearly turned over to find out, but the thought of Elspeth catching her looking was enough to stop her. Irritated, she focused on breathing until her whirling thoughts slowed and her body relaxed.

She was almost asleep when she felt Elspeth slip in beside her. Not long afterward, Elspeth started snoring. Charlotte buried her face in her pillow. If she closed her eyes, she could almost pretend she was asleep in her bed back home, years ago, with John slipping in beside her after a Saturday night at the pub, snoring at her back.

XXXI. In which Arthur gets cozy in a cave

With the coming storm, Ira's limp had been worsening for hours, but they'd kept going. Never mind the dropping temperature and gusting wind. But when it started raining, so hard they were soaked within minutes, Ira's pace slowed. He stumbled; Arthur caught him.

He had to shout over the rain. "Can't we get out of this wet?"

Jaw tight, Ira nodded. "There's a cave not far from here."

He leaned on Arthur the whole way. Fat raindrops pelted them. The cat mewled pitifully; fur matted with rain, she looked like a drowned rat. Hopefully Charlotte found shelter, too, Arthur thought. Storms always worsened her pain, but at least she'd be dry.

A handful of silver saplings grew at the mouth of the cave. Half of them were tarnished. Arthur bit his lip, but with the way Ira leaned on him he didn't think they could make it any farther.

The cave was small and sandy, well ventilated with a large opening in the ceiling forming a chimney, but mostly dry. Ira collapsed against a stony wall, nostrils flaring. He ripped off his knee brace and stretched his leg out, working his knee with his fingers, then dug through his bag for ointment.

Arthur shivered with cold and wet, but he scoured the cave for tinder. Naturally, there was none. He braved the pounding rain again, though the wet twigs and branches he gathered probably wouldn't light. With rain-smeared glasses, he stumbled back toward the cave. His right foot sank into a puddle, soaking his shoe and sock.

When he returned, arms full of soggy wood, Ira said, "I could've just—"

He waved a hand. A shrub sprouted, its leaves blooming and changing color and falling off all at once, until it was bare and dry.

"Oh," Arthur said in dismay.

Ira's mouth twitched, and that was something. The acorn still kept fresh greenery from creeping across his face. That was something more.

Arthur abandoned the wood he'd collected and built a little tent near the cave's chimney from the shrub's branches. It took him a while to get it to light, but he managed. He sat back with a small sense of accomplishment he didn't often feel unless he'd recently gotten a clock working. Freya rubbed against him in gratitude, settled by the fire to bathe until she was dry and fluffy, and curled up for a nap.

Now his damp clothes, which stuck to his skin in a deeply unpleasant way. Arthur dug dry clothes from his knapsack, wishing his journey hadn't involved quite so many wet socks. He tucked himself into a corner to change, further wishing he had a towel. The idea of putting dry clothes on his wet skin so they could stick right back to him was nearly as bad as being in wet clothes in the first place.

He wrung water from his hair. Droplets spattered his glasses, not that it mattered since they were smeared from the rain outside. He wiped them off on the dry shirt from his knapsack, grimacing, and dressed.

When he turned around, Ira was wrestling with his own wet clothes. Arthur reddened, but Ira didn't seem to be getting anywhere. His thick, furry fingers could no longer work the buttons and toggles.

"Would . . ." Possibly this was a terrible idea, but Arthur asked anyway. "Would you like some help?"

A brief pause. Ira nodded.

Arthur knelt before him, unbuttoned his trousers, and peeled them off. His stomach swooped as Ira's bare thighs appeared, then his calves, transitioning smoothly from human legs to wolf paws. Ira's chest heaved.

Arthur's tongue stuck in his throat, but he said, "About earlier . . ."

Ira looked away. "You don't need to explain."

"No, I—I do. I do."

Arthur had been thinking about it all day. Wondering why he cared so much what the villagers would think when he was deep in the forest and they'd never liked him anyway.

Standing, he reached for the first toggle of Ira's shirt. "It was nothing to do with you. It's . . . This is all very—very new to me. Everything about it. For God's sake, I've hardly even courted anyone. None of the young women in the village has ever been interested, and I've never . . . I thought I hadn't found the right girl. And now . . ."

He let out a breath, feeling foolish for never realizing. All those years longing so desperately for Cormac to notice him. Stumbling through every interaction with any man with nice eyes or an air of kindness. Attraction. Crushes. He'd read about love endlessly, dreamed about it, longed for it, yet he'd never understood his own feelings.

How could he have known, when none of his books showed romance as existing between anyone other than a man and a woman? When every marriage and courtship he'd seen had been the same? Only that single fisherman and his friend, living together in a shack with a single bed, might have given him the idea that romance could look different. But it hadn't, because his father had offered another explanation.

He wondered what his father would say about this now, or his mother. He wasn't sure he wanted to know, not that he'd ever find out.

What about Charlotte? His stomach twisted, but she wasn't here. For the moment, Arthur could imagine she'd understand. He finished undoing Ira's toggles in silence.

Ira shrugged out of his shirt, grimacing as he worked it over his injured shoulder. He was naked, now. Firelight gilded the feathered curve of his shoulders. His buttocks. His antlers and paws. His gnarled right leg, a map of scars.

He was beautiful.

He tugged furs from his pack, settled one on the floor of the cave and wrapped another around his shoulders. Arthur sat beside him.

"And now?" Ira said softly.

Arthur tried and failed not to let his eyes follow the trail of hair down Ira's stomach. Nether regions: thoroughly human. For now. He glanced hastily away, running a hand through his own damp hair.

"I'm not sure," he admitted. "But I know I care about you. And I find you—you're very—well, I think you're beautiful. And I wish I hadn't pulled away earlier."

Ira's eyes flickered over him. Fingers curled, he touched Arthur's cheek.

"Can I . . . ?"

Arthur shifted closer, and closer, and closer. Then he

thought, *Confound it*, and he crawled right into Ira's lap, straddling him as he had last night to shave away the greenery on his face. Ira's breath hitched.

Biting his lip, Arthur ran his fingertips over Ira's antlers. They were hard and bony, not as smooth as he'd expected. Ira's eyes fixed on his face.

Arthur flushed. "Sorry, I, er, I was wondering what they'd feel like. Can you, er . . . feel anything, when I . . ."

Ira shook his head.

"If you'd caught me this summer," he said hoarsely, "before the velvet sloughed off, I would've."

Arthur traced his fingers down the side of Ira's face. His cervine ears, silky soft. His neck. His uninjured shoulder, black with smooth, glossy feathers. Ira caught his hand, pressing it to his chest. He pressed tighter and tighter, his pulse raced, his eyes flickered over Arthur's face, so Arthur leaned in and kissed him.

A moment of surprise, in which Arthur thought he might have done it wrong and started pulling away. Then, with a soft growl, Ira pulled him back in. Arthur's stomach tingled. He looped his arms around Ira's neck and kissed him with more certainty. Ira's mouth was hungry on his.

His claws tangled in Arthur's hair. Arthur trailed a hand down his body. Ira inhaled sharply, but Arthur stopped at his stomach, liking its softness, its rise and fall.

Ira gripped him so tightly his claws dug into Arthur's sides. Arthur gasped into his mouth—but he found he liked it, the pressure, the slight stab of pain. With a low groan, Ira slid one hand lower and lower, trailed a curled finger over Arthur's inner thigh—

"Wait," Arthur breathed. "Wait, wait, wait."

Ira jerked away. "Sorry. I should've—"

Shaking his head, Arthur looped his arms back around Ira's neck. "It's not that I'm not enjoying myself. I'm, er, actually I'm enjoying myself very much. I just—I've never done this before. I think I might like to go slower than we were about to."

Letting out a breath, Ira leaned his forehead against Arthur's. "Of course. Whatever you need."

His breath was sweet like spring flowers. Outside, rain pattered thick and fast, but the fire was warm and bright at Arthur's back. He kissed Ira's scarred eye, then the unscarred one. His forehead. His nose. The metacarpal pad on his left hand, then the one on his right, then held Ira's hand just because he could.

Ira brushed a lock of hair back from Arthur's forehead. "When this is over . . . If we make it. If we save the forest . . ."

"We will." Arthur kissed him again. "And you, too."

The corner of Ira's mouth turned up.

". . . when everything's done, maybe . . . you could stay. I mean," he added, "of course you'll go home to your family, I know what they mean to you, I know they're really why you're doing this, I just . . . Maybe, afterward, you could come back. To the vale. With me."

Arthur's breath caught. His imagination bloomed with images of him and Ira, after they'd saved the forest, after he and Charlotte had made it safely home to the children. The vale would blossom, green and sweet with flowers instead of cold and white in eternal winter. Ira could transform at will, never worrying about whether he'd be able to change back. They'd wander the forest at leisure, no longer afraid, and at the end of each day they'd return to the vale, curl up in that little bed together, and maybe— Arthur's brain stalled out before he could delve too far into what exactly might happen in that little bed, but he'd read enough romance novels to have ideas, if ever he wanted to put them into practice.

"Why—" he started, but he wasn't sure how to finish the question. "I mean . . . you'd want that? For me to . . ."

Ira let out a breath, ran his hands through his hair. Strands came loose and fell around his face. Arthur tucked them behind his ears, which twitched toward him.

"I've been alone a long time, except for Calyx. Then you came. You're so . . ."

There it was, Arthur thought with a twinge of disappointment. The same trailing off that had plagued his entire life, although this time it at least suggested something positive.

Then Ira said, "You went back for me. Even after Calyx attacked—even worrying for your sister—you went back to the vale anyway because I needed help."

He touched Arthur's cheek.

"The way—what you said about your books. How they make you feel like everything will be all right, even when it's terrible?" He kissed Arthur's fingertips, one at a time. "That's how you make me feel. You give me hope."

Arthur's fingers tingled at the press of his lips. He'd always figured he made people feel, at best, nothing. Indifference. Annoyance. Contempt. That last morning in Seacliff, something akin to danger, like any man so much as seen being too friendly with him might be tarred with the same term Mrs. Young had lobbed at him.

Ira had kissed him like none of that meant anything. Like such thoughts had never occurred to him.

Like Arthur mattered.

When this was over, the two of them could return to the vale and create a world for themselves where Arthur could read his romance novels and repair timepieces and no one would say he was odd or useless or not much of a man. Where he was worth something.

The two of them, he thought, and his stomach twisted. Twenty miles from Seacliff, farther from Port Lorne—or wherever Charlotte and the children settled. Of course they could visit each other, but Arthur had never lived apart from his family. The thought of not seeing them every day, not waking to Sasha's raucous play, was intolerable. And who would take care of Charlotte? She needed so much help now, no matter how she resisted and denied it. He couldn't leave her.

What had he expected to happen should he ever marry? That his wife would live in the cottage on the heather-grown cliff with his sister and niblings? Well . . . yes. Of course he had. John had moved in with Charlotte's brother and mother. Why shouldn't any future wife of Arthur's? Why not Ira? As much as Arthur had dreamed of change, he'd never once dreamed of a life in which he did not live with his sister and the children.

Ira's forehead rested against his. "You don't have to decide now. I just . . . I wanted to say that. You could. If you wanted to."

Arthur touched his face. "What if you came back with me, instead?"

"I can't."

"It doesn't have to be Seacliff. We could go to Port Lorne. It's right by the forest, too, you could visit whenever you wanted—"

"I mean I can't leave the forest."

"No, I suppose that would be difficult, since you're its . . ."

Arthur paused, not quite sure what Ira was to the forest. Its spirit, perhaps.

Before he could continue, however, Ira said, "I mean I *can't*. Physically. I'm incapable of it."

Arthur opened his mouth, couldn't think of anything to say, tried to say something nonetheless, and gave up. A little unwillingly, he crawled out of Ira's lap and sat beside him.

"But surely once we replant the tree—"

Ira shook his head. "I've never been able to. I've never been beyond the forest."

Arthur's skin prickled. Until a week ago, he'd never been

beyond Seacliff, either, but he'd always known it was an option. One dependent upon money and transportation and any number of other things, but an option nonetheless.

He took Ira's hand, stroking the furry back of it with his thumb. "I'm sure we'll figure something out."

"I hope so."

Arthur kissed his hand. Despite himself, he chuckled ruefully.

"What?" Ira asked.

"I was thinking, it's a good thing Calyx wasn't here for all that. I can only imagine what it might've thought I was doing to you."

XXXII. In which everything goes to shit

Though the morning was cold and gray, the rain had petered out. Arthur was loath to leave the cave, not least because he'd fallen asleep reading a romance novel aloud, at Ira's request, and awoken in Ira's arms and didn't want to relinquish their comfort. But Ira kissed him, tugged on his knee brace, and was out of the cave before Arthur could object.

He couldn't object anyway, since Ira reached for his hand and held it as they walked onward. Ira kept smiling, and every time he did so, Arthur felt a thrill. He had done that. All right—probably the acorn had done it in part: No new greenery had grown on Ira's face or body overnight, nor did any sprout as they went.

Still, Arthur had had a hand in making Ira happy. It felt like quite the accomplishment.

The cat was considerably less pleased with the circumstances, having to pick her way through wet undergrowth, but the two men had all but forgotten her. Arthur's neck and hand throbbed periodically, but since he couldn't do much for the phantom pain, he squeezed Ira's hand for comfort whenever it happened, without mentioning it. The wild hunt may have gotten them off track, but feeling as he did now, he was hopeful of reaching the heart of the wood soon. He whistled tunelessly without realizing he was doing so. Ira smiled.

They had not gone more than a couple miles when Ira bent with a groan.

"Is it the tarnish?" Arthur asked.

Ira tried to straighten—then screamed, dropping to all fours. His eyes crumpled against the pain. Arthur fell to his knees beside him. If this was the tarnish spreading at the heart of the wood, it was far worse than it had been before.

"Ira?"

Ira clawed at the ground. His pack slipped from his shoulders.

"Clear-cutting," he said through gritted teeth. "They're clear-cutting. I can feel—"

He broke off with another scream. The ground trembled. The forest quaked with rage and fear, or maybe it was Ira's rage and fear, or both.

Ira's eyes flew open, his right eye the same milky color as his left. Their depths reflected a woodland hollow with trees cracking and falling as men worked at them with horrendous machines, no axes but brush cutters and feller bunchers.

He screamed again. In his scream was the roar of felled trees and the bellow of a stag and the anguish of a dying man. He fell to the ground, convulsing.

"What do I do?" Arthur cried. "Tell me what to do."

But there was no one to tell him what to do, no one to rely on except himself. He clenched his fists on his thighs.

Hands shaking, he shoved sticks and stones away from Ira. He folded one of their furs under Ira's head and turned him on his side. Ira groaned, tears streaming down his face. Despite the acorn, moss thickened, spreading down his neck and into his shirt. Lichens bloomed across his arms. Tiny toadstools burst between his claws and exploded with spores. Like the forest thought the pain would stop if Ira became part of it.

Arthur swore. He needed something to treat the convulsions, but he feared Ira would turn into a lump indistinguishable from the forest floor when he wasn't looking. He scrambled upright, searching the undergrowth in panic like the right medicinal plant would helpfully present itself.

Ira lurched to his feet, breathing hard. Tentatively, Arthur reached for him.

"Ira?"

Ira looked past him, both eyes milky white. He sprinted into the trees, shivering into a stag as he went.

The stag bugled, shaking the treetops. Freya hissed.

Arthur's mouth went dry. "Ira!"

Freya threaded through his legs, nearly tripping him, but he scooped her up and sprinted after the stag. The cat yowled as she bounced in his arms, clawing into his shoulder.

"Ira!"

Arthur followed the path of dying flowers left behind, his legs like jelly. The ground trembled underfoot, but he gritted his teeth and kept going.

Another bugle, and now men were shouting, too, as the stag burst upon them. Machinery screeched, groaned, and went silent. Horses screamed; several burst through the trees, buffeting Arthur. He cowered, clutching the cat tight.

The bugle shifted to a howl. Guns fired. Arthur's heart was in his throat.

"Ira," he croaked, and the trees opened up.

The work camp was a graveyard of trees and men. Arthur couldn't tell whether Ira or the forest itself had killed the men, but greenery crept over them with long, curling fingers. Around them, collapsed tents crumpled. Machinery belched acrid smoke.

In their midst stood a wolf with heaving sides. Ira was every bit the eldritch beast: massive, eyes white and glowing, moss tinging his ruff green in wolf form as it had grown across his face in human form. A woodsman approached, axe raised. Ira snarled and snapped.

Arthur sprinted toward them.

"Don't!" he cried, hardly knowing who he was saying it to, but it didn't matter; no one heard him.

Wolf and woodsman lunged at each other at the same moment. Ira yelped.

The forest responded.

The ground rumbled and opened, swallowing tents and machinery. Shocks of fern and bugleweed grew in their place. Roots bound woodsmen where they stood. Their clothes and skin hardened into bark, and they were trees, with the same misshapen limbs as those in the vale. Other woodsmen hacked at their roots, as if felling the new trees would turn their friends back into men. The trees screamed. The woodsmen stumbled away, turned, and fled. Distant screaming and crunching told Arthur the forest was having its way with the survivors.

His stomach churned. He hadn't wanted them to hurt Ira, knew it hurt Ira when they hurt the forest—but they were working men with wives and families at home. Trying to keep roofs over their heads and bread in their mouths, the same as the fishermen and cannery workers in Seacliff.

Freya scrambled out of his arms and vanished up a tree.

"Freya—"

In the woodsmen's midst, Ira shuddered. His form cycled from wolf to stag to raven to man and back, so quickly Arthur barely glimpsed each before it passed. Like Ira couldn't decide what form to take. His eyes flickered between white and hazel.

Swallowing, Arthur ran to his side. The wound in Ira's shoulder bled through its bandages.

"Ira—"

Arthur touched his arm, but Ira shook him off, still cycling through forms.

"Don't," he growled, as he turned briefly into something not quite human but not quite wolf or stag or raven, either. His eyes squeezed shut. "Don't touch me. I don't want to—"

His voice gave way to a deep, cervine groan.

The transformations stopped. He was a stag now, white-eyed and gold-pelted. Nostrils flaring, he turned toward Arthur.

Arthur swallowed. "Ira?"

"That's him!"

More woodsmen came running through the trees, armed with axes and rifles; they must have been working nearby. Several of them skidded to a stop by collapsed tents or humanlike trees, dropping their weapons to search for friends—until the stag roared.

The men ran at him, but Ira flung the first off with his antlers—shifted to a wolf, bit another's arm—shivered into a raven, flitting upward from a third's attempt to shoot him. Back to a wolf to launch himself at another's throat. Arthur's mouth went dry, but he could only watch, horrified.

Several men escaped, but that did not comfort him. He grabbed one's arm as they passed, struggled as the man tried to throw him off.

"Don't," Arthur croaked. "Don't go that way. The forest will—"

"Leave off," the man snarled, wrenching away.

He vanished into the undergrowth with his friends. The men screamed, but the screaming cut off in a crack of bone and crunch of bark. Arthur's stomach turned.

A stag again, Ira stood amidst the remains of the deserted work camp. His antlers were rusty with blood.

A boy with a mop of dark hair bolted from a collapsed tent. He wore a worker's clothes, but he couldn't have been more than seventeen. Snorting, Ira raced after him.

"Ira, don't!"

Trees shifted. The boy changed direction, but he was trapped between the stag and a thick growth of trunks. His face strained. Whipping around, he threw a rock. It bounced harmlessly off Ira's chest.

"Don't," Arthur cried, but the stag lowered his antlers and pawed at the ground like a buck during the rut. The boy backed into the trees. He swallowed. The stag menaced him, tossing his head.

Arthur squeezed between them. "Ira, *stop*!"

The stag stopped.

His antlers were too close to Arthur's chest. Arthur reached for him.

"Don't."

The boy pressed into Arthur's back, breathing raggedly. Arthur's hands fell to his sides.

"Don't. Ira, please. He's just a boy. You wouldn't harm a child."

At the moment, he wasn't sure of that. Ira wouldn't harm a child—but surely he wouldn't murder an entire work camp, either, and the bodies of the men he and the forest had slain were scattered around them. He wasn't Ira, now. He was the Lord of the Wood, taking his vengeance for the wood's destruction.

The stag snorted again, his breath hot. Arthur swallowed.

"Don't," he whispered. "Please."

The stag's nostrils flared. Slowly, he raised his head.

Arthur spoke to the boy over his shoulder. "Go."

The boy tensed. "What about you?"

"He won't hurt me." Arthur wasn't certain of that just now, either. "Go, now."

The boy rabbited away. Bellowing, the stag bolted after him. Arthur blocked his path, skidding on wet leaves. His knapsack dug into his shoulders. The stag turned on him.

"Ira—"

The stag menaced him until Arthur backed into a tree, antlers at his throat. Their prongs pricked him.

He swallowed uncomfortably.

"Ira, please." He moved his lips as little as possible. "It's me. It's Arthur."

The prongs pressed into his skin. He gasped, gripping the stag's antlers.

"Please." His eyes stung with tears. Ira didn't know him. "*Please.*"

Blood beaded at his throat. A droplet trickled down his neck. Arthur squeezed his eyes shut.

With a hiss, Freya launched herself at the stag. She clawed his cheek. He snorted and flung her off.

Then, with a scuffling and a rustling of leaves, the antlers were gone. Arthur slumped against the tree, rubbing his neck. His fingers were smeared red. He gulped down air.

In the dirt before him, Ira stared at him in horror. He was a man again—barely. Gray-green with moss and lichens, scar and hair speared with white flowers, antlers twined with leaves and rusty with blood. His face had twisted and lengthened into something like a wolf's and something like a stag's and something like a raven's. Blood stained the fur on his right cheek, where Freya's claws had raked across his face, and spotted his shirt where his shoulder was injured. Though his eyes were human, they had the expression of a wary animal.

Arthur breathed deeply, *in for four, hold for four, out for four.* He stepped forward, but Ira said, "Don't."

"Ira—"

Ira scrambled backward. "Keep away from me."

Freya mewled pitifully. Arthur scooped her up and held her close.

"It's all right. I'm fine."

He said nothing about the woodsmen unrecognizable as mossy mounds growing in the clearing. His stomach twisted.

Ira shook his head. "I could've killed you."

"You didn't."

"I wanted to."

His voice was hoarser than ever. Arthur's heart sank.

"Not you. The forest. Which I must admit," he added, hoping to lighten the mood, "rather hurts my feelings after all we've been through together."

Ira didn't smile.

"It doesn't matter. The forest, me—it's all the same." He scrubbed a paw-like hand over his face. "I have to go back."

"Back?"

"To the vale."

"Ira—" Arthur set the cat down and chanced another step toward him. This time, Ira didn't back away. "We've been traveling for two days. I know it's been . . . less than ideal—" possibly the greatest understatement he'd ever made "—but I think—I *know* we can do this. Everything will be all right."

Ira yanked the acorn off. Staggering to his feet, he stumbled: Like his face, his figure had changed. He was barrel-chested and hunched; his wolf's paws extended into legs. His knee brace buckled and slid down his right leg, no longer fitting. He swore.

"Nothing about this is all right, Arthur!" he snarled. "I can't even wear my knee brace."

He threw the acorn. It bounced off Arthur's chest and vanished in the leaf litter. Arthur fell to his knees in a panic, searching by touch until his fingers curled around its silver form.

Ira growled, deep and resonant, more animal than ever. "What good did it do? Look at me. It's so much worse now. I only left the vale because you made me—"

"I didn't *make*—"

"—and now I'm *this*. The fucking acorn didn't do anything."

Arthur clutched the acorn, getting to his feet cautiously. He'd never seen Ira so angry. Ira was frightened, really, Arthur knew that, but his heart hammered.

"It will. Once we plant it. It'll make everything better."

Ira lurched toward him, eyes glittering. "We'll never make it. I'll become a beast, all of me, and you'll die because the forest kills you, or maybe I'll kill you myself!"

His snarl chased crows from a nearby tree. They burst from the canopy and flew away, cawing, translucent and black-veined.

Ira followed them with his gaze. Chest heaving, he slumped against a stump and ran a hand over his beastly face. Arthur stepped closer, aching to touch him.

"Look at me," Ira repeated morosely.

Arthur cupped his furred cheek in a hand. Ira had a snout now, and fangs. He was so much more beast than man, and with that growth in his scar, and lichens clinging to the ruff of his neck. But his eyes were the same, one hazel, one milky. His breath was sweet in Arthur's face.

"You're still my Ira," Arthur whispered.

Ira squeezed his eyes shut. Touched Arthur's hand, so carefully, keeping his claws from Arthur's skin. "I just wanted to keep you safe."

"Then come with me," Arthur pleaded. "We must be closer to the heart of the wood than the vale by now."

Ira pulled away with a growl. "Don't you understand? I'm the greatest danger to you now. If this happens again—"

"Maybe it won't."

"—if I lose control, if the forest takes me over that way—there'll be nothing I can do."

Arthur dragged his hands over his face.

"I'm so sick of you saying that." Looking confused, Ira opened his mouth, but Arthur held up his hands. "I know—

the forest doesn't listen to you anymore. You can't do all the things you used to do. I know. You think there's nothing *you* can do? There's nothing *I* can do!"

Ira opened his mouth, but Arthur barreled over him.

"I can't support my family because I can't do anything useful. When Charlotte got sick, I couldn't do anything but keep the children quiet and bring her bread and water and make up the medicines *she* knew about, when she felt up to giving me instructions. I couldn't even make it through the forest on my own for more than a day and a half!"

His cheeks had gone red and patchy. He couldn't remember the last time he'd gotten really angry. Now that he'd turned it on, he didn't know how to turn it off.

"*I* can't do anything, and my God, I know that—but at least I try. I don't sit around doing nothing because I'm so convinced I can't do anything."

"Oh no?" Ira said quietly. "Isn't that what you told me you were doing back in Seacliff? Sitting around sighing about how you couldn't change your own life because you were too cowardly to do anything about it?"

Arthur whitened. "I—"

Ira staggered closer with another growl. "Isn't that what you did in the vale? For all your talk about needing to get back to your family—how hard did you try to leave before you looked in the basin? Before Calyx scared you off? How many times did you tell yourself the brambles were too thick, the danger too much?"

The words punched Arthur in the gut—because they were true. A scratch on the cheek had been enough to keep him from seriously confronting the brambles for days.

He clenched the acorn so tightly it dug into his palm. "I'm doing something now. Maybe I'll muck it up like I always do, maybe I won't make it, but I'm not turning back. Not this time.

If you won't come with me, I'll go myself. I'll make sure Lottie is safe. I'll save you even if you won't."

"Do what you must. I won't risk being the thing that kills you."

Ira limped away, but his leg buckled, and he collapsed. Arthur stumbled after him, wanting, despite himself, to offer aid or comfort. Snarling, Ira shivered into a raven whose feathers were stained green with moss. He hopped several times, flapping awkwardly.

Between the new greenery and the shoulder wound, Arthur thought he wouldn't be able to leave. But with an angry croak, the raven darted upward.

"Ira!" Arthur cried, but the raven didn't turn back. Ira could fly to the heart of the wood and save it this minute, if he'd listen to reason. But he was too scared to think straight, too scared to listen to Arthur any longer.

The raven vanished over the trees. A wave of tears threatened, but Arthur swallowed them and hung the acorn around his neck. Freya mewed at him. He hugged her to his chest, burying his face in her long fur.

He turned and walked into the trees, alone except for the cat.

XXXIII. In which Charlotte sees her father's portrait

Charlotte spent the morning in the less shabby of the two armchairs by the stove, relieved to sit with a cushion at her back. Whenever she needed something, the plant creature retrieved it, slinging itself through the tiny house to retrieve a mug, or a bowl of stew, or an extra cushion, and then sat in Charlotte's lap, clicking happily.

Resting seemed less objectionable in the wood, where there were no patients to visit, no cupboards to fill, no house to clean. Or at least the house was not hers, and neither were the cupboards. So it was a rare rest taken willingly and guilt-free.

Elspeth, however, spent the morning tearing the tiny house apart, searching every drawer, cabinet, nook, and cranny for any sign her sister might have been here.

She found nothing—no sign of Maggie, anyway. Of the Lord of the Wood, there was plenty. The usual odds and ends, or almost the usual, in the room that was kitchen, sitting room, and bedroom all in one. Sacks of root vegetables, braids of garlic and onion, bunches of herbs. A pair of boots hidden away in a cupboard rather than sitting by the door where Charlotte would've expected them. In other cupboards, drawers, and cabinets, sparse dishware, no more than two of each item, as if the Lord of the Wood didn't have much company. Other kitchen implements: pots, pans, a ladle, a kettle, various types of kitchen knives. A pipe with a store of tobacco so old the leaves had crumbled into dust. Charlotte had not expected the Lord of the Wood's home to seem so . . . normal.

In the drawer in the bedside table, Elspeth found an odd makeshift pillow, a roll of fabric tied atop a wooden block. They weren't sure what to make of that, nor of the fabric booties tucked in beside it. The booties were clean but torn. Perhaps the Lord of the Wood had a pet besides the plant creature; that was the best Charlotte or Elspeth could come up with. There was a whistle of some sort, too, though it wasn't like any whistle Charlotte had ever seen: ovular, with holes all along the sides and an opening at the top.

In the chest of drawers by the bed: a couple pairs of mended trousers; lumpy socks worn threadbare but out of use, stuffed into the back of their drawer; a handful of linen shirts, once pullover in style, cut down the front with toggles added. Beneath them, a block of paper, a stick of charcoal—and a stack of sketches.

"Sketches of what?" Charlotte asked. Elspeth had been sharing a running commentary of what she'd found, bringing over occasional curiosities—like the silver basin hanging overhead—to show Charlotte.

Now she perched on the arm of Charlotte's chair with the sketches, rubbing her lower back with a grimace.

"Are you all right?" Charlotte asked.

"Sore today, is all."

Charlotte's lips thinned. If she'd been sore, she would've thought little of it. Elspeth sore concerned her.

They leafed through the sketches together. Most were of the forest, or forest creatures, or creatures Charlotte didn't recognize but was certain must be particular to an enchanted forest. A squirrel-like creature with ancient eyes skirting up a tree. A frog in close-up, a study more detailed than most of the sketches. A tiny old woman with tree-bark skin and a shock of pale hair—many sketches of her, most often accompanied by a raven. There was the plant creature, too, taking various shapes on the page: a ball of greenery; a loose mass of plant anatomy; the shape of a hare or fox or bird or any number of other animals. Charlotte let one of its tendrils weave through her fingers as she examined the drawings.

Occasionally, a human image cropped up. Most of the humans were figures in full, sketched as if from a distance, but there were portraits, too. Elspeth paused at one such drawing, a little girl with light hair in twin braids.

"That looks like Gran, when she was small."

"Perhaps it is. She met the Lord of the Wood once, didn't she?"

Elspeth nodded, her gaze flickering over the page, taking in the girl's frock, her eyes, her nose and chin. "Got separated from her caravan once on a trip through the wood, long ago. Said the Lord of the Wood brought her back to 'em. Say, those must be Gran's folks."

Another sketch of the girl, this time waving from the forest's edge, amidst a small cluster of covered wagons, shawled women, capped men.

"Gran'd love this. She's only got a couple'a pictures, faded as anything . . . Maybe we'll find a sketch of Maggie in here. Then we'd know."

"Maybe," Charlotte said, but it seemed improbable. The paper was yellowed and brittle with age; the sketches were likely decades old. But with Elspeth so much calmer than she'd been all day, sounding almost hopeful, Charlotte couldn't bring herself to point that out.

They flipped through more and more sketches, until Charlotte's father smiled at them from the page. Her breath hitched.

Elspeth considered the drawing. "That's your old man, then? Looks just like you."

Charlotte's eyes stung. "That's what Arthur says."

She took the sketch from Elspeth, studying every detail. They had few pictures of George Throckmorton, all faded or blurry like the pictures Elspeth's gran had of her folks. Sometimes, Charlotte studied herself in the cloudy washroom mirror, trying to graft scanty memories over her own freckled reflection.

Now here he was. George Throckmorton, smiling out at her. He had broad cheeks and a high forehead. A rounded chin and matching nose. Deep dimples. Eyes that sparkled like Sasha's. Charlotte had always thought her daughter had John's eyes; now she realized they were George's. Her fingers tightened on the sketch, crinkling the paper. She handed it back to Elspeth. The plant creature curled over her shoulders comfortingly.

"There's more." Elspeth checked the remaining sketches. "Lots more. Like there were of that little tree person. And your new pet."

Charlotte's skin prickled as Elspeth paged through sketch after sketch of her father. George head-on. George in profile. George laughing, or reading, or sorting through plant matter, separating stem from leaf and flower. George looking over his shoulder, annoyed, and suddenly Charlotte remembered leaving church with him once, her tiny hand in his big one. A young woman with a nervous complaint, who often wanted his care, had stopped to ask if he might look in on her new baby. Her husband had interrupted, said she always worried over nothing and what must the doctor think, always coming to the house at odd hours for ailments that turned out to be naught? Quailing, she'd apologized to George for bothering him.

George had stopped her, given her husband a look much like the one in the sketch (if tinged with disdain), and said, *If you'll let me hand my own wee one off to her mother, I'll be over directly.*

Charlotte blinked back tears. She hardly remembered her father anymore, she'd been so young when he'd vanished, but now she could picture him clearly that day. How he'd been dressed, his lips pursing when the husband bowled over his wife's concerns, the warmth of his hand around Charlotte's.

The sketches were a gift. Yet the fact that there were so many of them had her reeling.

"I don't . . ." A headache threatened in its habitual place over one eye. "Why are there so many drawings of him? He only met the Lord of the Wood once. In all his stories—"

In all Arthur's stories. Her father had been gone so long, she only heard his stories in her brother's voice.

She shook her head, then stopped because it aggravated the burgeoning headache. "Are there any more?"

Elspeth shifted through the sketches. "None of your da. Here now, this looks more recent. Paper's just as yellow, but the charcoal's not so faded."

Charlotte took the paper and almost dropped it.

"Arthur," she breathed.

Her eyes darted over the page, drinking in his expressions, his posture, the fall of his hair over his forehead. Every sketch was Arthur sitting in an armchair, reading, and it was all so very *Arthur* that she started crying.

Her headache spread from its spot over her eye to the rest of her forehead. Different now, a crying headache, but with that threatening migraine throb beneath it. She ground the heels of her hands into her eyes.

Elspeth set the paper aside. "S'all right, Lottie."

"It's not the drawings," Charlotte said, though it was. "It's my head."

Elspeth slid off the arm of the chair. A drawer opened; papers rustled; the drawer closed. Cupboards opened and shut. Elspeth muttered, "Where'd I put that benighted kettle?" The plant creature slipped off Charlotte's lap. A moment later, Elspeth said in surprise, "Oh. Thanks."

Water being poured, the clink of a kettle set down, the hiss of steam. Charlotte's insides needled with guilt. She uncovered her eyes.

"I'm sorry," she said to Elspeth.

"What for?"

"You didn't find anything of your sister's. Just more about my family. And now you're making tea, because my head hurts, instead of continuing your search."

"Who says the tea's for you?"

Charlotte was mortified. Elspeth laughed.

"Of course it's for you, you numpty."

Charlotte wanted to object to the insult, but it felt so much like a caress she couldn't bring herself to do so. She rubbed her forehead without saying anything.

Elspeth's laughter faded. Wrapping her cloak around herself, she returned to her perch on the arm of Charlotte's chair. Rummaging through the house had warmed her; now she was shivering again.

"Don't think there's anything of Maggie's to find. If she'd been here recently like your brother, likely she'd've been in the sketches, or we'd've seen something sitting right out in the open. Less'n she took everything with her and got home, but I didn't come after her until a good week after she was supposed to've returned. Told you, I know I'm probably looking for a corpse. For a moment, those sketches made me think . . . but she wasn't in 'em."

She ran a hand through her hair. She was seated precariously, one leg swinging off the side of the chair. Charlotte touched her thigh, hoping to comfort her.

Elspeth gazed at Charlotte's fingers.

"Look, even if I hadn't already tore the whole house apart . . . you need someone to take care of you. That's me, long as we're together. Whether that's till our business is done, or . . ."

Charlotte longed to know what words clung to the end of that *or*, but she didn't ask. She patted Elspeth's thigh, then folded her hands in her lap so she wouldn't do it again.

Elspeth bit her lip. "Well, I'll take care of you. And I don't mind doing it, neither. That's all."

The water boiled. Elspeth retrieved Charlotte's medical kit.

"Which plant? There's one in here for pain, aye? Or more than one?"

"It's . . ." Charlotte couldn't remember the word. It danced at the tip of her tongue, but all she could come up with was *silverweed*, and that wasn't right. "Just bring me my kit."

"Sure, you don't expect a city slicker to know her plants," Elspeth said with amiable belligerence, but she obliged, then started closing the cupboards she'd wrenched open this morning.

"It's not that," Charlotte mumbled. "I can't . . ."

She shifted the things in her kit aside until she found the plant. The name of the dried white petals floated frustratingly close to the surface of her mind without breaching it.

Silverweed, her brain supplied unhelpfully, over and over. *Silverweed silverweed silverweed silver—*

She frowned, massaging her forehead with her knuckles. Elspeth turned from stuffing socks into their drawer and doubled back. She crouched before Charlotte, touching her knee.

"Find anything good down there? God staring back at you, maybe? You've been contemplating it long enough to be took for a monk."

Charlotte handed the not-silverweed to her. Elspeth took it with an air of bemusement.

"Meadowsweet, aye. That's the one, is it?"

"Meadowsweet," Charlotte echoed, both relieved to remember what the plant was (*not* silverweed) and mortified she'd been unable to do so on her own. "Yes. I couldn't think what . . ."

It would help with the pain. Whether it would help with the brain fog was less certain.

She fell asleep in the armchair, warm with meadowsweet tea. When she awoke, sometime early that afternoon, the plant creature had abandoned its spot by the stove and wrapped around the branches overhead. Elspeth was coming in from outside, stamping snow from her boots and burrowed deep into her cloak and the borrowed fur. She shook them out and hung them on the pegs by the door to dry.

"Built up some shelter for the animals. Ain't snowing now, but you never know. How you feeling?"

Charlotte settled deeper into the chair. The tea had burned away the worst of the pain.

"My headache's gone. And I think I can think now."

Elspeth kicked off her boots and knelt before her with a soft groan. Her hands were freezing, her hair damp. Her eyes were bruised like Charlotte's so often were, like she was exhausted.

"You ought to warm up," Charlotte said. "Is there any tea left?"

"So much pain earlier you couldn't remember a plant, but it's me you're worried about." Shaking her head, Elspeth peered into Charlotte's face. "You look better. Think the rest done you good."

"I will learn nothing from this."

Elspeth's mouth twitched. She squeezed Charlotte's hands and turned, stiffly, to build up the fire. Water dripped from her braid into her collar. Orange light flickered on her face and arms, outlined her figure through her shirt. Charlotte looked away, thinking of how she'd frozen Elspeth out the other day for suggesting they were the same. The way Elspeth had taken care of her since, though Charlotte had been frequently unpleasant.

"There was this woman," she blurted, in a low voice. Elspeth paused in sticking another log into the stove. "Ages ago, a couple of years after John's death. That is . . . I'd known for a long time that I . . ."

Her hands fisted in her apron. She'd never told anyone about this, not even Arthur.

"Her husband was a local boy. He'd moved to Glenwhistle looking for work, and he'd married her and brought her back to show off to his family. She was . . ."

She'd had a laugh that went through Charlotte like music and a smile that left her desperate to do what she could to see it again. Only Charlotte's sense of propriety had kept her from making a fool of herself.

"Well, I—I wanted her." Charlotte licked her lips. Admitting it felt like a crime. "I didn't do anything about it—of course I didn't, she was married, and even if she hadn't been—"

She hadn't been sure which was worse: that she'd wanted a *married* woman or that she'd wanted a married *woman*. She'd thought the woman smiled at her more than at others, clasped her hand too long during the sign of peace, but she'd told herself she was imagining it.

"After Mass one day," she said, "she asked if she might speak with me in private. About a medical issue, I assumed, but she took me around the side of the church and—"

The moment they were alone, the woman had pressed Charlotte up against the building. Starving for the intimacy she'd shared with John, taken with this beautiful girl, at once elated and terrified that she might want what Charlotte wanted, Charlotte had touched her face. The woman had taken her other hand and laid it on her bosom.

Elspeth turned to gaze at her. "She kiss you?"

Charlotte shook her head. "Her husband came around the corner looking for her."

Elspeth whistled, long and low. "What happened?"

"Nothing, thank God." Charlotte twisted her hands in her lap. "I was terrified, but she didn't bat an eye. She told him she had asked me to look at a rather concerning birthmark, and I managed to gabble something about it being nothing to worry about, and she thanked me and took his arm and went home. They left for Glenwhistle the next day. I never saw her again."

"Lucky for you." Elspeth looked away; Charlotte was relieved. "Lucky nothing happened, I mean. Last time a man caught me with his wife, I got a black eye for it. Didn't even know she was married."

Charlotte flushed; she had immediately wondered what, exactly, Elspeth had been caught doing with the man's wife.

Elspeth closed the stove door, adjusted the damper, and dropped into her armchair. "Why're you telling me this now?"

Charlotte let out a breath. "Because . . . I think I should. Because you've been good to me—taken care of me, like you said. The other day, when you said we were the same, I was afraid . . . No one knows this about me. I've never . . . I've been very careful. So when you said we were the same . . . I was afraid of what you might say."

It seemed foolish to have been scared, now. Of course she was afraid of what the villagers might say, but Elspeth was different. Elspeth had wanted to know what had happened. Elspeth had responded with her own story, or a piece of one.

"I know I hurt you," Charlotte said, "responding how I did. And you've been kind to me anyway. So I . . . I wanted you to know. You deserve the truth."

Elspeth was silent for so long that Charlotte's palms itched. She rubbed them against her apron. Maybe she'd made a mistake.

"Glad you trust me with it," Elspeth said. "You didn't have to, though, just because I been taking care of you."

"Maybe not. But I wanted to."

Elspeth dimpled. Charlotte's heart stuttered.

Then Elspeth slouched in her chair, gazing into the stove.

"He ain't back yet. Maybe he ain't coming back."

Charlotte didn't ask who she meant. "It's barely been a day. We can give it more time."

Elspeth unbraided her wet hair and combed her fingers through it. Charlotte watched, strangely fascinated; she'd never seen Elspeth without her braid.

"I don't know what time I have. Feelin' . . . Think the sickness is getting to me. Thought the acorn'd stop it spreading, but today I'm so . . ."

Charlotte didn't ask what she meant. Elspeth had looked achy and exhausted all day. She'd still managed her usual business, taking care of the animals and whatnot, but Charlotte knew from experience that it was only a matter of time before her usual business caught up to her.

"Let me see your scar."

The black veins were minute, not as extensive as Gracie Buchanan's had been, but Charlotte was almost certain they'd spread. She touched Elspeth's collarbone, worrying her lip with her teeth. The acorn had slowed the symptoms, certainly; Elspeth wasn't in such bad shape as those with wood sickness generally were this long after showing symptoms. But it hadn't stopped them.

Charlotte would try the acorns anyway. They were all she had. If they didn't work, she didn't know what would.

"I been thinking." Elspeth sat back in her chair, running a hand through her damp hair. "I could track him through the wood. It can't be that different than tracking any other beast."

"And you'd know all about that, I suppose, city folks being well-known for being master trackers."

Elspeth's mouth twitched. She rebraided her hair in silence, perhaps considering how little tracking knowledge she (presumably) had.

"How about this? You stay here in case he comes back. I know the journey's been hard on you. You could keep resting up, less'n you see him. You'll have your—whatsit, that green thing, seems like it's useful to you, gets you what you need and all that. I'll take the mule, no gig, just the mule, and I'll look for him. Whichever one of us sees him first, we make him come to the other one so's we can both get answers."

Charlotte's stomach clenched. As if she meant to leave this minute, Elspeth staggered up from her chair. Reached for her cloak on its peg.

Charlotte lurched toward her. At her distress, the plant creature dropped from the ceiling, swaying after her.

"You said you'd take care of me."

Elspeth paused, a fist clenched in her cloak.

Charlotte swallowed. She couldn't be alone in the forest. Not even here, where it seemed reasonably safe.

She couldn't be here without Elspeth.

The plant creature swayed at her shoulder, reassuring. Maybe things would be all right, if Charlotte only said what she wanted.

"I know you want to find your sister, or find out what happened to her. I want that for you, too. But I . . ."

Elspeth's gaze flickered over her. "What, Lottie?"

Charlotte squeezed her eyes shut, heart pounding. "I lost my father in the wood, maybe I've lost my brother— You already have the sickness, and it's getting worse. If you go out there . . . I can't lose you, too."

Slowly, Elspeth's fist unclenched from the folds of her cloak. Charlotte let out a breath.

"One day more." The plant creature wrapped a gentle tendril around her arm. "Stay with me. One day more. Then, if you want, if he's not back yet—"

Elspeth stepped toward her. Charlotte gulped down air. She'd thought, for a moment, that Elspeth would really leave. That she would vanish from Charlotte's life as suddenly as she'd entered it—never to be seen again, for the forest would surely disappear her for good.

Elspeth touched her cheek. Charlotte wanted to cry.

"Please," she whispered. "Don't go. Not yet."

Elspeth nodded. "All right, Lottie. All right. One day more."

XXXIV. In which Arthur falls into a fog

Arthur's arms were leaden after carrying the cat for hours, but he wouldn't put her down. She'd curled against his chest and started purring and hadn't let up.

His tears had dried, but he kept thinking: *Why did I ever come here? What was I thinking?*

Everything was a mess. He'd lost track of the days, but probably Mrs. Livingston's cousin was dead. The clock might've sold to someone else. Charlotte was in the forest, and maybe she was dead, too. Arthur's grand adventure had been danger and misery and a plant creature that had hated him on sight, and far too many wet socks, and injuries that, though magically healed, throbbed periodically, as did his back. The only good of the whole situation had been Ira.

Now Ira was a beast. And they'd said terrible things to each other. And Arthur would probably die alone in the forest, without reaching the heart of the wood, and so would Charlotte, and the children would never know what had happened, and Ira would be a beast forever—or until the forest succumbed to wood sickness, and he died, too.

No wonder Arthur had been so afraid of getting everything he'd ever wanted. Reality never lived up to one's expectations;

it burst the shining bubble of one's dreams. Better to never have a chance of achieving them. Then one could take comfort imagining they might one day come perfectly true. The wood might prove enchanting instead of bedeviling.

The one upside—if it could be called that—was that Arthur thought he understood, at last, why his father had not told them more about the Lord of the Wood. Why he'd spun a story of a forest prince, met once and left in gratitude. Had anyone asked Arthur about the Lord of the Wood now, he might've done the same.

The thought brought little comfort. It restored George's memory, but it sank Ira's: The reality of him hadn't lived up to Arthur's imaginings.

His stomach twisted. That was hardly fair, was it? Blaming Ira for being a person who got scared and angry and irrational. For not resembling the mental image Arthur had carried so long—not only of the Lord of the Wood as George had described him, but of the romance that might one day sweep Arthur away as it swept away the heroines in his novels.

Not for the first time, Arthur wondered what his father would've thought of what had happened between him and Ira. He wanted to believe George would've accepted it without question, the way he'd always accepted Arthur without question. He'd always seen things differently than most of Seacliff, perhaps because he—like so few villagers then—had ventured beyond it.

But Arthur remembered his father's hesitation when he'd asked about the old fisherman and his friend, the answers George had given. George had never hesitated before or since when answering his children's questions, not even (to Arthur's immediate regret) when Arthur had asked where babies came from. If George had hedged his answer, it must've been because he found the truth shameful. After all, he and Eileen had been a unit, and Eileen had been deeply uncomfortable with anything odd about Arthur the older he'd grown.

Not Charlotte, though. When she was twelve, she'd snorted and said, *How silly*, about their mother refusing to teach Arthur to bake biscuits, and taught him herself. When she was fifteen, their mother had found one of his novels lying around, and Charlotte had claimed it was hers. She'd pretended to read until their mother turned back to her needlepoint. That night, after Eileen had fallen asleep in the room she'd shared with Charlotte, Charlotte had snuck into Arthur's room and shoved the book into his hands.

I don't see how you can read anything so saccharine.

The sex scenes are quite good, Arthur had said, even though the sex scenes were the least important bit to him, and she'd made him flip to one to show her. He'd been mortified as she'd sat on the edge of his bed and read it with interest. With the same practicality of her later years, she'd told him she might as well learn about sex from his romance novels if their mother wouldn't tell her anything about it, as seemed likely. Eileen teased Arthur periodically about sowing wild oats, only asking that he didn't get any girls into trouble, but she'd told Charlotte that good girls needn't concern themselves with such things until marriage—even though Charlotte had pointed out she could hardly perform her marital duty if she didn't know what it was.

That was something, Arthur thought hopefully. Charlotte had always been there for him in a way no one else ever had. If anyone would understand about him and Ira, it was her. He didn't know whether he'd tell her, if she were to appear before him this moment—though it seemed an awfully big secret to keep—but he hoped he'd have the chance to decide.

"I will," he mumbled into the cat's fur. "I will. I'm going to replant the heart of the wood, and then—"

Then he'd find his sister, somehow, and he'd throw himself

at her and promise never to leave again. The wood would be the beautiful place of enchantment he'd always imagined, the cottage would be as he'd left it, and they'd all live happily ever after. Even if it was harder to pretend he wasn't lonely, now.

Freya squirmed in his arms. He set her down, stretching. His elbow ached; he'd had one hand clenched around the acorn at his neck the whole way. The acorn, warm and alive, was guiding him to the heart of the wood.

The forest was silent. Yesterday's wind had died away. No leaves rustled. No birds called. No creatures slunk across his path, although perhaps that was for the best: He didn't care to see another deer or bird with translucent skin showing its ribs or skull or vertebrae.

The silence unnerved him, however. Arthur held his father's watch to his ear to hear it ticking. The quiet, constant sound calmed him.

Ever more trees oozed black down their trunks. Arthur steered as far from them as he could. He didn't know what the ooze would do if it touched him, but he remembered it corroding the tip of his shovel days ago.

"Do you think we're close?" he asked Freya.

As usual, she didn't respond. Instead, she gazed up the trunk of a nearby birch, tail twitching. Claws outstretched, she shot toward it.

"Freya?"

With a chitter, a small green creature darted out of the foliage above. Blue cap mushrooms sprouted in its wake. The creature was a person, if people were a foot tall and mossy, with hair that trailed into their body and clothes or maybe *was* their body and clothes. It vaulted from the birch to a nearby aspen, skirted down the trunk with the cat in pursuit. Then it darted up Arthur's body.

He flinched at the tickle on his trousers, his shirt. The creature scurried up him like a squirrel. To his relief, the blue caps it trailed didn't follow, nor did the cat. Growling, she glared at the thing but sat lashing her tail at Arthur's feet.

The creature peered into his face with eyes as brown and ancient as a tree.

"Oh," he breathed.

The creature prodded him with a tiny finger and scampered over his shoulders, snuffling at his hair. He laughed.

Freya's tail lashed faster as her eyes followed the creature. She launched herself at it, clawing into Arthur. He yelped.

"Freya—"

Chittering, the creature sprang from his shoulder onto a branch overhead. Freya followed. She and the creature chased each other along boughs, blue caps sprouting behind them, until, with a final, impressive leap, the creature reached the shelter of its birch. It vanished in the birch's branches as if it had melted away. The tree's yellow leaves trembled, then stilled.

Freya mewled, her hindquarters wiggling, but Arthur dragged her from her branch.

"I wish you hadn't scared that thing off," he told her.

He'd liked its liveliness, after the silence that had grated on him since he'd parted from Ira, but the cat merely grumbled. He contemplated luring the creature back with . . . whatever such a creature might like, food or a shiny trinket like his father's pocket watch or—he didn't know what. But Freya would undoubtedly go after it again.

The blue caps the creature had left burst and shriveled. Spores drifted through the air. Holding his breath, Arthur stepped closer.

His stomach clenched. Internally, the toadstools were threaded with black. Examining the birch, he discovered it also had black veins creeping up from the base of its trunk. More blue caps clustered there, similarly veined.

Arthur hugged the cat and continued on his way.

After a while, they came upon a stream. From a distance, the sight heartened him. Perhaps he could follow it to the heart of the wood, or a good chunk of the way, and he'd have fresh water to drink and fish to eat (if he caught any).

Then he reached the bank. Most of the trees nearby oozed black. The water was black, too, and smelled mechanical.

His stomach turned. Not quite the saving grace he'd hoped for. His throat was dry; he was suddenly thirsty, with only that black water to drink because he'd already emptied his bottle.

He shut his eyes and focused on his breathing. He'd been traveling for hours. He might be as little as a day from the heart of the wood. Surely he could make it that long without food or water.

In the meantime, the stream could guide him, the sound of it a comfort though the sight of that black water wasn't. That would have to be enough, but the disappointment was hard to bear.

Gradually—so gradually that, at first, Arthur didn't notice—a mist rose. Then he thought his spectacles were fogging. He put the cat down and wiped his lenses on his shirt several times, to no effect.

Freya twisted between his ankles. He stumbled over her and fell.

Cursing, Arthur pushed upright. His back twinged. He winced.

The mist had thickened to fog. Now Arthur could barely see six inches in front of him.

"What is this?"

Freya mewled uneasily.

The stream still burbled to their left. That was something, Arthur told himself, but a fog arising in the afternoon, that he hadn't noticed until he was in the thick of it, made his skin prickle.

Around him, the forest had vanished. He could no longer see trees, stream, grass, or sky. Leaves crunched; his heartbeat pulsed in his ears. The cat kept underfoot until he picked her up. She burrowed into him.

Arthur didn't like that. He'd figured that, as long as she was nonchalant about the forest, there was nothing to worry about. Her apparent anxiety about the fog increased his own.

He fell to his knees, narrowly avoiding dropping her. His knapsack crashed over his head. He swore and shook it off. His back twinged so badly he couldn't get back up. In fact, he wanted to lie down on whatever nice, springy surface he was kneeling on. A thick bed of moss, maybe.

Bed. That sounded nice.

Freya seemed to agree. She climbed out of his arms and curled on the ground. In a moment, she was asleep.

"Freya?" Arthur gasped.

Gasping was all he could manage. The fog pressed on him like a physical thing. It should've been cold; wasn't fog cold? This fog was warm. Had it been pressing on him? It was comfortable, now. Soothing.

The fuzzy black animal beside him seemed to think so. He was almost certain he used to know what the fuzzy black animal was, but he couldn't remember. It was unimportant anyway.

He couldn't remember his name, either, but that seemed equally unimportant. All that mattered was that his back had stopped twinging (had it ever twinged to begin with?), the fog wrapped around him like a blanket, and he was pleasantly sleepy. He removed his spectacles, lay down, and closed his eyes, calm washing over him. He would lie down for a while, and when he awoke, he'd go back to what he'd been doing, whatever that was . . .

He frowned. Now he'd lain down, he was rather less comfortable. Something dug into his hip, a hard point that disturbed his rest.

He fumbled in his pocket and pulled out a rowan cross. His frown deepened as he gazed blurrily at it. It was important for some reason.

The fog grasped at him, but he shuddered it off.

"Not now," he murmured. "I'm trying to . . ."

Arthur shot upright, reaching for his spectacles. His sister. Charlotte had given him the rowan cross. He gripped it tight, its points digging into his palm, his mind clearer for focusing on it. He didn't know how long that might help. He was short of breath; perhaps breathing in the fog was doing this to him.

How had he ever thought it warm and comfortable? Fumbling for his knapsack, he wrenched a handkerchief free and held it over his nose. He shouldered his knapsack and scooped up the sleeping cat, hoping he could negotiate cat, cross, and handkerchief at once.

The fog's grasping fingers made him want to peel his own skin off. He shook his head, shuddering away from it. It came at him from every side, but he squeezed his eyes shut and trudged forward. He'd walked into it; he could walk out of it.

Lottie, he thought, clenching the cross. *Lottie, Lottie, Lottie—*

Something crunched underfoot. Several somethings. Arthur tripped but righted himself and kept going.

Then he was free. His mind cleared; his breath returned. Clutched uncomfortably in one arm, Freya awoke with a disgruntled *mrrf.*

"Are you all right?" Arthur asked. She headbutted him. "What do you suppose . . . ?"

He turned warily toward the fog. Now he was out of it, it didn't look like normal fog. It was vaguely gold despite the dimness of the forest, which was darker than it had been earlier. Stumbling through the fog, he'd lost time, and he wasn't sure how much—but it seemed more time than it had felt.

He'd lost the stream, too.

The fog dissipated. As it did so, strange spindly forms appeared on the ground.

Arthur stepped toward them, gripping the cross tighter than ever. Skeletons. In the moss were skeletons. Three people, a bird, a squirrel, one that might have been a fox. Each laid out as if its owner had lain down and fallen asleep like he'd nearly done.

His breath hitched. "Let's get out of here."

He jogged away, the cat bouncing in his arms. He didn't remove the handkerchief from his nose until he'd put distance between them and the fog.

xxxv. In which Arthur finds someone unexpected

It was nearly dark by the time Arthur located the stream again. Despite its blackness, the sight comforted him. Shrubs clustered nearby, closer to the water than he would've liked, but they looked healthy. He could shelter in them for the night.

"That's something," he told the cat. She headbutted his ankle.

He squeezed into the shrubs' midst. Twigs scratched his face, but once inside he found he could fit semicomfortably. If he curled on his side, he could lie down.

"It will certainly feel safer sleeping in here than out there," he said to Freya. "Even if it'll be awfully dark."

Nosing at the shrubs' roots, she ignored him.

He clambered back out, crept to the edge of the stream, and peered up at the break in the canopy. Stars glimmered between shreds of cloud drifting across the velvety sky. No rain tonight, probably. No wet socks. That was something more.

Sighing, he wondered whether Ira had made it home yet. He might've, if he'd flown the whole way. He might as well transform, now; he could hardly become more beastly than he already was.

Arthur swallowed. Yesterday morning, he'd been so afraid

Ira would remain a stag forever. He hadn't realized then how much worse it could be. How Ira could transform in other ways, losing himself to the forest's anger.

What must it feel like, Arthur wondered, to lose one's will—one's self—to the wood? His heart clenched. No wonder Ira had been so scared.

Letting out a breath, Arthur squeezed back into the shelter of the shrubs.

In the morning, he awoke stiff and sore with the cat tucked into his side. The stream burbled outside his shrubby shelter.

"What d'you think?" he asked. Freya stretched luxuriously. "Should we keep following the stream and hope for the best?"

Beginning her morning bath, Freya did not respond, except to hack up a hair ball. She resumed her bathing. Arthur's nose wrinkled.

He dragged himself from the shrubs, grimacing as his back acted up. His stomach rumbled. He gazed at it dolefully.

"I can't do anything for you right now," he told it. "I'm sure something in this forest bears fruit, but I don't know that I'd be able to tell a poisonous berry from a safe berry—assuming any berry in this forest *is* safe."

He imagined biting into a berry that spit black ooze instead of juice, and lost his appetite.

"Come on, Freya."

They set out, following the stream. Arthur kept one hand on the acorn and the other in his pocket, on his father's watch, but his mind wandered back to Ira. Ira touching him, tenderly and often, long before they'd kissed. Taking care of him.

Asking him to stay.

Ira going home without him because he was too frightened and angry to listen, even though he'd said Arthur made him feel hopeful. Ira accusing Arthur of never trying to change anything, which stung no matter how true.

Well, Arthur was trying now. He'd continue onward, replant the heart of the wood, and save himself and Charlotte and Ira whether Ira thought it possible or not.

The open sky above the stream didn't improve his mood: dingy gray like a used dishcloth. Freya crouched periodically in the grass, flicking her tail, and pounced at a spider or a late-season butterfly. Arthur sighed. She'd seemed much better company before he'd had another person to talk to.

His mood dropped lower the longer they walked. The water still smelled mechanical, the sky's color did not improve, he was hungry and thirsty, and he kept thinking with a shudder of yesterday's fog. At midmorning, feet aching, he dropped his knapsack and sat on a rock by the stream. Breathing deeply, he turned the rowan cross over and over, ran his fingers along its edges.

"We'll never make it, will we? I don't know why I thought I could do this."

Pressed against him, Freya didn't respond. Her ears twitched at a distant rustling.

The rustling came closer, and now it sounded bigger. Something was coming their way, and quickly. Arthur staggered to his feet and lunged for the nearest stick. He raised it like a sword, arms trembling.

A creature burst through the trees. Arthur dropped his stick, scrambling out of the way—then realized what he was seeing.

A horse. A massive gelding with a tan coat and flaxen hair and feathered feet. Except for the scarring on his hindquarters, he looked as he had when Arthur had last seen him.

"Maurice?"

"Uncle Arthur!"

His heart leaped. When Maurice turned, Sasha vaulted off his bare back. She barreled into Arthur with a laugh, hugging him tight. Behind her, Jonas dismounted more carefully. They stumbled, but Arthur caught them and pulled them into his arms.

It was a trick of the forest, it had to be, but Arthur laughed through his tears, kissing the tops of the children's heads over and over. They were reassuringly warm and solid. Freya arched against them, twisting between all of their legs.

Maurice stood guard. Two pillowcases were slung over his back with rope.

"I told you we'd find him!" Sasha said in triumph. "Hullo, Freya!"

"Did not," Jonas mumbled, sniffling into Arthur's neck. "You said we'd find Mama."

Arthur's stomach clenched. "How long since she left, duck?"

"She left Saturday to come find you with Miss Elspeth," Sasha said. "Miss Tierney has been looking after us."

"She was supposed to take us to the convent Monday morning," Jonas mumbled. "But . . ."

They scuffed their shoes.

"But we came looking for Mama," Sasha said. "Jonas wanted me to go home, but I wouldn't. I guess it's okay they came, though, since it was their idea to borrow Maurice."

Jonas looked up anxiously. "We'll bring him back when we get home, honest."

Arthur hugged them tight. "What day is it?"

"Wednesday."

The better part of a week since Charlotte had come after him. Arthur swallowed. He had to believe she was all right, wherever she was, for the children's sake as well as his own. *He'd* made it this far unscathed after only one day less since leaving the vale—although that had mostly been Ira's doing.

Then he processed something Sasha had said. "Who's Miss Elspeth?"

"She wears trousers." Sasha's eyes gleamed. "I want to be just like her."

"She's a stranger, kind of," Jonas said. "But she helped Mama up the hill last week. They came looking for you together."

Charlotte wasn't alone. Or hadn't been, when she'd left Seacliff. The Lord of the Wood wasn't traveling with her, but someone was. That was something, Arthur told himself, it was, it *was*, but his brain threatened to spiral into panic. He didn't know where Charlotte was, whether she was alive, and now the children were in the forest, too—although, while that worried him, he couldn't help but be grateful to see them.

A bandage was tied inexpertly around Jonas's arm. Arthur examined it, worried one of the strange, translucent animals had hurt them. The bandage was rusty with dried blood.

"What's this, duck?"

Jonas shivered. "These giant eagles chased us. One of them tried to eat Sasha."

"I tied the bandage myself," Sasha said proudly.

Arthur chuckled. She sounded as if she'd had a fun romp through a magical forest, with no concern for how the forest had tried to kill them. And while the eagles were terrible, they weren't infected, or hadn't been when he'd seen them.

"You did a marvelous job, just as Jonas did a marvelous job making sure the stormwings didn't eat you. Can I see?"

"You don't like blood," Jonas said.

Arthur's mouth twitched, but his skin prickled. "I've had some practice with it now."

His mouth puckered when he untied the bandage, however. A gash in Jonas's arm dribbled blood sluggishly.

"Do you have more bandages, duck?"

"I'll get them." Sasha dragged the pillowcases from Maurice's back with difficulty. He snuffled at her hair. She kissed his nose loudly and dragged her burden to Arthur. "They're in Jonas's."

Arthur had no idea which was Jonas's, since both pillowcases were identical, but he opened one, was immediately corrected, and opened the other. The corner of his mouth turned up. Each pillowcase held a bottle of water, a change of clothes, whatever dried or cured food they'd found around the house, and a few things—like the bandages—pilfered from Charlotte's medical supplies. Sasha's also had a kitchen knife; Jonas's, a pair of scissors and a ball of twine. The only things out of place were Sasha's old rag doll, Charlotte's favorite whistle, and one of Arthur's novels.

He clutched it briefly and set it aside in favor of the bandages. "What's the book for, duck?"

Jonas pinkened. "That was Sasha's idea. In case we found you and you were scared. That's what the whistle is for, too. In case Mama was scared."

"And the doll, for Sasha." Arthur wiped blood from their arm. "What about you, duck?"

They shook their head. "I didn't think anything would make me feel better in here. Until we found you."

Smiling crookedly, Arthur kissed their forehead. Their flush deepened, but they leaned against him when he finished rebandaging their arm.

"Let's take a look at you, Sasha," he said.

She was scratched and bruised but on the whole unharmed. Arthur dabbed ointment onto her scratches. With the children at his side, more or less safe and sound, a tiny flame of hope flickered to life inside him. They'd make it to the heart of the wood. They'd replant the tree, heal the forest, find Charlotte—and go home. Together.

"Right," Arthur said, with renewed determination. "Let's get on with it."

"Finding Mama?" Sasha asked, trying and failing to climb back onto Maurice. Arthur lifted her and the children's makeshift saddlebags into place, smiling. Her skinny legs splayed wide across the gelding's back, but she gripped his mane like she'd been born sitting there.

"I hope so," Arthur said. "Maybe we'll stumble across her on our way. But we're going to the heart of the wood to plant Granddad's acorn."

He offered Jonas a leg up, but they shook their head and clung to him. He squeezed their hand.

"Why?" Sasha asked.

"To heal the forest, duck. To make it safe for Mama. And for us. And . . ."

He faltered. He patted Maurice's withers and started jauntily forward, but Sasha had never met an unended sentence she didn't like.

"And what?"

Shame needled Arthur's insides, but Sasha's eyes gleamed with curiosity, and he couldn't bring himself to disappoint her.

"And," he said, in the best bedtime story voice he could manage, "for the Lord of the Wood."

Sasha gasped, which almost made the mention of Ira worth it. "You met him?"

"I'll tell you all about it," he lied, planning to do as George had done and tell them half-truths gilded in embellishments. "Probably we'll reach the heart of the wood before I'm done. It was a great silver tree . . ."

Jonas walked at their uncle's side, clinging to his hand; Maurice was on his other side, with Sasha proudly on his back; Freya trotted on ahead, tail held high. The ache in Arthur's chest gave way to a soft, golden warmth. He'd been reunited with his family, most of it, and soon—he gripped Jonas's hand tighter, determined for the children's sakes—he'd be reunited with Charlotte, too. His family was all he'd ever needed.

But as the afternoon darkened and died away, he kept thinking of Ira. Alone, back in the vale with no one but Calyx for company, with a stab wound in his shoulder and an aching leg and no knee brace.

Arthur's skin prickled. The things Ira had said to him, until this morning, had meant so much. Like something about Arthur mattered. But it had stopped mattering the moment Ira was scared.

Ira had so many reasons to be scared, Arthur thought. The creep of moss and lichens over his body, the transformations that left him different each time he turned back. The way he lost himself inside the creature or the forest's rage. He'd transformed anyway, over and over, to save Arthur.

Arthur hoped Ira would be all right, once the tree was replanted. Even if they never saw each other again, as seemed likely: Every budding friendship Arthur had ever had, having broken off so abruptly as they all did, had concluded that way. This time, at least, he knew why.

He gripped Jonas's hand so tightly that his nibling squirmed out of his grasp. He loosened his grip.

"Sorry, duck."

He spun his hopes for the Lord of the Wood into stories for the children, the same as his father had spun stories for him and Charlotte so many years ago.

XXXVI. In which Charlotte tests her cure

On Wednesday, with Elspeth looking after the animals, Charlotte was still in bed. It was a rare good day. She was tired, but not as bone-deep fatigued as she often was; her head didn't hurt, and the ache in the rest of her body was tolerable.

This was later than she normally stayed in bed on good days. At home, she would've been up before sunrise, but lying in a bed that wasn't hers, in a house that wasn't hers, was oddly freeing. There were no patients to see, no laundry to do, no children to tend to—she winced at that thought but let it pass—no villagers who might realize she was playing the layabout instead of going about her business as she ought.

At home, of course, Arthur tried to help, but he was also a constant source of worry. Charlotte knew he was lonely, though he never admitted it. She had figured out how to fit in with Seacliff long ago. It wasn't always comfortable, but she'd managed. Her brother never had; she worried he never would.

With that thought, she got up. Thinking about Arthur meant wondering, again, where he was and why he'd left the vale in the first place. Surely the Lord of the Wood had taken him home, she tried to tell herself, but optimism came hard to her. And it was difficult not to think that, if that *were* the case, she could've stayed home instead of gallivanting through the forest.

The plant creature skittered across the floor to greet her, small and vaguely dog-shaped. Picking it up, Charlotte carried it to the window.

She peered outside. Elspeth came around the side of the house where she'd left the horse and mule. Her shoulders were bowed, her eyes bruised like they'd been yesterday, but she stopped to listen to a wren trilling the gray winter dawn.

The corner of Charlotte's mouth turned up. It hadn't been all bad, coming out here.

Setting the plant creature on the floor, she turned to her work. The creature slung itself onto the counter beside her vials.

"No pets on the counter. I know you can grow tall enough to look from the floor, if you're interested."

The creature clicked but slid off the counter and grew, swaying at her side. She patted it and returned to the vials.

Since plant matter could not swallow things, she'd decided infused water might be the best way to run her test. Last night, with the plant creature's help, she and Elspeth had cracked the acorns, removed the skins, and ground the nuts. To their surprise, it had been like cracking normal acorns, except that the nuts came out gold. Ground, the nuts had become a golden powder that Charlotte had put in water overnight.

This morning, the water shimmered with gold specks. They'd made more than would fill the vials. Charlotte had wanted extra in case a course of medication was called for and in the hopes of treating Elspeth if the acorns proved effective on the plant matter.

"I hope this works," she murmured.

She pulled gloves on and poured acorn water into the vials of bark and leaves. The infected grass from the vial of ooze she moved into a fresh vial and watered that, too. It might've been worth testing the water directly on the ooze, but she'd leave that for later. First she wanted to see whether it did anything for her patients, such as they were.

Nothing happened, but that didn't dishearten her. Most medications needed some time before they took effect; cures often took longer. She'd check on the vials throughout the day, the next several days if necessary. If they showed no improvement in that time, she'd have to reevaluate. With Elspeth's symptoms developing so much more slowly than usual, Charlotte hoped several days wouldn't see her bed-bound like Gracie Buchanan.

Elspeth came in and slumped in her armchair. Charlotte joined her, resisting the urge to grab something to occupy her hands. The plant creature shrank back down and curled in her lap, winding tendrils through her fingers.

"It work?" Elspeth asked.

"I don't know. Medicine doesn't usually work that fast. It might take effect in fifteen minutes, or three hours, or it might take a course of several days."

"If it works."

Charlotte reached for Elspeth's hand. "If. But I'm hopeful."

Elspeth's fingers were cold and stiff. Scooting closer, Charlotte rubbed her hands to warm them.

"Thanks." Elspeth's hair lay in limp strands across her forehead. "What's got you so cheery today?"

"It's a good day. I'm less tired and hardly in pain."

"I'd've thought a good day meant no pain."

"I don't remember what it feels like not to be in pain. Anyway, the acorns—I don't know if they'll work, but I've spent years lamenting that nothing I had access to could even alleviate the sickness's symptoms, let alone cure it. Now I've got something new to try." Charlotte smoothed Elspeth's hair from her forehead, then sat back pretending she hadn't done it. "I don't know. Today I feel . . . hopeful."

She built up the fire, tucked Elspeth into a fur, and experimented with the ovular whistle they'd found in the bedside table. Positioning her fingers on this whistle was different than on her whistles at home, which were thin and cylindrical. A pleasant note in a lower tone came out, then a higher one. Her fingers fumbled at the unfamiliar placement of the holes, but she blew a few more notes. One screeched like a dying cat. The plant creature slung itself out of her lap and disappeared into the ceiling.

"Sorry," Charlotte called up to it.

Cautiously, the plant creature curled back down over her chair. It examined the whistle, which she held up for it before putting the whistle away.

Elspeth had been listening with her eyes closed, but she cracked a tired eye when Charlotte returned to her chair. "Took to that like a duck to water."

"I have a couple of whistles at home." Charlotte stroked the plant creature. "I used to play. Not all the time, of course, I had far too much to do, but I played when I could. John whittled my favorite one."

"You don't play anymore?"

Charlotte shook her head. "I get breathless so easily. And my fingers are stiff so often, or sore, or both . . . It's harder than it used to be. Most things are."

"Must be frustrating." Elspeth drummed her fingers on her knees. "That sounded pretty good, anyway. Mostly."

Charlotte's mouth twitched.

An hour had elapsed when she finally checked her vials. She'd found herself thinking periodically, *A watched pot never boils*, though taking such things literally was silly. The acorn water would work, or it wouldn't, and it would do so in its own time whether she watched or not.

"So?" Elspeth asked.

Charlotte's hands shook. She laid them flat on the counter and went through a few cycles of breathing. The plant creature swayed at her side, waist-high.

She reached for the vial of bark.

Hard to draw any conclusions. The bark was softened by having been left in water for an hour. It looked brown rather than gray or black, but she couldn't be sure that wasn't the lighting. The infected leaves were similar.

Charlotte shook her head. She should've realized; of course half-decayed bark and leaves would crumble in water.

She reached for the clean vial into which she'd put the blade of grass.

The grass was green.

Charlotte's heart skipped a beat. She held the vial to the window. The water no longer shimmered with gold specks, but no question: The grass was free of ooze and black veins. No dark tendrils unfurled in the water.

The sickness was gone.

"Well?" Elspeth croaked.

Unable to speak, Charlotte brought her the vial.

Elspeth whistled but broke off coughing midway through. Charlotte hovered, a hand at her back, until she quieted.

"I'll be damned, Lottie," Elspeth rasped. "You did it. What about the others, then?"

Charlotte handed them to her. Elspeth examined them.

"All right—harder to say. But it looks better, don't it?"

Not clearly enough for Charlotte's taste. The water in the other vials was brown with flecks that might've been desiccated plant matter or some remnant of the sickness. But they didn't seem as black as they'd been, and the grass—there was no question its sickness was gone.

Charlotte sucked in a breath, leaning on the back of her

chair for support. The anticipation had sapped some of her energy. The plant creature wrapped around her, offering more stability. She patted it gratefully; it had proven a good aid in the last two days.

"It's a good first step."

Elspeth laughed, stopped to fight another coughing fit. "First step! Lottie—"

Charlotte shook her head. "It's good, I'm not denying that, but we don't know if it'll work consistently. Or if there are any side effects. Or if it'll work on humans as well as plants, for that matter. But . . ."

Straightening with the plant creature's help, Charlotte pulled Elspeth's collar aside. The black veins at her scar had unwound farther, stretching up toward her throat and down toward her breast.

Charlotte swallowed. "I guess we're going to find out."

She found a glass in one of the cupboards and dipped it in the remaining acorn water, reconsidered and added more. Dosage. Another thing to figure out, if this worked.

"Start with this."

Elspeth downed it. "Now what?"

"Now we wait."

They passed a torturous hour in which Elspeth asked about her whistle playing and Charlotte named her favorite tunes. But their minds were on the acorns and the black veins at Elspeth's collar, her increased exhaustion over the last couple of days. The plant creature wound around Charlotte's feet, up her legs, over the back of her chair. Charlotte's eyes kept flickering toward Elspeth's shirt, but she forced herself to hold off checking until the whole hour had run out.

Elspeth sounded winded. "Well?"

"It's hard to tell."

Charlotte kept her voice light, but internally she panicked.

She couldn't tell whether the black veins had receded. Did it need more time, or a higher dosage? Both? Or was it simply not working?

She cleared her throat. She was a healer, for God's sake. This was the whole business of her life. Not something to panic about.

"We'll let you sit another hour and see what happens."

Another hour made no change, but another dose would empty their supply. Charlotte's hands shook as she gave Elspeth the rest of the acorn water. She had no more acorns to do a new batch. If this didn't work—

Stop it. She didn't usually panic so much when treating a disease.

But she'd never meaningfully treated the sickness. This was a new treatment, yes, a possible cure, and it had worked on the grass. But a blade of grass was not a human body.

It was agonizing. Elspeth slumped in her armchair with her eyes closed, her breath rattling. The plant creature swayed between them, its tendrils turning from Charlotte to Elspeth and back.

She's just another patient.

Charlotte busied herself doing what she could to ease Elspeth's pain and breathing, but it wasn't much.

Just another patient, she repeated like a mantra, *just another patient*, but it didn't work. Elspeth was not just another patient, no matter how Charlotte tried to convince herself.

At some point, Elspeth fell asleep. Charlotte moved her collar aside, holding her breath. The veins seemed less extensive.

She let out a breath and smoothed Elspeth's hair. Rather than waking her, Charlotte decided to give it another hour. To distract herself, she pored over the sketches of Arthur sitting every which way in his armchair but right, his nose in a book.

You'll never find me, his voice echoed in her head. She pictured his face ghostly in the terrible trees outside. She swallowed.

"I will," she whispered. "I will find you. I will."

She put the drawings away; they reminded her of the faces and voices in the trees. She pulled the plant creature into her lap. It shaped itself vaguely into different animals.

Elspeth awoke with a lazy stretch. Charlotte was at her side in an instant. The plant creature clung to the back of her chair, as if to get its own look.

"How do you feel?" Charlotte asked.

"Better." Elspeth breathed in deeply. "I can breathe. Ain't so cold anymore, neither."

"And the pain? The fatigue?"

"Gone," Elspeth said. "All gone. What about—"

Charlotte peeled back her collar.

The black veins had vanished.

She touched Elspeth's stitches, hardly believing what she saw. Smooth, unblemished tawny skin. The wound's edges weren't even red anymore.

She met Elspeth's eyes. "It's gone."

Elspeth's breath caught. "All of it?"

"All of it."

Elspeth whooped and leaped up from the chair. Charlotte laughed, half crying with relief. Elspeth must be feeling better, she thought, to move like that.

Elspeth whirled them around the room until Charlotte was dizzy. The plant creature slung itself out of their way and curled up by the stove.

They stopped by the door, faces flushed.

"You did it, Lottie."

Charlotte wiped her eyes on her apron. "Maybe."

Elspeth laughed. "Maybe, nothing."

"*Maybe.* It looks good, certainly, and your scar makes me hopeful, but I'll have to repeat the test on another person, if I can—we'll have to find more acorns—and you might need to repeat treatment to make sure the symptoms don't return—"

Elspeth gripped Charlotte's arms.

"Lottie. Take the win. You did it."

Charlotte's eyes darted over her face, down to her stitches. Half expecting the black veins to have returned. But they hadn't.

"You really feel all right?"

"Yes."

Charlotte couldn't stop staring. She'd lost every patient infected with wood sickness. Two hours ago, Elspeth had been exhausted, cold, her breath rattling. Now she looked like she'd never been sick a day in her life.

"I did it," Charlotte whispered. "I cured it."

"You did."

Elspeth's hands were warm on her arms.

Charlotte laughed. "I did."

Dizzy with her triumph, she grabbed Elspeth's collar, pulled her in, and kissed her.

A sharp inhalation. Elspeth braced herself against the door and kissed her back, hungrily, until Charlotte was breathless.

They stood forehead to forehead, breathing hard. Elspeth touched her cheek.

Charlotte squeezed her eyes shut. It had been so long since she'd done anything like this. Years. She'd been so concerned with maintaining—both her propriety and her ability to carry on—that she hadn't realized how much she'd missed it.

"Take me to bed," she whispered.

"You sure?"

"Please."

Elspeth's hand slipped into hers. She led Charlotte across the room and pushed her gently into the little bed in the corner, leaned in. Her kisses were soft now, like Charlotte was something to be handled carefully. Something precious.

One hand cradled Charlotte's face. The other traced down her neck, over her bosom, lower and lower. She pushed Charlotte's skirt up over her hips, worked at her underthings until her hand found its way between Charlotte's thighs.

Charlotte gasped and shuddered, tears spilling down her cheeks.

Elspeth pulled away. "We don't have to do this."

"I want to."

Elspeth wiped her tears away. "You're weepin', Lottie."

Charlotte sat up, sagging against her. "It's just . . . it's been so long. Since Sasha was born. John died so soon after, and I haven't . . ."

Elspeth kissed her forehead. "S'all right. We don't have to."

"I *want* to." Charlotte wiped her eyes. "Unless you don't want to."

The corner of Elspeth's mouth turned up. "Ain't the first time a woman's turned the waterworks on to me. I just want you to be sure."

"You must be dreadful, if women are always crying in bed with you."

Elspeth let out a bark of astonished laughter. Charlotte giggled wetly. Good Lord. She'd *giggled.* How long had it been since she'd done that?

"You must be dreadful," she repeated, "and I'll go on thinking you're dreadful until you prove otherwise, so unless you'd like a black mark on your record—"

"Can't have that, can we?" Elspeth murmured against her lips, pushing her back again.

Charlotte slid Elspeth's braces down over her shoulders. Elspeth sat back and tugged her shirt free of her trousers, pulled it over her head.

Charlotte's breath hitched. She touched the hollow of Elspeth's throat, the dip between her breasts. Cupped one of them in her palm. With a low murmur Charlotte didn't quite hear, Elspeth kissed her neck, her hand slipping back beneath Charlotte's skirt and between her thighs. Charlotte clung to her and breathed her name.

No black mark was added to Elspeth's record that afternoon.

XXXVII. In which Arthur forges onward, despite the forest's misgivings

Arthur had hoped they'd come across the heart of the wood that very day, but the forest was behaving oddly—if there were a normal way for an enchanted forest to behave. With the acorn as his compass, Arthur was certain the heart of the wood was somewhere straight ahead. The forest wouldn't let them go that way. It kept closing paths before them, opening others that pushed them farther west or east or south. The trees shifted so much that it confused him. He focused on the acorn.

"We *are* trying to help you," he said to the trees more than once, with increasing annoyance. The forest didn't respond, except to keep subtly shifting. The cat wound underfoot, mewling uneasily.

Wind clawed through the branches around them. Jonas shivered, drawing their coat tighter. Arthur squeezed their hand. He didn't feel half as hopeless as he had that morning. As long as he had the children, he could believe everything would be all right. They'd work their way north again. The forest had to let them through eventually, as it had let him into the vale, as it had regrown the bridge once it had understood what he was about.

Maurice didn't like the wind. His ears twitched at every

sound, but he didn't run off. He seemed to have taken a liking to Sasha. The day's journey had worn her out; she fell asleep on his broad back, her fingers tangled in his mane. Whenever she seemed in danger of slipping off, the gelding twisted around to nudge her back into place with his nose, whickering.

Arthur smiled fondly, but his smile faded as he thought, again, of Ira. He hoped Ira was safe back in the vale, that Calyx was comforting him if it could. He sighed.

Jonas spoke for the first time in hours. "What really happened, Uncle Arthur?"

Their thin face was creased with concern, although admittedly their expression had been such all day. While Sasha was intrigued and delighted by the forest—even its dangers, like the stormwings—Jonas couldn't wait until they were free of it.

"What do you mean, duck?" Arthur asked.

With a glance at their sleeping sister, Jonas lowered their voice. "You didn't answer Sasha's questions about the Lord of the Wood. You always answer her questions. Even the bad ones."

"There are no bad questions," Arthur said automatically, because his father had always said the same.

"Maybe not," Jonas said solemnly, "but Sasha has them sometimes."

Arthur chuckled.

"What happened?" Jonas repeated. "Didn't you really meet the Lord of the Wood?"

Arthur gazed straight ahead, considering how much to say. Before, he'd spun the children a tale of a fairy prince like the one he'd always dreamed of. He'd told them about the greenery sprouting at Ira's feet without mentioning it dying a moment later; a sentient plant creature without mentioning it had tried to kill him; a magical pool that healed wounds without mentioning he'd seen his father's spirit or that his hand and neck still throbbed periodically.

He'd told them stories, in short, like those Charlotte had worried about him telling: ones that glossed over unpleasant realities in favor of a dream and a wish.

"I met him. He wasn't what I expected."

"What was he like?"

"He was dreadfully grim, at first. He was . . . a person, not the figure Granddad always made him out to be. And he didn't wear flowers and leaves like in the story, but I don't suppose they'd be very warm at this time of year." Arthur gave a small smile without meaning to. "He was kind to me, mostly. He didn't think I was odd. He . . ."

He thought of Ira drawing him, over and over. Ira so earnestly telling Arthur he wasn't useless like he—like everyone—thought. Ira worrying that nothing he did would make a difference, the same way Arthur worried.

Ira touching Arthur's face. His claws tangled in Arthur's hair. His lips on Arthur's.

Arthur flushed, deciding not to share any of that. "He knew Granddad better than I thought."

Jonas's brow scrunched. "What do you mean?"

"They were good friends." Arthur ran a hand over his face. "Granddad never told us that."

Jonas's lips twisted. They picked at their lower lip thoughtfully. Arthur bent to grab a leaf and handed that to them to shred instead.

"You and Mama don't always tell us the whole truth about things."

Arthur looked at them in surprise, then chuckled ruefully. "I suppose that's true. We do try, you know. Lottie doesn't like to hide things from you if she doesn't have to, and neither do I."

Jonas considered this. "Maybe Granddad thought he had to."

Arthur cracked a smile he wasn't feeling. "Why's that, do you think?"

"You're too much like Sasha," Jonas said, to his utter shock. No one, least of all himself, would ever have said he was anything like Sasha. "Probably Granddad thought you'd walk into the wood for fun if you knew more about it."

"I might have. If I'd known . . . Well, I might have. He did promise to take me one day, but I was never old enough before he vanished." Arthur glanced at Jonas. "You really think I'm like Sasha?"

Jonas gave one of their small rare smiles. "Less annoying, though."

Sasha let out a snore so loud she might've been faking, but she never would've let her sibling call her annoying without jumping up to accuse *them* of being annoying instead. Maurice's ears twitched in her direction.

"She's not annoying," Arthur said, with nothing but fondness in his voice. "She's . . . well, she's Sasha."

She mumbled in her sleep. His face relaxed into a smile, a real one.

When Sasha awoke from her nap, Arthur focused on pushing north. The heart of the wood was that way; he felt it. They had to get through, no matter how hard the forest nudged them in another direction. Whenever a clump of trees appeared, he went through rather than around as best he could, following Freya. Jonas clambered over trunks and through brambles, uncomplaining about the scratches sustained. Arthur stopped periodically to dab ointment on their face and arms, and his. Astride Maurice, Sasha barreled through every obstacle—sometimes getting so far ahead that Arthur panicked, afraid that if he lost sight of her she'd vanish in the forest forever.

It quickly became clear, however, that Maurice barreling through was their best chance of getting past whatever obstacles the forest placed in their path. Arthur let Sasha ride ahead but begged her not to go too fast.

"Stay in sight, duckling. We need to stick together."

"Careful," Jonas said. "When I said that, she made me ride the horse."

Maurice snorted into their hair. They grimaced, wiping equine snot from their curls. Arthur gave them a handkerchief.

The temperature plummeted. Leaves crackled with frost.

Sasha shivered. "Why's it so cold?"

"The eagles you saw, duck. They bring storms, but they come too early."

"How do you know?"

"The Lord of the Wood told me."

Sasha's eyes shone with curiosity, but Arthur hurried onward, unwilling—as Jonas had pointed out—to answer any questions she might ask about the Lord of the Wood. He hadn't even told the children Ira's name. It let him pretend he could distance himself from the Lord of the Wood, though he'd worried about Ira almost constantly since they'd parted ways.

He couldn't shake it. Despite the way things had soured, he couldn't stop thinking of what had come before.

You have kind eyes like he did, he heard Ira saying, when they'd met. And later: *I think you're lovely.*

Ira had transformed for him so many times, though it always meant changing back different. He'd been so afraid to leave the vale, but he'd left anyway because Arthur had asked him to. That had to mean something, despite their falling-out. No one Arthur had ever attempted to befriend had done half so much for him, nor made it so clear they liked him despite his oddities, or perhaps because of them. For the first time, Arthur let himself hope that his parting from Ira didn't have to mean the end.

Maybe, after the heart of the wood was replanted, Arthur could find him. Maybe, no matter how angry they'd gotten, they could fix things between them.

XXXVIII. In which Charlotte meets the Lord of the Wood

Long after their lovemaking had finished, Charlotte was still rumpled in bed, curled into Elspeth's side. Elspeth, rumpled herself, stroked her arm and kissed her forehead, her nose, her eyes. The corners of her mouth lifted whenever Charlotte caught her gaze, but she'd hardly glanced away once. The sex must have left Charlotte looking positively taken apart.

"What?" she murmured. She was exhausted, but not in a bad way; for one thing, she felt like she might fall asleep and stay asleep.

"I dunno." Elspeth shifted, leaning over her. "Different, seeing you like this."

"Denuded of my clothing?"

Elspeth laughed. "You ain't hardly naked, Lottie, I barely got a thing off you but your drawers. I'll own I'd like to see you that way next time, if you're amenable."

"You really are dreadfully vulgar."

"You didn't seem to think it was vulgar when I had my tongue up your—"

Charlotte hit her with a pillow. Elspeth fell back beside her, chuckling. Charlotte kissed her into silence.

When they broke apart, Elspeth touched her cheek.

"Seeing you relaxed, I guess." She propped herself on her elbow, a hand on Charlotte's hip. "Feels like your mind's been going since the moment I met you, with all the things you gotta do and all the people you gotta take care of, even when you're in pain. And now it's quiet."

Charlotte's eyes prickled. She liked the weight of Elspeth's hand on her hip. She wanted to like the way Elspeth understood her, too, but she couldn't yet. It was mortifying, being known this way.

Elspeth watched her carefully. "It's like you think use is all there is to a body. Like you think you gotta earn rest, or . . . or someone caring for you. But it ain't, and you don't."

Mortifying, yes—but Charlotte wanted to learn to like this. She sighed, snuggling into Elspeth.

"I'd like to believe that," she said, "but it's difficult. I can't do as much as I used to, since my illness, and in Seacliff . . . Well, it's just how everyone thinks. How everyone lives—how can you live, otherwise?"

Elspeth bent and kissed her brow.

"Port Lorne, too, darlin'. But you know what? Gran and Granddad worked themselves half to death when me and Maggie was growing up. I watched 'em. Always told myself it wouldn't be that way for me. And it don't have to be for you, neither." She hesitated. "I'd make sure of it. If you wanted that."

Charlotte's breath hitched. Before she could respond, however, there was a flump across the room: the plant creature dropping to the floor. It scrambled toward the window, tendrils swaying.

Charlotte sat up, her back twinging. Her pain had been low all day, but the movement coming on the heels of physical exertion reminded her how easy it was to overdo things.

"What do you suppose has it so excited?"

"Dunno, but I'll see what's what." Elspeth reached for her shirt and boots. "Stay here."

"Not a chance."

Charlotte tugged her clothes back into place and reached for her cane. Elspeth grabbed the poker from beside the stove and slipped out into the snow with Charlotte at her heels. The plant creature slung itself after them, darting back and forth like an excitable dog.

Beyond the brambles, an angry howl split the snowy silence. Charlotte shuddered. The plant creature nosed at her hand, then went weaving back and forth again.

Another howl, louder and angrier than the last. Brambles withered and died, crumbling to dust. They left an opening wide enough for a horse, beyond which was a swinging bridge.

Limping off the bridge was something misshapen. The plant creature shot forward, bowling into the thing as it cleared the brambles. The thing fell with a crunch of snow and a curse. Elspeth stood in front of Charlotte, armed with the poker.

"Calyx—" A low growl. "Calyx, *stop it.*"

The plant creature whirled away and trotted happily back to Charlotte. It sat at her feet, tendrils waving.

"Calyx. Is that your name?"

It nosed at her hand.

The thing before them struggled to its feet. It was a beast, with a wolf's legs, paw-like hands, antlers, a fanged snout, and a face something like a wolf's and something like a stag's and something like a raven's. One leg was twisted, one eye scarred. Angry red streaks slashed across one cheek. Moss and lichens grew in the scar and the ruff of the beast's neck.

But he had black hair tied in a loose knot like a human's, except for the white flowers dotting it like stars. Human eyes, too, one hazel, one milky. Except that he was without shoes, he wore human clothes: trousers, a linen shirt with toggles—spotted with blood at the shoulder—and a fur cloak he had become tangled in.

With a snarl, he flung the cloak away. Charlotte gasped; the snarl gave her goose pimples.

The beast looked up. Elspeth stepped forward, raising the poker, but a tendril shot out and wrenched it away.

"Hey—"

Calyx whipped the poker so hard it flew over the remaining brambles. Elspeth whirled on the plant creature, but the beast's eyes fixed on Charlotte. His face slackened.

"Charlotte Throckmorton, I presume," he said, in a hoarse voice.

"Prentice," Charlotte said automatically, but her brain stalled out. Why did the beast know her name?

He nodded and trudged toward them. They backed away, but he merely went to the door. Calyx gamboled after him until he went inside. It stood uncertainly at the threshold, but Charlotte scooped it up and followed him into the house.

"Arthur was right," the beast said. "You do look like George."

Her heart beat painfully. "You've seen Arthur."

He hung his cloak on a peg, limped toward the stove, and sank into the shabbier of the two armchairs.

"I know he was here." Charlotte's voice shook. "His tools are here."

"He was here."

"Then where is he now?"

"I left him." The beast dropped his head into his paw-like hands with a low moan. "Oh, God. I left him."

Charlotte perched in the other armchair. Elspeth stood over her like a bodyguard. Calyx wrapped one tendril around Charlotte's arm, reached for the beast with another.

"Left him *where*?"

The beast dragged his hands through his hair, leaving it bedraggled. Calyx unwound itself from Charlotte to drape over his shoulders.

"In the forest. Alone."

They seemed in danger of getting no more from him, for he dropped his head in his hands again, his breathing quick and harsh in a way familiar to Charlotte. To her astonishment, she realized he was in the grips of a panic attack.

He was a beast, and he'd seen Arthur—but Charlotte was a healer before she was anything.

She bit her lip, touched the beast's arm.

"Lottie," Elspeth said sharply, but Charlotte said, "It's all right."

To the beast, she said, "Breathe with me."

He raised his face to hers. It was alarming: the fangs, the cervine ears on a face both canine and corvid, the human eyes at odds with all his animal features. The blood dried on one cheek, the moss and lichens growing from his fur. But his eyes were bright and scared, latched on to her desperately as so many eyes had been in her years of healing.

"Give me your hands," Charlotte said.

They were nearly paws, thick-fingered, clawed and furry, with metacarpal pads. Charlotte swallowed but gripped them. She didn't have to tell him to hold her gaze; he was already doing it. To her surprise, he started breathing the way she'd intended to show him, *in for four, hold for four, out for four*, before she'd begun.

"That's it. Together, now."

After several cycles, his breathing calmed. He let out a long breath. Calyx nuzzled his cheek with a vine.

"Did you teach Arthur that," he asked, "or did he teach you?"

Charlotte's eyes stung. That was why he'd known the breathing cycle: Arthur had taught it to him.

"I taught him." She gripped the arms of her chair, trying to order her errant thoughts. "Are you the Lord of the Wood?"

The beast gazed at her dolefully. "I am."

He bent over, massaging his gnarled right leg with a grimace, or what Charlotte thought was a grimace. With his strange, bestial features, it was difficult to tell.

Her brain had gone all numb and funny. Her thoughts swirled, a confusion of her father's stories, the beast before them—so different than the figure in the tales—and question upon question about Arthur. How long he'd been in the vale. Why he'd left. Why the Lord of the Wood had, evidently, gone with him, and why they'd parted.

"You seen a girl?" Elspeth asked in a strained voice. Charlotte reached for her hand. "Would've been—hell's bells, I don't know—three weeks ago now or so. Looks a good bit like me, except she's taller, and fairer, and her nose's crooked."

"Arthur's the first human I've seen in almost thirty years," the beast said. "I was trapped here. Until he came."

A muscle ticked in Elspeth's jaw. Her fingers crushed Charlotte's. She'd known she was probably looking for a corpse, but she'd thought she'd find it. She'd thought the Lord of the Wood would know what had happened.

"If you haven't seen her," Charlotte said, "isn't there any way to—to find out what happened? To see where she is?"

The beast dragged a hand through his hair and launched to his feet. Calyx swayed on his shoulders. Charlotte tamped down a prickle of jealousy. She'd come to think of the strange little creature as hers in the last couple of days, but it was clearly his.

The beast brushed past to retrieve the odd silver basin.

"This." He filled it with water, growling when some sloshed on the floor. "Spill a drop of your blood into this, and you can see where she is now." He set the basin on the table and sat. "It won't be pleasant."

Elspeth didn't move from Charlotte's side. "Is it safe?"

"Safe, yes. But it may be disorienting."

He held out a pocketknife.

"What d'you think?" Elspeth asked Charlotte in a low voice.

"I think, if we want to find our siblings, we have to take whatever he can give us."

Elspeth approached, took the knife without touching the beast's fingers, screwed her face up, and pricked her finger. A drop of blood splashed into the water.

Elspeth froze.

"Elspeth?"

She didn't answer. She stood just as she'd been, face screwed up, hand over the basin, blood slowly dripping into it.

Charlotte grabbed her in alarm. At her distress, Calyx slipped from the beast's shoulders and wound up her side instead, clicking fretfully.

"What's wrong with her?"

"Nothing." The beast retrieved bandages from a cupboard and shrugged out of his bloodied shirt. The bandages on one shoulder needed changing. "When she's done looking, she'll come out of it."

Nonetheless, Charlotte fussed over her. She bandaged the bleeding finger and kissed it. Then, more to have something to do than for any other reason, she asked the beast, "Do you need help?"

He paused in the middle of packing his wound with fresh bandages. With his hands so paw-like, it seemed difficult.

"Yeah. Thanks." He avoided her gaze as she finished the work for him. "I'm sorry I left him."

Her skin prickled. She thought of her brother alone in the forest. "Why did you?"

"I was scared." He scrubbed his face with a paw. "The forest took me over. I thought I might . . . I should've listened to him. He tried to calm me down, but I wouldn't—"

A sharp inhalation cut him off: Elspeth had come back to life. She glanced around wildly, gulping down air.

Charlotte touched her back, worried by the sudden change. "Are you all right?"

Elspeth shook her head. She cast Charlotte off and paced the room, fingers clenching and unclenching at her sides. Calyx curled a comforting tendril around Charlotte's arm.

"Elspeth?"

When she finally spoke, it was to the Lord of the Wood, venomously. "You said I'd see her. You said. Wherever she was."

"You would," he said in confusion. "You must have. What did you see?"

"Nothing," Elspeth spat. "Not a damn thing. Not even a body."

Charlotte reached for her. With a sob, Elspeth buried her face in Charlotte's neck. Charlotte kissed her head, tamping down her worry for Arthur and the fear that she, too, might see nothing in the basin.

"What did you see?" she asked, when Elspeth's sobs had quieted. "If not Maggie, what . . . ?"

"A tree." Elspeth's voice was muffled. "It spat me out at a mossy tree."

Charlotte's heart sank. "Like the ones . . . ?"

Elspeth shook her head against Charlotte's neck. "Just a plain old tree. The one where I found the acorn, right there with the stump of the first tree behind it. I called for her, I went wandering all around, but all I saw was the leftovers of that work camp what vanished. Like I was stuck in a nightmare, trying to find Maggie, but all I could find was trees."

"She's there," the beast said. "If that's what the basin showed you, she's there. One way or another."

"I'm telling you, I didn't see her."

"If—" Charlotte's arms tightened around Elspeth "—if it's a body you're looking for, it might be buried."

Elspeth sagged against her. Then, straightening, she pulled away. A lump swelled in Charlotte's throat. Elspeth had already stayed here longer than she'd wanted because Charlotte had asked her to.

"Lottie—"

"I know. Go."

Elspeth unclasped the chain from Maggie's acorn and hung it around Charlotte's neck.

"We'll find each other again," she said in a low voice.

Charlotte nodded, wanting to cry. Elspeth kissed her once, hard.

"You take care of her," she said to Calyx. It touched her hand.

She nodded at the Lord of the Wood and stalked outside. A moment later, the horse raced around the side of the house and galloped through the brambles and over the bridge, with Elspeth on his back. Then they were gone.

Charlotte swallowed. The spot over her left eye started throbbing. "Calyx, can you get my painkillers?"

The plant creature crept away, to root through her medical kit, and back.

The beast's expression was unreadable. "I see Calyx has taken a liking to you."

Charlotte took her painkillers, patting the creature swaying beside her. "I found it outside, half frozen. I think it was grateful someone brought it in where it was warm."

The beast ran a clawed hand through his hair.

"I banished it from the house. It . . . didn't take to Arthur like it has to you." He emptied the basin and filled it with fresh water. "If you look—if you describe what you see—we might be able to find him."

Charlotte's fingers curled into fists. "You know where you left him, don't you?"

The beast closed his eyes briefly. "That was yesterday morning. He might be anywhere by now."

"But you know where he was, and surely you know where he was going?"

"To the heart of the wood. What your companion called 'the first tree.' But many paths lead there. And for all we know he may have lost all of them. But if you look—"

"Can't you do it?" Charlotte's stomach churned, thinking of Elspeth unnaturally still until she'd wrenched free of the vision. A vision that had not shown her Maggie. "You'd likely recognize the place, surely you know this forest like the back of your hand—"

"I won't be able to see him. I'm not his blood."

Charlotte sucked in a breath and stood beside the basin. The beast handed her the knife. Her fingers were stiff; she did not prick so much as dig into her fingertip. Her head fuzzed—*silly*, she thought blearily, *I'm a healer, I can stand the sight of a little blood*—but she managed. A single drop of blood dripped into the water.

She was in the forest, alone.

Charlotte froze, disoriented by the change. Trees surrounded her, their leaves edged in unseasonable frost. The temperature had dropped drastically, but, to her surprise, her body did not react. Her pain hadn't lessened, but the cold hadn't worsened it as it so often did.

"What do you think of all this cold, duck?" a voice said, and Charlotte's heart leaped. Arthur, scratched and dirtier than she'd ever seen him but all in one piece as far as she could tell. "Doesn't it make it feel like Christmas?"

Her heart dropped into her stomach. Clutching his hand was Jonas. Sasha rode alongside them, atop the same massive horse that had pulled Arthur and his cart into the wood in the first place.

"Children?"

"It's September," Sasha said. Jonas merely pressed into their uncle's side. Kitty Tierney ought to have taken the children to the convent, but here they were in the forest.

"Yes, duck," Arthur said, "but it *feels* like Christmas."

Sasha wrinkled her nose. "It doesn't feel like it to me. We haven't had a tree or stockings or carols or *anything*. It's just cold."

Tears welled in Charlotte's eyes. Her children were cold and lost in the forest with her brother. It seemed as if it had been inevitable. She'd come here for so many reasons, but among them had been the hope that her action would prevent Sasha from searching for Arthur herself. Charlotte ought to have known: Whether she'd entered the forest or not, Sasha would have. To find her uncle, if her mother wouldn't; to find both of them, if she would.

"Arthur—"

Charlotte reached for him. Her hand passed through his arm like he was a ghost. Shuddering, she pulled back. Her family had fallen silent, even Sasha, whose small fists curled in the horse's mane like she'd never let go.

Think, Charlotte told herself. The Lord of the Wood had said they might find Arthur if she could describe where he was. All right. So she had to describe it, and "there were a lot of trees" certainly wouldn't do.

She followed her family, searching for anything that might stand out. Rowans surrounded them, veined in black and dripping, interspersed with goat willow and thickets of holly. A single yew rose from the gloom and sank back again as they passed.

That single yew stuck in her mind like a burr. A rarer tree, but odd to see *one* instead of a handful scattered among the other species.

Charlotte examined it. Like the other trees, the yew was veined in black, but no ooze dripped from its branches. The veins followed the grooves of the bark, neater than the chaos of veins she'd seen on skin and bark and leaf before. The leaves were a sickly green, not gray like those of other infected trees or the leaves she'd collected for her tests.

Burned into the trunk was a symbol. A circular knot, cracked through the middle. Ooze bubbled up through the crack without spilling. Maybe she could touch it safely, since she didn't seem quite real here. She reached for it—

She was standing back in the Lord of the Wood's house.

Her fingers were so stiff they ached, but the painkillers had reduced the throb over her left eye. She leaned on the table, breathing hard. Calyx rustled in concern.

"What did you see?" the beast asked urgently.

Her head fuzzed. She swayed. Calyx slithered from her shoulders to support her.

"The children. The children are with him."

"Where?"

A wave of nausea swept over her. She squeezed her eyes shut, trying to focus on what she'd seen.

"A yew tree. There was a symbol burned in the trunk, a shield knot, I think, but it was cracked."

Swearing, the beast struggled to his feet. "I have to find them. Now. I'll fly if I have to—I can hardly get any worse than I am—"

Charlotte straightened slowly. "Fly?"

He stumbled toward the door. Charlotte grabbed her medical kit and cane from their spot by her chair and followed him outside.

"If you fly, how do I come with you?"

The beast turned on her, his eyes faintly angry. "You don't."

"But—"

"It's dangerous. If anything happened to you— Stay here. I'll bring him back."

"Absolutely not," Charlotte snapped. "I spent days at home waiting for him to come back. I spent days here waiting for you to come back. You've already left him once—"

The beast flinched, but she ignored him.

"—and it's not just him anymore—my *children* are with him, for God's sake. If you think I'm going to sit here twiddling my thumbs, hoping nothing's happened to them . . . I have a mule, I can—"

The beast dragged his hands over his face.

"You Throckmortons," he growled. "A mule won't keep up with me, but maybe—Calyx?"

The plant creature rustled importantly.

"You'll need to follow me," the beast told it. "And you'll need to carry her."

Calyx unwound from Charlotte and exploded with growth. New vines and branches grew and thickened, wove through each other, until the plant creature was twice the size and vaguely the shape of a horse. It tossed its faux-head proudly.

Charlotte touched its viny leg. "My goodness. I didn't know you could do that."

"It's never done it before. I don't know how long it'll hold."

Vines wrapped around Charlotte and lifted her onto Calyx's broad, leafy back, then formed into a chair. More vines slung across her lap and chest and around her medical kit and cane.

"Keep up," the beast said to Calyx.

He shivered into a raven—larger than a normal raven, with moss creeping through his feathers. He perched on the plant-horse's neck, head cocked at Charlotte.

Her skin prickled. Something like wonder sprouted through the determined practicality she kept herself cloaked in. She stroked the bird's back.

The raven took off. The plant-horse reared up—Charlotte gripped its mane of tendrils with a gasp—and *leaped*. It cleared the vale in one bound, flying over the remaining brambles. Ahead, the raven croaked encouragingly. Out in the forest, the plant-horse slung itself forward, somewhere halfway between galloping and swinging through the trees. Charlotte clung tightly as it followed the Lord of the Wood through the forest to find her children and her brother.

XXXIX. In which Arthur has an encounter with a bear

Arthur and the children straggled onward. Despite the acorn, he thought they might be going the wrong way. Ever more trees dripped with black ooze as they passed. The few animals they saw showed skulls, ribs, and pelvises through their skin.

Jonas pressed so close to him it became hard to walk. Freya rubbed against their legs over and over, mewling. Sasha, quiet, clung to Maurice's neck. The gelding's pace slowed until he was almost creeping. With his size, it would have been funny, if the forest hadn't crawled with unease. If the forest hadn't been so *silent.*

It was a wintry silence, cold and muted as if a foot of snow had been on the ground, though it wasn't. Branches encased in ice looked like glass. Frosted leaves crunched underfoot.

"Look," Jonas whispered.

All around them were trees like those in the vale. Twisted into human shapes. Arthur shuddered away from them, picturing Charlotte's face in a gnarled trunk.

She wasn't a tree, he told himself. She was fine. Wherever she was.

The anthropoid trees made it harder to believe.

"Who are they?" Sasha whispered.

"No one, duck," Arthur said, though he knew otherwise. "They're just trees."

"They're not shaped like proper trees," Jonas said.

The iced-over branches stuck up at odd angles, like arms raised in terror. Knots and cavities gaped like eyes and mouths. Roots thrust up as if all the trees had been frozen in the midst of fleeing some disaster. Half-dead birds, translucent and skeletal, whistled thinly from branches. Other birds, entirely dead, littered the leaf mold.

Arthur shivered, clutching Jonas's hand and walking so close to Maurice that he kept bumping into him.

Perhaps the forest had had a reason for preventing them from coming this way.

The human trees persisted. They ought to have heeded the forest, Arthur thought, and not gone so persistently northward, but he wasn't sure they could've reached the heart of the wood otherwise.

He wasn't sure they'd reach it in this case, either. He couldn't stop imagining them turning into trees themselves and wished, for the first time, that the children weren't with him. Pointless, that. He couldn't have sent them home through the forest alone. They were here, and that was that.

The ice kept the black ooze from spreading. That was his only comfort.

"Who's that?" Jonas asked suddenly.

"Who's—"

A boy. Overgrown with moss, his skin and clothes hardening into bark. And Arthur recognized him.

The boy from the work camp.

The back of his head melded into a trunk. His hair had transformed into the thin, threadlike roots of a parasitic vine. His face was human, throat and chin and nose and forehead skin instead of bark, but veined in black. Crystalline ice feathered across his features, clinging to his eyebrows and lashes. His lips were blue with cold, his eyes horribly open but so fogged with ice it was as if he had grown cataracts.

Arthur had saved the boy from Ira only for him to suffer this fate instead. "Oh, no."

"Who is he, Uncle Arthur?" Jonas repeated.

"A woodsman." Arthur drew closer. "I'd hoped he'd gotten away."

The boy was dead. He must have been. Surely he could not have grown so cold as to turn blue and survived.

But behind their icy film, his eyes shifted minutely.

"Hello?" Arthur wished he knew the boy's name. "Are you . . . Can you . . . Can you hear me?"

The boy's mouth opened, barely. He let out a sound that might have been an attempt at words.

Arthur touched the acorn at his throat. Perhaps it could stop the boy's growth as it had Ira's. But it hadn't reversed Ira's growth, and the boy seemed too far gone for anything less.

Arthur unclasped the acorn's chain nonetheless, but the boy's lips moved. His paltry breath fogged the air. Arthur stepped closer, straining to listen.

"What?"

The boy's lips formed a word so quietly Arthur might have imagined it.

"Run."

Something crashed through the underbrush behind them. Its roar shook ice from the trees with a tinkling like broken glass.

Arthur stepped back, shielding the children. "Oh—"

It was a bear. Arthur had never seen one, except in books or ancient carvings. But there it was, towering over him on its hind legs, far larger than he'd imagined a bear could be. Half its skull, its vertebrae, and one scapula were visible through its skin. Black ooze dripped from its eyes, as if it had been blinded.

If it couldn't see them, it could smell them. It stopped, rearing to sniff the air—God Almighty, it was twelve feet tall—then lowered and shambled toward them. Freya darted away through the trees.

"Run," Arthur said to Jonas, nudging them behind him. "Run!"

Jonas froze, unable to do anything more than cling to his hand. Arthur flung them toward Maurice. His back spasmed horribly, but he shoved Jonas onto the gelding's back.

"Get them out of here."

Maurice snorted and whirled around, but Sasha hurtled off of him.

"Uncle Arthur!"

Before Arthur could stop her, she'd run past, waving a stick and hollering. The bear ambled closer in utter disregard for her weapon. The boy in the tree closed his eyes exhaustedly as more bark solidified at his throat and chin.

A rock hit the bear in the face. Jonas, dismounted and trembling but already armed with another. Roaring, the bear changed direction. Sasha chased it, beating it with her stick and shouting, "Don't! Hurt! My! Sibling!"

Desperate, Arthur hurled a stone at the bear and dodged as it came toward him. He grabbed Sasha around the waist and threw her at Jonas.

"Go, now!"

Maurice screamed but circled the children, shaking his mane as if to encourage them to grab on. Arthur broke away, throwing more rocks and silently praying he'd find the children if he lost them.

"Go!"

Then he stopped worrying about whether they were listening, because the bear reared right over him.

He didn't even have a stick to beat it off. All he had was a single remaining stone, which seemed more likely, at this point, to anger the creature.

Dropping to all fours, the bear snuffled his shirt. Its breath scorched his skin. He swallowed.

With another roar, the bear lunged at him. He yeeted the stone at it, uselessly, and tried to dive aside—too late.

Claws raked across his chest and stomach. The children screamed. His fingers scraped in the leaf mold for another stone, a stick, anything with which to defend himself, but all he could do was throw a fistful of wet, dirty leaves at the creature. He didn't know where the acorn had gone.

The bear grabbed his ankle with its massive jaws, whipped its head around, and threw him into a tree. He gasped, winded. Blood trickled from his chest, his stomach, his ankle. His clothes were shredded and filthy, his glasses askew, the children were screaming and throwing rocks, bark had grown up the boy in the tree's face until all that was visible was one dead eye.

In the distance, a stag bugled. The bear turned from Arthur with one paw raised over him, confused. Black ooze dripped from its eye onto his torn chest.

Arthur turned his head, barely, blearily. The fluffy shape of a cat leaped over a fallen log and sped toward the children. The last thing he saw, before he lost consciousness, was the blurry form of a stag bounding after her.

XL. In which Arthur has a reunion but also, unfortunately, wood sickness

Arthur ached. His neck was throbbing—dully, but the throbbing had escaped containment. His chest throbbed, too. And his stomach. And his ankle. And, well, his whole body.

Nice to know he was alive enough to feel pain. He hadn't been sure when the bear grabbed him that it wasn't the end. And it was a dull pain, not the sharp stab it had been when the bear's claws raked across him. That was something.

He shivered. The pain spiked. He was wrapped in furs, but the cold he remembered from before—the cold that had frozen the blood oozing from his chest and stomach—was bone-deep now. Something heavy and warm rumbled on his chest. He hoped it would warm him up.

Now there was a voice. Rather, the voice had been there, but he'd been too busy picking out feelings to notice. The voice rose to the forefront, soft and soothing and achingly familiar.

". . . and this door opened in the wall, and Odette found that secret room of Mrs. Wellsley's. You remember I told you about the secret room the other week. Anyway, Odette found it, but we don't know what's in it yet."

Her radio program. Charlotte was recounting the latest development in her radio program, no different than if they'd been at home on a Saturday morning, drinking coffee and swapping stories. Arthur's mouth curled into a smile, or tried to.

"Of course that was Friday. If we don't get out of here soon, I'll miss the next episode. Not that worse things aren't likely to befall us."

When she paused, he imagined her sitting across from him at the kitchen table, taking a sip of her coffee.

"Still," she said. "I'll hate to miss it. What if they finally reveal Mrs. Wellsley's secret? I won't know a thing about it until the following week, and by then I'm sure I'll have lost the plot entirely."

Arthur wriggled his fingers. They were so stiff he wasn't sure they'd moved.

Her breath hitched. "Arthur?"

He tried again.

She clutched his hand. "I'm here."

He opened his eyes.

Everything was blurry, of course; he wasn't wearing his glasses. He wasn't sure where he was. Not where he had been. The canopy blurred darkly overhead, but around him glowed firelight.

And at his side was his sister.

"Lottie," he croaked.

She squeezed his hand. He struggled to sit up. The rumbly thing on his chest *mrowred* disapprovingly and hopped off him. Freya. She arched into Arthur's hand before trotting off to curl up beside the fire.

Charlotte helped him sit up and slid his glasses onto his face.

Her features leaped into focus. She looked so like she had when he'd left the house that he could've cried.

Then he saw Calyx piled behind her.

Arthur jerked away. Pain jolted through him. "What's it—has it hurt you? Are you—"

A lazy tendril unfurled in his direction.

"It's all right," Charlotte said. "I know what happened. But Calyx has been a great help to me, and it's not going to hurt you—is it?" she asked the plant creature, in much the same tone she always told the cat to get off the table.

The tendril waved from side to side. Arthur still remembered leaves sealed over his face, vines biting into his ribs, tendrils down his throat.

"Are you . . . quite sure?"

Faint clicking, which did not raise his confidence.

"Calyx." The clicking died away. "Yes, I'm sure."

The tendril stretched toward him. Nervously, Arthur let it wrap around his finger.

"Bygones? I'll forget the whole thing if you will."

The tendril shook his finger and retreated. Arthur let out an astonished chuckle and started coughing.

"You're here," he rasped, when the coughing had died away. "You've got eldritch creatures eating out of your hand. Of course you have." He prodded her shoulder, reassuring himself she was real and unharmed. "You're not hurt?"

She laughed wetly. "Heaven's sakes, Arthur. Half your torso is being held together by stitches and bandages, and you want to know if I'm hurt?"

"Are you?"

"Of course not. I didn't get mauled half to death by a bear."

"And the children?"

"They're fine. More or less." She kissed his knuckles. "Seeing you get torn to bits didn't do them any favors, but they're not hurt."

Letting out a breath, Arthur leaned against her, careful to avoid squashing any of Calyx's appendages. Charlotte wrapped her arms around him and rested her head on his shoulder. Knowing she'd come after him had been one thing; finding her sitting beside him, taking care of him as she always had, was quite another.

His eyes prickled. "I've missed you so much. I can't believe you're here."

"Thank God I am." Charlotte's voice wobbled. "Ira was panicking so badly he couldn't have done anything for you himself. Jonas had to do the stitches, my hands were so stiff by the time we reached you, but I was able to talk them through it all right."

Arthur's stomach dipped. "Ira . . . Is he here?"

"Mmm."

She let go of him. He wished she hadn't. They had things to talk about, and he didn't want to talk about them. Easier to go on leaning against each other, glad to be sitting together.

"Let me see your bandages," Charlotte said.

He tugged the furs from his shoulders, shivering so violently his teeth chattered. His father's acorn hung from his neck. He touched it, relieved. He'd dropped it at some point in the confusion with the bear.

His bandages were tidy but spotted with blood. Charlotte peeled them away to replace them.

Arthur sucked in a breath and started coughing. Black veins crept across his torso from the gouges the bear had left. Coughing made his injuries throb worse than ever, but he couldn't stop for several moments.

Charlotte's jaw tightened, but when she spoke it was in the same calm, soothing tone she used on all her patients. "It's not as bad as it could be. The acorn's slowed the spread. I wish . . . I found a cure for it. The sickness."

"You did?" Arthur wheezed. "Then—"

"I don't have any more." Charlotte fiddled with John's wedding ring—or Arthur thought so, before realizing she was fiddling with a silver acorn, hanging beside the ring, that matched his own. "There's this woman I've been traveling with. She had the sickness. We tested the cure on her, and it worked. But we used it all up, and I haven't . . . It's the acorns, but—"

She gestured around them. They were in a grove of young silver oaks. There was no black ooze, no half-skeletal animals, no unnatural silence—but all the trees were tarnished, none fruiting.

"Ira thinks replanting the heart of the wood will cure you, too, but we have to get there first."

Arthur let the mention of Ira go by without comment. He wanted to see him—wanted to deal with the way they'd left things—but first, he wanted more time with his sister.

He fished around in his pocket for the rowan cross, handed it to her. Her breath caught.

"It did keep me safe," Arthur said, and he told her about the fog.

She turned the cross over and over in her fingers, eyes bright. "I suppose we'll never know why Dad had this."

Arthur smiled crookedly. "I think there's a lot we'll never know. Why he didn't tell us he was friends with the Lord of the Wood. Or what he'd think of—"

He broke off, skin prickling. He hated feeling so uncertain of the one person who had always been there for him. Mrs. Young's single, angry word echoed in his head; Arthur knew what Seacliff would think. But he wouldn't care what they thought, if only Charlotte understood.

Her eyes flickered over him. "What he'd think of you and Ira?"

Arthur's stomach clenched. His palms were clammy.

"You know?"

She gave a small smile. "It's the way he talks about you.

And . . . it explains a lot. About you. You were always so lukewarm on courtship, no matter how much you dreamed of romance."

She didn't sound angry, or disgusted, and there was that small smile, but Arthur's mouth was dry.

"And . . . you're not . . . you don't . . ."

Charlotte chewed her thumbnail. Like Jonas's lip picking, the nail chewing had been a nervous habit for a long time, but Charlotte had grown out of it two decades ago.

Arthur tugged her hand from her mouth. "What is it?"

"I loved John," she blurted.

"I know," Arthur said in confusion.

"I still do." Charlotte fiddled with John's ring. "But I'm . . . I've always . . ." She cleared her throat. "Elspeth . . . the woman I've been traveling with. The way it is between us . . . It's like how it is with you and him."

Arthur's heart stuttered. He'd always thought them so different, he and Charlotte, but here they shared one thing that seemed rather important.

"I've always known," she said tightly. "I've always . . . admired other women that way."

Arthur wrapped his arms around her. She relaxed.

"I never knew," he said, "until him. Where . . . where is he?"

She helped him to his feet. "I should warn you. I don't know what he looked like when he left you, but . . ."

Arthur's legs wobbled, and he was half bent over, but he could stand. Sort of. Charlotte handed him her cane; Calyx supported her. She seemed perfectly comfortable with it, and bygones were bygones and all that, but Arthur wouldn't be anything like comfortable with Calyx for some time.

Charlotte nodded to their left. Clinging to the furs, Arthur peered through the trees.

Sasha and Jonas ran back and forth, kicking leaves at each

other. A beast with a scarred eye and a twisted leg slunk between them, growling. He had a wolf's tail now, too, Arthur noticed with a pang. Moss and lichens grew more thickly over his scar and in the ruff of his neck than ever.

Sasha whacked the beast in the side with a stick. With a pained howl, he fell to the ground. She threw the stick down and jumped on him, tickling him as he pretended to die a slow, dramatic death.

Arthur's heart fluttered. Ira was playing with the children.

"I can't say I cared for him at first," Charlotte murmured, "but he's not so bad."

Arthur didn't respond. His skin buzzed, his ears rang, and he wanted nothing more than to run to Ira and hold him.

But he was being held together by stitches and bandages. He was mostly standing because of Charlotte's cane. And he wasn't sure how Ira would react to being run to and held.

When the beast had gone still, Sasha poked him in the stomach. "Ira?"

He snorted in her face, making her fall off of him. She laughed.

"No fair!" Then she spotted Arthur. "Uncle Arthur!"

Ira scrambled to his feet, gazing at him. "You're all right."

Arthur let out an *oof* as Sasha flung her arms around his middle. He bent, groaning.

"Gently, dearest," Charlotte said. "Your uncle isn't entirely in one piece."

Jonas hugged him, too, more carefully. Arthur hugged them back with one arm, his throat closing up, but he was aware of Ira's eyes on him all the while.

"Come along, children," Charlotte said. "It's past your bedtime."

"Bedtime?" Sasha said in a scandalized voice. "How do you even know what time it is? We're in the *forest*."

"Your uncle's pocket watch. Come, now."

Charlotte squeezed Arthur's arm, nodded at Ira, and dragged the children back to the fireside with Calyx supporting her.

Ira had stridden toward Arthur like he, too, might fling his arms around him. Instead, he stopped several feet away, shoving his hands into his pockets. The lichens growing in the ruff of his neck thickened before Arthur's eyes.

Arthur fumbled for his acorn, but Ira stepped closer and stilled his hand before he could undo the chain.

"Don't. It's all that's keeping the sickness from spreading faster." His eyes were red rimmed and baggy. "Your sister says her companion's sickness didn't even show up for a week because she was wearing one, but she hadn't shown any symptoms yet. We're not sure how long it'll keep yours at bay."

Moss and lichens tinged his arms green. Still a beast, but becoming increasingly plant matter, too.

"Charlotte has an acorn now, too," Arthur said. "Surely—"

Ira shook his head. His hair hung messily around his face, like his knot had given up. "We tried. The chain won't fit me, with . . ."

He gestured at his ruff, thick and furry and green with growth.

"There must be something—" Arthur started, but Ira wrenched away.

"Don't— Why do you always—"

He paced, not limping as badly as he had when they'd parted. He had a new knee brace, one of vines woven tightly together about his transfigured leg.

With an effort, he stopped pacing. He ran a hand through his hair.

"Then," Arthur said, unable to help himself, "if you flew to the heart of the wood with her acorn—"

Ira shivered into a raven. One of his wings was fur rather

than feathers—winged in shape, but useless for flight. He hopped several times, flapping, but barely made it a foot into the air before sinking back to earth.

"Oh," Arthur said in dismay.

Ira shivered back into the beast he'd been, winced and rolled his shoulder. "I aggravated my injury flying here anyway. Charlotte was kind enough to change my bandages again. We'll walk. In the morning."

His eyes kept flickering to Arthur's face and away.

"Here," he said suddenly, "you shouldn't be on your feet."

As he had in the cave the other day, Ira waved a hand, but he slumped almost before the gesture had been completed. A vine wriggled from the dirt, trembled, and died.

"What happened?" Arthur asked.

Ira leaned against a silver sapling with a grimace.

"Used too much energy getting here. Harder to grow things from nothing when I'm injured anyway." He stroked the sapling's trunk and spoke to it. "Could you . . . ?"

The sapling quivered. The silver trunk shivered and melted, reforming into a mass of low-hanging branches that wove through each other until they'd formed a little bench. When it wasn't trying to kill him, Arthur thought, the forest's magic was really something. Perhaps Ira didn't consider it *his* power the way growing something from nothing was, but Arthur doubted a tree would've helpfully made a seat that way at his own request.

"Thanks," Ira said to the sapling. Its upper branches dipped as if in a bow.

Ira offered a hand like he thought Arthur might slap it away. Arthur took it gratefully and sat on the silver bench.

"You can sit, too," he said. "If you want. I don't mind."

Ira bit his lip but joined him. The bench was so small their thighs and shoulders bumped together.

They gazed through the haze of slender silver trunks around them. Ira clenched the bench's edge, leg bouncing like he was anxious. Not the way he so often was, his fear masked as anger, but the way Arthur usually was. It reminded Arthur how scared he'd been throughout their time together—and how badly Arthur had handled it the last time they'd seen each other.

He touched Ira's thigh. The bouncing stopped.

"Listen," Arthur said softly, "I'm sorry for getting so mad at you."

Ira's brow furrowed, but he said nothing as Arthur squeezed his thigh and let go.

"You were scared," Arthur continued, "and I knew you were scared, and I should've—I don't know—let you be scared for a bit, or kept trying to calm you down, or, well, I shouldn't've gone off on you like I did."

Ira hesitated.

"I needed to hear it," he said. "And I don't know that you could've calmed me down. I think I needed time away. I just wish I hadn't left you undefended to get it."

Arthur's expression softened, but Ira looked away like he couldn't bear it. His leg started bouncing again.

"I'm sorry," he said in a low voice. "For everything. Even before—in the vale—every time I was scared, I lashed out at you."

He hunched, dragging paw-like hands through his bedraggled hair. Before he could think about it, Arthur tucked the loose strands behind a cervine ear. The ear twitched toward him.

"The longer we spent together," Ira continued, "the more I felt like a person. But then the forest took me over, and it felt like the Lord of the Wood was all I was or ever could be. I was so scared, Arthur, I was so afraid of hurting you—but I hurt you anyway, saying what I did."

"You were right, though."

Ira glanced at him. "No."

"Yes." Arthur smiled bitterly. "Everything you said about me—it was true. I've always been too scared to change my own life. This is the first time I've ever really tried to do something. To see things through."

"I don't think that's true." Ira reached for his hand, fingers curling uncertainly around Arthur's. "Charlotte told me how you cared for her, growing up. How you asked that woman if you could repair clocks for her, even though you were afraid to knock on her door."

Arthur opened his mouth but closed it again without speaking. He *had* been afraid, knocking on the Livingstons' door that first time, twelve years old, with Charlotte's small hand in his—but he'd done it anyway. Because someone had needed to put food on the table. Because Charlotte had been a child and needed looking after.

He glanced back through the trees, where she sat by the fire with Calyx, telling the children a bedtime story. His eyes stung. She'd been taking care of him far longer and better than he'd ever taken care of her. She'd come into the wood for him.

At last he said softly, "I've never thought of it that way."

Ira gave a tentative smile. "I could tell. You're more than you think you are, Arthur. You did what you had to for Charlotte then, and you've done what you could for me since the moment we met."

Arthur's throat was thick with things he didn't know how to say. *When you came, it felt like spring*, he remembered Ira saying. *Like you woke me up*. Arthur felt like he'd been awoken instead, like Ira had unlocked doors and solved riddles that had been a mystery all his life.

Angling toward Ira, Arthur looped his arms around his neck. Ira's breath hitched.

"I'm glad you came back," Arthur whispered.

Ira's eyes flickered over his face. "I had to."

Hesitantly, he touched their foreheads together, relaxed when Arthur pressed against him. He stroked Arthur's face. As always, his furry fingers curled in to keep his claws away.

Arthur sighed, oddly contented considering the state of him. "How far to the heart of the wood?"

"A couple hours, if we stay on track and keep a good pace."

"That might be a tall order for some of us just now."

"Calyx can carry you. It carried your sister the whole way here. I think it'll be able to carry you both, so she doesn't wear herself out walking. It'll need the night's rest first, it's never grown that big before, but I think it can do it. And the children have the horse."

Arthur smiled. A real smile, this time, at the thought Ira had put into the well-being of his family. He kissed Ira's furry snout. Ira huffed a laugh, his breath sweet like spring flowers.

Behind them, Charlotte cleared her throat. Arthur pinkened, but she gave them a small smile.

"There's supper, if you're up to it. Mind you don't wake the children."

XLI. In which Arthur plants an acorn, which does not go as expected

The next morning, as they headed for the heart of the wood, Charlotte told Arthur about her journey, and Elspeth. It distracted him from his unease at being wrapped in Calyx's vines, far too high above the forest floor, and the bone-deep cold and all-over ache he felt despite the cat purring in his lap. Charlotte fiddled with the acorn Elspeth had left her as often as she fiddled with John's wedding ring. At their side, on Maurice's back, Sasha regaled Ira with a dramatic retelling of her own adventures in the forest.

At midmorning, a horse riding the other way at a smart trot caught up to them. It skidded to a halt, its rider dismounting almost before it had stopped: a woman with tawny skin and a black braid, improbably wearing trousers.

Charlotte cried out, struggling to dismount Calyx. The plant creature helped her down.

The women flung their arms around each other. Arthur had been worried when Charlotte cried out, but now he relaxed; this must be Elspeth.

"Told you I'd find you," Elspeth breathed, pressing her forehead to Charlotte's.

To Arthur's astonishment, his sister melted into her. Of course Charlotte had told him the nature of their relationship, but to see her like this—forgetful, for once, of all eyes that might be on her—was a shock.

Charlotte's fingers curled around the other woman's collar. "And—your scar—is it . . . ?"

"Sickness ain't come back, Lottie, I'm fine."

Sasha launched herself at them. "Miss Elspeth!"

Charlotte pulled away, pink cheeked, as her daughter hugged Elspeth tight. Elspeth laughed.

"How now, my little bug! Here I thought your mam told you to go to the convent if'n we didn't come back."

"Jonas and I had to find you," Sasha told her solemnly. Hanging back with Ira and Maurice, Jonas was as pink as Charlotte, but they nodded when Elspeth smiled at them.

"Guess it's just as well." She tugged one of Sasha's pigtails. "It was on account of hearing your voice I found you all so easy. Must be entertaining the whole forest, huh?"

Noticing Arthur, and his bandages, she whistled.

"Didn't quite find you in one piece, did she? You're the brother, I take it."

"Yes," Charlotte said, too loudly, and Arthur was even more astonished. Charlotte was *flustered*. "This is Arthur. Arthur, this is Elspeth. Did you find Maggie?" she asked Elspeth.

Elspeth shook her head. "That's why I was coming back. I made it to the tree, but there's a work camp been setting up all morning, and I don't think I'll find Maggie long as they're there. I tried to make out like I was another worker, but they chased me off when they realized I was a woman. They won't let anyone near that stump who's not part of the camp. They mean to uproot it."

Ira's jaw tensed.

"What do we do?" Arthur asked.

Before anyone could answer, Ira groaned and bent double. Charlotte stepped toward him, her brow furrowing in medical concern. Tendrils shot from Calyx's sides.

Ira screamed. Charlotte flinched away, shielding the children.

"The hell's wrong with him?" Elspeth asked.

Arthur dislodged the cat, struggled out of his seat, and slid down Calyx's side awkwardly. He leaned against the plant creature, rubbing his chest; his heart and lungs strained. "The camp must've started working. He can feel it. Whatever they do to the forest, he can feel it."

Ira's eyes flashed white, filled with images of logging machinery. Arthur knelt before him, cupping his face in his hands. "Stay with me."

Ira's eyes squeezed shut. With a moan, he leaned into Arthur's chest. Arthur wrapped his arms around him, hugging him tight like that could squeeze the pain out.

"How close are we?" he asked.

Ira shuddered in his arms. "Close."

"Just back that way," Elspeth said.

"We have to get to that camp," Arthur said. "We have to stop them uprooting the stump, or he'll—"

Ira went rigid. Arthur gripped him tighter, certain he was about to transform and run off to murder woodsmen. "Stay with me, Ira."

Ira shot to his feet. His eyes rolled; his nostrils flared. Arthur clung to him, repeating, "Stay with me—Ira, please—" but suddenly he was clinging to a stag's mane.

Mostly a stag. The stag had a wolf's tail, and fangs, and its pelt was shaggy with moss and lichens. Calyx's tendrils waved in alarm. Freya hissed.

"Ira—"

The stag shoved him aside with its nose, tossed its head,

and bounded away. Arthur staggered, heart pounding so hard he felt sick.

"Come on," he rasped to Charlotte. "He said we were close. We can catch up to him. If he distracts the workers, we can—"

She nodded. "Stay here, children."

"I want to come," Sasha said immediately, but Elspeth lifted her onto Maurice's back.

"Not this time, bug. Who'll watch the horses if you come with us? Or the cat? Mind your mam and stay here. We'll be back soon."

The three adults climbed onto Calyx's back with the help of its tendrils.

"Follow him, Calyx," Charlotte said, and the plant creature slung itself through the trees. The humans ducked to avoid getting whacked in the face by branches.

Ahead of them, the stag bugled—but this camp seemed better prepared for the Lord of the Wood. Instead of screaming and the distant crunching that signaled the forest was doing away with survivors, orders were barked back and forth. Guns fired. Arthur bit his lip so hard he drew blood.

They broke through the trees and found chaos. Men ran back and forth with guns and powder, trampling recently erected tents.

"Get a net!" one of them roared, sprinting past Calyx without noticing.

In the midst of the camp, Ira stood snarling, a wolf now—mostly. His front legs ended in a deer's hooves. A clump of woodsmen faced him, aiming with shaking hands, but no one seemed to want to take the first shot, and Arthur was struck, again, with the thought that these men were merely workers trying to get a paycheck in a world that demanded one.

But they were about to destroy the forest, too, and kill Ira, and he couldn't let that happen.

"Ira!" he cried, but Elspeth sprang from Calyx's back and dragged him with her. The second Charlotte had dismounted, too, Calyx threw itself at Ira. It lost its shape as it went, loosening into a mass of foliage. Vines shot toward the nearest woodsmen and dragged them away.

"Let the eldritch monster handle it," Elspeth said. "It's like you said. He's keeping 'em busy. They're not gonna bother about us with a shape-shifting beastie bent on killing 'em right in their midst."

She was nearly right. Most of the workers surrounded Ira, but a handful were by the stump, working shovels and machines.

The stump was so massive it seemed impossible that anything could uproot it. Yet, reluctantly, its roots relinquished their grip on the soil. Tarnish spread across each one as it was loosed from the earth. Nearby leaves wilted and dropped with increasing speed as more roots emerged.

Elspeth swore and pulled a knife from her belt. One of the workers came at her, shovel raised, but she jerked it away from him.

"Go on," she spat at Charlotte and Arthur, and she raised her knife at the other workers converging on her. They backed her into the mossy trunk of a stunted tree—one of them struck at her—but Charlotte clenched her jaw and tugged Arthur onward.

Two workers abandoned Elspeth and jogged after them, but ravens burst from the trees and descended upon them. Charlotte cowered. Arthur spotted a tiny brown rider with a shock of white hair riding the largest bird.

"Maud!" he cried.

"Go on, boy," she called back, in her voice like a tree's creaking. "My birds'll keep 'em busy."

The pair of workers sprinted away, swinging shovels fruitlessly.

The ravens clawed at their hair. Maud cackled and swooped away to help Elspeth.

Another bugle. Calyx had been netted and was trying to tear itself free. Ira was a stag, mossy and fanged and alone, surrounded by woodsmen.

A hand gripped Arthur's shoulder, yanking him back. "What—"

One of the workers, trying to stop him from replanting the tree. Charlotte tugged the worker's arm, but he threw her off. She hit the stump with a yelp.

"Lottie!" Arthur cried.

Halfway across the clearing, the stag's head whipped around at him. Ira kicked free of the woodsmen and raced toward the stump. The worker gripping Arthur's arm swore, let go, and fumbled for his abandoned rifle.

A shot rang out. Ira collapsed, legs kicking uselessly, and shivered abruptly back into a beast. Arthur's breath caught.

Everything fell silent, as if the forest were inhaling.

When it exhaled, it exhaled explosively.

Trees burst from the ground, growing ten—twenty—fifty feet in a matter of seconds. Branches speared woodsmen through the stomach. Vines whipped around their ankles or wrists and dragged them away. The camp rang with their screams. Maud's ravens wheeled through the sky, croaking.

In seconds, the clearing was regrown. In seconds more, the new trees and flowers drooped and died, dripping black ooze.

The woodsmen and their machines were gone. Birds sang in the canopy as if nothing had happened, but their song cracked and broke and went silent. One at a time, they fell from their perches, their small, translucent forms showing delicate skeletons.

In a flurry of black wings, Maud's ravens landed in the dying greenery, but they had a faded quality. Calyx shrank until it was nothing more than a sprout, a single vining tendril with a handful of thin, pale leaves.

In a patch of sunlight, collapsed against the silver stump, Ira slumped with blood blooming across his side. Maud hobbled toward him. Calyx slithered out of the net and followed.

Arthur jerked toward him, but Charlotte, getting to her feet shakily, said, "The acorn."

Arthur nodded, clutching the acorn tight. The tarnish spread before their eyes, but the stump's heartwood was silver. It would have to be enough.

He knelt with difficulty, pulling off the acorn and its chain. Without it, the thin black veins threading from his wounds unwound farther across his skin, so much faster than they'd spread before. Charlotte sucked in a breath.

"It'll be all right," Arthur told her, but without the acorn breathing was a lot harder. "It'll be fine."

Praying he was right, he pressed the acorn to the heartwood. The acorn glowed, then melted into the stump. They waited, holding their breath.

Nothing happened.

XLII. In which there are multiple transformations

Panic welled in Arthur's chest. He pressed the spot where the acorn had vanished, but it was gone. Tarnish still spread. Ooze still dripped down the dying trees, same as the black veins creeping across his stomach and chest and up his throat. Blood still spilled from Ira's side.

"No." Arthur's breath rattled. "No. No, this isn't—"

"Maybe something was wrong with that one," Elspeth said doubtfully. "Maybe mine—"

Charlotte was already clasping it around Arthur's neck in place of their father's. "Absolutely not. His sickness has spread quite far enough."

"What do you want to do, Lottie?" Elspeth asked. "Acorn's not gonna stop his sickness spreading, just slow it down some."

"It'll give me time to get more. To make more water."

"Lottie, please," Arthur rasped. "Please. He'll die without it."

He tried to remove the acorn from his neck, but Charlotte gripped his hands. Her eyes widened: Despite the acorn, the black veins did not slow. Each breath he took rattled worse than the last. His lungs struggled to expand and contract.

His sister's voice wobbled. "Why isn't it working?"

"Reckon nothing'll help now." Elspeth touched Charlotte's shoulder. "I'll stay with him, if you want. You should get out of here, before the whole forest goes."

"I'm not leaving without the two of you."

"Things're different now, Lottie," Elspeth said gently. "There's nothing to be done for him. And the kids are out here, too. You want them safe, don't you?"

"Yes, but—"

"She's right." Arthur extricated his hands from her grasp, his fingers stiff and cold. "You could make it safely away with the children."

Charlotte's eyes welled with tears. "I came here for you."

He smiled crookedly. "I know. It's the best thing anyone's ever done for me."

That he would die in the forest anyway, in the end, didn't matter. It was enough that she'd come after him. That she'd done something so deeply impractical, with so little hope of success, simply because she loved him and he'd needed her.

His own failure was harder to bear. For thirty years, Ira had been resigned to his fate. To dying because his forest was dying, because they were irrevocably bound together. Arthur had made him believe it didn't have to be that way—but there Ira was, lying on the other side of the stump, dying anyway.

Arthur pushed to his feet and stumbled toward him, coughing.

"Arthur—"

Every step was agony. He hunched, clinging to the stump for support as he rounded it.

Maud turned her wrinkled brown face to him as he approached. Like her ravens, she had a faded quality. Not translucent, not veined in black, but glimmering in and out the way the wild huntsman had. Her silver eyes dimmed. With one withered, vanishing hand, she clutched Ira's fingers.

Blood matted in Ira's shirt, his fur. His ears twitched as

Arthur approached. He turned his head weakly, nostrils flaring. Calyx twined thinly around one wrist. Blood stained the stump red.

Arthur knelt at his side, numb. Then, suddenly, not numb at all. His skin prickled, tears coursed down his cheeks, and he pressed his forehead to Ira's and wept. They'd made it here. They'd *made* it, yet it was ending this way. Ira raised a clawed hand to touch his cheek, but it fell back to his side.

Around them, leaves wilted and dropped from trees. Vines crumbled to ash. Dead birds rotted away until nothing remained but skeletons. Calyx's leaves curled, blackened, and dropped off.

Arthur's breath hitched. His fingers curled in Ira's fur, his chest buzzing with sudden hope. They still had one acorn.

He fumbled with the chain, but his fingers had gone stiff and aching. Behind him, Charlotte had approached cautiously, despite their efforts to send her away.

Kneeling beside him, she undid the chain and handed him the acorn. "What are you thinking?"

"I think," Arthur said, "he's the heart of the wood."

"Of course he is." Maud's creaky voice had a faded quality like her form. "He and the tree. Twin anchor points. Like binary stars."

Then this would work. They were bound to each other, Ira and the tree, both necessary to keep the forest alive. As the tree was the one that had been dying, Ira hadn't been so concerned with himself. The tree had been replanted; now Ira would be. It would work.

It had to work, because if it didn't, Ira was going to die. And the forest, and Arthur, would die alongside him.

Ira was barely breathing. Arthur kissed his forehead.

"Come back to me," he whispered, and he pressed the acorn to Ira's heart.

As the other had at the stump, the acorn glowed, then melted into him.

Silver light snaked from his heart and wound around him. Charlotte stumbled back, dragging Arthur with her. Maud shuffled after them. Calyx unwound feebly from Ira's wrist, fell to the ground, and inchwormed away.

The humans shielded their eyes. The silver light wound faster and faster, glowing so brightly they could barely see Ira.

He lifted into the air.

Light shone from his paws, his antlers, his face. The blood matting his fur streamed back into the wound until his shirt was clean and his body uninjured, except for the twisted leg and scarred eye. He transformed back into a man, more human in form than Arthur had ever seen him.

Around him, the silver light shone on the trees. The black ooze on their trunks vanished. Their withered leaves regrew in a burst of greenery. The skeletal birds at their feet erupted into flight in a flurry of feathers and down and birdsong. Maud's ravens joined them, solid again. Calyx unwound in a spool of fresh greenery.

Arthur's chest tingled hopefully. Charlotte squeezed his hand. Elspeth wrapped an arm around her waist.

The light lowered Ira to the stump. Arthur stepped toward him, but, in a single burst, the light twisted up from his body and into a tree: a silver oak growing from the stump in moments instead of years. Silver grew over Ira's body, as the moss and flowers had done so many times, until it encased him. No more than a human face protruding from a silver trunk. The hopeful tingling in Arthur's chest soured to dread.

When it was a young tree some twenty feet tall, with a spreading crown, the oak stopped growing. Silver acorns shook free of its branches, showering the ground. The surrounding flora was soft and green and sweet smelling. Maud poked through the grass with her cane, gathering acorns. Her ravens stalked after her. The light faded.

In the oak's trunk, silver gilded the contours of Ira's face. Calyx nosed at the trunk like a confused dog.

"Arthur?"

He staggered toward the tree without answering, chest tight. Swallowing, he touched Ira's cheek. His skin was hard and silver, no different from the rest of the oak.

"Ira?" Arthur whispered.

The tree did not answer. He leaned his forehead against it and cried.

There was a tug at his trousers. Predictably, the children had left their hiding place. Sasha gazed up at him much more seriously than was her wont, the cat clutched disgruntled in one arm.

"Look, Uncle Arthur. You're all better."

It wasn't quite accurate: He was riddled with the bear's claw marks. But his breathing had eased; he was no longer cold, and his joints no longer ached. The black veins were gone. Sasha prodded his stomach, avoiding his bandages, to show him.

He attempted a smile. "I see."

She hugged him tight. His abdomen ached, but he hugged her back.

Charlotte caught his eye as he turned from the tree, bit her lip like she wanted to say something, but she merely took his hand. Elspeth nodded at him, her jaw tight. He gave her the smallest imaginable smile, but his heart was shattered. He'd thought he would save Ira, not doom him.

Behind them, there was a crack like thunder and a flash of light. They whipped around. With another crack, the tree split—and Ira stumbled out.

He heaved a breath, gazing down at his own body. His skin was sun-bronzed, his hair inky dark, one eye scarred, one leg twisted, all human in form. He was clad in flowers and leaves like he'd always been in George's stories, but no moss or flowers or silver grew from his skin.

Arthur's heart leaped.

"Ira?" he croaked, half expecting it to be one of the wood's tricks.

The Lord of the Wood shivered into a stag and bounded through the clearing, tossing his head. Into a wolf that howled then raced to the tree, muscles bunching under his fur. A raven spiraling into the sky with a croak. As he returned to earth, he shivered back into a man and landed with a stumble, shifting his weight to his left leg as woodland flowers blossomed at his feet.

For the first time in thirty years, he'd changed entirely back.

He laughed, strode toward Arthur, cupped his face in his hands, and kissed him.

Before Arthur could respond, Ira pulled away.

"You saved me," he said.

"It was Elspeth's acorn." Arthur's lips curved into a smile. "Would you kiss me again?"

Ira smiled, too, his eyes flickering over Arthur's face. He pulled Arthur back in, hands fisting in Arthur's hair, and kissed him. Arthur kissed him back, overwhelmed by the press of Ira's body and the pleasurable pain of his fingers and the desperate crush of his lips. They kissed and kissed and kissed, and Ira's fingers tightened in his hair, and Arthur held Ira so hard that he lifted his feet off the ground.

Then he stopped, because his injuries throbbed and he worried he might've popped his stitches. He set Ira down, carefully, and touched his face.

"I won't lie," he said breathlessly. "I miss the antlers. And, er, well, the claws. A little."

Ira let out a huff of laughter. "I can put them back, you know. Now and then. If you want."

Beside them, Maud cleared her throat. They broke apart. Arthur's ears pinkened. Ira laughed.

"If you two are quite finished," Maud said.

Ira smiled. "For now."

"Sorry," Arthur said, too giddy to be sorry at all.

Elspeth raised an eyebrow. Charlotte bit back a smile. Sasha, ever disgusted by "kissing books," looked nauseated. Jonas blushed but kept glancing between their uncle and the Lord of the Wood as if they hadn't realized men kissing other men was an option.

Ira slipped his hand into Arthur's. Calyx wound between his legs like a cat.

Arthur squeezed his fingers. "What now?"

"Now," Charlotte said, "we find Elspeth's sister."

XLIII. In which goodbyes are said (for now)

Charlotte touched Elspeth's cheek, concerned. Elspeth's jaw had gone tight, but at Charlotte's touch, she let out a long, low breath. Her eyes dimmed.

"How, Lottie? This is all I saw in that basin. The stump, a tree—that's it. I didn't see Maggie."

Ira untangled his fingers from Arthur's, nudging Calyx out from underfoot. "What exactly did you see? Which tree? If something happened to her here, if you can remember exactly what you saw, I can find out."

Elspeth seemed even more suspicious of him now that he looked human. Charlotte squeezed her hand, wishing they were alone. They'd found her brother alive, more or less in one piece, in better shape now than he'd been when they'd reached him—but no sign of Elspeth's sister. Although Charlotte had forgotten herself before, so relieved to find Elspeth in the wood, she couldn't comfort Elspeth much with so many people around.

"Which tree?" Ira repeated.

Elspeth bit her lip. So many trees had grown in the last few minutes. What had been a dying clearing was new-growth forest. Young trees of all kinds—birch, holly, rowan, goat willow, aspen, hawthorn—all with leaves that had budded, opened, grown, and started turning yellow or orange or red. Moss and lichens bloomed on their trunks.

"Let's take a closer look," Charlotte said, though she shuddered at approaching the new growth. Calyx wound around her for support.

The ooze, the veins—all of it had cleared up. The trees were healthy. Nonetheless, the forest's magic made her shiver. Never mind that the forest no longer wanted to kill them; it had done away with the work camp. Somewhere in Port Lorne and cities like it, wealthy men who already owned more than anyone could humanly use would learn of their plight. Undoubtedly, they'd start planning their next camp, determined to remove the heart of the wood, destroy the forest, and gobble up the land for factories or grand estates.

But the men who had done the work had been working men in need of money. And likely none of their families would ever see any, now. Perhaps they'd known that. Known, like the fishermen in Seacliff, that their provider was as likely to kill them as support them.

Perhaps knowing that hadn't mattered, because they'd had no other options.

Elspeth's grip tightened as they moved through the trees.

"None of 'em are . . . I don't recognize any of 'em." Her breath hitched. "There are too many. There are too many trees now."

"Here." Charlotte turned Elspeth toward her, cradling her face in her hands. "Breathe with me a minute, hmm?"

They all did it together, even Maud, breath sighing out of her like wind in the leaves. *In for four, hold for four, out for four.*

Elspeth's breathing steadied. Charlotte wiped her tears away.

"Now, close your eyes and picture what you saw."

Elspeth let out a breath and did as instructed. "It . . . it was the tree where I found Maggie's necklace, but it looked like it'd grown thicker. Mossier."

"Her necklace?" Ira asked.

Elspeth plodded through the trees.

"The acorn. It was our gran's—yours, I guess, she said you gave it to her when she was a little girl lost in the wood. Maggie wore it everywhere, but when I found it on this tree I figured she'd left it for an offering, for safe passage." She shook her head. "I could've sworn . . . When that woodsman struck at me, I thought one of the trees struck him back. Could've been the same one."

Through the new growth, a tree appeared. Stunted, but thoroughly *tree*, not human in form like the trees they'd fought to get into the vale. It was bent and twisted, carpeted with a thick layer of moss. The thin, whiplike branches of a willow spilled from its crown, blooming with little white flowers not unlike those that had bloomed in Ira's scar before he'd transformed.

"That one," Elspeth said in a hushed voice. "It's that one. Them flowers weren't there before."

Ira ran a hand over the branches, laid his palm against the trunk. He cocked his head, listening intently.

"It's not a tree. It's a person."

Elspeth's jaw clenched. "The forest turned her?"

Ira shook his head. "It isn't someone the forest was protecting itself from. That's why it doesn't look like the others. It's someone the forest wanted to protect from something else. The same way it tried to protect me all those years, by making them a part of itself."

"Why?" Charlotte asked.

Ira shrugged.

"We can ask, if I . . ." He ran his fingers over the bark, murmuring, "It's all right. You can let her go. She'll be safe now."

Moss shifted and slipped downward, creeping away through

the grass to crawl up the trunks of other trees. The white flowers wilted. The bark shuddered and melted into skin and clothes, the whiplike branches turned to hair, and the tree was a young woman with mousy-brown hair, a crooked nose, and skin a shade lighter than Elspeth's.

"Maggie," Elspeth breathed.

The next moment, her expression twisted into horror. Rather than straightening, stretching, awakening—whatever any of them had expected Maggie to do once no longer a tree—she tilted forward and collapsed. Her skin was waxy, her breath shallow.

"Maggie!"

Elspeth caught her, eyes wide with panic. Maggie bled spectacularly from a wound in the back of her head.

With Calyx's help, Charlotte knelt beside them. "Let me see."

Her stomach twisted. No *head wounds often look worse than they are*, this: Maggie had been bludgeoned. Charlotte couldn't fix this.

She met Arthur's eyes helplessly. He'd gone pale at the sight of all that blood, but he blurted, "Maud! Maud—your pool—did you bring any—"

"Of course I did." Maud clicked her tongue, pulling a vial from her skirt. She nodded at Ira. "He *would* bring humans into battle with him, never mind how fragile you all are."

She gave the vial to Charlotte. Its contents were silver.

Charlotte held it to the light. "How do I use it?"

"Pour it over the wound," Ira said. "That's all."

"Might not work as well as you hope," Maud warned. "Best on fresh wounds. Which I suppose this is, in a way, but if the girl's been a tree all this time it's likely older than it looks."

"She . . ." Elspeth swallowed. "She's been missing for weeks now."

Charlotte uncorked the vial with difficulty, turned Maggie's head, and dripped silver fluid onto the wound. Beside her, Elspeth was rigid as stone.

Wherever the liquid spilled, skin knit itself together and new hair grew. Charlotte had never seen anything like it. With access to this, she could save anyone who had an accident that might otherwise cost their life.

Maggie's skull stitched itself up until it looked as if the wound had never been, except for the blood sticking strands of hair together. With the last few drops of liquid, Charlotte wiped the blood away. It stained her apron pink.

Shaking, Elspeth stroked her sister's hair. "Maggie?"

Charlotte felt for a pulse. Maggie's chest rose thinly, but her skin looked less waxy than it had before. "Her pulse is all right. Let's give it a minute."

Slowly, Maggie's color and breathing improved. Elspeth held her, rocking her on and off. She kept stopping, like she'd realized rocking someone who'd recently had a head wound wasn't the best idea, then continuing like she couldn't help herself. Charlotte slipped an arm around her, hoping to comfort Elspeth as they waited since she couldn't do anything more.

Maggie's lashes fluttered.

Elspeth gripped her hand. "Maggie?"

"Elspeth?"

Maggie's eyes were deep and blue. She sat up slowly, brow furrowing, and clutched her head.

"How you feeling?" Elspeth asked anxiously.

"Like I got run over. But I'm . . . How'm I . . . What are you doing here?"

Elspeth hugged her tight. Like a disgruntled cat, her sister tried to squirm free.

"Elspeth—what . . . ?"

Elspeth's voice was muffled in Maggie's shoulder. "I thought I'd never see you again."

"You've been missing for some time," Charlotte said.

Since Elspeth was too busy squeezing the air out of her sister to explain, Charlotte explained in her stead. As she did so, she examined Maggie's head, face, throat, and pulse, and periodically had Maggie curl her fingers or flex her feet.

"What we don't know," she said when she'd finished, "is what happened to you in the first place. Let's try standing you up."

Calyx helped her get Maggie to her feet. Maggie swayed; Calyx steadied her. Charlotte would've offered her cane, had it not gone flying when Calyx had slung itself toward Ira upon reaching the work camp. She didn't know where it had ended up, but she missed it already. Just now, however, Maggie needed Calyx's support more than she did.

"How do you feel?"

"Dizzy." Maggie squeezed her eyes shut but abruptly opened them. "Oh—that made it worse."

Charlotte helped her sit back down.

"I was almost home," Maggie said slowly. "Made it all the way to the first tree. After nightfall, it was. Thought I'd sleep by the stump. Always felt safe here. But I found a work camp—big one, fires burning and all, trees cleared away that'd been here when I passed through with Bess on our way to Seacliff."

She rubbed her forehead, frowning.

"There was this big machine. Don't know what it's called. Sitting right there by the stump, though, and I could see they meant to uproot it. So I thought . . . while I'm here, why don't I bollox their plans a bit?"

Elspeth snorted. Her eyes were red, but she was calmer now that Maggie no longer seemed in danger of imminent death.

"You? What'd you do, huh? You always were the good one."

Maggie smiled crookedly. "Think you got a monopoly on making trouble, do you? I found a fire poker and stuck it in the thing's gears. Had it pretty well in there, too. But the foreman caught me at it, tried to get the poker away from me, and when he couldn't, he walloped me instead. That's the last I remember."

Elspeth pulled her in for another rib-crushing hug. "I hope the forest walloped *him*."

Charlotte touched Elspeth's arm. "Gently, dearest."

"I think it did," Ira said. "Maybe that's why the first camp was destroyed before they'd started uprooting the stump. Because your sister tried to stop them, and they hurt her for it. The wood has long had difficulty recognizing those who mean it no harm—but when a human tries to help it like that, it knows. And she had the acorn. It would've recognized that."

Maud bid him goodbye and flew off with her ravens. Calyx helped Charlotte, Arthur, and Maggie onto its back; regrowing with the first tree had renewed its energy. Freya jumped up beside them, ignoring the plant creature when it tried to shudder her off. Elspeth mounted her horse; the children were back on Maurice.

"Where to?" Ira asked.

"Port Lorne's closest," Elspeth said. "God knows we could use a breather after all that. I need to be getting Maggie home to Gran and Granddad anyhow."

Ira nodded. "We'll take you as far as that. Nearly as far. Calyx shouldn't be seen like this."

Light as they were traveling, and with Calyx's size, they had reached the edge of the forest by late afternoon. Before them stretched pastureland, empty now. It crested and dipped downhill, but the first lights of Port Lorne twinkled beyond the rise.

Calyx deposited Charlotte, Arthur, and Maggie on the

ground. Elspeth dismounted her horse and made Maggie get on it instead.

"Guess we're hoofing it from here," she said, then frowned at Charlotte. "Where's your cane, darling?"

Charlotte flushed at the endearment, slightly embarrassed that everyone had heard it but pleased at how easily it had come.

"I lost it," she said with a grimace. She wasn't sure how long the walk was down into Port Lorne, but she dreaded it already.

Elspeth considered the distance between them and the city. "What d'you want to do?"

Until she'd asked, Charlotte had planned to simply grit her teeth and walk to Port Lorne as she was, never mind any pain or fatigue that resulted. Even now, *I'm sure I can make it* was on the tip of her tongue, where *I'm fine* had dwelled for so long.

Likely she'd never return to the pre-illness version of herself. That frustrated her—angered her, sometimes—but she was so tired of pretending. Pushing through until her symptoms worsened, indulging in misguided self-flagellation as if it were somehow her fault that she'd gotten sick, just because the place she'd grown up thought she ought to do so.

Arthur touched her arm. "Lottie?"

He'd offered her help from the beginning and never thought less of her for needing it. Elspeth had done the same, before they'd even known each other's names. Accepting their help—needing it at all—didn't mean Charlotte was weak or worthless. It just was.

"It's going to be difficult," she admitted at last. "I'll need some support."

Elspeth nodded, but before she could respond, Ira said, "Here."

He bent, pinching thumb and forefinger together in the dirt, and straightened again. Thin strands of greenwood followed him upward, braiding together into the shape of a crook. They aged and hardened in an instant, sloughing bark and leaves until the smooth, shining wood of a new cane was left behind.

Ira handed the cane to Charlotte. It was the perfect height for her, comfortable to grip, with tiny flowers and leaves carved or stamped or, well, *magicked* into it. It would give her the support she needed to walk down into Port Lorne—and if it wasn't enough, she knew Elspeth and Arthur would willingly pause a moment to figure out an alternative.

"Thank you," she said. "It's beautiful."

To her surprise, Ira's ears pinkened. She smiled; he seemed a far cry from her first impression of him.

Elspeth's eyes flickered over Charlotte's new cane. She hesitated, then said to Ira, "You're welcome to join us."

He gave a thin smile. "Thank you, but I'm . . . It's best if I head home. There's your mule to tend to."

"We'll see you on our way back?" Arthur asked.

Ira kissed his forehead. "I'll be waiting."

Arthur smiled thinly back at him. Charlotte reached for his hand. Calyx swayed at her side, its tendrils waving alternately between her and Ira.

Ira huffed a laugh. "Go with her, if you want. Mind no one realizes what you are."

Calyx brushed against Charlotte hopefully.

"You'll be a houseplant," she warned. It leaped into her arms and wrapped around her. She laughed in surprise, burying her face in its appendages. She hadn't imagined leaving it and was glad she wouldn't have to.

Shrinking down, the plant creature wound itself around Maurice's bridle to hide. Maurice snorted and pranced, not liking that, but Elspeth calmed him. She walked, holding Charlotte's hand. Together, they all set off across the pastureland—except Ira. He stood in the tree line, gazing after them.

Charlotte moved closer to Arthur, on her other side, and lowered her voice. "Why isn't he coming with us?"

"He can't." Arthur avoided her eyes. "He can't leave the forest."

"Oh." It seemed like all there was to say.

They reached the top of the pastureland. Port Lorne spread below them, a maze of cobbled streets, tenements, factories, shipyards, and shops.

Maggie sighed. "Green Streets. Lord, but it does feel an age since I seen it."

"It's *been* an age," Elspeth said. "We'd best keep moving. Gran'll go off her nut if we keep you from her."

Charlotte's breath hitched at the sight of the city below. The harbor to the west, the great masted ships so different from the fishing boats in Seacliff. The smoke rising from the factories, reddish in the late-day sunlight.

Beside her, Arthur was pale and silent, his eyes damp.

"You'll see him again," she said. "When we pass back through."

"Yes."

"Perhaps you could bring him something from Port Lorne."

"Perhaps."

"C'mon," Elspeth said impatiently, leading her horse downhill by the bridle. The children trotted after her on Maurice, the cat at their heels.

Arthur turned, gazed at Ira for a long moment. The Lord of the Wood was a distant, shadowy figure, half lost in greenery.

Then Arthur turned back, gripping Charlotte's arm tight. "All right."

She kissed his knuckles. Leaning on each other, they straggled downhill, toward the great port city about which their father had told them so many stories.

Six weeks later

On a chilly morning in late October, Arthur was lugging the Throckmorton-Prentices' boxed-up things through the workshop when a wagon emerged from the forest. Hitched to the wagon was Maurice, gifted to them (officially) by Agnes Livingston, and in the driver's seat was Elspeth.

Keeping a lookout from the garden wall, Sasha sang out, "She's here!"

Charlotte hurried through the workshop, trailed by Jonas. She ran to the wagon and kissed Elspeth full on the mouth almost before it had stopped moving.

"Brought you a gift," Elspeth said, when they'd pulled apart. From a heavy earthenware pot in back, Calyx emerged. It slung itself joyfully at Charlotte; she caught it in her arms with a laugh. They'd left it with Elspeth's family in Port Lorne when they'd come home, since they would shortly return.

Sasha jumped off the wall and clambered into the wagon to hug Elspeth.

"What d'you think of driving?" Elspeth asked. "Sit right in my lap and I could teach you."

Charlotte made an offended sound.

"I don't think Mama will let me," Sasha said.

Elspeth laughed. "When's that ever stopped you, bug?"

"Could I learn, too?" Jonas asked shyly.

Charlotte looked at them in astonishment, and Elspeth laughed harder.

"C'mon, now, Lottie. Living in Port Lorne, best for 'em to learn sometime."

Arthur smiled, glad to see them all happy, but something ached inside him. He'd been so busy preparing for the move that he had not yet traveled back to the vale. Ira had visited once, a couple weeks ago, appearing as a stag just within the trees. Arthur had run and clung to him this same way until Ira had peeled him off so they could walk together through the wood. At sunset, Ira had seen him to the tree line, shivered back into a stag, and vanished in the forest's depths.

Hopping down, Elspeth started loading boxes into the wagon. Arthur joined her, wanting desperately to ask about Ira, but he couldn't bring himself to do it.

Elspeth caught his eye. "Spending his time traveling the forest, your man. Making sure the sickness is truly gone. Clear-cutting ain't stopped, but replanting the first tree's slowed it some."

"I'm glad," Arthur said softly. "Has, er, has anyone else who turned into a tree been . . . ?"

Elspeth shook her head.

"He hoped they might, but no one's walked out alive but Maggie. Workers in Port Lorne are throwing a fit, let me tell you. With three camps gone already, the rest of 'em won't go back without a promise of more money, and money to their families if they vanish. There's talk of unionizing." She opened and reclosed a box that hadn't been shut properly. "Ira's looking forward to seeing you. On our way back through."

Arthur returned to packing the wagon in silence, pausing when his back spasmed. His throat and cheek throbbed, too. Despite the magical healing, after all these weeks, they pained him periodically. He still couldn't lift too much, with the wounds healing on his torso. Charlotte had caught him filling each box to bursting and immediately repacked them lighter.

When they'd spent several days with Elspeth's family in Port Lorne to recuperate back in September, Arthur had hardly enjoyed it. Everyone else had seemed happy. Maggie, grateful to be home, and Elspeth, grateful to have her there. The children, especially Sasha, who had found the city so new and exciting that it had been difficult to keep them from running off to explore. Agnes, when they'd wired her; she'd wired back to say Gracie's sickness had cleared up—though it had left her with fatigue, pain, and dizzy spells, whether because she was an old woman or because she'd had it for so long—and to ask that they please bring the clock back with them. Charlotte, who had gotten on with Elspeth's grandfather in particular, though he and Elspeth's grandmother both delicately referred to her as "Elspeth's friend."

Granddad McIntire was a skinny, balding little man with medium brown skin and a magnificent beard, a loud laugh for someone his size, and an interest in the medicinal qualities of plants. He'd been fascinated by Calyx, who'd been disguised as a houseplant in the room Elspeth shared with Maggie until now.

While Charlotte and Granddad McIntire had pored over the plants in Maggie's garden together, Arthur had kept Granny McIntire company in the kitchen, reading romance to her. She'd gotten into it herself in the last decade, but her fading eyesight made it hard for her to read. He'd stumbled over the sex scenes, not entirely sure it was appropriate to read them to an old woman, until she'd told him peevishly that she had six children and knew perfectly well what sex was, so he might as well let her enjoy herself.

(He'd almost stumbled worse after that, but she was so strong-willed that he didn't dare skip such scenes lest she catch him at it.)

Despite the embarrassment, sharing the novels had been a comfort. So had fixing Granny McIntire's old clock, which she'd asked him about upon learning of his affinity for timepieces. It was the first timepiece he'd seen, apart from his father's watch, since leaving home.

Otherwise, Port Lorne had held no charms for him. The McIntires' house was loud and crowded, overwhelming. The city was a noisy labyrinth whose factories belched out such smoke that Arthur could hardly believe he'd ever minded the smell of the cannery. Elspeth's cousins teased him without him realizing that was what they were doing—until Elspeth overheard and sounded them out for it. And he couldn't stop thinking of Ira alone in the forest, unable to leave it, without even Calyx for company. Now, he longed to see Ira so badly that he was sick with it.

At last the wagon was loaded. Arthur, the children, the goat, the chickens, Calyx (in its pot), and the cat were safely ensconced in back. Charlotte was beside Elspeth in the driver's seat. Elspeth flapped the driving lines, and they were off.

Arthur twisted around for one last look at the cottage in which he'd grown up. Already he missed Seacliff a little, despite the years of loneliness, the lack of friends, the constant feeling of inadequacy. He missed the cottage with its memories of his parents far more.

If the cottage shared his pang of regret, however, it gave no sign. Its white clapboard sides receded and vanished in the thick foliage of Shiftleaf.

With the heart of the wood restored, the forest was at the height of its autumnal glory, girt all in reds and golds. The paths shifted, more as if the trees were going about their tree business than as if they wanted to lure one into their depths and prevent one's escape. Rabbits and squirrels scurried through the undergrowth, opaque and unveined. Birds sang in the canopy or flew past on their way south. The air was chill, but no unseasonable ice or snow coated the ground.

When they reached the swinging bridge, Ira was waiting for them.

Arthur gave a wordless cry, leaped from the wagon, and scurried across the bridge to fall into his arms. Ira held him and kissed him and only pulled away, laughing, when Elspeth called out, "Oy! Some of us would like to cross!"

Ira pulled Arthur off the bridge, holding his hand. The wagon crossed, the children jumped out (Sasha flung herself at Ira), and Elspeth and Charlotte dismounted and loosed Maurice from his traces. The horse moseyed over to the nearest patch of sunlight and set about grazing. The goat and chickens joined him. Calyx clambered from its pot and slithered about the vale, curious about the changes to its old home.

The snow had melted. It had swelled the stream and left behind a soft green carpet of clover and moss. Like elsewhere in the forest, the trees were red and gold instead of barren as they'd been before. Ira's clothes were autumn leaves and flowers. Arthur wondered idly whether they'd be more difficult to remove now.

They unloaded enough of their belongings to stay a couple nights. Sasha darted back outside to explore. Jonas followed to make sure she stayed in the vale. Elspeth and Charlotte made small talk with Ira for a while, then wandered into the forest alone for reasons Arthur pretended not to understand.

He and Ira sat in companionable silence on matching stools outside. The children chased each other, Calyx, the cat, the goat, the chickens, and sometimes Maurice around the vale. Ira filled a page sketching them. He kept glancing over as if he meant to say something, but he kept not saying anything.

Arthur couldn't stand it. "How have you been?"

Ira gazed around, smiling. Arthur had thought him beautiful before, but with that soft smile, he was more beautiful than ever.

"Good. The forest is whole again." His smile faded. "It won't last. They're scouting new areas to fell."

"We won't let them," Arthur said at once, but Ira shook his head.

"We probably can't stop them. But perhaps we can stall them. Prevent them from felling so much."

"If we can't—" Arthur turned out his pockets "—we'll replant the tree. No matter how many times they cut it down."

In his pockets was a bounty of silver acorns. Ira's lips twitched. He turned out his own pockets; they were full of silver acorns, too. Charlotte had given most of hers to Kitty Tierney for safekeeping, in case the sickness ever returned, and told her how to use them to cure it. The rest she'd bring to Port Lorne for the same reason.

Arthur edged his stool closer to Ira's. Giving a small smile, Ira reached for his hand.

"I've missed you," he said.

Arthur kissed his fingers. He'd missed Ira so much it made him ache constantly. He didn't know how he'd bear leaving him.

This was precisely why he never pursued anything. Why he let his dreams remain just that: shining bubbles of fantasy, never to be popped by the ugly realities of life. He could've dreamed of romance and happily-ever-afters forever. They would've been perfect and beautiful and free of all sorrow and difficult decisions.

They didn't speak of what would happen when the family left for Port Lorne. It hung over them like a cloud, but they talked of other things. What the children had been doing. (Jonas had been shadowing their mother at her work more consistently; Sasha had become determined to know the name of every plant that grew on the edge of the wood.) What the McIntires' house in Port Lorne was like and how Calyx liked it. What romance novels Arthur had been reading. He'd found himself returning to the one with the monstrous love interest over and over but couldn't quite bring himself to admit it.

When Charlotte and Elspeth returned from their walk, Arthur brought his sister to see their father's grave.

(Unlike Ira, he told her in advance what they were doing and asked whether she wanted to see it.)

They gazed at the headstone in silence. Charlotte sat on one of Ira's stools, which Arthur had brought in case she needed it. She had been less resistant to rest and help since their adventures. Seacliff hadn't appreciated that, but Arthur certainly did.

"It's nice," she said stuffily. "The flowers are . . ."

"They were like that even before. The ground was covered in snow, but the flowers bloomed anyway."

"Do you recognize them?" Wiping her eyes, Charlotte gave a tiny smile. She pointed. "Sweet amber. Wild garlic. Meadowsweet. Heal-all. They're all medicinal."

They fell silent again.

"I still miss him," Charlotte said.

Arthur took her hand. "So do I."

Her voice got very small. "I wish I remembered him as well as you do."

"Well, anytime you'd like to talk about him—we'll talk about him so much you'll feel just as if you remember him that well."

Charlotte bit her lip. "Maybe . . . we can talk about John sometimes, too. And Mam."

She'd never offered that before, or asked for it. The few times Arthur had mentioned John over the years, she'd shut down.

He kissed her hand. "Certainly we can. There's sort of a way to see them, too. Ira has this basin—"

"I'm familiar."

"—and we can see our memories, really see them. And each other's. If you'd ever want to."

"I don't know if I'm ready for that much," Charlotte said softly, "but maybe one day."

The children tumbled into view, followed by Elspeth, whom they fended off with sticks and laughter. Giving an uncharacteristic yell, Jonas lunged at her. She took the stick between her arm and ribs, falling to the ground, and died dramatically, with a great deal of weeping for the cruelty of the world.

Arthur smiled. "I think she'll be a good influence on Jonas."

"She'll be an absolutely dreadful influence on them," Charlotte said fondly.

Ira sidled into the scene, laughing, and took them away to see an old fox's den that looked as if it had recently been in use. Now the forest was as it should be, Sasha in particular had liked exploring its edges, though Arthur and Charlotte had never let her go too far or alone. She'd badgered Ira all afternoon to take her exploring in more depth, and he'd finally obliged.

Arthur's gaze followed them until they were out of sight. He sighed.

Charlotte glanced at him. "You could stay."

Arthur's skin prickled. "I couldn't, though."

"Why not?"

It was deeply distressing that Arthur couldn't think of a single reasonable response.

"Well—you. And the children. I couldn't leave—"

Charlotte took his hand.

"Do you think you'd never see us again? We could visit as often as you liked. Or you could stay with us, whenever you wanted. Now the forest isn't so dangerous, we could travel back and forth all the time."

Arthur paused. "But—your income—"

"That will be a difficulty. But Mrs. Livingston's money is quite a good start, and it isn't as if I'll be alone. Elspeth will provide for us, too. She says Port Lorne has more opportunities. And we'll have a roof over our heads and a garden to feed us, and her whole family to help us, and you and Ira right here in the wood if we need more."

Charlotte smiled mischievously. Arthur's first confused notion was that Sasha looked a lot more like her than he'd ever thought.

"Besides," she said in a low voice, "it would be nice to have somewhere to send the children for a few days when Elspeth and I want some privacy."

He flushed at her tone. "Charlotte!"

She giggled. He stared. He hadn't heard her giggle in years. Perhaps Elspeth had been a bad influence on her, too.

If only she'd be a bad influence on him. He certainly needed one.

"But," he sputtered, "but—"

His sister's laughter faded. She took his hand.

"Arthur, what is it you're afraid of?"

Something cracked inside him. Something that had long been held together by his romance novels and daydreams, stories where happily-ever-after came surely and perfectly after true love's kiss, where no one ever quarreled or resented each other for petty reasons regretted long after death. He swallowed.

"What if," he said, "what if it's terrible? What if we fight all the time, or get tired of each other, or find we can't stand each other? What if the sex is dreadful? What if—"

"What if it doesn't stand up to your novels?"

Reddening, Arthur nodded. Charlotte squeezed his hand and let go.

"You can't expect to find out if you don't try. You can't expect your life to change if you never choose to change it."

"But I *did* choose that. I decided to take on Mrs. Livingston's job, didn't I?"

"After trying to make me decide for you," Charlotte said with a smile, but Arthur pressed on.

"I went into the forest—I left the vale—I chose to keep going even when Ira didn't want to! I just—" He ran a hand through his hair. "I thought it'd be easier now. I've had my adventure, for heaven's sake, I've *made* decisions—why must it still be so hard to decide? Why can't I be—I don't know—brave and bold and *certain* now?"

"Wouldn't that be nice." Charlotte's smile faded. "I know your books are like that. My radio program is, too. But it's not like that, really. There's not one moment where you make a choice and now you're a different person. You have to keep choosing to be that person, again and again."

Her hands scrunched in her apron.

"I feel it myself. I care about Elspeth, I was so glad to see her, but . . . the whole time she was gone, I kept thinking, what if we stayed? How well do I know this woman? It won't be like it was, living with her family in the city after being alone together in the forest. It's so impractical to *want* to go, when I've never lived anywhere else, and the children have school, and . . ."

Charlotte let out a breath.

"It's seemed so much easier to go on the way we've been. The way I've been. I've had to keep reminding myself it's worth it, I'll be happier, and I'll have more help on bad days—between Elspeth and Maggie and their grandparents and cousins, there'll always be other people to help with chores or watch the children. And I think it will be good for the children, too. Sasha already thinks it's a wonderful adventure."

Her smile was brittler than before.

"It is exhausting, I admit, to keep reminding oneself of such things. To keep deciding all over. But it seems that's how it is." She squeezed his hand again. "So you'll have to choose, you see, and I'm afraid it won't be for the last time."

"But—"

Arthur hardly knew what he was objecting to. To having to choose. To whatever he chose popping the shining, golden bubble of his dreams, leaving him with rubbery scraps that no longer resembled what he'd imagined.

"You care about him," Charlotte said, "and he cares about you. And if for any reason things don't work out—you'll always have a home with us, you know."

They stayed for several more days. Each time someone (usually Elspeth) suggested it was time to move on, Arthur begged off for increasingly weak and ridiculous reasons. Charlotte shook her head but let it stand.

Elspeth, however, grew increasingly belligerent.

"Not that this ain't nice," she said at supper one night, in a voice of extreme begrudging, "but it's only going to get colder the longer we stay. Maybe the forest is healed, but that don't mean we want to be caught traveling through it in the dead of winter because you won't shack up with your boyfriend and you won't leave him, neither."

Arthur flushed. Luckily, Ira had stepped out for more firewood, so he didn't hear her comment. Perhaps equally luckily, he returned before Arthur could sputter out yet another half-hearted protest to their continuing on to Port Lorne.

Long after everyone else had fallen asleep, Arthur sat in his armchair and gazed into the stove's glowing depths, thinking about Ira and his family and the empty cottage back in Seacliff and the oak tree he was in now and the house in Port Lorne he'd soon live in unless he decided otherwise.

In the other armchair, Ira shifted. He'd fallen asleep after listening to Arthur read several chapters of a romance novel. Although the read-aloud had been Ira's request, Arthur had insisted on choosing the book himself lest Ira choose the one with the monster love interest.

A strand of hair fell into Ira's eye as he shifted again without waking. Arthur tucked it back into place. He loved Ira's hair.

When the family left the next morning, Arthur didn't go with them.

He removed the rest of his things from the wagon, though Sasha stomped her feet and told him, repeatedly, that he *had* to go.

"Penny won't go without you," she said tearfully, tugging the goat toward him to prove it. "See?"

"Wheest, my little bug." Crouching before her, Elspeth unwound her arms from the disgruntled goat's neck. "With your uncle here, don't you know how much more often you'll be able to visit? Think of all the things Ira might show you, foxes' dens and robins' eggs and all sorts. And your mam won't even be here to tell you no."

Sasha glared at the adults but made no attempt to drag the goat anywhere else. "I *guess*."

"You can visit all the time," Arthur said anxiously, hoping saying it would make it so. "Anytime you want."

"Even when I'm supposed to be in school?"

An affirmative would clearly make her less resistant to the idea of her uncle's no longer living with them, but Arthur couldn't bring himself to respond in a way he knew would never fly with her mother.

"We'll see," Charlotte said.

When his luggage was safely in the house, and the goat back

and support, even when I go many weeks at a time without messaging because I forget time is passing.

Shout-out to my sisters, who I felt probably should've gotten a dedication in this book because it's a sibling book. But then the dedications started getting long, and I couldn't bring myself to cut any of them. So Lucy and Kate, you'll have to live with a special paragraph in the acknowledgments just for you. I would enter an enchanted forest to find you. Let's ignore the fact that I love trees to begin with.

When I was twelve, I wrote a book that was a lot like this one in many important ways, although entirely different in terms of premise. I lovingly hand-bound it and gave it to my parents for their anniversary, then later took it back "to revise" but never revised it and never gave it back. Sorry about that, Mom and Dad. This book is basically that book, only miles better. I hope you enjoy it. Don't talk to me about the fade-to-black sex scene. I'm pretending you didn't read it.

Finally, thank you to Henry, Eli, Nate, and Emmy. Love you guys.